CW00419176

DOWN... BUT NOT OUT

Ian Cook-Abbott

GCW Book Co.

Copyright © 2021 Ian Cook-Abbott

All rights reserved

The characters and events portrayed in this book are fictitious. Any similarity to real persons, living or dead, is coincidental and not intended by the author.

No part of this book may be reproduced, or stored in a retrieval system, or transmitted in any form or by any means, electronic, mechanical, photocopying, recording, or otherwise, without express written permission of the publisher.

ISBN-13: 9798710824641
ISBN-10: 1477123456

Cover design by: Joel Lindley of Simply Legends
Library of Congress Control Number: 2018675309
Printed in the United States of America

Commenced in 1997, this really should not have taken so long. Along came Bebe, followed later by Joey and Jay and the book went on hold until Lockdown 2020. My thanks and love to Anne and the younger C-As for their support and patience.

Down... but Not Out is a work of fiction. The 1997 England – Australia ODI series did take place and contextual references are made to some real cricketers but the key characters and the events herein are figments of my own imagination and are not based on real people or real events. Any errors are all of my own making.

Thanks to Joel Lindley of Simply Legends for the cover artwork.

CHAPTER 1

Saturday April 12 1997

It all started to fall apart around the time Elisa flew off to New York, and the first book signing was just the start of it. I got the call from the English Cricket Board on the first day of April. The date should have been an omen I suppose, not that I am overly superstitious. In any case the book should have been ready a couple of months before but, as it was part of a set and one of them had had to be completely overhauled, the launch date had been shifted back. To be honest I did not have a great deal to do with the one that bears my name. My hand had been forced by the ECB, who strongly hinted to me that my involvement in the project might go a long way towards my rehabilitation and an eventual recall to the national side. And that had been my goal since being dropped two years previously over a well-reported incident allegedly involving recreational drugs during the Ashes tour Down Under – to date, my only tour with the full England team. The whole thing was a sham. I am no angel, but I would prefer to be punished for what I did do rather than the rumour of what I might have done. More importantly, I had done nothing on that tour – certainly nothing that should have seen me dropped in the way that I was. Anyway, the book-signing sessions were going to be the final acts of repentance so far as I was concerned.

I had dropped Elisa off at Heathrow, still puzzled at why she was so keen to take this assignment when for the past year she had tried desperately hard to avoid overseas trips and had spent an increasing amount of her time working from home. I understood that having moved to a new magazine she felt she had to show commitment, but she had told me that this new post was a more senior position and one where she could begin to dictate her own terms. The assignment was, admittedly, a good one and I imagine she had had to fight for it, although she denied that. Toadlust had come from nowhere to take the top slot on the Billboard charts and the British papers and magazines were suddenly full of them. Musically, they were not so different from many of the other punk/metal bands doing the rounds, but they seemed to revel in confrontation. The band's lead singer and guitarist were said to be siblings and there was a wild rumour that their father was a Member of Parliament, and possibly a Cabinet Minister. The band had apparently refused to speak to anyone except *Smashed*, and in her role of News Editor, Elisa felt she ought to go to interview them. As an editor, I thought she could have sent someone else, but apparently not.

I parked in Greek Street, as close to the bookshop as I could, slotted a handful of coins into the meter and, noting from its clock that I had a few minutes to spare, slipped into a little old-fashioned café for a cup of strong, black coffee. I took it out onto the pavement where the proprietor had arranged a couple of plastic garden chairs around a small, circular, metal table. The dark black coffee smelt delicious as it wafted from the cup in the stiff spring breeze. I had bought an expensive coffee maker for Elisa at Christmas but neither of us had mastered it and after a couple of weeks it was put back in its box. A decent coffee and a few minutes with the papers are luxuries I struggle without.

The pavements were filling up with lunchtime pedestrian traffic and I found myself people-watching: a couple of down-and-outs were arguing over something they had discovered in a litterbin just across the road from me; an old lady in what looked like a coat of genuine fur passed them, apparently holding her breath; a cycle messenger swooped dangerously in and out of the cars that were crawling along the road and a little group of punks stood obligingly for their photographs to be taken by a well-dressed Japanese couple. It seemed odd to see them still in their anarchy armbands and spiked hair all these years after the bands had got fat and hung up their guitars. Or maybe it was just me - too old and out of touch at 27. That worried me. I resolved to ask Elisa when she called from New York.

I checked my watch again and found I had another ten minutes, took a sip of the still scalding coffee and carefully re-folded my newspaper to the sports section. The Guardian had been running a preview of the season all week and I had noticed a mention of Surrey in one of the headlines when I picked the paper up on the way into town. Scanning down the page I found the article in the bottom right hand corner and folded the paper again. I was interested to see what the papers were going to make of the changes at The Oval. Not only had Mark O'Brien relinquished the captaincy but there was Alan Dench's surprise move south from Worcester.

O'Brien had been good enough to win a couple of England caps some fifteen or more years earlier and had been a popular skipper since his own move south a year before but the captaincy had taken its toll on his batting and, after a pretty dismal year for him, he had stepped down at the end of the season. A genial Irishman, he had been a positive force in the dressing room and in the bar afterwards, despite the results on the field. Dench's arrival was not anticipated as keenly.

It had not been greeted with universal acclaim at The Oval when it was announced as a possibility in early March and he had yet to appear at pre-season training as the management had agreed to allow him to continue his winter training programme up in the Midlands. Few of us had had any personal experience of him, aside of course from the games we had played against him. Off the pitch he was the type to leave the ground pretty much as soon as stumps were drawn and I had never heard of him staying for a drink after the game, although that tradition does seem to be fast becoming a thing of the past. It was what we had read about him, and the rumours we had heard, that fuelled the dressing-room gossip. The cricket writers had either been in the game before Dench or played alongside him. There seemed little love lost between the two camps. He is about ten years older than I am and as a boy I had watched him from afar and developed a sneaking regard for his self-centredness, his almost un-British arrogance. We seem to prefer our sporting heroes to be flawed and humble. Dench is technically almost perfect and frequently stands accused of playing for himself and not the team. Quite why the management at Surrey decided to offer him terms was a mystery to all. After too many inconsistent years we had had a pretty decent season last time out, with a Sunday League title and a third place in the championship. And on paper, despite a number of departures, we still had a strong-looking squad.

The Guardian piece was written by a former Worcester team-mate, Larry Helm, who seemed equally surprised at the move, pointing out that if it really was for personal reasons as Dench had claimed, it probably had to do with money – and not the money that Surrey were paying him. I knew nothing of that but agreed with Helm's view that Dench was not needed in a side that already batted down to number ten. I also agreed with Helm that with '*England bad boy, Johnny Lorrens*' coming in at eleven, Surrey did *only* bat down to number ten, and smiled at his suggestion that perhaps Dench was being brought in for me. Helm is a good journalist, respected by the players, but even he could not resist regurgitating the 'bad boy' label. I needed to change that perception fast, if I was to regain my place in the England set-up. The article was illustrated with two photographs: one of Dench perfecting a classic cover-drive and one of me, looking a little worse for wear, beer in hand, exiting a club. It made me reflect that, contrary to the old adage, not all publicity is good. I caught a reflection of myself in the café's plate glass window. The shoulder-length blonde hair was greased back today, the features on my broad face were just ever so slightly blurred, and I felt under my chin, suspecting a slight doubling there. But there was still a sparkle in the blue eyes. I did wonder, though, if the image staring back at me looked like a top-class, international sportsman. I resolved to kick start the gym membership.

As I finished my coffee the first drops of cool April rain spattered gently across the newspaper. I nodded my thanks to the proprietor, who had appeared to take my empty cup, and started down Greek Street. Turning left into Manette Street, I had to wait as a rusty old van backed out of Orange Yard. I looked down into the dingy lane as I passed but Borderline's doors were already closed. Elisa and I had had some good evenings in there and, smiling at the thought, I followed in the Transit's wake of blue exhaust, trying to hold my breath. I turned left into Charing Cross Road and slipped between the slow-moving traffic to the opposite side. I looked at my watch as I pushed open the heavy plate-glass door to Sporting Books and was pleased to see that it was one minute to eleven o'clock. I like to be punctual.

There were a few early shoppers browsing amongst the densely packed shelves and a few more already clutching green Sporting Books carrier bags, standing around looking a little lost. I avoided them and headed across to the back of the shop where I could see a table that had been set up in a corner and, sitting behind it, the burly figure of Terry Court, the ECB's public relations man. I get on with most people, given the chance, but Court had never extended me that courtesy. He not only persuaded the Board to involve me in the project, but he also assured them that I should attend half-a-dozen of these signing sessions around the country. I was going to have to spend six sessions like this with him – a prospect I did not relish. But as Elisa kept reminding me, if it got me back in the England set up then it would be worth it. Maybe, although I was not at all sure that this was going to get me back in the side. With the Australians due in the country any day and the Ashes up for grabs again, I was desperate to regain my place. A few days with Court was perhaps an acceptable price to pay.

As I neared the table, Court ostentatiously checked his watch. I chose to ignore him and dragged a chair to the opposite end of the table. Sitting down, I picked up the top copy from the neatly stacked pile in front of me. I had seen a poor photocopy of the front cover artwork, but the actual book looked and felt surprisingly good. The photo on the dust jacket, of me in mid-delivery, was taken at Sydney in January 1995 – my only England appearance so far – on the third day when I took 6 for 38. I stared at the photo and reflected back on that tour – bittersweet memories.

The ECB was publishing a new set of training manuals covering all aspects of the game, including my one on spin-bowling. It might seem surprising that with my being rather out of favour I should be considered appropriate to 'author' any of these manuals; truth be told we have been struggling to find world-class spinners for a while so I guess I was something of a reluctant choice. I certainly was not getting carried away with any thoughts of a swift return to the fold.

Sporting Books had purchased a batch of fifty, which they wanted signing for their stock. I signed these first and then for the next hour or so I personalized copies for customers – in the main truanting teenagers and elderly men. Court left me alone for the most part and busied himself with a briefcase full of papers. At twelve on the dot he stood, eased on his ECB blazer and advised me that I could stop signing. I looked at the small queue and indicated that I was happy to carry on until the last few had been satisfied. Court raised his eyebrows and muttering something under his breath, stalked off. I signed another dozen or so books before a young fellow wearing a Sporting Books polo shirt came up to whisper in my ear that he was about to announce the signing session closed. He put all the loose copies save the one I was holding into a cardboard box and took them away with him. I thanked him and was just flicking through my copy of the book when a shadow fell across the table.

'Am I too late to get a copy for my boyfriend?'

I carried on flicking through the pages without looking up. 'Sorry, yes. Just finished,' I replied.

There was a pause and a rustle before she spoke, a little closer to me.

'Would you sign here for me, then?'

I let the book close in my hand and raised my eyes. I gulped. She was gorgeous. Long, jet-black hair, worn to below the shoulders. Wonderful, laughing, almond-shaped eyes of the most translucent blue. Flawless skin and lips made for eating. All of which I noticed a good while later, for she had opened her white, knee-length leather coat and the blue silk blouse beneath to reveal her breasts.

I looked at the biro in my hand and, fixing her right in the eye, I felt the skin tighten across my face as it reddened. I stammered something about a biro not being suitable. To be honest I cannot really remember what I did say; I do know that I hoped no-one had seen her and when she had gone so had my copy of the book. I supposed that I must have signed that for her. As I left the shop, I could see her playful smile as if it had been etched on my retinas. Lauren? Laverne? Lorraine? She *had* said, but I could not remember. I felt uncomfortable – no-one had had an effect like this on me since I met Elisa Wilton two years before. Nevertheless, I could not shake the image of her.

My pulse was still racing as I walked down Charing Cross Road towards Leicester Square and, nearing the familiar red and blue Underground sign, I suddenly remembered that I had promised Elisa that I would try to pick up *The Two Bear Mambo*, the Lansdale book she was missing, at Murder One. I backtracked a couple of hundred yards to the store and reached it just as another shower began to pepper the pavements. I quickly found the paperback she had requested and also picked up a copy of *Strangers on a Train* to replace the one I had lent my father. I was trying to get him out of his trash reading habits and although I was achieving some success, it was costing me a few of my favourite novels; sending them to him overseas meant they rarely came back. I paid for the books and, turning out of the shop back down towards the Underground, had only gone a few paces when I remembered that I had driven up that morning and that the car was parked a few streets in the opposite direction. The girl had rattled me.

Checking the dashboard clock as I swung left into the Harleyford Road, I saw that it was just gone one o'clock. Elisa would be a couple of hours into her flight and probably already on her fourth or fifth drink. For a regular flyer she is a remarkably nervous one; another reason why she had sought a job that was not going to demand that she spend half her life abroad. Besides, drink and Elisa do not mix well, or rather perhaps they mix a little too well; she had been trying to dry out and was doing well, but I was sure that her flying fears would get the better of her. She had promised to call the moment she reached her hotel and, knowing that my day was going to be severely disrupted by the signing session, I had told her to call me first at The Oval. I expected to be late home. The magazine was almost ready to go to print but I had some loose ends to tie up on the cricket grounds article and was hoping to be able to include some news on the proposed building works. I parked up close to the pavilion entrance and dashed across the few yards of glistening tarmac as the rains came in a fresh wave.

The subdued light inside the old pavilion contrasted sharply with the bright glare of the sun reflecting on the puddles in the forecourt. The slightly musty smell was at odds with the freshness of the spring day outside. There is a stillness in the old building out of season that to this day I still find a little eerie; there is so much history attached to the place that I half expect to see the ghosts of cricketers-past wafting through. I never have, although I have heard some mighty strange noises when the place has supposedly been empty.

I mounted the first flight of stairs and pushed open the heavy, half-glassed door into the Long Room. As a kid I used to spend lunch and tea breaks gazing at the old paintings of the Surrey greats. The names sounded at once familiar yet distant: Hobbs, May, Laker, Sandham and Surridge. On the left-hand side of the fireplace hung the 1911 portrait of the pavilion. There I could see the legendary professional, Jack Hobbs, surprisingly depicted amongst the club dignitaries – a formal painting of a time when amateurs were rather more respected than the players. Not, of course, for their cricketing abilities but for their privileged backgrounds. On the right-hand side, on its easel, the still incomplete painting which was commenced a couple of years before to celebrate the one-hundred-and- fiftieth anniversary of the Club. Surrey's own Sagrada Familia.

I paused in front of it and smiled at the strangeness of it. The pavilion was pretty much exactly represented but the little figures all seemed to have over-large heads. This painting too reeked of money but in a different way. The project was in part a method of raising funds. Senior members of the playing staff from the early to mid-nineties were clustered together towards the left-hand side, whilst a few of the Honorary Members and assorted VIPs were depicted standing in front of the white boundary fencing. The bulk of the rest of the figures were Members who had paid for their likenesses to be inserted into the seating plan. And it had not been cheap. A number of the current squad were dotted around the painting. After close to ten years at Surrey I was still just a blurry oval of pinkish paint at the extreme top right of the painting. There had recently been talk of trying to get the thing finished and at one stage it looked as though current players' wives and girlfriends were going to be slipped in next to them to fill up the gaps. The Finance Committee had questioned this and so only time would tell whether the pinkish blur next to me would transform itself into Elisa or not.

I carried on up through the pavilion until I came out onto the top deck and paused to lean on the railing for a moment. The ground looked superb. The outfield had been cut into a chessboard of varying greens and a couple of members of the ground staff were rolling the square. Over in the corner under the watchful eyes of the huge, green gasometers a little cluster of overalled workmen were re-roofing the old scoreboard. Its days had seemed numbered when it was announced that the side terraces were to be demolished and replaced with matching double-decker stands but a small group of Members had quietly approached English Heritage and managed to get it listed. The

Club was now obliged to keep it and pay for its renovation – which was badly needed. There was talk of moving it, but no-one could decide where to move it to. I had heard that it was a requirement that the successful building company incorporate it into the new stand on that side of the ground.

My gaze drifted round to the far side where the tumble of old stands stood humbly at the Vauxhall End. Plans had been drawn up a few years before which showed a magnificent new structure, a huge, white five-tiered monster curving gracefully around that end of the ground, linking with the two side terraces. Money proved to be the object and despite winning much praise from the architectural critics, the design was put on hold. There had been talk of selling naming-rights for a new stand, but I could not see any company wanting to associate themselves with the Vauxhall End any time soon. Fosters already owned naming-rights rights to the ground itself and I presumed that this would be a further stumbling block. If building ever did go ahead at the Vauxhall End the architect would have to blend in with the new double-deckers that were destined to replace the open terraces on the east and west sides of the ground. This part of the ground's redevelopment was scheduled to go ahead, however, the old post-war terraces long past their sell-by date. The plans I had seen for those showed a strong dash of modernism but empathy with the history and tradition of the pavilion.

The rain, which had briefly given way to apologetic sunshine, started driving even harder as I turned away from the railing and mounted the steps two at a time up to the very top of the pavilion. With various renovations going on around the ground during the winter months I had been pushed from corner to corner until I finally ended up in the library. Now with the season about to start I supposed that the computer would be uprooted again as the Members would need access to the library once more. Given that I had no previous experience in publishing, the Club had really been very good to me; when I decided at the end of the previous season to have a winter off, they had suggested that I edit the club magazine. I had contributed a column to The Mail on Sunday when I toured Australia a couple of years before but that was it. And even then, that appointment had been curtailed after the events in Sydney. I still harboured thoughts of writing on the game after my playing days and this seemed like a good chance to see what I could do. In the meantime, I hoped that I would be allowed to continue editing the magazine over the summer at least.

I tried the handle, but Sally had apparently gone for the day and had already locked up. I heard the telephone ringing as I fumbled for my keys but by the time I had got the door open, the telephone had gone silent. I slipped off my jacket, flipped the switch on the kettle and rattled about for a few seconds in the cupboard where Sally kept the makings. I threw a teabag into the only clean mug I could find, tossed in a couple of spoons of sugar and, waiting for the kettle to boil, hunted in the little fridge for some milk. I sniffed a couple of cartons before finding one that was useable and reminded myself to remind the cleaners that there was life up at the top of the pavilion. I poured boiling water and milk into the mug, mashed the bag with the wrong end of a dirty spoon and set it down on my desk, which was actually a rather wobbly trestle table. I turned on the computer and, waiting for the steaming tea to cool, fumbled in my jacket pocket for the pack of Marlboros that I had found in the glove compartment earlier. Thinking better of it, I crumpled the pack and sent it arcing towards the bin.

The fax machine on Sally's desk purred into life suddenly, breaking the silence in the room. I ignored it at first and focused my attention on my e-mail inbox. I had not been in for a couple of days and saw that I had seven new messages. I moved the mouse with my right hand as I adjusted the brightness control of the screen with my left. The library, with its wall of glass, afforded wonderful views of the playing area and, above the Vauxhall End, the London skyline, but the glare made staring at my computer screen uncomfortable. I took a swig of the piping hot tea and clicked on the first message. It was from Carlisle, our new Australian coach. We had had an inconsistent few summers at The Oval and, despite a decent season the previous year, the Cricket Committee had finally decided to get out the stiff broom during the winter. A couple of the senior players decided to call it a day and the club had reduced the playing staff from twenty-two down to eighteen. Rumour had it that an important sponsor was making ugly noises about pulling out of the deal and the Club was desperate not to lose them. Carlisle was acknowledging my request to interview him for *Oval Eyes*, the Club's newly restyled magazine. I had a couple of questions for him that I was really keen for answers to, for I was worried that the playing staff had been cut back too far and the talk in the dressing room was that Thoren Investments, the new shirt sponsor, was already exerting undue influence in the boardroom on cricketing matters.

I made a mental note to plan my questions ahead of our appointment as I selected the second message, a reminder from Marketing that my copy was due first thing Tuesday. That meant I would have to catch Carlisle on Monday at the latest. The third message was one that I had been waiting for, from RIBA. With the redevelopment of the side terraces moving into its final planning phase I wanted to give it maximum coverage in the magazine and who better to comment on the aesthetics than the Royal Institute of British Architects? I quickly scanned down the text and was pleased to see that they had addressed the main points that I had asked them to consider. They waxed lyrical about the plans-on-hold 'Iceberg' but cautioned over 'the rather mundane matching, two-tier stands at right-angles to the square' and the 'necessity of ensuring that the highest standards of construction are met'. Well that seemed pretty obvious even to me, and RIBA clearly felt the Vauxhall End redevelopment should have been prioritised, but I would at least be able to write up the ground development piece at home later in the weekend. I reached for my tea and looked over to the next desk where the fax paper was still curling lazily out of the machine. My curiosity pricked, I eased back my chair and stepped over to see who it was from. If it looked urgent, I supposed that I would have to track Sally down.

Sally Framsell was a new arrival at The Oval and had been brought in as liaison officer for the new building project. She reported directly to the Building Committee, which had been set up once the decision to redevelop had finally been made. We had only been sharing the library space for a couple of weeks, and either one of us had invariably been out, but in the brief time we had spent together I quickly decided that she was alright. This was her first job proper after studying psychology at university. I thought it odd that she had taken the job even though she apparently hated cricket, but then I suppose that you do not have to like carrots to be a greengrocer. Either way, she had a ready laugh, said she liked a drink, and shared my enthusiasm for curry, all of which made me warm to her.

I uncurled the sheet and saw that the message was addressed to Barry Miller, the chairman of the Building Committee. It was from Willby Construction and appeared to be a tender for the new double-decker stands. The name was instantly familiar as they had been the successful bidders to build the Iceberg, but as far as I knew, the date for tenders had passed and the Building Committee was already preparing a short-list, with recommendations, to present to the full Board. It looked as though Willby had cut it too fine and that seemed like a crazy error for a company which had been commissioned to build the now-postponed Iceberg project. Heads were surely going to roll at Willby HQ for this. I was just about to let the roll of paper drop from my hand when the message ended abruptly, returning the library to silence. I tore the paper against the serrated metal strip and scribbled across the top:

Sally – looks like Willby won't be!! See you Monday. Think I'm with Carlisle for an hour or so first thing – Johnny x.

I returned to my computer, saw that two of the remaining messages were internal memoranda with little relevance to me personally and clicked on the sixth e-mail. It was from Elisa – just a couple of lines and an attachment. I swallowed the last mouthful of tea as my eyes skipped over the words:

I'm gonna miss you, darling. Hope you miss me too – if you know what I mean. I'm due back Tuesday evening, late. Don't wait up, but if I'm in bed before you get in, don't be afraid to wake me!!!

When we first got together, and she was still travelling a lot, she always used to leave little post-it note messages around for me to find whilst she was away – some funny, some cute and some simply unrepeatable. I could survive a couple of days without her and in the summer I was away a fair amount too, but I am at my best when she's around. The next few days, with Elisa in the States, would be the longest we had been apart for a year or more and I did not much relish the prospect. There is more stress in professional sport than a lot of people realize, and she has a really grounding effect on me. All that aside she is also very enthusiastic in bed and I have no problem with that. I opened the desk diary that was propped up against the monitor at the ribbon marker.

I found Tuesday and was pleased to see that I had nothing in the diary for the evening. I closed Elisa's message and as I did so, remembered the attachment – I would have to go back to that. I moved on to the last one.

It was from Ken Lovell of the Mail on Sunday. It was a brief message but one that made me catch my breath. He said he had it on good authority that Richard Lees was standing down from the selectors' panel.

CHAPTER 2

Sunday April 13 1997

I managed to get a few things done on the Sunday; a few things that had been nagging away at both of us. You know the sort of thing – garage cleared, hedges trimmed and if the lawnmower had been working, I would have got the grass cut as well. I had forgotten that it had been put away after it broke down towards the end of last summer and of course we had neglected to do anything about it. If I had discovered that it was not working earlier it would have been possible to go and get a replacement but it gave me the excuse to get a cold beer from the fridge and to spend half-an-hour flicking through the material that the schools had sent in for my piece on schools' cricket. Elisa would not let me hire a gardener but neither of us got the time to do the gardening ourselves. As I gazed out from the patio, down the length of the garden I wondered whether I should get someone in for a couple of days to blitz the place whilst Elisa was in New York.

I must have missed the call when I was out in the garden and when I came inside in fading light I got straight onto Elisa's PC and started to put the article together. Either way, it was the blinking red light on the answerphone by the front door that attracted my attention at about ten o'clock. I was on my way upstairs with an armful of ironing that I had neither the time nor the inclination to do, and I let it drop to the floor in a heap and reached for the 'play' button.

'Hiya, lover......are you there? Pick up if you are...... look I've gotta dash, the band are doing an interview on the Letterman Show later and I've blagged my way in. Sorry about last night – jet lag.... be good! Byeeee!!'

Bugger it! I had missed her the night before, having waited until nearly 10:00 p.m., at The Oval, came home to find a quick message on the machine and now I had missed her again. She had only been gone a day and I was already pining – which surprised me. The next call surprised me even more.

'Johnny? I guess I've got the right number. It's Summers. Long time no speak and all that. You're not in by the looks of it so I'll be brief. Got some good news. Lees has stepped down, or so I am told. Get back to me if you can coz I've got an idea. Same number as before. Say 'hi' to Elisa for me – if you're still together? Speak soon.'

Suddenly I was glad that Elisa was not here, or at least not when Summers had called. I had nothing really against him even though he was largely responsible for me losing my England place. The cannabis incident in Sydney back in '95 was all rumour and conjecture, stirred up by the press and not quashed by the tour management because they were unable to link me to the more serious betting incident – something that could have really rocked the game. They couldn't prove my involvement in that, because I wasn't involved but there *was* an element of truth in the cannabis story and that gave them a way to be rid of me. I had had a couple of discreet draws at a gig when I was out with a shoulder injury for a few days, but the official version had me smoking grass in the SCG dressing room. Had Elisa been home, she would have ripped Summers apart. The bet was all his idea and he admitted it afterwards. To be fair to him, he also said that I had had nothing to do with it, but as we were teammates at Surrey and since we roomed together on tour it was clear that I was guilty by association. In truth, I knew about the bet beforehand but declined to join him. I would like to be able to claim the moral high ground, but I was strapped for cash at the time and in any case thought he was probably wasting his money, though I might just have had a punt if I had had the readies.

I spent a few minutes trying to find his telephone number but could not even find the address book. Remembering that Elisa had transferred all of our contacts onto the PC, I spent a few more minutes trying to find the electronic address book but, failing to locate it, I decided to call him from the office the next day. He had left Surrey under something of a cloud, but I supposed they still had his contact details.

Summers clearly had kept *his* contacts. I wondered how he had heard about Lees' departure from the selection panel. It had certainly been mooted for a couple of months and England's disappointing showing over the winter in Zimbabwe and New Zealand may have speeded things up, but nothing had appeared in the Sunday papers to my knowledge, despite Lovell's e-mail to me. Lees had managed the Australia tour that Summers and I had been on and although he had walked away from the position when his contract expired the following summer, he had agreed to remain on the selection team. I was not going to get excited over my chances because I had not had the opportunity of speaking with the other two selectors. Given that Lees had once promised me that I would never get back in the team all the time he had anything to do with it led me to hope that his departure might not be the worst thing that could have happened.

Summers and I had not spoken for at least eighteen months and quite what this idea of his might be I had not the faintest idea.

CHAPTER 3

I slept fitfully and awoke Monday morning for the final time just ahead of the alarm, slammed my open palm onto the button as it started to ring and pulled the covers up over my head to block out the light. The bed felt big without Elisa and it was odd to think that several thousand miles away she was probably asleep. It was two o'clock in the morning in New York and for a moment I thought of calling. I had tried the hotel a couple of hours earlier, but the desk could not get an answer from her room. I reflected grimly that she may not have been very keen to go but that she seemed to have come to terms with things pretty quickly. I resolved to give Ralph and Kitty a call after breakfast to see if they had heard from her.

I am not at my best first thing until I have had a cup of tea or two and prefer a quiet breakfast with a newspaper or book to a full-scale debate. Elisa is unreasonably cheerful in the mornings and ready to take on the world, so it was quite nice to be able to potter quietly and to catch up on the stack of mail, some of which had lain unopened on the breakfast bar for the best part of a week. Whilst the tea brewed, I set about the pile of letters, dividing the junk mail from the rest. That cut it down to about twenty-five pieces that I had to attend to; a mixture of bills and personal stuff. The bills could wait until later and, as I mashed out the teabag against the side of the cup, I started on the more interesting looking ones.

There were a couple of 'good luck' cards: one from the Supporters' Club and one, I was sure, from Elisa. The Supporters' Club sends one every year to each member of the squad with a specially composed poem for each player. They are invariably excruciatingly bad and this one was no exception. I will not repeat the whole thing here, but it ended:

> So, here's best wishes to Johnny Lorrens,
> Let's hope he scores his runs in torrents!

If I was the sensitive type I might have been offended. I joined them in hoping for torrents of runs, of course, but knew they were more likely to come in a very fine spray. I closed the card and reached for the other one; the one of a cartoon dog. The one with the lipstick kiss inside. The one that smelt of her favourite perfume. I smiled as I raised it to my nose. I had been disappointed not to have been able to get hold of Elisa and more so that her old habit of leaving me notes when she was away had, until I opened the card, seemed to have become a thing of the past. I glanced up at the photograph of the two of us

17

that she had pinned to the felt-covered notice board on the kitchen wall over the breakfast bar. It was taken just after we met – Sydney or was it Melbourne? I had been caught in mid-blink and looked as drunk as a lord. She looked absolutely gorgeous.

On a whim I reached over to the wooden block on the worktop against the wall and selected the largest of the three pairs of scissors. I stood to remove a drawing pin from the top edge of the photo and carefully snipped Elisa from it. I returned my own half of the picture to the board and slipped Elisa into my dressing gown pocket intending to transfer her to my wallet later on. I had never carried a photo of Elisa around with me and to my knowledge she had never had one of me. Absence making the heart grow fonder I suppose. The jarring tone of the telephone made me jump and I hurried out of the kitchen, down to the front door and grabbed at the receiver.

'Johnny? It's Mark.'

Summers. I looked at my watch. Not even eight o'clock.

'Johnny? You there?'

'Oh, yes sorry. Mark. How *are* you?'

'Fine, fine. Listen, is this convenient? I can call back.'

I realized that I must have sounded unfriendly if not downright rude. 'Sorry, Mark. Yes, it's fine – thought you were Elisa for a moment.' I heard him say something in reply, but his voice was muffled. 'Say that again – I can barely hear you.'

'My fault, mate. Is this better?'

I told him that it was and puzzled again as to why he was calling – and at this hour.

'I've got to be quick, Johnny, and I guess you are wondering why I'm getting in touch after all this time, but I wondered if you could spare an hour or two.'

I was losing patience already. It was largely his fault that I got in the trouble I did, and in any case, it was his decision to drop all his old friends. I had had some sympathy at first and had tried to get in contact, but he had chosen not to respond. He had been banned from representative cricket for three years following the Sydney incident, which I thought was unduly harsh punishment since it effectively killed off his career just as it had started – one Test cap certainly did not reflect his quality. Surrey had dropped him like a hot potato and the last I heard he was trying to use his notoriety on the after-dinner circuit. That was at least eighteen months ago, and this was the first time he had bothered to call.

'Johnny? I need help, mate. Just an hour…'

I had misgivings and had Elisa been home I would probably have refused to even meet him. But she was several-thousand miles away. And Summers had once been a good friend.

'Johnny?'

'Okay. Make it tonight if you like. Surrey Tavern at six?'

'Anywhere but that old dump,' he said quickly. 'West End would be better.'

'Flamin' heck, Mark. Do you want my help or don't you?'

'I really appreciate it – but the Tavern is just too close to home; too many memories. I just try to avoid the place these days.'

He did not sound convincing, but I did not really mind meeting him in the West End; with Elisa away I did not have the inclination to rush home to an empty house. Besides, Summers was always very persuasive and usually got his own way. I could feel myself getting sucked in again. Against my better judgement I agreed.

'Good man. Listen, gotta dash. Porcupine at six-thirty,' and he was gone.

I had to smile. The Porcupine in Charing Cross Road was a bigger dive than the Tavern. And he had managed to change the time as well. I replaced the receiver and reflected that I was rather pleased at the thought of seeing him again.

I drained the last drops of tea from the mug, placed it in the sink with the dishes from the previous evening, and went to run a bath. My right shoulder had been playing up for a couple of weeks; ironically, ever since the start of pre-season training. It had been good to rest it over the winter and the break had restored my enthusiasm for the game, but the lay-off had given time for the muscles to seize up. A winter off was what I had needed really, what with the likelihood of an international career on long-term hold and a niggling injury I just could not seem to shake. I felt a little guilty that after seven months away I was coming back perhaps more unfit than I had ever been, and I had to see Carlisle at eleven. No doubt he would have something to say about it. I had met him in Australia when he was the Queensland coach. Under his leadership the state had won three Sheffield Shields back-to-back with a squad largely made up of bits and pieces cricketers. At Surrey, he had inherited an ageing team of former internationals, a sprinkling of youngsters and me. He had made his opinion of me perfectly clear at his introduction to the team a couple of weeks before. A less than high opinion that was compounded by the unfortunate events of that evening.

The Club had invited players, wives, girlfriends and office staff to a cheese and wine do in the pavilion museum to welcome Carlisle. I had accepted the invitation and had expected to be working at the ground on that day. Elisa was to have joined me after an editorial meeting at *Smashed*, and when she called me at three o'clock to say that she could not make it I was disappointed but not totally surprised. In her line of work she has to be flexible, as the recent dash to New York proved. Apparently, she had heard that a secret gig was due to go ahead up in Camden and, through her contacts in the Immigration Service, she had discovered that Neil Young had arrived the day before ahead of a European tour. Elisa derived six from a pair of twos and suggested I meet her at the Underworld immediately. I cried off from the cheese and wine with a sudden migraine and enjoyed a thoroughly wonderful evening with Elisa, Mr Young and about five-hundred other lovers of fine music up in

Camden.

I got a call from Sally the next day, a Saturday, asking after my health and with the information that Carlisle had adopted a pretty aggressive stance, singling out various under-performers on the playing staff. Not unfairly, I felt, he pointed up my less than flattering batting average, suggesting that in this day and age I had no chance of regaining my England place until I worked out which end of the bat to hold, which would have been funny if it were not also true. I had heard similar mutterings from the selectors before about this but the jury generally seems to be out on the matter, with growing calls for selecting bowlers on their bowling abilities and that approach would not harm my chances. I resolved to have a chat with Carlisle to see if we could work on this weakness anyway. At this stage I was confident that we could have worked together. When, a week or so later, the door of my temporary office flew open and Carlisle burst in, frothing at the mouth, I could see we had a problem.

'You little shit!' he screamed. 'Don't you ever pull a stunt like that again or you are finished here.' He flung a magazine at me and flew back out the way he had come.

Sally came out from under her desk and I managed a nervous smile. 'See,' I ventured, 'I think he does like me.' I picked up the magazine, which had slid off my desk in the wake of his exit and saw that it was the latest issue of *Smashed*. I already had a sinking feeling as I turned the mashed pages with an attempt at indifference.

'Oh, shitola! That really helps,' I muttered as Sally came to look over my shoulder at the large colour photograph of Neil Young in the news section. The front row of the audience was nicely picked out in the stage lights but just in case there was any doubt, the caption beneath it cleared things up.

Neil Young in Camden – attracted a veritable who's who of the London pop scene and beyond. Seen frugging away furiously at the front, former England cricketer and all-round bad boy, Johnny Lorrens.

'They always say there's no such thing as bad publicity,' Sally offered cautiously. I remained silent. 'Are you in big trouble?' she asked quietly, trying to suppress a giggle.

'I don't know about that, Sally, but I was absolutely not frugging.'

She laughed. 'Sod him if he can't take a joke.'

'My thoughts exactly. Probably not a good time to tell him about the dirty fork.'

'Another obscure Python reference?'

I nodded.

'And the dirty fork is...?'

'My knackered shoulder and general state of unfitness,' I replied with a grin.

I turned the taps off and had just stepped into the bath as the phone rang again. I decided to leave the answerphone to record the call and as my own voice drifted up the stairs towards me, I lay back and closed my eyes. The tone of Sally's voice made me sit up sharply. I clambered back out of the bath and dripped my way down the stairs.

I managed to get to The Oval in a little over an hour. Thankfully the rush hour traffic had eased a little and I saw by the cricketers clock on the pavilion wall as I slid to a stop that it was just gone ten. When I reached the library, Sally looked as frazzled as she had sounded on the telephone earlier.

'What's all the fuss, Sal'?'

'Barry Miller,' she replied.

'Oh, he's in today, is he? Good effort.'

'Was,' she corrected me.

Miller was her boss, head of the Building Committee and almost never around. Still only around forty, he had played as a batsman for Surrey for ten years or so, the end of his career overlapping mine by about two seasons. He had been another one deemed good enough to win just the one England cap but had played at a time when the selectors were flip-flopping about in search of a quick batting fix. Back then the 'One Cap Club' was bolstered by a number of very good county players who were never given the chance to cement a place in an England team enduring a long run of mediocrity. He always seemed a little bitter about that and had never been really popular with his teammates. He eventually retired early, under something of a cloud, to start a career in project management. By chance, he had arrived back at The Oval to coordinate the new building project and his arrival had ruffled a few feathers. By all accounts he was on a fat daily consultant's fee.

'They're in the Committee room now,' Sally explained. 'Miller was jumping up and down about that fax.' She had mentioned a fax message to me in our earlier conversation and I had professed ignorance. I suddenly remembered the one that had come through Saturday afternoon.

'There *was* one late Saturday,' I replied. 'I'd clean forgotten it. Came from Willby Construction. I left it on your desk.'

'Well it's not here now. What did it say?'

'Well obviously I didn't read it properly as it was addressed to you, but it looked like a tender for the new stands. Anyway, why does it matter – they missed the cut-off didn't they?'

'Yes, they did, but for some reason Miller's got a bee in his bonnet over it. He came in here first thing before the meeting and asked if I'd had any messages. I gave him half a dozen that had come in over the past few days since he was last here. He flicked through them and said there was one missing. I thought it a little odd that he would not say who it was from, but I assured him that I had given him all the messages that I knew about. He then suggested I call you to see if you had taken any.'

'He didn't mention Willby by name?'

'No, but he seemed to be expecting a fax.'

'Well I shouldn't worry Sal', it was probably something personal. Funny where that Willby fax went to though. Have the cleaners been in?'

'Yes, did you mention it?'

I said that I had and wondered secretly whether they had been a little over-zealous and binned the message by mistake. I left Sally still fretting over the call she had to make to Miller and went in search of Carlisle. When I came back an hour later she seemed much more relaxed.

'I've just made a tea, would you like one, Johnny?'

I nodded. 'You seem happier. Miller took it well, did he?'

'Not bad. Seems to think *you* lost it, but I tried to persuade him otherwise. He cancelled the meeting anyway.'

'What?'

Sally looked taken aback at my sharp response. 'The fax. He reckons you probably lost it. Asked me if you had read it but I thought it best to say that you hadn't.'

'Yes, but how could he cancel the meeting? Weren't they supposed to be awarding contracts today?'

'They were, but Miller was taken ill not long after speaking with me and they've put it back to later in the week.'

'Thanks,' I muttered, taking the mug of tea that Sally held out to me. 'A lot of fuss over a message and then he goes off sick. Seems odd to me.'

'It does,' she agreed. 'More to the point, how did it go with your mate?'

I looked at her. She was smiling wickedly.

'Oh, Carlisle,' I said breaking into a smile myself. 'Let's just say that it could be an interesting season. I was meant to be interviewing him for the magazine, but we spent most of the time talking about me; my attitude, commitment, fitness – all that sort of stuff.'

'And what did he conclude?'

'You find this funny, don't you?' I laughed.

'Yes,' she said totally unabashed. 'All this fuss over a game.'

'It might only be a game, but it's my job.' I was still laughing, and she had tears in her eyes. 'And it's not *only* a game. It's bloody cricket!'

Tears rolled down her cheeks. 'I know,' she managed between sobs, 'but you get so indignant about it.'

'The bugger said I can't bat, didn't he? Said I didn't know which end of it to hold. I think I've every right to feel a bit indignant.'

Sally produced a tissue and dabbed at her eyes. 'Now I am no expert, but he is not completely in error there, is he?'

She had a point there. I picked up a rubber band and pinged it at her, making her splash tea over the papers she was working on. I slipped out of the office quickly as a handful of paper clips came my way.

The first pint was delicious. I had worked on the schools' piece at home over the weekend and spent half an hour in the office putting the finishing touches to it. I had then spent all afternoon on the Carlisle interview, struggling to put a five hundred-word article together from the tapes I had made. As I had told Sally, most of it was about me and I certainly was not going to put what he had said about me in the magazine. Not that *Oval Eyes* under my editorship was simply there to toe the party line. I had ruffled a few feathers in the first couple of issues and printed a couple of items that were not exactly flattering to me personally, but with my England place apparently a little closer, I was not going to mention the fact that the new coach had thanked me for making his job a little easier. He told me that he did not have to worry about where to put me in the batting line-up; even suggested that, if my shoulder was right, the scorecards for the whole season could be ordered from the printers with me at number eleven.

I found a table in a quiet corner and, placing my pint on a cardboard mat, pulled a sheaf of papers from the pocket of my Harrington and rummaged about for a pen. The day had turned quite chilly and every time the street door swung inwards it brought with it a sharp gust of icy air. I looked about for another free table but could not see one. Zipping up my jacket, I shivered and started to read the Carlisle piece again. I got half-way through and found myself drifting off again, thinking about what he had said. I could not account for why my batting had become so poor. Confidence has a lot to do with it of course and, in the nets, I had always been told that I looked the part. Out in the middle it was a different story, however. Earlier in my career I had sought advice from anyone I could and had tinkered with lighter bats and heavier bats, short and long handles and different guards and pick-ups. The result was always the same and my number eleven position at Surrey, provided I kept bowling well, looked mine for the foreseeable future. But whatever the current thinking, poor batting was not going to help my chances of a recall.

I had just returned from the bar with a fresh pint when a large, heavy set man sat down opposite me. I looked up, nodded and returned to my papers, underlining and circling with an orange highlighter pen. After a couple of minutes, a cough from across the table made me look up. The big figure opposite me was smiling benignly.

'You gonna sit there and ignore me all night, you rude bastard?'

The two years had taken their toll on my old friend. His thick, curly brown hair was turning grey and had thinned noticeably. His once, chiselled features looked slightly puffy and his eyes looked rather rheumy, although as he laughed, a glimmer returned. It was his size that amazed me. He is well over six feet tall and must have weighed fifteen stone when we played together. I could only see him from above the table, but he must have added another five stones since we had last met. My reaction must have been evident.

'Yeah, I know, who's been eating all the pies?' he said, laughing heartily. The table vibrated gently as his huge stomach wobbled against it with mirth.

I fumbled in my embarrassment for something complimentary to say. 'You, by the looks of it,' I managed, realising that I had failed in my quest. He did not seem perturbed. 'Where have you been hiding? I heard you had gone abroad.'

'I spent a bit of time coaching in Zimbabwe – until the political situation got out of hand. Travelled a bit. Do you remember how we'd go on tour and complain that we'd never seen any of the places we'd been to? Well, I decided to retrace my footsteps and went to India, Sri Lanka and then over to Oz and New Zealand.'

'Sounds great. And what did you reckon?'

'Waste of time. I realised almost immediately that what I had really enjoyed was the camaraderie on tour. Travelling on my own just felt kind of lonely. I met people, of course, but it wasn't the same. When you are on tour you moan about not having any freedom – but you forget that wherever you go there are people waiting for you; people that want you to be there – want to know you. On tour you are like a VIP. On your own you feel like a bloody nobody again.'

I was beginning to wonder if I had done the right thing in agreeing to meet Summers again. 'So, you came back home then?'

He motioned me to wait and stepped up to the bar, returning seconds later with two fresh pints. 'Yes, by way of America. And that's where things started to look up. I ended up in New England for a couple of months and then when I got home, I bumped into an old mate who sorted me out a job up in the City. Pay's not too good but I get to eat and drink out a lot.' He laughed loudly again and patted his stomach.

'I never saw you as the City type, I must say,' I said, smiling.

'Takes all sorts, and in any case, I was running out of options. I tried to get media work immediately after the Sydney business, but the ban seems to have been extended beyond the playing arena.'

'Yeah, I am really sorry...'

He cut me off with a huge upheld palm. 'Say nothing. It was my fault entirely. After all the papers we had signed I should have known better, but I just could not resist those odds. I mean, 300 to 1.'

I had often wondered about that day and whether the whole thing had been a sting operation set up by the International Cricket Council. There had been some dubious results in Indian domestic cricket a year or two before Sydney and of course there was the famous 1981 Ashes series when Rod Marsh and Dennis Lillee successfully backed the 500-1 odds offered on an improbable England win. The ICC belatedly had introduced increasingly stringent laws aimed at eradicating match-fixing. It was no longer acceptable for a player to bet on any game involving his own team and punishments for doing so had become increasingly harsh. The ironic thing about the Summers Incident, as the papers called it, was that he had had no influence on the outcome of the game, which was an unlikely Australia win and besides, was not playing in the match. He was not even twelfth man. I still felt guilty, and Summers knew it. I *was* playing in the match and would likely have joined him in the bet but could not lay my hands on the cash. Summers laid his bet, returned to the dressing room and picked up his winnings after the game. When I saw him next in our hotel room that evening, he was packing for home. Somehow news of his bet against the England team had raced around the ground. I was adamant that I should own up to my part of the bargain, or at least admit that I knew about his plan, but he would have none of it. I guess I got a comeuppance of sorts later on in the tour but nonetheless still felt a sense of debt towards the big man.

'Did you get to keep the money?' I had always wondered.

'That's what paid for the world trip. I really thought that I'd get away with it as I was not involved in the match. That's why you came under suspicion, I suppose. They reasoned that I'd need an accomplice or two and as we were mates...'

'That's ridiculous. I mean, you were only sticking on a couple of hundred Aussie. At those odds it was worth the risk surely.'

He grinned sheepishly. 'I put on a bit more than that actually.'

'You old bugger,' I said with a laugh. I took a long gulp of the cold beer. 'Do you miss it?' I meant the cricket.

'I do, yes. Not too proud to be in the One Cap Club to be fair – no offence, mate.'

I waived a hand to dismiss his apology. At least I had a chance, albeit a very slim one, of adding to *my* solitary appearance.

'I could have...' My old friend's eyes seemed to well up for an instant, but he took another huge gulp and drained his glass. 'Another?'

'My round,' I insisted. When I got back with the drinks he was flicking through a well-thumbed diary.

'What are you doing tomorrow night?' he asked.

'Nothing planned. Depends how much you make me drink tonight. Elisa's in New York – gets back late tomorrow.'

'You two still together?' He seemed pleased.

'Married,' I said, indicating the gold band on my finger.

'Strewth!' he exclaimed. 'Like, I mean, congratulations. She managed to get you, did she?' He nodded thoughtfully. 'Never saw her as a cricket widow.'

'Who's in New York?' I said indignantly.

'Steady, only messing. Listen,' he said, returning to the little diary, 'if you can come round to my place tomorrow, I want to talk to you about this idea.'

I had forgotten about his idea. He would not let on what it was all about, but I had the impression that it was no big deal. I sensed instead, a loneliness and a desire to rebuild some old bridges. I agreed to go to his place, and he scribbled down his old Wimbledon Hill address.

CHAPTER 4

Tuesday April 15 1997

I awoke to a hammering noise that I first thought was emanating from the garden. Keeping one foot in bed I stretched out towards the curtains and, reaching under them, pulled the window closed. When the hammering did not stop, I realised it was in my head. I flopped back into bed with a groan and closed my eyes. I knew I would have to take some Nurofen but the thought of getting up to find some was none too pleasant. I ran my furry tongue around the roof of my mouth and could still taste the greasy kebab that I had picked up at a disreputable little place close to Epsom station. I peered at my fingers in the semi-darkness of the bedroom. I sniffed at a nail and drew back sharply from the stale onion stench. I gulped back an urge to be sick and squinted at the clock. Still only seven. I began to see sense in Elisa's vegetarianism. My current state was, of course, nothing to do with the drink.

With what felt like superhuman effort I swung my legs out and tested the carpet gingerly with a foot. Not too much movement from the floorboards. That seemed to be a good sign and, rising slowly to allow the blood to find its own level, I inched carefully towards the door. I found a half-full box of tablets in the bathroom cabinet and took the stairs gently, holding onto the handrail for good measure. I had reached the bottom stair when I noticed the blinking red light on the answer-machine. I stabbed at it with a finger as I passed and had reached the kitchen door before the message cut in.

'Hi, lover. Only me. Sorry I've not been in touch. This place is a madhouse but I've got some great stuff on the band. Think they're gonna be huge. Look, I guess you're asleep so I'll ring off but will be back later. Don't forget – wake me even if I look dead! Love ya!'

I swayed in the kitchen doorway as I listened to Elisa's message. Just the sound of her voice sent a little tingle down my spine. As the message ended the machine announced the time it was recorded. Six-fifty a.m. I had just missed her and supposed that it was the telephone ringing that had awoken me. Well, she wanted me to wake her, which was good, because that was what I planned to do. I was pleased that I had missed her as much as I had. It was a good kind of empty feeling because I knew it was only temporary. And I knew how she and I normally responded to being apart for a few days. Sex was better than ever. And it was usually pretty good. I felt a little miffed though that she had only just managed to find the time to call.

After the first mug of tea I started to feel a shade better. I spooned in a couple of extra sugars and took my bowl of cereal into the living room. The place looked a mess and I resolved to tidy up before Elisa's return. I channel-hopped for a few minutes as I finished the cornflakes before taking a leisurely shower. I felt much more normal after that and decided to take the train up to town. In any case, I suspected that I was still over the limit.

Summers had persuaded me the night before, with little opposition, to try a private club he knew of in Wardour Street; a dingy little basement place, with peeling, black-painted walls and low ceilings. It was called 'The Trip' I think, or at least, Monday nights were. It was one of those places that have a different club night each day of the week. There was a tiny little bar serving spirits and expensive bottled beers at the bottom of the stairs and at the far end, a small stage. When we arrived, a four-piece band were just finishing their first set. They were all dressed identically in black: black roll-necks, black jeans and black Chelsea boots, topped off with black Ray-Bans and black pudding-bowl haircuts. On the bass drum skin in horror-film lettering, *The Sons of Stepford*. Like me, they were clearly into the Nuggets stuff from the mid-sixties and equally clearly had a small but very enthusiastic following. I made a mental note to tell Elisa about them. I stayed with Summers until gone eleven, but he was speed drinking and I could feel myself wilting. Besides, my little chat with Carlisle was still ringing in my ears and I thought it politic to beat a hasty retreat.

By the time I got on the Waterloo train at Epsom and found an empty seat I was feeling a whole lot better. I unfurled my Guardian and turned straight to the sports pages. The pre-season build up was continuing and there was a good piece about the Test match grounds. Old Trafford had been re-instated, having missed out on a Test the previous year and Worcester was still being talked of as a possible seventh venue. The Oval plans were mentioned and gave the impression that contracts for the building of two new double-deckers had already been approved. It mentioned the name of the architect who had produced the plans and the architecture critic, Ursula Hamilton, expressed surprise that designs from Foster, Rogers and Hopkins had all been overlooked in favour of those by an unknown twenty-five year old, Frederic Prinz. He had apparently 'impressed with his innovative use of in-situ con-crete,' which meant very little to me, and his prior claim to fame rested solely, it seemed, on some public toilets in Hackney. Whilst the appointment of Prinz had been revealed a while back, Willby Construction was mentioned as the main contractor. All very odd, I reflected, as I carefully tore the article out to show to Sally later.

The gentle rattle and roll of the train soon had me dozing and I awoke with a start as the doors hissed open. I lurched upright, saw that we had pulled in at Vauxhall and I just had time to dive off before the warning beeps sounded. Relieved that I did not seem to have been recognised – I was not feeling my best and assume that I was not looking too fabulous either – I put my head down and trotted down the two flights of stairs in the centre of the raised platform, slipped through the ticket barrier and headed off down the Harleyford Road, narrowly evading the Big Issue seller who was lurking in the station exit, on the lookout for customers. Nothing personal against her; more a reaction against the magazine, which had 'taken up my case' after the drugs incident and argued that I was a good example of how recreational drugs can be enjoyed without damaging a high-profile sports career. They seemed to overlook the fact that it had no doubt contributed to the ban that only now, two years on, was just possibly on the verge of being revoked.

I picked up a bundle of mail from the office on my way up to our eagle's nest at the top of the pavilion, pausing for a moment at the railings on the top deck to enjoy the view of central London, glimmering in the milky spring sunlight, and to wave ostentatiously at my Surrey colleagues who were jogging around the perimeter of the playing area, led by Carlisle. It was cold even for early April and the twenty or so figures, clad in all the layers they could find, looked like a Michelin Man convention, puffs of steamy breath dotting their progress in the chilly morning air. Although my shoulder was probably going to need some physio, I could in all honesty probably have joined them, but I still had to deliver the final copy to Marketing, and frankly, I cannot stand jogging. I decided that it would look good to volunteer for training the next day – before I was ordered to.

Sally glanced up as I entered and jerked a thumb at a steaming mug that she had evidently just placed on my desk. I dropped the Guardian article onto hers as I passed. 'You could have told me it was all settled,' I said with a grin. 'I could have put it in the magazine.'

Sally looked at the piece and as I spooned in a couple of extra sugars, I could hear her mouthing along as she scanned down the page.

'Where did they get this from?' she mumbled under her breath, and then a little louder and without looking up, 'You look awful, by the way.'

I busied myself with the stack of mail, which was mainly of the autograph hunting variety. As a kid I had plagued the counties with beseeching letters at the start of each season, in the hope of being sent the official team autograph sheets and in the knowledge that, armed with these, I would not have to spend depressing hours lying in wait for the players in the car park after close of play. Some of the counties were unfailingly generous. Leicester and Hampshire, for example, always sent very attractive sheets, embossed with the county badge, and covering letters. Some, however, sent poor photocopies which, to my discredit, went straight in the bin. I made a point from the moment I turned professional of replying to every letter and where possible, to accede to requests, in addition to signing the couple of thousand official sheets and dozens of bats that the Club arranged at the start of each season. I could only think off-hand, of two requests that I had not complied with: to sign a photograph purportedly of me sent in by a fan – I had to send it back as it was actually of a retired Essex player – and one that *was* of me, taken with a strong zoom lens, emerging starkers from the showers at Chesterfield. Oh, and the young lady's breasts just a couple of days before.

Sally was talking on the telephone and I had not been paying attention until she raised her voice a little. 'That's what it says, Barry. And before you ask, no, nobody from the paper spoke to me.' She paused and I saw a flicker of her eyes in my direction. 'No, nobody spoke to him either,' she said in a quieter voice.

She looked a little embarrassed when she came off the telephone and purposefully evaded my gaze. I continued to stare at her and smiled as a pink hue spread slowly from her neck until it covered her face. She looked up suddenly with a flash of defiance. 'What are you staring at, Johnny?'

I laughed. She looked lovely when she was in a temper. 'You,' I answered. 'Was Miller shocked?'

Her colour was returning to normal as she rummaged in the mini rucksack which she always carried with her. She pulled out a mobile phone and began to tap away at the keyboard in front of her. 'Not shocked, no. Annoyed maybe. Said it was some reporter jumping the gun.'

'You are not satisfied with that?'

'No,' she started uncertainly as she began to dial a number from her computer screen. 'The meeting is tomorrow apparently. Barry said he was better. You know – the postponed Building Committee meeting?' She suddenly held a hand up to stop me from replying. 'Mr Prinz, please. No, I'll hold, thank-you. My name? Ursula Hamilton. The Guardian.'

I must have looked alarmed. She covered the mouthpiece with her hand. 'It's not traceable; no-one knows my mobile number.'

I still had not a clue what she was up to when Prinz evidently came on the line.

'Hello, Frederic. Ursula Hamilton here, from the Guardian.' She quickly looked at the newspaper article on the desk in front of her. 'My editor just asked me to call you up to confirm what you told me on the phone yesterday afternoon,' she winked at me and held up crossed fingers, 'that The Oval commission will be your first sports arena. That's right isn't it?' She nodded into the handset as she looked at me. 'Oh, your second? Beijing, China? I didn't know that. Well thanks very much, that was all. Oh yes, I forgot to ask, are you pleased with the choice of building contractor, have you worked with them before? Oh, you have... China, I see. It must have been exciting when Barry Miller called with the news.' She winked again, then suddenly beamed as she gave me an excited thumbs-up before ending the call. She sat back looking both triumphant yet uncomfortable.

I sat perfectly quiet for a second, took a mouthful of tea before speaking. 'What the hell was that all about, Sally?'

'Good, wasn't I?' she said with a broad grin.

'Weird was the word that came to mind, if I'm honest. What's with the Ursula Hamilton business?'

'It's a fix – the whole deal with the new stands. Don't you see? First the hoohah over that fax and now this leak in the paper about Willby.'

'Well I know it looks odd seeing that the meeting has not even happened yet...'

Sally interrupted. 'Odd doesn't begin to cover it. I asked him whether he was excited when Barry Miller called with the news. He corrected me immediately. Sir Kenneth Parslow called him yesterday, directly after the Building Committee meeting. Sir Kenneth is the Surrey President.' Sally gave me a challenging look.

'I know who he is, Sal, but I thought that meeting didn't happen.'

'Precisely. Prinz already knew that Willby had the contract to build to his design. The meeting was to have been yesterday but was cancelled and I reckon Willby had already been chosen. It was a done deal, but they neglected to tell Parslow that the meeting was cancelled at the last minute. Sir Kenneth goes ahead and makes the call to Prinz.'

'And Prinz goes public during the interview with Ursula Hamilton because as far as he's concerned it's now in the public domain.'

'And that suggests Parslow is in on it too,' Sally murmured, half to herself.

I let out a long, low whistle. This did look odd indeed. I resolved to give Elisa's father a call.

Summers met me at Wimbledon station at seven-fifteen as arranged, greeting me like a long-lost friend. He looked bigger than ever in the ticket-hall crush but was a good man to follow in a crowd; the rush hour hordes scattered ahead of him, leaving us a clear passage to the forecourt. After the teeming station building it was a relief to get out into the crisp evening air. I have never liked being in crowds and to this day cannot bear to be cooped up in small places; something that goes back to being stuck in an old tree stump at infant school, and probably why I am happiest, in the wide open, out on a cricket pitch.

Despite the chilly air I could feel my shirt sticking uncomfortably to my back and hoping Summers had not noticed, I quickly brushed a hand across my moist brow. He looked round as I was wiping my hand with a handkerchief.

'Not still struggling after last night, are you? You've lost your touch, old boy.'

'I'm fine. Though I must say it took me a while to get over it this morning.' I asked him what time he left the club as I dashed after him between a pair of buses that were moving away from a stop just past the station.

'Oh, not long after you. I walked that little redhead down to the taxi rank and picked up a gypsy cab for myself.'

He had been teasing with a young woman in the club, but it did not seem to be going anywhere. I did not like to ask about relationships as I had heard on The Oval grapevine that his long-term partner had walked out after the betting scandal erupted. In fairness to her, they had had to put up with an army of reporters camped outside their flat for days. In all honesty, though, she had always seemed to me something of a gold-digger and I was not surprised that she had gone. Summers had always battled with his weight; successfully whilst he played for Surrey, but I began to wonder if he had found comfort in food and drink when his career disintegrated. I caught up with him on the other side of the road. He was apparently checking something on a piece of paper and looking at the shop-front before him.

'Have you been to this place before?' I asked.

'Kind of,' he said distractedly. 'Ah, this is it. Can you spare a minute?' Before I had time to answer he had pushed open the plate-glass door of a small, fancy looking wine bar and disappeared inside.

By the time I reached the bar he was all smiles and heading back for the street door. He tapped the side of his nose, conspiratorially. I gave him a confused look, but he simply smiled and indicated that I should follow him. By the time we climbed up to the Village I could see the bad shape he really was in. He had removed his suit jacket and his light blue shirt had big David Attenborough sweat patches under the arms and down the back. He was panting heavily as he leant against a lamppost. In between great gulps of air, he asked whether I had eaten.

I said that I had not whereupon he simply uncurled a big, fat finger from around the lamppost and pointed towards a curry house on the opposite side of the road. I nodded my agreement and a couple of minutes later we were munching through the mountain of poppadoms that had arrived at the table shortly after us. Summers was still steaming across the table from me as the waiter approached carrying a tray upon which were two unlabelled brown bottles and a pair of half-pint glasses, frosty and straight from the fridge.

'Did you want these now, Mr Summers?' the waiter asked deferentially.

Summers smiled and nodded. As the waiter moved out of earshot Summers looked at me conspiratorially, inclined his head slightly towards the newly arrived drinks, and wheezed, 'Try that, Johnny, tell me what you think.'

I was intrigued. I shrugged and poured the orange-tinged liquid into a glass, wiped my mouth on a napkin and took a sip. Apricot. The flavour was superb. Clean, fruity but very definitely a beer. Summers was looking at me, nodding knowingly.

'Good, is it not?' he said smugly.

'Good? Its bloody lovely, mate.' I picked up the bottle, turned it around looking for clues, before asking, 'But what is it?'

'My saviour,' he replied picking up his bottle and planting a loving kiss on it. I laughed with him but before I could speak, he continued. 'Try another,' he said as he gently inclined his head towards the waiter who was hovering by the bar.

During the meal we tried another five different beers, all very different, but all wonderfully flavoured. Blackberry followed by strawberry, then peach, blueberry and raspberry. I was intrigued by the cloak and dagger of it all: the unlabelled bottles and the collusion of the waiter. Summers would tell me nothing until we finally reached his flat. He left me in the huge living room whilst he went to put the kettle on. I sat on the sofa for a couple of minutes, gazing about the room, before spotting a stack of CDs next to the stereo. Wondering if his tastes had changed, I went to take a look. They had not. If anything, they had worsened. He still had the Elton John box set that he had played to death on that Australia tour, but he seemed to have belatedly discovered Simple Minds too. He really was a hopeless case. He came into the room as I was returning the pile to their shelf.

'Put something good on, Johnny,' he suggested.

'I didn't bring anything, mate,' I said grinning.

'You still arrogant about music?' he puffed. 'We can't all be as well informed as you, you know.' He thrust a scalding cup of coffee in my hand with a smile and trusted his weight to what looked like a very long-suffering old armchair.

I took the seat opposite him and simply opened my hands towards him.

'It's a long story, pal,' he said, 'but in essence, I think I have discovered gold dust in those beers.' He went on to explain that they were all made by a micro-brewery in a small New England town that he had happened by chance to spend a night in at the tail end of his round the world trip. The brewery was working at full capacity to satisfy its customers in Vermont and parts of New Hampshire and had never considered shipping beyond that region, let alone overseas. Summers, with his City contacts and, he felt, finger on the pulse, reckoned the beers would be a big hit in London. I began to feel uneasy and he must have seen it.

'Don't sweat, Johnny, this is not the hard sell. I don't want your money.'

I tried to look like I of course never expected that he did. But I was wondering what he did want. He told me.

'You liked them, yes?' I nodded that I did. 'I can get most of the backing, from up town – that should not be a problem. What I need is an angle. And you, my old friend, are it. You see, the beers are from New England and you will be returning to the England set-up later this summer – the press are already talking of 'New England' now that Lees has stepped down. It's perfect!'

He made it sound simple, although the New England angle sounded a little weak to me. It was also flattering, but I was clearly not as sure of my return as Summers appeared to be. I voiced my concerns. 'The one snag in your campaign to have me re-selected, is firstly that I am still officially banned and that secondly, the selectors have made it perfectly clear that there is no room for rabbits in the team.'

Summers waved away my words with an extravagant wave. 'Crap,' he said simply.

'It's in all the papers,' I argued.

'The ban we may not be able to do anything about immediately, although with Lees gone the mumble is that your chances have improved dramatically. But anyways, there's more talk now about bowlers who can bowl, and that, my old friend, you most certainly can. The batting, however, we can do something about.'

At this, I laughed out loud. I had spent hours and hours in the nets to

32

no avail. Before I could say anything he had heaved himself out of the arm-chair, padded in his stockinged feet over to the large bookcase of video tapes which dominated one side of the room and, after running a stubby finger along their spines, selected a battered Sony video cassette.

As the tape rolled, I saw that it was of me in the nets at The Oval and judging by the training strip I was wearing it was not more than a couple of years old. I looked at him quizzically, but he said nothing. After a few minutes of what looked to me like pretty good stroke-play, the image cut to a succession of clips of me in trouble out in the middle. The tape suddenly ended and I looked at Summers once more.

"Well, what do you reckon?' he asked.

'I did not know I had such a big fan.'

'Keep the size out of it,' he said with a smile. 'Did you notice no differences about you in the nets and you in the middle?'

'Obviously, but what of it? We've known all about that for years.'

Summers paused before answering. 'Look again and focus on your front foot.'

He rolled the tape again and watched me as I watched the nets footage. I looked relaxed – comfortable even, which in the nets did not surprise me. I had a fairly open stance and played strongly through the arc, from the front foot; a little cross-batted at times, but effective. When the real action started, however, I suddenly saw what he meant. I was markedly stiff and had closed my stance to the extent that when I played forward my leading foot was either preventing a free swing or causing me to use too much bottom hand. I looked back at Summers who shrugged.

'Don't ask me why none of us spotted it. I guess you were taking wickets and so your lack of runs was not seen as a huge problem. But look again at how that more open stance gets you out of trouble,' he said as he rolled the tape a third time. As the tape ended, he flicked off the television with the remote and, leaning back comfortably into his chair, he looked over at me and said casually, 'I think we can probably do something about that grip as well.' He took a sip of coffee before continuing. 'We'll have you opening the batting for England before you know it.'

'I still haven't seen anything about Lees' departure.'

'Trust me,' Summers replied, lighting up a large and smelly cigar.

'Besides, I thought it was bowlers that can bowl now.'

'And that, my friend, you can,' he grinned.

I made my excuses around midnight although I had planned to get away earlier. We had a few more of his New England beers and I would gladly have stayed for more except that in the morning I had more to do on the magazine and then an early training session and wanted to appear fresh for it or at least get there on time. Marketing had asked me to clarify a couple of points in the schools article and I had taken the opportunity to ask them if I could add an update to the piece on the ground re-development but those pages had been set and could not be changed.

I walked in through the front door and almost fell over Elisa's suitcase. A little thrill ran through me – I had really missed her. I almost ran up the stairs and was about to slip quietly into our bedroom when I stopped, my hand on the doorknob. I took a quick sniff at my armpits, winced and veered off to the bathroom for a quick squirt of deodorant. I then ran a toothbrush over my teeth and undressed silently, dropping my clothes into the washing-bin in the corner.

As I eased the door open gently, its underside whispered against the carpet and in the soft glow from the landing light I could see her stir softly. Now I could see her platinum-white hair – her latest style, halo-like on the dark pillow. And I could smell her familiar and lovely scent. She was wearing the *Balahe* I had bought her for her last birthday – a perfume she kept for special occasions.

Summers had asked me the night before if I had a recent photo of Elisa on me. I told him that I had only an old one from when we first met and that she had since recently gone platinum-blonde. I had flicked through some bits and pieces in my wallet to find him the photo I had taken from the kitchen board. The one that, on a whim a couple of days earlier, I had sprayed with a dash of *Balahe*. He said that's how he remembered her before putting it to his nose and saying something about her still smelling good. I had taken the photo back and could just detect a scent of the perfume and remembered the trouble it had been to find. I told him that I had tried just about everywhere to locate a bottle; Elisa had discovered it on a trip to Finland but baulked at the price. I eventually had tracked it down to a small shop in Bond Street.

Before slipping into bed beside her I glanced at the alarm clock on the bedside table. I groaned inwardly; it was almost one o'clock. I nuzzled up against her and kissed her faintly on the shoulder. She continued to breathe deeply, and I decided to let her sleep even though she had ordered me to awaken her. I whispered a good night and rolled over slowly to set the alarm. As I settled down, I felt her stir again and turn over towards me. I could feel her breath, warm on my back. In her sleep she moved closer until I felt a hard nipple glance against my back. I was on the point of waking her up when I felt her hand brush my thigh.

CHAPTER 5

Wednesday April 16 1997

I very nearly overslept, what with the sex when I got home and the sex we had when the alarm went off at seven o'clock, and I showered with a dull ache in my groin that, by the time I left the house, had turned into a pain in the lower abdomen. Elisa and I had said probably less than a dozen words to each other since she arrived home and most of those were unprintable. Unless the pain wore off I was going to be useless in the training session and I could have handled a couple of hours more sleep as well, but I had promised to edit the schools' piece down as Marketing had managed to sell some more advertising space at the last minute and I would need a little time at the computer to put the finishing touches.

I looked in on Elisa again just before I left but she was fast asleep. Fast asleep and naked, with the covers down around her knees. My complaining lower regions were the only thing that prevented me from joining her, so I simply placed the welcome home card I had written out on the pillow next to her. It felt good to have her back home and I was surprised to find myself looking forward to hearing all about her trip. I also wanted to have a chat with her about the Willby/Prinz business to see if she knew what the normal procedure was. Her stepfather, Ralph, was a retired architect and had written books on the subject. I was still sure that Sally was making a mountain out of a molehill.

She was already at her desk when I arrived a little after nine. I made a couple of mugs of tea and switched on my computer as I waited for them to brew. 'Any more scandals yet?'

She gave me what I presumed to be her withering look. 'Not yet, but the Building Committee meets at eleven so I imagine we will not have long to wait.'

'Conspiracy theorist,' I muttered, which produced a grin. She returned to the papers she had been studying when I arrived. 'Sally, I'm going to have a word with Elisa's stepfather, Ralph – about this Willby deal. He's an architect, or rather, was,' I continued. 'See what he thinks. I'll bet you we find this is how it's always done.' Sally had explained to me when we met that, jobwise, she had come pretty much straight from university and was sure that her lack of experience in the building area would have counted against her when she applied for The Oval post. It clearly had not. I even wondered wryly if that might have been in her favour.

'Thanks, Johnny. Maybe you are right, but it seems a funny way to do business to me.'

I quickly cut out two hundred words from my article and hurried out of the door for the training session. I had read an interview with a successful writer who had claimed that editing her own work and cutting words was like killing her own babies. I found it easier than I had expected but then maybe my words were not as good as hers. Sally said that she would call Marketing for me to tell them I had edited the piece and promised to let me know what happened at the Building Committee meeting.

After the first three circuits of the outfield I was struggling. We had jogged the first lap, alternated between jogging and sprinting on the second and sideways skipped much of the third. I had quickly fallen from the leading group to take up last place. Carlisle dropped back through the pack to urge me on. I had doubted his man-management skills from our first meeting, but he evidently had something, for I responded to his encouragement by working my way back through the pack until I was back with the leading group. His calling me a 'limey wuss' may have had something to do with it. Either way, by the end of the hour my lungs were screaming for mercy and it was with great relief that I felt the first few generous drops of forecast rain. At Carlisle's cue we dashed for the cover of the Barrington centre, and the indoor nets.

Although I had not played any representative cricket over the winter months, working on *Oval Eyes* in the pavilion had given me ample time to get into the nets and even at the quietest times one could normally find someone decent to bowl to. I had spent most lunchtimes in the nets deep in the bowels of the Bedser Stand and felt, bowling-wise at least, as good as I ever had, apart from the sore shoulder. Having spoken to Summers the previous evening I was keen to see if his theory about my batting stance was correct, although I was unlikely to find out today as the rain had forced Carlisle to abandon his plans for a practice match out in the middle in favour of the nets session.

We were split into groups of four or five. In my group were Gus MacLaine, our returning overseas player, the regular opening pair of Rennie and Driver, and our new recruit from Worcestershire, Alan Dench who, like me, was making his first appearance at training. I had not had the time to speak with him beforehand as I had rushed in from the office with seconds to spare but I could see that he was in good shape and as he padded up to bat first, I moved over to introduce myself.

'Alan, welcome to the club,' I said, offering my right hand.

He looked up uncertainly, took my hand and smiled thinly. He seemed uncomfortable.

There was an awkward pause. 'I'll let you get on then,' I continued. 'If you fancy a drink later…'

'I don't,' he interjected firmly. 'Drink, I mean. Thanks all the same.' He returned to his preparations. I stood for a second feeling a little awkward but was saved by MacLaine's booming baritone.

'Johnny! How's that lovely wife of yours?'

I turned to face him. He appeared to have grown in the close season and I had to crane my neck back to focus on his huge, sun-browned face. He had a barrel chest, weighed in at around fifteen stone and stood over six-feet-six in his socks. I had faced him in the middle just once, in that fateful Sydney Test, and did not envy the other counties having to face him this summer. I was just relieved that he had not been selected for the Ashes tour, so that if I was picked, I would not have to bat against him then either. His height and speed made a lethal combination and although he was at his peak as a player, he had been overlooked by his selectors as he too had taken time away from the game. In his case, to try to break into movies after a cameo role in an Australian crime film that had been a surprise massive hit in America.

'Lovely, the last time I saw her,' I replied, returning his bear-like embrace. 'She's just back from the States too – she was covering the Toadlust tour.'

'Is she still with *Burn Out*?'

'No, *Smashed*. She's on the editorial side now, which in theory means more time at home. That was what she told me, at any rate. Then this Toadlust thing came up and she was off like a shot.'

'Can't blame her, mate,' the big man replied, tweaking at his drooping Zapata moustache. 'I got back just a couple of days ago myself and believe me, they are going to be huge. I saw their arrival at JFK on telly – it was like Beatlemania. It's got to be *the* story at the moment.'

'Yeah, but are they any good?'

'Not the point, Johnny, and you know it. Daddy's the PM, or something, what does it matter if you can't play.'

'I heard Home Secretary,' I corrected him. Elisa had said she would do a bit of digging on that rumour on her trip Stateside. Either way, their very vocal pro-drugs stance must have been acutely embarrassing for the old man.

'Whatever,' he shrugged as he acknowledged Dench's wave of the bat from the far end of the net. 'Let's see what this sad old git is made of,' he muttered to me with a mischievous grin as he ran in towards the waiting batsman. It did not take the Australian paceman long to work up close to his ninety-three miles per hour top speed, even off a much-shortened run.

It was said in the game that he practised obsessively and Dench's footwork certainly looked good. Some said he had a weakness against spin but sadly that was not evident against me. His first movement to my leg-spin was a step forward; against MacLaine his first was to get onto the back foot, which gave him just a fraction of a second extra to play his shots. After he had delivered a couple of dozen balls, the big Australian sidled up to me.

'Looks good, doesn't he?'

'He should do,' I agreed. 'He topped the averages last year remember. And he *has* played for England.'

MacLaine grinned widely. 'So have you Johnny,' he said, as he turned to bowl to Dench again.

Driver followed Dench into the net and looked as assured as he had at the close of the previous season. Left-handed, and a natural striker of the ball, he had made his debut for England a couple of years before me at just twenty years of age at a time when Surrey had been very much in favour with the selectors. It had happened earlier in the nineties when Surrey had provided up to six players for the squad and as then, it had had serious repercussions for the county's season. Central contracts had been mooted for a couple of years but, with little solid evidence to suggest it was an expensive experiment worth undertaking, England's international standing had remained disappointing. There was the ludicrous likelihood of contracting a dozen players for twelve months, finding that six were so out of form that they could not be considered and having to select and pay six others. Driver had come into the set up not long after contracts had been returned to the 'maybe not' pile and had played a handful of matches before being found wanting technically at the top level. He had worked hard since and I fancied that at twenty-two his chance would come again. He is a great team player, serious about his cricket, but the joker in the dressing room. In looks his opening partner, Kevin Rennie, is identical but is his opposite in almost every other way.

Rennie at thirty-seven was clinging on to his first team place and had finished the previous season with a respectable average, but an old knee injury had been causing him to miss matches. He had wintered in the Sydney Grades but had not been too successful and in the nets he looked ill at ease against both MacLaine's speed and my spin; even Dench's looping medium pace seemed to be causing problems for him. I noticed Carlisle at one point staring glumly in Rennie's direction. Carlisle had the reputation of being able to make ruthless decisions and I felt that Rennie's nineteen years at The Oval might not be enough to save him if his run of poor form continued. Rennie could be self-centred and cantankerous, but I liked him. What he lacked in natural talent he attempted to make up for with grit and determination. Some said that the right-hander played for himself, that he was selfish. Either way, I hoped for his sake that he could battle his way back into form. I had the feeling that the arrival of another opener in Dench might be the writing on the wall for Rennie.

I showered quickly after the net and decided to call in on Sally before returning home. I found her sitting at her computer screen. She did not respond to my cheery greeting.

'Nice cup of tea?' I enquired with mock condescension. She and I drank gallons of the stuff.

'The Building Committee meeting has ended,' she said quietly.

'Oh yes?' I said above the boiling of the kettle. 'Did our friends Willby get the commission... again?' I asked with a smile.

'Surprise, surprise – yes they did,' she said without humour. 'Want to know something a little stranger? Guess who came in with the lowest quote.'

I suddenly knew what she was going to say. 'Not Willby?'

'In one,' she said.

I said nothing. The whole thing was starting to look murky.

'Are you going to speak with your in-laws?' Sally asked.

'Tonight,' I replied grimly.

With the final copy off my desk and with the marketing team, I decided to call it a day at a little after two o'clock. The rain had all but stopped as I ambled down the Harleyford Road on my way to Vauxhall mainline station. As I passed St Mark's Primary School a small group of children was being formed up into pairs, lining up at the gate. Their young teacher was struggling to keep control and I caught her eye as I came level with her.

'School trip?'

She laughed, sweeping aside a tress of black hair which had fallen across her face. 'Meant to be going on a boat on the Thames – if we can get there in the next half-hour.'

'Good luck - at least it's clearing up.' I said, nodding towards the big blue patch that had opened up above us.

'I hope so; they've been really excited about it for weeks.'

As I reached the busy junction at the Royal Vauxhall Tavern, the tethered balloon in the park at its rear started to gently rise, steaming slightly as the sun began to burn off the moisture left by the morning's rain. I timed my arrival perfectly, the Epsom train pulling in as I stepped up onto the raised platform.

I had the carriage almost to myself, slumped into a window seat and tried Elisa at home on the mobile but could not raise an answer.

The training session had taken it out of me, and I resolved to start jogging again. I distinctly and, for the first time, could feel every one of my twenty-seven years. Not that twenty-seven is old of course – although Elisa likes to remind me that she is still only twenty-five – but after ten years of pretty much continuous cricket it is perhaps not surprising that some toll has been taken. I spent the thirty-minute journey flicking through the Australian film magazine MacLaine had left in the dressing room. There was a spread on 'Sydney Carve Up', his low-budget movie that had taken America by storm. MacLaine played a heavy and he was proud to say that they let him 'use' his own moustache. He had received good reviews for his part, and he had promised to get me tickets for the London premiere which was scheduled for mid-June.

The house was silent when I opened the front door. Elisa's suitcase was still lying in the middle of the hall and I assumed she was still in bed. I made a couple of mugs of tea and, leaving mine in the kitchen, carried the other upstairs. I peered around the bedroom door and saw the covers tumbled over the floor – but no sign of Elisa. Backtracking, I returned to the kitchen and only then saw her note pinned to the notice board.

Got a call from the office – something's come up – give me a call when you get in.

I groaned as I read it. It was starting all over again. I took a swig of tea and dialled Elisa's work number from memory. Her last job had become so all-consuming that at one time it had threatened to tear us apart. I admired her work and recognised her desire for, and right to, a career but where my calendar was public knowledge almost a year in advance, Elisa would have to go dashing off at the whim of her editor. At *Burn Out* she very nearly had and at one stage, in the space of three weeks, she had been to Australia twice, Egypt once and New York four times. We had had some heated exchanges about it but in the end I think she shared my view that it was time to move on and get into the position where she was sending other people around the globe. That is why I was so surprised at her keenness to get the Toadlust gig after just a few weeks at the new magazine. I had to admire her judgement, though, if what MacLaine said about them was true.

Her secretary informed me that Elisa's meeting was switched to a restaurant at the last minute and wondered if I wanted to leave a message. I decided not to and flicked through the recently discovered address book by the telephone for Ralph and Kitty's number. They were home and would be happy for me to stop by and I was on the point of leaving when the telephone rang. It was Summers, calling from a pub judging by the hum of noise in the background. He was a little vague but said he was sending me something and that I was to be sure to open it on my own. He really was a big kid at times and I guessed that it would be a sheaf of his un-tellable jokes.

Kitty opened the door and beckoned me inside before wiping her paint-covered fingers on her ancient smock. 'Johnny, it's so good to see you,' she enthused. I noticed spatters of paint in her greying hair. 'Excuse my appearance, I'm trying a new technique – come and see.'

She led me excitedly into her studio at the back of the house, a bright, airy room that overlooked the red-brick patio and the sweeping lawn. I could see Ralph, stripped to the waist, digging at the end of the garden in the wild-flower meadow.

'It's big, Kitty,' was my first not very constructive assessment. 'And nice.' I was digging myself in deeper.

'You don't like it, Johnny, do you?' she said with a challenging grin as she picked up the whip, dipped it into the tray of red emulsion and started to flay the canvas that covered most of the floor space.

'I was just wondering where you were going to put it. I mean, it's huge.' It must have measured ten feet by ten. I ducked as she drew the whip back again. 'I'll let you get on, Kitty. See how Ralph's doing.' She was too engrossed to answer.

Kitty and Ralph are both in their late fifties and are what I suppose would be described as bohemian. Certainly they are still into all the hippy stuff and have never really let go of the 1960s. Elisa always maintains that they were in a band together in their teens, but the pair has always denied it to me. Kitty does play the piano and I have heard Ralph sing in the garden, but there the clues dry up. Whenever I ask Elisa, she becomes evasive and her parents will not let on. Since my parents emigrated to New Zealand around the time Elisa and I married, Ralph and Kitty have become important to me, surrogate parents almost.

Ralph plunged his fork into the just-dug soil when he saw me approach. 'Seen your mother's latest?' he asked with a wry smile.

'Could hardly miss it, could I? Where's it going to go?'

'I told her it would look good in the attic,' Ralph grinned. 'That's why I'm banished down here.'

I laughed. He asked after Elisa and I told him of her last-minute call from the office. He tutted supportively and asked how I was getting on.

'Surrey have issued contracts for phase one of the ground redevelopment and if the lottery funding comes through it could all be underway by October. I am going to cover it for the magazine and may come to you if I get bogged down by the technicalities.'

'Feel free. Any time,' he replied. 'I saw in the paper that they chose Prinz. He's good.'

'I'd never heard of him, and he's not done much before,' I started.

'I seem to recall a Chinese project a year or so ago,' Ralph mused. 'Anyway, he's produced plans before for competitions and they've always looked decent. Nothing too adventurous, and he is known to work for his clients.'

'Meaning?'

'Well, some of us can be a bit precious at times. About our 'art'. Prinz is malleable. He'll try to please his client, which is great when money is tight, and I assume that Surrey is not awash with cash.'

'Correct, if my pay packet is anything to go by.'

Ralph grinned and bent to pick up the fork he had discarded. He looked very fit for his age, and the muscles in his forearm rippled as he thrust the tines into the firm, damp soil. My silence seemed to make him stop again. 'Have you seen his plan?'

'Yes, it looks fine. Very simple; double-deckers on both sides of the ground to replace the existing terraces. Strange thing, though. Prinz knew that Willby Construction had won the contract to build two days *before* the meeting to select the building contractor was actually held. Prinz got the call from Sir Ken Parslow, the Surrey President, on Monday but the meeting was postponed until today. It was in the papers yesterday – the day after the meeting was originally due to take place.'

Ralph paused and leant on the fork. 'That's not so unusual; the successful builder is normally tipped off ahead of the official announcement. When lottery money is involved the lottery people have to be brought into the loop.' Ralph made rabbit's ears with his fingers. 'Though maybe Prinz should have kept quiet until the official announcement. Either way, they have chosen well – Willby have built some very good stadia and in several different regions.'

'The other funny thing, though,' I continued, 'is that Willby got the contract even though they missed the tender deadline by twenty-four hours.'

Ralph looked up sharply. 'Really?' he said with what seemed like sudden interest.

'Yes, and then they were revealed in the press twenty-four hours before the Building Committee met to award the contract.'

'Sloppy business,' Ralph muttered, as he picked up the fork again.

CHAPTER 6

Thursday April 17 1997

I was in bed when Elisa finally arrived home and feigned sleep as she climbed in next to me about twenty minutes later. I had heard her rummaging in the kitchen cupboards for a midnight snack and when she lay down next to me, I could smell a combination of alcohol, cigarette smoke and warm toast. I felt a little put out over the way she had rushed off again but realized too that I was being rather childish about it. Eventually I broke the silence. 'How did your meeting go, love?'

Elisa gave a little jump. 'I thought you were asleep,' she said, sitting upright and turning around to face me. 'Good, I think.'

I sat up too and turned on the table lamp by my side of the bed. Half past midnight according to the alarm clock, already poised to go off at seven. We were playing Sussex in a one-day friendly at The Oval later and although I was being given a few more days to get match fit I had decided to make the effort along with the rest of the boys.

'Surely you haven't had time to get all your copy in – I thought they would at least give you a couple of days to get over the trip.'

Elisa paused. She already had an apologetic look in her eyes.

'They're sending you away again.'

She nodded. 'But I can say no,' she began.

I could feel my anger rising but I knew it was an irrational response. I guess it was a bit of jealousy too but also I wanted her around – to be around her. 'Where to this time?' I asked, attempting an encouraging smile.

'New York again. Toadlust are staying on for a hastily arranged tour and there is even talk of a movie project in L.A. I know it's a pain in the ass and it could be for up to a month...'

'What! How the hell can it take a month? Sounds like you're joining the band.'

Elisa looked a little crestfallen. 'They've signed a book deal and as it's with a sister company of ours and I know them already, they've asked me to do it.' Before I could say anything, she continued. 'They are big now and are possibly going to be huge. The book could sell hundreds of thousands and I'm on a guaranteed twenty-five grand with points on top.'

I closed my eyes, lay back and said nothing.

'Johnny,' she pleaded. 'It's money for old rope. We'd be mad to turn it down. With your shoulder...'

I jerked upright. 'Don't bring *that* into it. It's simple – if you want to do it, fine, do it. But I really have to get some sleep now. I've got a job to do, too.' I turned my back on Elisa and lay there brooding, sleep seemingly impossible as my mind raced.

My alarm rang for about half a minute before I twigged that it was morning. I sat up and stretched and noticed that Elisa's side of the bed was empty. Rolling out into an upright position, I retrieved my dressing-gown from the peg on the door and shrugged it on as I trotted down the stairs. I had determined to be a little more adult about Elisa's trip and had convinced myself that it was my own failed attempts at rock superstardom that had induced my negative reaction. I had played in a band for a couple of years before turning professional with Surrey. Nothing too much to report save for a top ten indie single. *You Kill Me* had received some good airplay and garnered a few nice reviews – and had shifted a few thousand copies – but that was all a good few years after we had called it a day. The Phoenix Arizonas had originally split when our new agent had advised us to go full-time. I already had made a handful of second eleven appearances and felt my future was at Surrey. Besides, I knew my drumming had limitations and we had already experimented heavily with synthesized drums in the studio. In truth, I could see my own days were numbered. I pushed open the kitchen door.

Elisa was sat at the kitchen table eating a bowl of cereal. She looked stunning, her platinum blonde hair styled into an aggressive crop, her cream kimono wrap gaping just enough for me to see her breasts curving down towards the two dark smudges that I could make out through the silky material. I suddenly realised that it was the first time I had really seen her since she had arrived back from New York.

'Like your hair,' I said, running my fingers through the soft white layers, as I made my way to the kettle. She was engrossed in a book. 'What are you reading?'

'*Ulysees*. James Joyce. It's awful,' she smiled as she closed the huge volume with a soft thud.

'Why read it then?' I replied, suddenly remembering the Lansdale I had picked up for her at Murder One. 'Hang on a second.' I ran back up the stairs to the spare bedroom which had become the office, picked the book up from the desk and returned to the kitchen.

'This is the one you wanted isn't it?'

'Oh, thanks Johnny. Yes, that's the one – I'll read it on the plane. Can't see myself finishing this though,' she said, tapping the James Joyce with a forefinger.

I leaned over her, picked up *Ulysees,* opened it at random and started to read. Gibberish. 'Flamin' heck, what is he on about? Bin it?' I asked with a smile, with the book hovering over the flip-top bin.

'No,' Elisa cried out. 'It's Crispin's favourite – it's what makes him tick, so he says. If I'm going to get inside them, I am going to need to know what makes them who they are.'

I laughed. 'Nutters, if this is the stuff they read. And if the first single is representative of their work.' *Sniff Your Glove* was not only articulate and offensive, it was also quite utterly mad. I really did not relish the thought of Elisa spending any more time with them, but I had decided on a new mature approach and said nothing. 'When are you going back to New York? I forgot to ask last night.'

'It is, I'm afraid to say, totally representative. You haven't heard *Skin-flick Aromatherapy* yet. That's the one that they released in the States last week – the one that caused all the fuss.' Elisa gently removed the hand that I had slipped into her gown. 'And my flight leaves at two o'clock so we will have to be quick.'

She stood up, pulled down the kitchen blind and let her kimono slip to the floor with a sensuous rustle. My towelling gown rustled gently in sympathy, and her cool hands were a welcome reminder of what I had enjoyed the previous morning and what I would miss for the next month. I wondered if I could sneak off for a few days with her – there are always gaps in the fixture-list. As she eased my gown off of my shoulders and darted her tongue in my right ear, I pushed the debris of her breakfast aside and lifted her up on to it. I suddenly realised that the kitchen was virgin territory.

It was as good as ever, if a little rushed. At the last minute I had rather clinically reminded her that we ought to use protection. She had simply gripped me tighter and whispered something lurid and wonderful and we carried on regardless. We had talked about starting a family several times but not for a few months. I guess she had decided that the time was right. In the light of this momentous moment I felt a little shabby rushing around immediately afterwards to get to a game that I was not even playing in.

The postman had made a deposit at about the same time and I gathered up the bundle as I made a dash for the door.

Sussex was a team in deep trouble and the season had not even started. I sat at the balcony's open windows enjoying the unseasonably warm April sunshine – a welcome change from the cold, dreary wet weather we had had for the past few days – and watched a procession of Sussex batsmen wearing a furrow in the outfield between the square and the Bedser Stand. Their dressing room was right next door to ours and I could hear the discontent quite clearly. That, and bats being flung. I smiled to myself. It was, after all, only a friendly.

I had spent an hour in the nets with the second eleven and had missed the first hour of play, after which they had reached 37 for the loss of only the left-handed New Zealander, Lewis. In the hour that followed it was carnage and after twenty-five overs the recently renovated scoreboard read 49 for 7. I felt a little pity for Sussex. They had been in advanced negotiations for the installation of permanent floodlights at their historic Hove headquarters, apparently seeing day/night matches as the way forward. They were the first county to take this route but unfortunately this planned investment in the future coincided with a disastrous slump in form that was still continuing. A members' revolt in the close season had led to a new cricket committee and a drastic cut back in the playing staff which threatened to leave them badly exposed should they start getting injuries. If this was Sussex at full strength I did not fancy their chances this year.

After the seventh wicket I climbed up to the top of the pavilion to call in on Sally. She had not been there when I stopped by first thing and had locked the door, preventing me from checking my mail. I was annoyed that I had left my keys at home in the rush to leave. I suspected that there might be some amendments needed to the first drafts I had sent over to Marketing. Sally was at her desk this time and as I entered she looked up from the telephone and smiled, nodding towards the kettle. I took the hint and while she finished her call, I made the tea.

'Mark Summers called this morning,' she said with a quizzical look. 'Asked if you'd received the letter he sent?'

I nodded as I crossed the room to my desk where I had placed my rucksack. 'Probably some of his dodgy jokes. Did he have anything else to say?' I looked in the rucksack but then remembered leaving the bundle of letters in my locker in the dressing-room.

'No. He said you would probably want to call him later. Oh, and did you get a chance to talk to Elisa's dad?'

I was busy mashing teabags. 'Saw Ralph yesterday,' I said over my shoulder. 'He seems to think that the fact that Prinz knew about Willby in advance is nothing out of the ordinary. Apparently, the architect and building contractor are often given the nod on the sly. Ralph thought Prinz was probably not meant to go telling the press though.' I handed Sally a mug of tea.

'What did he think about Willby missing the deadline but still getting the contract?' she asked, offering me a cigarette from the crumple pack she took from her drawer.

'Still don't, thanks,' I refused with a grin. 'Must say, he was a little more interested in that. It seems that Willby have a good reputation in the sporting world. He said it is quite possible that their verbal quote had been accepted and that the committee had already decided to award them the contract. It could have been a slip up at their end. In short, it seems from what Ralph says, we've got the best people even if it all got a bit messy. Want another?' I nodded towards the mug that she had quickly drained.

She handed it to me absentmindedly and when I returned with the refill she was still looking off into space. 'Penny for them,' I prompted.

'What? Oh, yes,' she mumbled. 'Something doesn't seem right, Johnny.'

'Well as Ralph said, it's messy, but we ended up with the right builder.' I looked at my watch and saw that it was just gone two o'clock. If it was on time, Elisa's flight ought to have taken off.

'I'm not so sure. Miller was frantic about that fax the other day. Willby were a day late sending the original fax in – the one we apparently lost. I have been through all the communications on file and can't find any record of a verbal quote from anybody. They were all either by fax or letter. Once Willby missed the deadline their tender should have been null and void, yet Miller was bouncing around the office, apparently waiting for word from them. And then there's the actual quote.'

I drained my second cup, gave my watch a lingering look for Sally's benefit and reached for the door handle.

'You think I'm worrying about nothing, don't you?'

I nodded. 'We've got the best people which means we will get the best results. End of story. With respect, Sally, we are both new to this game...'

'Exactly!' she exclaimed triumphantly. 'That's why I was hired. Miller figured he could pull the wool over my eyes.'

I was getting a little impatient with her and made to leave the room. I had the door open and a sudden appeal down below suggested another Sussex wicket had fallen. Sally rose from her chair, grabbing a handful of papers.

'Look,' she said, thrusting them at me. Five quotes in the thirty-million bracket, and here is Willby's.'

I took the sheet of paper from her. 'Twenty-seven and a-half.' I read aloud. 'Confirms what Ralph said. We've had a result.' I handed it back to her.

She looked annoyed. And I was getting that way – with her.

'You go and play your game,' she said dismissively. I'm going to have a word with Miller about all this.'

At the break Sussex were teetering on the brink. Having set us just 85 to win, we were very quickly 68 without loss. Driver looked in fine form and even Rennie who had been struggling in Australia suddenly looked confident again.

I spent the rest of the afternoon on the balcony, catching up on all the news from my team mates, who had almost all been wintering in sunnier climes, and trying to make conversation with Alan Dench who had not, although he would not be drawn on what he had been doing. I was beginning to wonder if the murmurings about him on the circuit were not at least partly based on fact. He was apparently not the most popular player on the Worcestershire staff, a suggestion which had been borne out the previous season, his benefit year. Rumour had it that he had not even made enough to cover his own expenses which seemed incredible. At thirty-seven he was coming towards the end of his career and I had asked Carlisle during the interview why Surrey had signed him. Carlisle simply said that the decision had been made before he took up the coaching position. It hardly seemed a ringing endorsement for the new arrival. Personally, I hoped that Rennie would find some form and keep Dench out. Nothing personal against Dench; more a sense of solidarity with the Surrey veteran.

Giving up on Dench I started to read through the first draft pages of Elisa's *Toadlust Tour Diary*. It was only a working title, but it did not strike me as particularly inventive considering the Toadlust reputation for excess. Elisa had assured me that she would come up with something better. *Smashed* was going to print a hugely abridged version in the next issue and planned to use the article as a teaser for the book which was to be rush released once the band returned to London for their first major U.K. tour in June.

The game looked unlikely to last much beyond two-thirty and I checked with Carlisle to see if he wanted me to hang around afterwards. He said that we could knock off as soon as it was over, so I decided to call in on Sally before I left to see if she had calmed down. When I reached our perch under the pavilion roof, she was just closing down her PC.

'Half day?' I said, poking my head around the door.

'Not really; I'm meeting Miller for a drink.' She turned up her nose as she said this.

'Is he in today?' I asked with mock amazement.

'No, I called him up at home. He suggested we meet for a "chat"!'

'That'll be nice.' She did not reply. 'What are you going to say to him?'

'Don't worry, Johnny, I am not going to do anything stupid. I'll just probe around a little.'

'What did you say that made him invite you out for a drink?'

'I just said that I wanted to be clear on what our story was in the event of press enquiries.'

That seemed fair enough. 'He thought that a good idea?'

'He seemed to. Asked me if Ursula Hamilton had called.'

She must have seen the alarm in my face.

'I played dumb. I said she had not, that I didn't know who she was, and that I would love to have a drink with him.'

I did not like it. But then I knew of Miller's reputation and Sally did not. Miller had quit the game while he was ahead, but also after a couple of unsavoury incidents during away games. One involved the barmaid of a hotel in Manchester and the other was with a pair of prostitutes in Leeds. In both cases the women alleged that Miller was physically aggressive towards them. Nothing was proven and it never even reached the papers, but he disappeared from the scene soon after.

'Do me a favour, Sally. Be careful.' I said it lightly, but I meant it. I thought she was a little naïve – a little too trusting – and was about to tell her about the rumours but decided against it. They were never actually proven.

'I'm a big girl, Johnny,' she said as she slipped her jacket on.

I waved as I turned to go.

'Thanks though,' she said, blowing me a kiss as I closed the door behind me.

I nodded and trotted back down the steps.

Summers was already at the bar as I arrived and as I squeezed through the heaving masses, I saw him turn to order more drinks. By the time I reached him he had secured two more pints of cloudy, yellow lager.

'Hoegarden. It's Belgian,' he explained, handing me one.

I had had it several times, but I let him think he had introduced me to something new. It is a habit I have and one that really annoys Elisa. If I open a present and discover that it is something I already have I can never bring myself to say so. I cannot bring myself to disappoint the present-giver who has clearly considered their purchase. Elisa says I just do not like confrontation. I guess she has a point. I also find it difficult to say 'no' and Summers was about to unveil a plan that had me feeling very uneasy the more I thought about it.

He had called me up as I was leaving the ground on my way out to celebrate the easy win over Sussex with the guys. He sounded excited but that was always how he was about even the most trivial things. I remember in New Zealand back in late 1994 where, rather unusually, we were warming up for the Ashes series. We were playing Central Districts in Napier; Summers was twelfth man and I was on a day off. He had sneaked out of the ground at lunch to photograph the Art Deco buildings which litter the little seaside town and was back almost in time to continue with his duties. I say almost, as I had had to answer a call from the middle for a spare bat, in my civvies. It did not go down well and more or less sealed his fate. Not on the scale of Gower and Morris' biplane exploits back in '91, but he did not get another game on the tour after that.

'You should give Elisa a call – get her to join us.'

I shook my head. 'She's gone away again,' I shouted over the screams of a bunch of young people just along the bar from us. I did not want to talk about that. 'How come you can get out this early anyway?' I asked, nodding towards the clock behind the bar.

'I told them it's business. And it might be.'

I must have looked a little blank.

'I work for City Sports – the spread betting outfit?'

I had heard of them. 'Ideal job for you isn't it?' I said, patting my stomach.

'Steady!' he admonished with a grin. Raising his voice over the general noise he continued. 'It's a crap job. Money's okay but they really are a bunch of arseholes.' He paused, took a large gulp of lager and continued. 'Actually, the money is not good either – or at least, not good enough to get my beer venture going...'

I steeled myself for what I had initially expected the other day. He was after money, and it must have shown in my expression, for he suddenly held up his palms.

'No, no, no. I am not after money. I told you that already. But I could use your help. Look, down that one and let's go somewhere quieter.'

We strolled down through Covent Garden market, leaving the din of the Nag's Head behind us. I asked him how he had got involved with City Sports and he explained that he had been making a few appearances on the after-dinner speaking circuit on his return from America and had been approached after his turn at a City charity dinner. He had been at City Sports for several months and although he was officially one of their cricket analysts he spent a lot of his time out wining and dining clients. That partially explained his ballooning figure. He was only now taking his first steps in the market-making side of the business.

At the Strand we paused for a break in the traffic, crossed to the south side and descended into the Coal Hole. It was quieter, less smoky and there was a corner table free. When I returned with the beers Summers was busy with an electronic diary.

'I was going to invite the two of you over this weekend but if Elisa's away I shall have to find another day.' He looked up sharply. 'By the way, did you get my letter?'

'I did, yes.'

Summers was looking at me – clearly expecting a certain response. I should have admitted that I had not opened it but did not.

'Interesting was it not?' he carried on.

'Very.' I busied myself with my beer.

Summers looked puzzled but thankfully let it drop. He evidently had other things on his mind. 'Your batting average is terrible.'

Whilst his statement was unequivocally true, I bristled at his forthrightness but before I could say anything he had continued. 'How would you like to help me make a lot of money?'

'Now why would I want to do that?' I said indignantly, still smarting from his analysis of my batting.

'Because then I can properly launch 'New England Beers' and make you plenty of money when we use your ugly mug to promote it.'

'So far so good,' I replied cautiously. 'Where's the catch?'

'That's the beauty of this plan – there is none. You bat to the best of your ability – I clean up on the spreads – we make a killing on the beers. Simple.'

It was clearly far too simple for me. I had not a clue what he was on about. Summers bought another round of beers and, lowering his voice as he checked that we were not being overheard, he outlined his plan.

'Your one-day average is well under three runs per innings. When you get picked for the three one-dayers in May, City Sports will be quoting a 'Johnny Lorrens Performance Index'. Do you know how spread betting works?'

'In theory, yes,' I replied.

'Well let's recap – just in case. In a simple example we might quote a price on, say, England runs in a one-day international. Fifty overs at 4 runs per over, say, suggests a total of 200. Take into account the opposition, match conditions and current form and we might open at 210/215. A punter who thinks England will do better than that will 'buy' the spread at 215 – someone who feels they will score less, 'sells' at 210.'

'That's how I understood it,' I said.

'Good. Well let's follow the example through.' Summers was warming to his task. He took a huge gulp of beer and continued. 'The stake might be our minimum which is a pound or our maximum one thousand pounds, or anywhere in between. If England makes 250, the buyer at 215 makes 35 'points'. Each point is worth the value of his stake. The guy with the one-thousand pound stake walks away with a cool thirty-five grand.'

'Yeah, and the seller at 210 loses forty thousand. So what? City Sports makes a killing.'

'Hold on, that's what I'm coming to,' Summers said impatiently. 'In the case of a performance index on an individual, points might be awarded for each wicket taken, catch held and run scored. If my theory about your batting is correct, you are going to score more runs than usual this year. I'm going to quote a price on you that is high enough to induce some sellers. And I will sit on the other side, buying.'

'Two problems with that master plan,' I said brightly. 'Firstly, I have not been picked yet, and secondly, my career is over if this ever gets out.'

Summers looked disappointed. In me, I thought. 'Johnny, I am confident that you will be picked – but if you are not, we forget the plan. As for your second point, you would be doing nothing wrong. The opposite, in fact. You would be scoring more runs for your country. How can that be wrong?'

He had a point. I was not making any financial gain from it. Not directly at any rate. 'So, it doesn't really matter whether I like it or not?'

He shook his head with an almost apologetic smile. 'Not really, mate. I'd just feel happier in the knowledge that when you go out to bat you know I've got money riding on you.'

'Bloody hell, Mark – that's a bit heavy,' I protested. 'I haven't had a chance yet to try out the new stance out in the middle.'

'Don't!' he exclaimed, spilling beer as he banged his glass down on the table. 'Not yet at least. I'm sure I am right about that but do me a favour – keep things as they are until the one-dayers – that'll help me to establish the right price. If you go getting runs before the internationals that will ruin the whole thing.'

'Mark,' I groaned, 'how can I *not* try the idea out for Surrey? If I know that I can do something to improve my...'

'Your crap batting has not caused you too many sleepless nights so far, has it?' he snapped. 'So why does another month matter? Anyway, with the batting line-up at Surrey you might not get to bat much before then.'

'And I might not get to bat in the one-dayers either,' I retorted.

'Oh, I believe against the Aussies that you very probably will bat in all three,' he said with a grin.

He was very probably right. England had just come back from a disappointing winter that at least finished more strongly than it started. Drawing a two-match Test series in Zimbabwe was a shock but losing the ensuing three-match one-day series was little short of a disaster. Things did improve in New Zealand but the sense that England was a team struggling to find itself prevailed. On the back of such an inconsistent winter, England was faced with the undisputed leaders in Test cricket, Australia, and Rodney Marsh still arguing for the traditional five-Test series between the two old rivals to be downgraded to one of three matches only. For once I could see some sense in what he said; we really were not adequate opposition at the highest level.

Ironically, the only bright spot seemed to be our prospects in the three-match one-day series that was due to get underway in little more than a month time. Australia had had by their standards a lean time in the limited overs format over the past couple of months, but they were still ranked number one, and they always seem to reserve their best for us. That series at least promised to be a little more even than the Tests.

'What makes you so sure that I am going to be recalled?'

Summers paused as he took another large mouthful of beer. 'Simple. The selectors have got to give the squad a real shake up, you have served your 'time', and our old mate Lees has retired. All the omens look good,' he said with fluttering hands.

'My only concern is all the press about England not having depth of batting. The Times the other day was still arguing for bowlers that can bat...'

'England needs a good leg-spinner,' Summers interrupted. 'Shane Warne's injured, but they've got this guy Pocket who Benaud is raving about. Cotton has had enough opportunities for us to prove himself, but I think he'll get the axe and you will come in – crap batting and all. Except your batting might surprise a few people. Of course, you are going to have to bowl well through April.'

'Okay, so let's assume I get picked. What happens next?'

'I work out a price on you, stick it on the screens and wait for the sellers. Meanwhile, I will have a couple of punters ready to buy on my behalf. People I can trust.'

I still did not feel easy about it. 'And what might this price look like?'

'Off the top of my head...' Summers started mumbling under his breath as he gazed up towards the ceiling. '70/75. And that is based on 10 points for a wicket, 5 for a catch and 1 for each run. I've taken into account your averages in one-day cricket to get this price. You take on average, one-and-a-half wickets per game, a catch every three and an impressive two point something with the bat.'

He knew more about me than I did. But I knew the batting average as it had haunted me for a long time.

'Over a three-match series that would suggest a price around 56,' he continued. 'But I need to be careful to pitch the price right. Too high, and I cannot make much, if anything, from it and besides, my bosses will think I've gone mad. Too low and we'll be swamped with buyers. I do not want any excess attention drawn to this index at the office. That could spoil everything. That's why I want it to look pretty well matched in the books.'

For a moment I lost interest in the pricing of the spread. I was more interested to know how many runs Summers thought I might get with the new stance. He paused again, emptied the remaining half pint down his neck and stood to return to the bar. 'Over three innings, I would not be surprised to see you acquire at least thirty.'

I laughed. 'Shitola! I don't think I have ever scored more than thirty in a season. And what if I don't get there? You lose.'

Summers was straining to get back to the bar. 'Have confidence, young man! And if things are looking grim I would simply have to turn the position round. Cut my losses.'

My head was starting to swim with the speed drinking as I watched Summers' huge form weave surprisingly gracefully across the floor to the bar. He had been a graceful batsman with wonderful footwork and sinuous, wristy stroke play. The papers often referred to him as the finest bat of his generation to have failed to secure a second England cap. I felt a pang of guilt as I watched my old friend order the drinks. His career in tatters, his body looked several sizes too big for him and he was clearly drinking heavily. And all because of a lousy bet; a bet that I might have placed as well. And here I was, possibly on the verge of getting my place back. And maybe getting sucked into his plan.

CHAPTER 7

Monday April 21 1997

The answerphone cut in for the umpteenth time. I flicked off my mobile and dropped it back into the jumble of clothes and equipment in my coffin, careful not to be seen by anyone with it in my hand. I had left a couple of messages earlier, but Sally had not replied. She seemed to have taken Friday off work and I supposed she must have gone away as I had tried her at home over the weekend but not managed to catch her then either. I was keen to hear what Miller had wanted to discuss with her and it flashed through my mind that he might have sacked her. I was just wondering whether he could actually do that when I heard a muffled roar from the pitch outside. My stomach flipped as I waited for the call. I get nervous before every innings, even friendlies like this, but the first bat of the season is always particularly worrying.

Sven Molander stuck his big, blonde, half-Swedish head into the dressing room from the balcony and nodded, smiling grimly. 'You're on, mate,' he said, with still a trace of Stockholm in his voice, even after ten years in the English game.

I reached for my bat and gloves and, attempting a cheery wave, headed for the door and the long walk down the stairs and through the Long Room. 'See you in a minute,' I called as I went. I heard Carlisle say something about my attitude towards our second friendly of the season, but the closing door muffled his words. I sensed it was not complimentary.

Lord's looks marvellous at any time of the year, and at the start of a new season with the grass lush and green and the stands gleaming in their newly scrubbed whiteness it is a scene in world cricket that is hard to beat. Some of the West Indies' grounds are surrounded by wonderful scenery, the Sydney Cricket Ground looks magnificent and the Melbourne Cricket Ground is awe-inspiring in its vastness, but Lord's is Lord's – the home of cricket. And it took ages to get out to the middle.

The weather had returned to type and I was wrapped up in all the sweaters I could find in the house that morning. I had only managed to find three and suspected that Elisa had sneaked a couple off to New York with her where they were expecting sub-zero temperatures before she went. She had called on Saturday to say they were right. It was absolutely freezing apparently. She also said that the tour was due to start today, in Washington and that she had managed to talk her way onto the tour bus. The tour was a prospect that had haunted me from the start, and the thought of her actually travelling with them made me feel very uneasy indeed. I would not have been happy before reading Elisa's notes, but having read how they had stripped and tied to a lamppost a reporter from Melody Maker who had written something derogatory about them, I felt even unhappier. I consoled myself with the thought that the Melody Maker reporter was male and hoped that they would treat a woman rather better.

'One please,' I said, holding up a single finger to the umpire. He nodded and told me that it was right arm over, five balls to come. What he failed to mention was that it was also likely to be bloody fast. Middlesex had signed a young West Indian who had played a couple of Tests earlier in the ongoing series against India in the Caribbean. His slower ball was around 88 mph.

As I bent over my bat, I found myself wanting to shift into the more open stance that Summers had noticed me use in the nets, but Hendriks was already half-way through his very long, very straight run. I was mesmerised by the first ball. I could not concentrate, and maybe that is another part of my batting problem. I can remember playing for my home club, Wimbledon, when I was about sixteen. We had no sightscreens in those days, but the pavilion was painted white to give the batsman a chance. On that occasion I was at the striker's end with the bowler at the start of his run up, when I saw a woman pushing a pram at the far end of the ground, around about long-on. She was about to pass behind the bowler's arm and I clearly recall thinking that the movement ought to be putting me off. I was spot on. Suddenly there was a rattle behind me, and I had been bowled.

I did not see Hendriks' first ball either, but I heard it fizz past me at about head height. In the hands of someone as fast as Hendriks the spinning seam knifes through the air and you can actually hear it going past. It can be a quite chilling sound. Oxymoronically, I was already beginning to feel warm under all the sweaters despite the bitter April day. The second ball was much fuller but outside the off stump. I left it. More because I didn't even see it rather than any wise shot selection. I saw the next one though. Short and straight, I had no time to move and felt the thud as it crashed into the top of my helmet. It hurts even with all the protection we wear nowadays, and my ears were still ringing a couple of minutes later as I walked back to the pavilion. As Hendriks approached for the final ball of his over, I opened my stance up a little. I knew Summers had told me not to, but I was angry about the beaning and excited that he might have hit on something. The ball was maybe a little too short for the shot, but it was the first of the over that I had seen well enough to even try to hit. I stepped back and swung, connected and felt that lovely sensation, a sensation I rarely feel out in the middle, as the leather cannoned off the sweet spot. Unfortunately, extra cover was awake and clung on despite hands that were almost blue with cold. I was more disappointed that my experiment had to be abandoned than I was about the duck.

I sauntered off the field with Gus MacLaine, the not out batsman. The big Australian was in a good mood. That would change the moment he got the ball in his hand after the interval. 'Been practising?' he asked with a smile.

'Good, wasn't I?' I replied.

'You'd better have a lie down after that. Long innings for you.'

'I see your boys are due in later this week,' I said, referring to the Australian tour party. He had made himself available for the Ashes tour but had been overlooked. At twenty-five he would surely get another chance.

'Screw them,' he said with a smile. 'Hope they lose.'

I gestured for him to go through the little, white pavilion gate ahead of me. 'You don't mean that,' I ventured.

He looked over his shoulder as he started up the steps towards the Long Room. 'Nah,' he drawled, 's'pose not. Bastards though, all the same.' Being dropped had clearly hurt him, but Australia's loss was definitely Surrey's gain.

Lunch was taken between innings and I fuelled up on a stack of peanut butter and jam sandwiches and about four mugs of hot, sugary tea. As we took the field I could feel the liquid sloshing around inside me and, glad that I did not have to open the bowling and feeling just a little uncomfortable, I took my place at first slip, next to the jittery figure of Ronnie Lenderman. He had been keeping wicket for as long as I had been in the side and in the early days we had roomed together on away matches until his constant chatter and nervous habits got too much for me. Somehow, I managed to persuade someone else to take my place and I got a room with Summers. Lenderman is an excellent keeper and is a genuinely nice guy – but he just never stops. Even now with MacLaine marking out his run he was still chuntering on about the new gloves he had bought, and how the old ones had had much less padding in them and did not let his hands breathe. I nodded in the right places and concentrated on MacLaine. We had a system so that he could let us know what type of delivery he was going to send down. A roll of the head clockwise meant bouncer – a scratch of the left cheek indicated a yorker and so on. Lenderman had been so busy talking that as MacLaine started to hurtle in, he whispered out of the corner of his mouth, 'What's this one?'

'Nothing,' I replied. There had been no signal. MacLaine leapt into his delivery stride, grunted and sent the ball on its way. The batsman prodded forward uncertainly and the next instant I was tumbling to my right. As I rolled away I looked at my outstretched right hand and was rather surprised to see the ball gripped tightly in it. Suddenly I was mobbed.

'That just about atones for your woeful display with the bat,' Rick Pallant said with a huge grin as he slapped me on the back.

'Thanks skip,' I said, as I rubbed the grass-stained sleeve of my sweater. 'That was a complete fluke, to be fair.' I laughed.

Pallant got the team into a huddle. It was his first season in charge and after Rennie he was the next senior player on the staff. He had the reputation for being rather straight-laced, but there was a lighter side to him as well; you just had to get to know him. I had the feeling that he was going to be a good captain. Someone in the papers had said that we were like a superbly tuned racing car without a steering wheel and there was more than a little truth in that. Although we had won the Sunday League the previous season and come third in the longer format, we had been amongst the most noticeable underachievers on the county scene for much of the previous decade and more. With our long, successful history it was clear to all that we should have won more County Championships since 1958 than the solitary 1971 victory. Last year aside, we had had too many underwhelming campaigns. With much speculation around the Championship being split into two divisions, our recent inconsistent form suggested we could be borderline for division two unless improvements were made. Sadly, we had not looked like potential winners for a good while. Mark O'Brien had stepped down at the end of the previous season after just the one campaign in charge but no-one held him responsible for our lack of success and to be fair, although Leicestershire were easy winners, second, third and fourth were tightly bunched, but still some way off. O'Brien's batting form had suffered in his year in charge and I just hoped that Pallant could lead the team without it destroying *his* average.

I looked around the circle of faces in the huddle as Pallant urged us on. MacLaine looked really fired up by the wicket. Lenderman looked tiny next to him and was all ticks and twitches. Rennie and Driver were next and apart from the age difference and a few more wrinkles on Rennie's face, looked like twins; immaculately turned out, both with their collars starched upright. Molander towered over everybody except Maclaine, his big, smiling face lapping up Pallant's words. O'Brien was next, and if there was any sense of regret over his abdication I could not see it. His thick, crinkly blond hair was trying to escape from under his chocolate-coloured Surrey cap and his sunglasses rendered his expression totally impassive. That was his general style, I reflected; I had played alongside him since he was brought in from Warwickshire to captain the side the previous season but have never felt really close to him. After a few drinks one night he did talk about being glad to get away from Birmingham but quickly closed down and I never pushed him. I could not fault him as a skipper, though, and felt that he was too hard on himself given the successes we had had. Hopefully, with the weight lifted he could provide a boost to our top order and at 38 this might be his last chance to prove his worth. Carl Gaye, our number three batsman was looking towards Pallant but had a glazed look about him. He is the most laid-back member of the team – which was maybe a product of his West Indian upbringing. He had moved to London when he was about ten-years of age and fifteen years later he had become a firm favourite with the fans. A mighty hitter of the ball and a brilliant cover fielder, he is also the team pin-up. At least that is what Elisa told me. Stuart Snipe, our other opening bowler, was in another world; I guess he was already planning his first over. Only twenty-one, he is a big-framed Lancastrian who made no bones about wanting to wear the red rose. He also never gives less than his best for Surrey. I liked this bunch and was just thinking how lucky I was when Pallant clapped his hands.

'Let's get into them, lads,' he said, as the incoming batsman approached the wicket.

As the huddle dissolved, I turned to go back to the slips when I heard Molander's voice from the direction of square-leg. I swung around and saw him talking earnestly with Alan Dench. Dench was waving him away as if he was bored. I suddenly realised that Dench had been missing from the huddle. I was puzzled. He really was not trying to blend in with the team in these early days. Carlisle had given him a start at three so maybe he was thinking of keeping Rennie and Driver together at the top of the order and slotting Dench in at first down. Or perhaps he was just having a closer look at Dench. His stubborn 53 would have done him no harm, but maybe the rumours were true. Maybe he was as selfish as had been said. Or was he just finding it difficult to settle? I had heard that he was commuting from Worcester still and that there might be marital problems. Even so, I could not help feeling that he could have made more effort.

The wickets started to tumble shortly after and with Middlesex well short of their target and only three men left, Pallant at last threw the ball to me. Stomping around the outfield for the best part of forty overs in what felt like arctic temperatures, I had started to loosen up when Pallant had given me the nod a couple of overs before. I still felt stiff and very cold and the first couple of balls were just awful. A wide was followed by the rankest long hop I have probably ever bowled in a professional match. Bad enough that the Middlesex batsman had so long to decide where to hit it that he shaped to play about three different shots before the ball reached him. Ultimately, he looked relieved just to drop the bat on it. Maybe I lulled him into a false sense of security, for the next ball, my third of the season, was a bit of a shock. It was meant to be a googly, but we will never know – largely because it never pitched. The batsman's eyes lit up and he launched himself into a most impressive straight drive, but he was too eager. Through with the shot too soon, and I like to think my beguiling flight catching him unawares, he tried to correct, jabbed his bat down hard succeeding only in hurrying the ball onto his stumps. My colleagues refused to acknowledge any skill on my part. The Middlesex batsman, Jensen, headed off towards the pavilion with an embarrassed grin.

After the match most of us stayed behind for a couple of beers with the Middlesex boys. My three wickets had wrapped the game up and given Surrey an easy win. My second and third victims were admittedly tail-enders, but the deliveries were good – and they were both clean bowled by googlies.

In a conversation further along the bar I thought heard someone mention Summers, and I suddenly thought about his spread betting plan. Three wickets and a catch today – that was 35 points. If I got picked for the one-day internationals and I made 35 points each game, his 70/75 price looked modest and that was without my batting on which he seemed to be banking. Of course, the opposition was going to be a hell of a lot tougher than today's, but it got me thinking. I did some rough numbers in my head and worked out that, as Summers had suggested, if I played to my one-day form and played in all three matches I could expect to accrue 56 points, but this would be a huge step up to one-day internationals where I was unproven. Given a lot of luck and with batting improvements, perhaps 70/75 was not completely ridiculous. I still was not entirely happy about the plan, though – certainly not the part where Summers wanted me to keep using the old batting stance until the internationals. It was more than that though. The authorities had tried to stamp out any player involvement with the betting fraternity and although Summers was an old friend, I could not help feeling very wary. The trouble was, I still felt that I owed him for my silence over his Sydney bet. Uneasy as I felt, and whilst I had no plan to bet myself, I also knew that I was going to help him.

CHAPTER 8

Tuesday April 22 1997

We were given the Tuesday off after the victories against Sussex and Middlesex and with the magazine now with Marketing I found myself with some time on my hands. I had planned to take a drive down to the Cotswolds to see my brother and had set the alarm for eight o'clock. That would allow me to get out by half-nine and miss the rush hour on the M25.

Before I could set off, though, I had to do a couple of favours for Elisa. She had called the previous evening whilst I was on my way back from Lord's to tell me that they had reached Washington and that the tour bus had been mobbed at the hotel when they arrived. It had apparently been terrifying and at one time she had felt the pressure of the crowd starting to tilt the bus. She sounded a little drunk and I supposed that she had had a couple to steady her nerves. That was another thing that worried me. When we had first met, she was drying out and after a long battle she had reached the stage where she could trust herself to have the odd social glass of wine. They say that once an alcoholic always an alcoholic and that it is not possible to become a social drinker again. Elisa had to my mind proved that theory wrong. I just hoped that all the good work was not coming undone. She had always been a little cagey about her drink troubles, but I had the impression that it all stemmed from the time when she was playing in bands herself.

As I turned Elisa's computer on and waited for the screen to come to life, I rummaged through the stack of CDs in the cardboard box on the desk next to it. Elisa always kept a jumble of old favourites, new arrivals and a few of her own too. She had played guitar in a girl group that had formed when she was at Exeter University. They had started off as a bit of a joke band, but they got the support slot to Belinda Carlisle when she played in Plymouth and were spotted by a small London label. Within about three months The Marnies had been given the full makeover, a manager, agent and most importantly, a deal. Their sound was also worked on and they ended up sounding more like the GoGos than their earliest influence, The Runaways. Elisa and the four other girls left Exeter before their finals to tour their debut album around Europe. They never really made it, but you can still find their CDs in the shops.

I found the one I was looking for and slipped it into the mini-hifi. 'She doesn't know it was me' was their biggest hit. It just scraped into the top forty and was one of only a couple of numbers on which Elisa sang lead. I am biased, but she had a far better voice than the lead singer and I think they would have done better had Elisa been more confident about singing the lead more often.

As the opening chords sounded, I turned my attention to the screen in front of me.

Elisa had forgotten to take a copy of the *Smashed* article with her to show the Toadlust people and had called to ask me to get a copy to her. She also hoped that I was coping without her. I was coping but I would have been happier to have her at home. She had sounded very up-beat and that strangely made me feel a little lower. I quickly found the folder she had entitled *'Toadlust'* and opened it. There were about a dozen documents but the lettering on the icons gave little away. Elisa could not remember which one I needed so I started opening them one by one. There were just two to go when I heard the telephone ringing downstairs in the hall. I looked at my watch and decided to wait to see who it was first. Time was running on and I really wanted to get going down to Bledington. The cursor was hovering over the icon that was simply accompanied by a question mark, when I heard Summers' voice from the hall below.

'Good news mate. Look at The Guardian, page 42. Give us a call sometime. Bye for now.'

I made a mental note to pick up a copy and turned back to the screen. My hand must have moved slightly as I listened to the call and the cursor was hovering over the final document, one entitled *'Smshdart 1'* – Smashed article 1, perhaps? – that had to be it. It was the document I had been looking for. I made certain the printer was powered-up and printed off a copy. As the three pages churned slowly out, I found a large manila envelope and addressed it to Elisa's colleague at *Smashed*, who was apparently going to fax it to one of the hotels on the tour. I put a couple of first-class stamps on it to be on the safe side and closed the computer down again. I posted it in the box at the end of our road and it was just a few minutes later that I realised that I could have emailed it. But if Elisa could not get near a computer I supposed faxing it might be the better option after all.

The traffic on the M25 was fairly light and I made good progress until I reached the M40 junction where the pace slowed. We crawled along for about ten minutes and then suddenly everything was flowing smoothly again. The sun was shining, I had the sunroof of the Vauxhall open and Jay and the Americans blasting out of the stereo. It felt like the first day of a holiday and I was looking forward to seeing Jack again. Elisa and I had spent a week with him in February, but we had not seen him since. He has a telephone, but I sometimes wonder whether he knows how to use it, and I had called him the night before and invited myself down. Only for a couple of hours, but I thought I might take him to lunch at the King's Head on the green in the centre of the village. He would probably tell me that he had far too much work to do – he was studying to become a structural engineer and was always immersed in technical books. My mother had called me from New Zealand a couple of weeks before. She seemed worried about him, said that he never called or wrote and asked me to keep an eye on him. He is twenty-five but I still see him as my little brother, and I was happy to go and see him so that I could put mum's mind at rest.

I think he had had words with her too because he seemed curious as to why I was coming down at such short notice, so I said that I had the plans for The Oval redevelopment and thought he might be interested to take a look. He sounded sceptical but did not try to put me off.

I stopped in a Shell station just outside Burford, had settled my bill with a credit card and was on the way out of the shop when I noticed the newspaper stand and remembered Summers' call. Picking up a copy of the Guardian, I queued once more and flicked through to page 42 as I waited to pay. I scanned down the page which had mainly racing and boxing news until I spotted a piece by Larry Helm. Guessing that this was what Summers had read, I handed over the right money and left the shop still reading the short article. Helm had obviously spoken to Richard Lees about the book that Lees was planning to write about his days as a selector. Half-way across the forecourt I suddenly stopped. I had seen my name a couple of lines below where I was reading and jumped ahead to see what he had to say. Lees had apparently been the selector most opposed to giving me my place back, yet here he was saying that I was sure to get back in to face the Australians. Not only that, but he even argued that my lack of runs should not be held against me. This was indeed an about face on his part – but a very welcome one. I just hoped the other selectors were Guardian readers.

Jack was sitting on his own at a small, round table in a corner, over by the old inglenook fireplace. He raised a hand in greeting, and I mimed drinking an invisible pint. He smiled and nodded. I knew exactly what he would have and ordered two pints of Hook Norton. As the young barman pulled the drinks I gazed around the bar. Nothing had changed at all since Elisa and I had last been here; in fact, it looked like nothing had changed in the last hundred years. We used at one time to visit Bledington quite frequently – certainly when Jack first moved into the village. We did not always stay with him as he only had a tiny little one-bedroom cottage up by the ancient church, and although we did not mind sleeping on the sofa bed in the living room, Jack's habit of getting up in the middle of the night could be disturbing at best – embarrassing at worst. Elisa preferred a little more privacy, and the four-posters in the bigger suites at the pub were superb.

I paid for the drinks, nodded hello to the landlord who was flying past to the restaurant, carrying a tray loaded with meals, and walked the pints over to Jack's table.

Jack may be two years younger than me, but most people take him for several years older. His hair turned grey when he was twenty, but it is his more serious disposition that seems to fool people. As long as I can remember he has been the studious type. Where I got involved with rock groups and cricket, Jack turned to computers and classical music. Where I quit school with a couple of A-levels, Jack had gone on to a degree and was now half-way through his engineering Masters, seemingly set on becoming a structural engineer. I know my mother had been worrying about him being twenty-five and having never had a proper job and that she would be relieved once he got his career going. She would be even more relieved if he found himself a girlfriend.

He got up to shake my hand. Although we were close, we were not demonstrative in our affection towards each other.

'How was the drive down?'

'No problem,' I replied. 'At least, not after a little hold up as I got on the M40. Cheers!'

We both took long drafts of the nut-brown beer. It was brewed locally and always tasted wonderful. 'Here, before I forget, take these. I'll only lose them.' I handed Jack the sheaf of papers I had been clutching – the plans for the new stands at The Oval.

Jack accepted them and started to unfurl them. 'Ah! Willby Construction,' he said with a nod, reading from the panel set into one corner of the plans. He spread them on the circular table and pinned them down with our two pints.

'Heard of them?' I asked.

He answered without looking at me. 'Yeah, they're probably one of the bigger building firms when it comes to stadiums, although most of their higher profile stuff has been built in the Far East. Where money is no object. What's this costing?'

'They tendered for twenty-seven and a half. They were the cheapest.'

'No surprise there. Mind if I smoke?'

I indicated that I did not. Besides, the low-ceilinged pub was filling up with late lunchers and the air was already heavily streaked with cigarette smoke. 'Are they any good?' I asked. 'Ralph seems to think they are.'

Jack raised his eyes. He paused for a second. 'Yeah, I guess so,' he replied rather ponderously.

'Jack, is there a phone in here?' I suddenly remembered that I had left a message with Jackie Kray in the Club Office and had left my mobile in the car. Jack directed me to the payphone and I quickly dialled the number. Jackie was at lunch, but I was informed that my message had been taken up to the library and that the door had been locked. Sally had not appeared for work again. That made it three days, now. I thanked the receptionist who suggested that I contacted Barry Miller. He had apparently been in but had a meeting in Slough with some seating suppliers. It was just possible that Sally had gone with him, or even that she had decided to tack on an extra day or two to make a long weekend. I really thought she would have called to let me know how the chat with Miller had gone the previous Thursday.

When I got back to Jack he was still poring over the plans. 'They should look great when they're done,' I said, sitting back down.

Jack was silently studying the sheet in front of him. 'What scale is this?' he muttered to himself, as he referred back to the corner panel.

I let him get on with it and gazed around the pub. Elisa really liked staying here and I thought I would book us up a couple of nights as a surprise on her return. I drew my Surrey diary out of my jacket pocket and flicked through to the fixture list, trying to find a spare couple of days.

I looked back at Jack. His face was screwed up with concentration, his grey hair and small, round spectacles making him resemble some eccentric professor. His faded corduroy trousers and ancient-looking flannel shirt simply reinforced the impression.

He suddenly sat up straight and folded the plans up. 'Thanks for bringing them down. I'll have a closer look later – that's, if I can keep them? They look interesting.'

We had another drink and then moved through to the restaurant for lunch. Jack was fairly quiet during the meal. As the dishes were being cleared away, he lit up another cigarette. 'Mum sent you down, didn't she?'

It was more an accusation than a question and my delay in responding as I searched for the right answer told him he was right. 'They just want to be sure you are happy, Jack.'

'Well you can tell them that I am fine, thank-you very much.'

I paused for a moment. 'Why don't you give them a ring?'

'What, and get the Spanish Inquisition? No thanks!'

'There's no need to be mean,' I protested. 'Think of it from their point of view...'

'They moved to bloody New Zealand, didn't they? What did that tell me about how much they cared? And all they want to know is have I got myself a girlfriend yet. Well, the answer to that is no, *definitely not*.' Jack downed the remains of his pint and looked pointedly at his watch.

We had had this conversation before, and it usually got us nowhere. I took out my wallet and withdrew from it forty pounds, which I placed on the table in front of me.

Jack leant forward and picked up two of the ten-pound notes, thrusting them back towards me. 'And I don't need your charity either.'

'It's not charity, Jack. It was my invite, remember?'

'When you come down because *you* want to – then you can pay. Otherwise...' he let his words trail off.

I sat and looked at him for several moments. It was pointless trying to argue with him when he was in one of these moods and I could see why mum and dad were concerned about him. With his attitude it was hard to see him ever holding down a job – or getting a partner. I wondered if he wanted either anyway. And he seemed to be very bitter about them emigrating to New Zealand. In a funny way I too had felt a little let down, hurt even, by their decision. After all, it was a decision based only on a holiday they had taken there to see friends. But to take it as an intended snub seemed rather childish. I decided not to pursue the matter and, in any case, wanted to get back to London before the chaos of the evening rush hour.

I stood slowly and, taking my jacket from the back of the chair, held out my hand to him. 'Keep in touch, Jack. And if you fancy a day at the cricket any time...'

He slowly extended his hand and grimaced. He hated cricket and in all the years I had been professional he had never been to see me play. 'Sorry, Johnny, I think I'm busy then. When is it?'

I laughed. 'You bugger.'

I was at the door when he suddenly called out. 'Did you want these?'

I waved my hands. 'Keep them. I'd be interested to see what you think.'

'Like I've got time for these as well,' he grumbled, as he re-folded the plans. But I was glad to see he said it with a grin.

CHAPTER 9

Thursday April 24 1997

Terry Court was on a charm offensive, and I did not know whether I preferred him that way or his normal surly manner. Certainly, it was a big change from the last time we had been together at the first book launch. Today he could not do enough for me. He had a Caffe Nero coffee ready on the table for me and had arranged a load of books so that I simply had to cruise along the table, scribbling my name across my photograph on the title page of each one. This was all a pleasant change and it got me wondering why.

After the accusations of pot-smoking in the dressing-room, it had been Court's task, as head of public relations on the tour party, to put the England Cricket Board's case, and it was clear from the start that they had decided I was guilty. After all, they had failed to link me with the betting incident even though they suspected my involvement. The cannabis story had first appeared in one of the Sydney newspaper's gossip columns just after the Test Match. The tour party had moved on to Melbourne by the time the news broke, where I had been picked to play against the Victoria State side. It was apparently Court's suggestion that I be pulled from the team whilst the matter was investigated, which seemed to me like being presumed guilty until proven innocent. Court got his way and a couple of days later I was told that I was no longer required to stay with the tour party and that a flight home would be arranged for me. I tried to find out who had put up the evidence against me and vehemently denied smoking anything at all in any dressing-room. No mention was made of the gig earlier in the tour where I *had* had a couple of discreet draws – and I certainly was not about to mention it. Court had seemed to gloat at the prospect of sending me home, but I spoilt his fun by rejecting their offer, saying that I had decided to stay on for a few weeks holiday. What I did not say was that Australia's Channel 9 had approached me to join their commentary team for the remainder of the series. And that really annoyed the ECB, and in particular, Terry Court.

With hindsight it may not have been my finest decision. It was bad enough that I had seemingly disgraced the game and the name of English cricket – a charge I thoroughly refute by the way – but to be seen to be profiting from my misdemeanour put me almost beyond the pale. Court was sent to see me at the first match I covered with the threat that I may never be selected again. Not good news, of course, but armed with a fairly hefty, new Australian salary and bolstered by some high-profile appearances on Australian chat shows, I was revelling in my new-found notoriety. I told him where to go and he made it clear to me that he was positive that I was involved with Summers in the bet. I suggested he prove it if he could – with my fingers crossed that Summers would not mention the fact that, but for a lack of ready cash, I might have been.

The one really good thing to come out of the whole mess was the coverage at home, particularly in the music press. I suppose the general perception of cricket is still that it is a bit 'public school' and for most people it is not as cool as our other national sport, football. Since the roistering days of Ian Botham, the press has searched in vain for a replacement. Suddenly, without any planning on my part, I seemed to have given them what they wanted. Newspapers and magazines either sent Australian stringers or they sent their own reporters out to interview me. I was caught between playing it all down in the hope that I could persuade the authorities to reconsider their verdict and playing it up out of sheer bravado. Certainly, I did not admit to the pot smoking during the Test, but I perhaps did not always protest my innocence as loudly as I could. Strangely enough, the most damaging article also had the best outcome.

The tour had reached Canberra where a day/night match against a President's XI was due to be televised and I was in my hotel waiting for a call from the front desk to tell me that my transport to the ground had arrived. The phone rang and the desk said they had a young English lady in the lobby for me. I laughingly told them to send her right up. When I opened to the gentle knock, I was for a second, rendered totally speechless. Standing before me was the most beautiful woman I had ever seen – and since the drug story broke, I had met quite a number of women. She was a little over five feet tall, had a shiny, black Louise Brookes' bob, elfin-like features with a little nose that curved ever so slightly upwards at its tip and gorgeous, sparkling green eyes. She was wearing a loose-fitting white cheesecloth shirt that was slashed to the waist, a pair of khaki combat trousers that had been cut off just below the knee and a huge pair of Doctor Marten's.

I invited her in and as she bent forward to pick up her little suitcase, I could not help noticing that she had neglected to wear a bra. She introduced herself, said that she was a freelance journalist and told me that she wanted to do a fairly in-depth piece. She hoped that she could follow the tour for a few days to observe and to conduct a series of informal interviews. She explained that she was in Australia to research a book on the INXS singer, Michael Hutchence, and had become interested in my story after reading the papers. I was absolutely entranced by her but, trying not to show it, I gave the impression of finding it all a bit of a chore. I desperately wanted her to stay around for a few days but said I would have a chat with the people at Channel 9 to see if they were okay with her spending time with us. Whilst we were talking, I received another call to say that my lift had arrived, and I arranged to meet the girl again in the bar that evening.

Elisa and I had sex together for the first time about an hour after close of play that night. I already knew she was the girl for me. She did her article

– and I did just about anything she asked, some of which was probably a little ill-advised. Certainly, the photo session on Bondi beach was. It was Elisa's idea to have me in swimming trunks, cup of tea in one hand and pantomime spliff in the other, surrounded by a group of ten topless girls from the beach. The photograph looked great on the cover of *Mad For It*, who bought the article, which was also syndicated around the world. The story helped Elisa too, because the Hutchence book, which she had struggled to place, was snapped up not long afterwards. I received another snotty letter from the ECB over the spliff, and with the benefit of hindsight I can see they had a point. Trouble is, I was hooked – on Elisa.

The other spin-off from the sudden surge of media interest was that top-ten indie hit I mentioned earlier. My band had split nearly a decade before, but Elisa had contacts in the recording business and managed to arrange a one-off deal for the single to be re-packaged and re-released. We had put it out originally off our own backs and with our own money and it had sunk without a trace. This time, with the Bondi Beach photo on the sleeve and with a fair amount of airtime, *You Kill Me* at last crawled into the charts. The Phoenix Arizonas never did manage to get any reunion gigs arranged but we all met for a beer one evening to toast the single's success.

As I sat sipping the scalding coffee and waited for the session to begin, Court continued to tidy piles of books on the long table in front of me. A couple of times he checked that I was okay and I began to suspect that he was under orders from above. I smiled at the sudden about-turn and hoped that perhaps Summers was right, that I was on my way back. There was another piece in the papers that gave me hope, this time from one of the remaining two selectors, Gerry Brevin, to the effect that England needed to diversify its bowling attack. He went on to say that batting ability was less important than finding the right combination of bowlers.

The bookshop was rapidly filling with lunchtime shoppers. It had been easy to find, bang in the middle of Leadenhall Market in the City of London, although I had over the years driven past the market countless times without ever noticing it. Today, I had decided to take the Tube up from The Oval and had strolled down from Bank. I was struck by all the new building work that was either finished or nearing completion. There were some really good structures going up all over the City and again, I had never really taken the time before to think about them. Since I had begun to follow the re-development plans at Surrey, however, I had started to look at buildings in a different light. If I had had more time, I think I would have spent the rest of the afternoon wandering around but I had a stack of mail to attend to back at home and had picked up another pile earlier from my desk. I had also found a note stuck to my computer screen telling me that Carlisle wanted to have a chat with me. He knew about these signing sessions, but I got the impression that he did not like me missing training for them. I rubbed at my shoulder, remembering that it was still sore – although that was more due to the lengthy net session I had had the night before.

The Surrey Championship season had still not started and although I get very little opportunity to get to Wimbledon these days I do keep in touch and try to get to a net every now and then. The previous night's session had lasted for nearly three hours and I had bowled for most of it, the shoulder holding up well. I had also managed to get my pads on for a bit and immediately focused on Summers' idea. I was now conscious that my stance in the nets has always been more open than it is out in the middle – and for the first time I could begin to understand why things in practice sessions seemed so much more comfortable. The challenge was going to be to transfer this knowledge onto the pitch.

Court gave a little cough and I quickly looked up to see that the rope which separated us from the queue of shoppers was being un-hooked. The snake started to inch forward, and I reached out to take the first copy. Most of the people said very little aside from who the dedication was for. Some of the younger men wanted to have a few words about the game and almost all wished me well or said they hoped I got my England place back. One old boy bought three copies, he said for his grandchildren, but thought I was a disgrace to the game. Luckily, he was the only one – or at least, the only one brave enough to tell me.

As I continued to sign, my mind started to wander, and I found myself thinking about Sally. She had planned to meet Barry Miller on the Thursday of the previous week, but I had not seen him either since then. Sally was not returning calls to her home and I decided that either I tracked down Miller or went knocking on Sally's door. I supposed that her drink with Miller had been unremarkable or else she would surely have called to tell me. Quite where she was though was now becoming troubling.

'Hello, again.'

The voice was familiar, and I looked up with a start. For a second, I was looking at Elisa. She was wearing the long, white leather coat again and I was relieved to see that it was buttoned up this time. It was the girl (Lisa? Laura?) from the last book-signing session. A new, bleached-blonde hair colour, a good deal shorter, but the same wonderfully mischievous smile and I found myself grinning stupidly back. I looked down at her hands but could see no book.

I groaned. 'What do you want me to sign this time?'

She threw back her head and laughed. She even had a wonderful laugh. And perfect white teeth, almost as dazzling as her cropped, newly peroxided hair. Her blue eyes sparkled. 'Don't worry,' she said, before lowering her voice. 'I work up in the City and saw you were in here today...' Here she paused and I saw a flicker of uncertainty in her eyes for the first time. I said nothing, preferring to let her flounder. 'I don't suppose you fancy a drink later.... no, I expect you are far too busy. Look, sorry, let's forget this.' She turned to go, and I found myself grabbing out for her sleeve.

'I'd love to,' I replied, not quite believing that I was saying it. 'Where do you suggest?'

She mentioned the name of a bar quite close by and I said I would be there a little after one. As she left, I felt a little surge of excitement mingled with a prickle of guilt. But I told myself that I had done and would do nothing wrong and that I was just going to have lunch with a girl. That was all. A girl who was not only beautiful, but whose name I did not even know. It sounded great but it did not look good.

The signing over, I left Court to wrap things up and I headed off in search of the Jamaica Inn, which the girl had told me was in a little alley off of Cornhill. I had to ask for directions as Cornhill seemed to have an alley turning off every few yards. The ancient little russet-coloured building looked quite out of place, hemmed in on all sides as it was by larger, more modern office buildings and as I approached the doorway I noticed the step had been worn away to almost nothing. Inside, my eyes took a few moments to adjust from the bright sunlight to the more subdued lighting and I thought suddenly that she might not be there. For a second, I could not see her, and feeling a little foolish, I was about to turn around and leave when I caught sight of her at a corner table. Her hair almost glowed in the sombre colours of the bar.

'I didn't think you would come,' she said with a shy smile, handing me a cold bottle of Becks.

'If you had not had your coat buttoned-up I might not have done,' I replied.

She gave a little embarrassed giggle and looked away. 'Ah-hem,' she coughed. 'Let's forget about that, can we? I had had a couple of drinks.'

'Well I will try to forget it, but that may be a little difficult.' She looked up at me from under her long, black eyelashes. She seemed pleased. 'Anyway,' I continued, 'what were you doing drinking that early?'

'It's never too early to drink,' she said, her teeth flashing white.

'A girl after my own heart. Cheers!' I replied, clinking bottles with her. 'You are a cricket fan, I take it?'

She reddened slightly. 'Not especially, no, but I saw you were doing a signing and wanted to say hello.'

It was my turn to redden. 'Well, I am very glad you did,' I began.

A mobile telephone warbled and for a couple of rings I waited for her to produce one before suddenly realising that it was my own. Apologising, I fumbled inside my jacket and answered. Reception was poor and nodding in the direction of the door, I stood up to take the call outside. It was Jackie Kray.

'Look I'm really sorry, but I've got to rush back to The Oval. Seems there's a problem,' I said, as I came back to the table. Jackie had sounded upset and asked if I could get over immediately.

'No worries. I understand,' the blonde replied, although I thought I detected a hint that she felt I was grabbing at an excuse to escape.

'Are you free later?' I asked, trying to make amends.

'No, not tonight. Another time maybe.' She looked disappointed.

'Give me your number – I'll ring.' I could not believe I was saying it.

As I hurried down Cornhill towards Bank underground station, I slipped the business card she had written her number on into my wallet. I suddenly realised that I still did not know her name and took the card back out to check that. She had scribbled a number on the back of someone else's card. The name on it was male and he clearly worked for an investment bank. That was little help but looking at the number it seemed to be for her home – at least, it began with 0208, suggesting outer London but that did not mean she lived anywhere near me.

I was back at The Oval within twenty minutes and went straight to the Club Office. Jackie Kray was there on her own, sitting at a computer screen. She looked up as I entered, and I noticed that she had been crying. She spoke before I could say anything.

'It's Sally. She's dead.' Her red eyes started to fill again.

I stood there rooted to the spot. I had heard the words, but I could not understand them. 'What?'

'Hit and run. Just down the road from her flat. I'm so sorry, Johnny.'

I slumped into the seat next to her. I felt a little sick and gulped heavily a couple of times. Jackie leant forward and laid a hand on my arm. 'You going to be okay?' she asked.

'How did you find out? Who called?'

'I called *her*. Miller asked me to give her a call at home as she didn't turn up for work this week. Last time we saw her was last Thursday. Seems she met Miller for a drink, and no-one had seen her since.'

'Who told you about the accident?'

'I spoke with Sally's mother. She was at Sally's flat – she seemed terribly upset.'

So was I, even though I had only known her a few weeks. 'What did Miller say?' I suddenly asked.

Jackie frowned. 'He really annoyed me actually. I called him on his mobile to tell him about Sally. He seemed more put out than upset.'

'Bastard. But that's Miller, I'm afraid. I don't think it's anything personal against Sally. They probably didn't know each other that well. He's never here and Sally was up in the library with me. They probably only met a handful of times.'

'Are you going to be okay, Johnny?'

'I guess so. This is so bad, Jackie. She was a great girl – what a waste. And you say it was a hit and run?'

'Her mother said it happened late. Sally had apparently popped into a late-night shop for some milk and was hit crossing the road. She died shortly after reaching the hospital.'

'Where did this happen? I don't even know where she lives...lived.'

'Putney – a little flat off the High Street.'

'And Sally's mum didn't think to let us know?'

'She said she assumed we knew,' Jackie replied, frowning.

I left the Club Office in a daze and went in search of Carlisle, who had said he wanted to see me. I found him in the sports centre and waited until he had finished with one of the second eleven players. He took me to one side.

'How was the signing?' he asked.

'Okay. Court seemed in a better mood.'

'That's the ECB guy?'

I nodded.

'That's a good sign, Johnny. Perhaps the ECB are warming to you again?'

'We'll see,' I replied. I could not get the mental image out of my mind of Sally, lying broken in the road.

'Thanks for stopping by. Look, I want you to concentrate on your cricket again. I know you've got to do these signings, but with the magazine as well there just seems to be too much on your plate at the moment.'

'The magazine is ready to print – there won't be another one for a couple of months,' I protested.

'But when there is, you will be up to your neck in it. Anyway, I'm not suggesting you stop for good. Just for the summer.' Carlisle was clearly trying to be reasonable, but I was still rattled by the news about Sally.

'No, sorry boss. I don't want to stand down,' I said flatly.

Carlisle's tone abruptly cooled. 'Well I have taken the liberty of standing *you* down.' With that, he turned on his heel and stormed back to his net session.

I left the ground in a sad, bitter mood and travelled all the way home without even opening the newspaper I had picked up earlier. I checked the answerphone but there were no new messages. Elisa had not phoned for a couple of days, but I was getting used to the gaps between her calls. I flipped the kettle on and went upstairs to the bathroom. As I passed the open door to the study, I saw out of the corner of my eye that Elisa's computer was still on. The screensaver was spiralling away and had presumably been doing so for a couple of days. Annoyed at the waste of electricity I went in to turn it off.

Elisa gets very upset with me harping on about conserving resources and I felt a little guilty at having not noticed that it was left on. When she brushes her teeth, she needlessly leaves the water running the whole time. I will reach over her and turn it off, which really pisses her off. I gave the mouse a gentle nudge and the screensaver vanished. The screen was displaying the contents of the folder that Elisa had asked me to check a couple of days before and I was just about to close it when I noticed the icon that was simply titled with a question mark. Intrigued, I double clicked and waited for a second whilst the screen filled.

I sat down on the swivel-chair as the document appeared before me. There was just one sentence. I read it once quickly and then a second time slowly, word by word.

I woke up to find C's hand in my pants. I thought about screaming but seeing that there were already half a dozen people already in the room, I pulled him down on top of me – it was exciting knowing that we were being watched. I loved it – decadent, dangerous and very Chelsea Hotel.

I sat there stunned for several minutes. I felt betrayed. And humiliated. I simply could not believe that Elisa would do that to me.

On an impulse I ran back down the stairs and pulled the telephone lead from its socket. I did not expect Elisa to call, but I certainly was not in the mood to speak to her if she did. I suddenly had the craving for a cigarette, and the desire to get blind drunk. But there was no-one to get drunk with – and I had thrown the cigarettes away. A vindictive thought flashed through my mind, and I fumbled in various pockets until I found what I was looking for.

I reconnected the telephone and dialled the number in front of me. It went to a messaging service. I left a brief message and my mobile number, pulled the lead from the wall again and went to make a cup of tea.

The kettle had only just boiled when the mobile rang.

'It's Lori. That was quick.'

Lori. I had her name at last. 'Look, this thing you've got on tonight – can you change it?'

I don't know if I sounded desperate or whether she had fabricated the appointment, but she agreed to meet me. She said she lived in Kingston, so I suggested The Ram, a little old-fashioned pub on the river, opposite the police station.

As I climbed into the mini-cab I had called, I had a fluttery feeling in my stomach. Images of Sally bleeding and Elisa screwing tumbled around and every now and then Lori's beautiful face came into focus. What the hell was I doing?

CHAPTER 10

I arrived home in the early hours with surprisingly mixed feelings, and as I let myself in the front door, I reached over to reconnect the telephone again, feeling a little ashamed at having tried to avoid Elisa's call. There was no point running away from the situation and if I knew where she was staying, I think I would have called her. I had scribbled the cities she was visiting in my diary's margin, but she had not known in what order the tour would visit them and she did not know many of the hotels they would be using before she flew out. Since she was not keeping in touch I did not know where to start.

I made a large mug of tea and took it into the living room along with the stack of mail that had been steadily building over the past few days. Flipping on Sky News, I slumped down into my favourite armchair and with half an eye to the screen, I started to work my way through the pile.

My head was still humming from the drink and from the loud music in the little bar we had ended up in. I had never heard of it before – a little trendy place across the other side of town from the Ram. We had had a couple of drinks in the pub before getting a bite to eat at a vegetarian place just along the road. Like Elisa, Lori was a strict vegetarian and although I am not usually keen on meatless meals, I had to admit that the food was excellent. After the meal Lori had suggested the Chewy Bar.

The place was tiny and absolutely rammed. We got a drink at the bar and stood against a wall to one side. It was difficult to hear each other and even though we were away from the bar area we seemed to be on the direct route to the toilets. When a table was suddenly vacated, Lori grabbed my hand and we just managed to claim it ahead of another couple. It was just big enough for our two bottles of lager and, squeezed between similar tables on either side, we were forced to sit almost in each other's laps. Sat this close to her I was reminded once again of how much alike she and Elisa were. Elisa had changed her hair from black bob to peroxide crop a few months before. The most obvious difference were the eyes; where Elisa's were green, Lori's were the most striking blue. They were of similar height and build and even seemed to share a sense of humour. Lori and I apparently shared the love of the same films and she seemed to be pretty knowledgeable about cricket too, certainly for someone who professed little interest in the sport. I had not mentioned Elisa at all since we met, but seated at the little table, Lori had suddenly stopped smiling.

'Are you married, Johnny?'

I wished she had not asked that and found myself fumbling with the soggy label on my beer bottle. 'At the moment,' I replied.

She looked at me quizzically, so I continued to tell her of Elisa's sudden focus on her work and of the lack of contact and I even mentioned the words I had discovered on the computer. She had waved away my worries and said something I could not hear. I shouted over the music, asking her to say it again, and she leaned forward, putting a hand gently on my shoulder. As she spoke directly into my ear, I could feel her lips brush against my skin, and her soft, warm breath. I felt a little shiver of excitement. She was telling me to confront Elisa with what I had discovered and not to let it fester – it could all have an innocent explanation. She went on to tell me about her own marriage which had ended acrimoniously. She had married a Frenchman when she was just seventeen and after a couple of happy years in Paris, he had started to knock her around. She had left him, filed for and got a divorce, before discovering that it was the side-effects from the anti-depression drugs he was taking that had caused his character change. By the time she had discovered this, he had re-married.

'You've seen that Hitchcock film, *Strangers on a Train*?' I asked.

'That's the old black and white one – where the two guys agree to commit each other's murder? Yes, definitely. I love that film,' Lori replied, her eyes sparkling in the bar's dim lighting.

'Makes you think doesn't it?' I said with mock grimness, pretending to strangle my beer bottle.

Lori laughed. 'I don't think things are that bad yet, Johnny. Speak with her. Try and find where she's staying and give her a call.'

I was suddenly disappointed that she was seemingly keen to get Elisa and me back together.

As I sat waiting for the one o'clock bulletin, I thought about what she had said. After the drink I had suggested a coffee, but Lori seemed to think that there would be nowhere open. I found myself offering her a coffee at home and for a second I thought she looked disappointed in me. She had suddenly smiled and said that she had an early start that morning. She would not let me see her home, but she did say she would like to meet again. We had kissed goodbye – a simple platonic kiss on the cheek – yet I still felt guilty. I think, because I had invited her back to our place. I felt strangely relieved, now, that she had refused.

I was still opening letters when the London news bulletin started and was only half-listening when I heard the words 'hit and run'. I looked up sharply, but the item had finished. I wondered if it was about Sally and started to sink into a blue mood again. I pulled out the sheet of paper from the stamp-less envelope in my hand and read it several times until the words finally sank in. I suddenly felt very uneasy –and slightly nauseous. It was a handwritten note that seemed to come from beyond the grave. I must have picked it up at The Oval a few days before, because it was from Sally. I quickly read it, but the alcohol was making comprehension a little difficult.

Dear Johnny,

I am really worried. Please come up and see me when you are in next. I must speak to you. I don't know who to turn to. M is a monster – but I will tell you more when I see you. Better still, call me at home on the number below.
Love Sally.

Images swirled in my mind of Sally lying in the road, bleeding, and of Miller. She was meeting Miller that night. 'M' had to be Miller, didn't it? Had he tried it on with her? It certainly sounded like he had. And he had plenty of previous. I decided that I would call her mother to see if Sally had said anything to her. In a way though, I realised that it did not really matter. Sally was dead. But I also realised that Miller should not be allowed to get away with it if he had assaulted her. And knowing what I did about Miller, the rumours I had heard, I was not too surprised. She must have gone out for that drink with Miller to confront him about something and I was pretty sure it would have been about the Willby contract. She said he was a monster but surely not monstrous enough to run her down in cold blood?

CHAPTER 11

Saturday April 26 1997

Carlisle had allowed me to sit out the first Championship match of the season, a home game against Somerset, but I decided to show willing by popping in to support the lads on day four. My shoulder was responding to treatment, but it was decided that I should focus on the one-dayers where I would have less bowling to do, at least in these early stages of the season. Somerset had scored a big 450-plus in their first innings and we were clinging on in our second but losing wickets consistently throughout the day. I had just walked into the dressing room as the 8th wicket went down. We were in big trouble. The mood was tense, Carlisle was fuming and my mobile warbled. I made a hasty dash for the corridor, hoping the gaffer had been too absorbed in proceedings out in the middle to have noticed.

A strained, barely audible voice started to speak before dissolving into tears. For a second I thought it was Elisa and had awful visions of what might have reduced her to this state, but before my mind could conjure up any, more detailed images, the small voice returned.

'It's Lori – look, I'm sorry to have called. I shouldn't have.' The line went dead.

'Damn!' I cursed, immediately realising that I did not have her number with me. I would have to call her from home.

It took for ever getting back to Epsom. The match had finished close to four o'clock, which meant that after sitting through Carlisle's harangue, and feeling relieved that I had only been a spectator, I was on the road bang in the middle of the rush hour. The traffic crawled nose-to-tail through the dismal south London streets until finally I reached the beginning of the three-lane section of the A3 at Roehampton. Both the Vectra and I gave a huge sigh of relief as we managed to get into fourth gear for the first time since leaving The Oval over an hour before. I was home within twenty-five minutes and immediately went in search of Lori's number.

She did not answer until close to nine o'clock, but when she did I was relieved to find that she sounded a lot more like her normal self. She would only say that she had had a shock and did not know who to turn to, but that everything was now okay. I suspected that she was putting a brave face on it but wanted to see her and asked if she would like a quick drink. My heart gave a little flutter when she instantly said yes. We agreed on the Ram again and I rushed around for a few seconds with a flannel and toothbrush.

My mobile rang again as I was ready to leave. It was Lori. Something had cropped up and she could not now meet but could we do it tomorrow instead. Disappointed, I tried to sound cheery and said, of course. That was all very sudden – and rather odd. I wondered for a moment whether she was living with someone else. We arranged to meet in the evening after our first AXA Sunday League match of the season.

CHAPTER 12

Sunday April 27 1997

She beat me there by just a few minutes and I found her still at the bar ordering drinks. Her eyes seemed to light up when I came in through the door and she kissed me directly on the lips. It was the first time she had done that, and I liked it.

'You won today!' she said, clinking my glass, as we took the drinks over to a table in the window.

'We did – early days but it's been a good start to the one-day season,' I replied, surprised that she even knew we had had a game – a 1-run win over Somerset at The Oval in our AXA opener.

'And you took 3 wickets but didn't bat?'

'You are well-informed. I didn't know you were such a fan,' I grinned at her, flattered by her apparent interest. 'At least Carlisle was happier after the Championship drubbing.'

Lori's eyes sparkled in the subdued lighting and she told me excitedly about some goings on at her office. I had the impression that this small talk was an effort to cover over our earlier phone call, but I did not want to broach the subject. It was Lori that did so when we were on our second drink.

'I'm really sorry about that call, Johnny. I shouldn't have made it.'

I waved my hand. 'Don't apologise. I'm just sorry it took me so long to get back to you.' I explained that I had not had her number on me and that I had got tangled up in traffic on my way home. 'What was up?' I asked gently.

She seemed about to change the subject but suddenly got an intense look about her eyes. 'It's Phillipe. He called me today – from Paris.'

'Your ex?' I asked, wincing supportively.

She nodded. 'I haven't seen or heard from him for years and then today, out of the blue, he calls up.' She stopped talking and sat staring morosely into her drink, scratching nervously at a soggy beer mat. 'Probably my fault for telling you about him.'

I remained silent for several seconds to give her the chance to continue but she said nothing. She had previously told me that she was married at seventeen and that the marriage had lasted a couple of years, but I had no idea how old she was, although I would have guessed at about twenty-five. 'What did he have to say for himself?'

There was a long pause before she answered, and I could see her eyes welling up again. 'This is really embarrassing, Johnny,' she said quietly without raising her eyes.

'Is it anything I can help with?'

She looked up and smiled at me through the tears that were now beginning to fall gently down her cheeks. 'Is your *Strangers on a Train* offer still open?'

'Could be,' I replied, smiling with her. 'What's he done?'

She suddenly sat up straighter, took a swig of the cold lager, and wiped her eyes with the cuff of her sweatshirt. 'He is being a total bastard. I have not seen or heard from him for five years and now he's trying to blackmail me. When we met he was a struggling photographer. He did a bit of freelance work for one of the motor sports magazines, but he was predominantly a glamour photographer.' Here, she paused for a moment, took another gulp of lager before continuing. 'Rather ill-advisedly I sat for him – to help him out really. The shots were never meant to be published, at least that is what we agreed.' Her voice tailed off and she went back to fiddling with her beer mat. A pink flush crept across her face.

'And I guess now he has fallen on hard times and is threatening to publish?'

She nodded and spoke without looking at me. 'Says he can get a few thousand francs for them from one of the top-shelf magazines.'

'Ah,' I said, and Lori's head snapped up. She looked up at me sadly and nodded again.

'It would kill my parents, Johnny. I mean, the pictures are pretty explicit. If it wasn't for them I don't think I'd mind so much, but unless I can get ten thousand pounds together pretty quickly he will sell them.'

'Blackmailing bastard!' I said a little louder than I intended, and Lori's head dropped as heads turned towards us. Speaking more quietly, I continued. 'Can't you go to the police – or at least get some legal advice? You're not thinking of paying him, are you?'

'I just don't know what to do,' she said with a note of despair in her voice.

I reached out across the table and took hold of her hands. She looked up at me, clearly on the verge of breaking down. 'Let's go,' I said, starting to pull her up.

'Where?' she asked limply.

'My place.'

CHAPTER 13

Monday April 28 1997

The alarm sounded bang on six o'clock and I fumbled around until I found it – it wasn't in the usual place. For a second I wondered where I was but quickly realized that I wasn't in the usual place either; I was on the sofa in the living-room. Lori and I had driven straight home from Kingston and I had made us a couple of strong brandy coffees to go with the toast that Lori accepted. She had slowly brightened up and by midnight when I went up to change the sheets on the bed she seemed back to normal. I was just about to pull the bottom sheet from the bed when I heard the door open behind me. She gently pulled my hand from the sheet and turned me around to face her.

'Don't change them,' she said. Her face was just inches from mine. 'I want to be able to smell you tonight.'

I went all Hugh Grant for a second, stammering something about it being better to put clean on. She silenced me with a soft, lingering kiss on the lips. I pulled away a little more sharply than I had intended and caught a look of hurt on Lori's face. 'Well, I'd better be off – Canterbury tomorrow... first B&H match... there's a new toothbrush in the bathroom cabinet – help yourself.' I left the room without looking back. I immediately both regretted it and felt a little proud that I had been strong enough to resist – although with Elisa's current form I wondered why I bothered. She rang so infrequently and when she did it seemed to be just to get me to do an errand for her. And moreover, I still wanted to speak with her about what I had read on her computer.

I made as little noise as possible in getting ready, partly out of consideration for Lori and partly to avoid having to face her. I had woken up in the early hours and for a fleeting moment had thought about going upstairs to join her but quickly thought better of it. By seven-thirty I was packed and ready to go. I checked my coffin one last time to ensure everything was there and having placed it in the trunk of my car, I suddenly realized that I had to do something about the sleeping girl upstairs. I assumed that she had to go to work too.

I did not really know what I could do to help; the business with her ex-husband seemed to me to be a matter if not for the police, then at least for a lawyer. I climbed quietly back up the stairs and eased the bedroom door open a couple of inches. Lori was fast asleep. In the half-light seeping through the dark blue curtains she looked more beautiful than ever. I stole into the room and stood for a couple of seconds just watching the bedclothes gently rise and fall in time with her breathing. She looked so peaceful that it was almost hard to believe that this was the same person who had been on the verge of completely breaking down the night before. Controlling another urge to jump in with her and mindful of the time, I leant down and planted the softest kiss on her forehead.

In the kitchen I scribbled her a note and left it propped up against the kettle. I quickly read it and added, after my name:

The offer's still there: you do mine and I'll do yours!!

Smiling to myself, I picked up my mobile from the worktop where it had been recharging overnight, collected my Surrey blazer from the coat–peg by the front door and let myself silently out of the house. As I went to close the door behind me, I tapped my pockets: wallet but no house key. I went back to the kitchen counter where I normally deposit everything from my pockets when I come in but could not see my door key. Grabbing the spare we keep on a peg, I dashed back out to the car.

I reached the M25 within twenty-minutes and was pleased to see the traffic flowing freely. I slipped in between the fast-moving vehicles and eased my way up to eighty. The morning was clear and bright, the sky a weak, pastel blue, streaked with a few puffy, pink-tinged clouds. In the fields that sloped down towards the motorway on my left, where the sun's warmth had not yet penetrated, the grass was still a frosty blue. Prospects for a full day's play looked good. It also looked like being another three-sweater start.

I groped around for the mobile amongst the debris on the seat next to me and barely taking my eyes from the road, tapped out a number. Summers picked up almost immediately. I had remembered that he had called me at The Oval the day before but had not found the time to return the call.

'Elisa back yet?'

'No, she's not. She did at least call yesterday – from San Antonio – but I missed *her* as well.'

'I hope you're behaving yourself while she's away,' Summers said with a laugh.

'Of course, mate – although I have just left a gorgeous blonde in my bed, but that's another and very long story. Anyway, you rang?'

'I did, mate, but the blonde sounds more interesting.'

'It's not, I can assure you.' I was annoyed that I had mentioned it. There really had been no need to. 'She's just a friend of ours who dropped in and de-cided to stay. I slept on the sofa,' I added quickly. I must have sounded guilty.

'It's okay – I believe you. Nearly. Anyway, tell me about Alan Dench.'

'Sorry?'

'Alan Dench. How does he look?'

I paused for a moment wondering where this was leading. 'He looked good yesterday – although Somerset's bowling was pretty average. Why do you ask?'

'No drama, Johnny, just keeping abreast of things. I hear on the grape-vine that Dench is being considered for a recall, him being top of the averages last year.'

'I wonder if he's heard something too,' I replied, remembering his sudden commitment to the team's cause the day before. 'He seemed remarkably buoyant yesterday.'

'Yes, he must have thought his last chance had gone. Do you know what sort of deal he's got with Surrey?'

'No idea at all, but you surely remember how they kept that sort of information quiet.'

'I just wondered... my source tells me that he has money worries.'

Summers had mentioned this before, but I had no knowledge of Dench' private affairs and really did not see of what interest they were to Summers either. After the call I was left with a slightly uneasy feeling. I certainly regretted mentioning Lori, but I also realized that my discussion with Summers could technically have contravened the ICC guidance around consorting with bookmakers. I resolved to call Summers again later to tell him that I was happy to meet up with him but that I was not willing to get involved with forecasts or even player assessments. Feeling better already, I moved over to join the traffic filing off for the A2 Canterbury turn-off.

I reached the St Lawrence ground at just gone nine o'clock, parked and strolled across the car park towards the pavilion. A couple of the Kent players were chatting together just inside the pavilion doors and stopped when I walked between them.

'Morning, Johnny, you okay?' asked Flowers, their wicketkeeper.

It was like someone had died. 'Great, thanks,' I said with a smile, and as an afterthought I added, over my shoulder, 'bad luck for today, by the way!'

I climbed the stairs to the away dressing-room and struggled through it with my bat and heavy coffin. The normal hubbub died away almost instantly; a few furtive glances were shot in my direction and then the volume gradually increased until it had reached normal intensity again. It was all rather like the scene in American Werewolf in London, where the two American hikers enter a pub, deep in the Yorkshire moors. I walked over to one of the last remaining free places and dumped the coffin down next to Lenderman on one side and Molander on the other.

'Morning lads!' I said heartily. They each murmured a muted good morning.

Lenderman turned away and busied himself with something in his locker. Molander maintained eye contact and I thought I detected a pitying look.

'What's with everyone today – do I smell or something?' I asked with a grin.

'You haven't seen it, have you?'

'Depends what it is,' I replied, feeling the first stabs of unease.

Molander bent down and rummaged in his bag for a second before coming up with a copy of The Star. With a moistened finger he quickly flicked through the pages until, finding what he wanted, he folded back the paper and silently held it out to me.

I swallowed hard as I felt the nausea rise into my throat. I was conscious of everyone looking at me. My eyes stung and I felt the sweat breaking out on my forehead. Molander ostentatiously turned and started a conversation with Pallant and I had that uncomfortable sensation of being alone in the crowd. I slumped into the empty seat and tried again to read the article.

The report was of the Toadlust gig in San Antonio. They had apparently played to a sell-out crowd at one of the colleges and there had been some trouble over what the paper described as a 'lewd act' onstage. The police had been in attendance anyway to help with crowd control and had interviewed the band afterwards. It was the photograph of a very wasted looked Crispin that was worrying me, however. He had been caught backstage, according to the caption, which read:

> *Toadlust singer, Crispin LeDare, seeks comfort from new girlfriend, Elisa Lorrens, wife of England cricket maverick, Johnny Lorrens.*

Crispin was sitting on a flight case with one arm draped around Elisa, his head resting on her shoulder. She looked half-cut too or had perhaps been caught in mid-blink. I hoped.

I re-folded the paper and dropped it quietly onto Molander's bag, and trying very hard to be casual, started to change. I hoped nobody noticed my trembling hands. Pallant shot me a quick glance over Molander's shoulder and I smiled back.

'Okay, Johnny?' he asked a little awkwardly.

'I'm fine. The Star is being a little over-dramatic,' I replied, nodding towards Molander's copy. I was itching to call Elisa up – if only I had known where to get hold of her.

'You going to be alright for today?' Carlisle had appeared behind me.

'No problem, Gaffer. Paper's full of crap.'

'Good man,' Carlisle said, slapping me on the back.

I could not concentrate on his pep talk, my mind crossing the Atlantic and conjuring up all manner of painful images. It all rather looked like the sentence I had discovered on Elisa's computer had some truth to it. But why she had felt the need to write it down was beyond me; unless she wanted me to read it. I even wondered if she had asked me to look for her article knowing that I would probably stumble across it. Perhaps she could not bring herself to tell me face-to-face. It might also explain why she had been so vague about the tour details and why she had hardly called. For some reason, I had the sudden urge to speak with Lori and when Carlisle finally clapped his hands and opened the dressing-room door, I quickly slipped into the shower-room and stabbed out my home number on the mobile. After six rings the answerphone cut in and I heard Elisa's voice. It had the effect of sobering me up pretty quickly and I suddenly realised that I did not know what I was going to say had Lori answered anyway. I flicked the mobile off, threw it in my locker and trotted off after the rest of the team, catching up with them mid-way to the square.

We had lost the toss and Kent had elected to bat on what looked like a very good wicket for this early in the season. After ten overs my fears were confirmed, with the Kent openers rattling along at nearly six an over. I was surprised how well I managed to concentrate. I do not think Elisa ever escaped from my mind, but I was able to remain fixed on the game at the same time.

Snipe eventually made the breakthrough and removed both openers in the same over. Thereafter Kent struggled and limped to 212 for 7 from their fifty overs. I bowled six overs with only minimal pain in the shoulder and took 2 for 20. Back in the dressing-room at the interval I sat by myself, nursing a mug of steaming tea with a sudden craving for a cigarette. The rest of the team seemed to realise that I wanted to be left alone and I was glad when Rennie and Driver eventually left to start our reply, giving the others something to focus on.

I sat quietly, weighing the mobile in my hand – wondering who to turn to. I thought about calling Elisa's office before reconsidering – I did not want to get into this with them just yet – and was about to dial Ralph and Kitty's number but suddenly wondered if they knew about Crispin already. Had the affair started on Elisa's last trip to New York – or was it earlier than that? She had been very keen to get the job. I felt more miserable than I could ever remember feeling before.

On the A2 that night, I put my toe down and raced back towards London. I was relieved that I had not been needed with the bat as we had cruised to an easy win. I do not think that in the state of mind I was in that I would have been much use.

The road was fairly empty and I made good progress. As I filtered onto the M25 the radio DJ was burbling about the new Toadlust single.

'*Skinflick Aromatherapy has been deleted from our playlist*', he announced almost triumphantly, '*so we are going to play you a track from their forthcoming album, Smell Your Fear. For the first time on the airwaves, I give you, in its place, at number seven, Toadlust with Sucker.*'

My immediate instinct was to reach for the off button, but I was intrigued. Aside from the Sex Pistols' *God Save the Queen* twenty-odd years before, I could not recall any other records that had been banned from the radio. Maybe a Frankie Goes to Hollywood, but I was not sure. *Sucker* sounded like Thrash Metal to me; Thrash Metal with Noel Coward on vocals. It was truly awful, and I do not think that my feelings for Crispin were swaying my judgement. It was also pretty clear to me what *Sucker* was about which made me shudder to think what the lyrics of the banned single might be like and wondering why the radio station thought this track any more appropriate. My disappointment with Elisa was magnified and, feeling the dark gloom of earlier falling around me as the sun sank in the western sky, I pushed in the cassette and cut Toadlust off.

Jay and the Americans accompanied me for the rest of the journey and by the time I reached Epsom with Jay launching into their wonderful version of *Cara Mia*, I felt in better shape. Certainly, I felt like a drink and someone to talk to and I decided on a whim to drive up to Wimbledon and call in on Summers. I thought for a moment that I should call first but decided not to waste the time. Besides, he might decline. Although that seemed highly unlikely.

Twenty minutes later I was parking up outside his flat. In our early days at Surrey we had been inseparable mates and I had many happy memories of evenings spent here, discussing with equal enthusiasm both cricket and girls. I saw a light on in the living room and paused at the door to check my watch before knocking. Nine o'clock; not too late.

Summers looked a little taken aback when he saw me.

'Johnny!' he boomed. 'What a surprise! Come in.'

I started to ask if it was convenient and he waved away my questions as he fought with the thick coconut doormat which seemed to be hampering the opening of the door. He finally succeeded in sliding it out of the way.

'Bloody mat! Nice to see you, mate', he said, shaking my hand with a bear-like grip. 'Drink?'

I nodded, as he showed me into the living-room. The furniture was Art Deco, one of Summers' weaknesses, and the walls were covered with mementos from his playing days. In pride of place was a large glass frame above the fireplace which held his England blazer. In the alcoves to either side of the fire he had put up framed scorecards and I quickly found the one for the game against Durham where he had scored 312 – his highest ever. In the bay window stood a wonderful thirties sideboard with a selection of framed photographs on top. There were Surrey line-ups, one of the two of us in the England touring party and a few family shots. I recognised one of his late parents and one of his brother. There were some people I did not know, one of a couple in ski-gear, which I took to be of Summers and a girlfriend, although it was difficult to tell with the goggles and scarves on.

'You had a good win today and I see you are still managing to avoid batting,' he said with a grin, holding out a bottle. 'Try this – almonds!' He thrust the bottle into my hand. 'Let me take your coat.'

'Almonds?' I was not sure that would work. Took a sip. It didn't. 'Not sure about this one I said,' waving his hand away as I took my jacket into the hall where I remembered pegs by the door. Another Deco unit there, again with framed pictures on top. One of Summers in the only Test he played; one of a Surrey line up from the early 90s and, as I was just running a finger through the light film of dust on top of the sideboard, I noticed a thin, clean line where a photo frame had evidently recently stood. Summers appearing behind me made me jump.

'Steady tiger – it's only me,' he boomed as he brushed his hand over the unit. 'Must have a good clean up in here,' he added.

As I turned to follow him back to the living room, I caught a faint whiff of sweetness. I put the bottle to my nose.

'You have to drink it, Johnny,' he grinned.

'What aftershave are you wearing these days, Mark? Smells like Opium?'

He hesitated for a fraction of a second. 'It's a deodorant I picked up in some poncey shop in Brighton. Need to get me some Right Guard,' he said tautly as he produced another beer from the fridge. 'Grapefruit.'

'Thanks, mate, couldn't drink the almond one and yes, you do need to go back to the Right Guard,' I agreed with a laugh.

I took a long drink from the bottle and at first could only taste beer. I was about to say so when the citrus aftertaste cut in. 'Now that is excellent, Mark – another one from New England?' I asked, looking for clues on the customary unlabelled bottle.

He nodded. 'You see why I'm so keen to get the deal done to import them?'

I could, but that reminded me of my concerns over the spread betting. 'That's something I wanted to talk to you about actually.'

'Not having second thoughts?' He looked anxious.

'Not really second thoughts, no. Though I am not happy about trying less than one-hundred percent for Surrey...'

'Just don't play with the new stance,' Summers quickly cut in. 'That's all I'm asking and although you said to me that knowing that you can probably bat more effectively with the new open stance makes you feel obliged to try it, all I am saying is don't try it just yet. There's plenty of time later in the summer.'

He was almost pleading with me. 'How much is this worth to you?' I asked.

Summers looked a little taken aback and seemed to consider his response for a few seconds. 'It's not just the money – although that's a big part of course. I left the game suddenly as you know and with no money to speak of; what little I had went on the round the world trip. The City Sports job is not too well paid and is just not for me in any case. I am just sorting the financial side so that I can go back to the beer company and jump start this import business. I simply need to buy your spread with a decent stake and hope that I'm right. Then I can repay the loan. Sorted.'

The way he put it sounded easy. 'Will that really give you enough?'

'Well we need to negotiate your share, naturally.'

'I don't want anything, Mark. I just want my place back in the team. The other thing I am concerned about is you calling me at The Oval.' He looked immediately crestfallen, but I stopped him from cutting in. 'I am more than happy to meet up and talk at home – as friends, but if I am caught taking calls from you at work, I'm for the high jump. I know you call as a mate, but Carlisle would see you as a bookie if he knew where you work now.'

He looked relieved and waved his hands.

We chatted about the bet for a couple of minutes and I expressed my concerns over him placing too large a stake on me but Summers assured me that he would be able to trade his way out of it if he was wrong about my batting. I also pointed out that I might not actually get a bat even if I played all three matches. He laughed at this but reminded me that England had batted all the way down to eleven in each of their last nine one-day matches. He tapped his nose and said he had a 'contingency plan'.

'Heard from Elisa yet?' Summers abruptly changed the subject.

'No – not to speak to,' I replied cautiously, wondering if he had seen The Star whilst quickly scanning the room for newspapers.

'Strange behaviour. If you don't mind me saying,' he added almost apologetically.

'I don't understand her, Mark. She made a big fuss out of wanting to stay at home more then suddenly jumped at this Toadlust job. And now she never calls and said she can't leave an itinerary. Then this thing in the paper today.'

Summers was about to take a sip of beer and suddenly looked up at me. 'What thing in the paper?'

'The Star; they had a story about Toadlust's gig in San Antonio where the police were called. There was a photo of ... Elisa. She looked half-cut – like she's fallen off the wagon.' I had been about to tell him that the paper was suggesting she was back with LeDare but could not bring myself to say it.

'So, she had a drink or two? Where's the problem?'

I paused before continuing, wondering why I was telling Summers.

'It suggested she was playing away.'

Summers threw his big, curly head back and laughed. I was a little taken aback by his reaction – and a little offended, but before I could reply he held up a big hand and continued. 'You surely don't believe what you read in that rag, Johnny! Come on, give Elisa some credit. I agree she could have kept in touch more, but you know her better than that. Even I do. Or are you suggesting that she has previous?'

I felt guilty of betraying Elisa and found it hard to look Summers in the eye as he sat in the chair opposite almost challenging me to disagree with him.

I started to get up. 'I guess you're right,' I said, feeling a little embarrassed, and wanting to change the subject. 'Maybe that was just the press stirring things up.' I had decided anyway to call Elisa's office in the morning to see if they could track her down for me.

'Call her up, mate – have it out with her,' he suggested.

As I started to open the front door, I bent down to move the coconut mat that had got tangled up earlier, but the door opened easily over it. I looked quizzically at Summers.

'Odd,' he said simply, his eyebrows raised. 'Johnny, just call her office and get things sorted. Don't go brooding on it – at least hear Elisa's side if you really think there is any substance to it.'

I got home a little after midnight, and, not feeling like sleeping, I poured a double measure of brandy into the coffee I had just made and took it into the living room where I flicked on Sky News. They led with a story about cloning and I was about to switch the set off when the next piece came on about the funeral of a gangland boss in Chicago. I suddenly remembered that Sally's funeral was in a couple of days' time and decided that whatever happened and however difficult the call might be, I would phone her mother later that day. I had arranged flowers a few days before but was so wrapped up with everything else that it had almost slipped my mind. I also remembered that Barry Miller had said he would attend and that thought did nothing to dispel my gloom. I resolved to call Jackie Kray as well, since she was due to represent the Club, to see if Miller did attend. If I had understood Sally's note correctly, at best Miller had no business attending and at worst he should be locked up. I went to bed forgetting about Elisa, but even angrier than I had been when I arrived home.

On the newly made bed was a single sheet of pink filofax paper, folded in half. I picked it up and a little thrill ran through me when I realised it was from Lori. With all the events of the day I had completely forgotten that she had spent the previous night in the house.

Johnny, thanks so much for being there for me – and yes! You get rid of Phillipe and I'll sort your problem out too!! Love you – Lori xxx

My spirits lifted, I neatly re-folded the paper and placed it in my wallet.

CHAPTER 14

Wednesday April 30 1997

The ball slammed into the boundary boards with a thud and a smattering of applause rang round the almost empty ground. As I slid to a muddy stop, I looked up at the electronic scoreboard on the Bedser Stand and saw that Gloucerstershire had reached three figures. And it was only the nineteenth over. I threw the ball in over the stumps to Lenderman and trotted back round to my position at deep square leg, glad of the exercise and the chance to keep warm. It was the second game of our Benson & Hedges campaign and but for the damp, cold weather The Oval would have surely been a little fuller. It has often struck me as odd, that a game still deemed important enough to get national coverage in all the dailies, can sometimes only attract a couple of hundred people. Until we get cricket stadiums with roofs, which given their irregular shapes and the huge expense involved looks most unlikely, it is always going to be the same. MacLaine's next delivery was another short longhop and I found myself haring round the boundary again. The umpire signalled 'four' and as I looped the ball back in towards Lenderman, I saw Pallant give me the signal to warm up.

As I started my routine of bends and stretches, I could not help glancing up to the library at the top of the pavilion – to the office that I had shared with Sally. I had not had the courage yet to call her mother about Miller and felt angry with myself that I had not even called to offer my condolences. I resolved to phone her during the interval.

At the end of the big Australian's over I removed two of my three sweaters and handed them to the umpire. He tucked my folded cap into one of the deep pockets of his white coat and advised the batsman 'right arm over.' The batsman made an adjustment to his guard as I took a deep breath before my first delivery of the day. I was conscious of Lenderman bobbing up and down behind the stumps like a nervous jack-in-the-box at the other end, and of Pallant at first slip clapping his hands in encouragement. The batsman settled, I gave my left ear a quick rub, and I started in towards him on my six-stride run-up. The ball looped away from me, pitched on a good length on middle, and as the batsman strode forward to meet it with a neat forward defensive stroke, it bit into the wicket and turned at a vicious right-angle towards Pallant. A murmur of surprise from the almost empty ground was quickly drowned out by the exhortations of my teammates. Crowther, the Gloucester batsman on strike, looked up at me with a grim smile and a nod of appreciation. I bent down to rub my hand in the footmarks that Stuart Snipe had made in his opening spell, returned to the end of my run-up and looked up to receive the ball from Dench who was fielding at cover.

I was about to start in for my second delivery when Crowther suddenly stood up and stepped away from his wicket, gesturing towards the Vauxhall End with his bat. Umpire Farmer, his large bulk accentuated by the layer of sweaters I had provided, shifted round testily to look in the direction Crowther had indicated. From pitch-level, the asymmetry of the stands at the Vauxhall End is not ideal for batting against despite an attempt to paint everything down there white. It is a messy tumble of ancient stands, some open, some roofed. Frankly it is a bit of a mess. Filled on a big match day, the constant crowd movements are even more off-putting. For a Benson & Hedges zonal match it would be closed, but there, in the very centre, right behind the bowler's arm, was a group of people in high-visibility jackets. Farmer called out in his bluff, West-country burr for them to move out of the way. I took advantage of the delay to give the damp ball a wipe with the towelling square I keep tucked into the waistband of my whites, and as I prepared to come in again, I absentmindedly rubbed my right ear, telling Lenderman to expect the googly. The ball looped in, a little faster this time. Crowther took a very short step to meet it, played for the turn and looked aghast as it carried straight on, through the gap he left between bat and pad and on to his stumps. We had the breakthrough at last.

I did not have too much luck after that first wicket despite getting a lot of turn. O'Brien put down a very difficult chance at point and I had a couple of good LBW shouts turned down by Farmer, although I was at least economical and finished my tenth over having given away just 29 runs. MacLaine came back from the Pavilion End for another spell and snapped up three quick wickets, but it was Snipe replacing me at the Vauxhall End who mopped up the Gloucester middle order with a spell of 4 for 11 from three overs. Gloucestershire struggled after that but credit to them, they managed to last their full fifty overs, ending on 222 for 8.

I was glad to get back to the warmth of the dressing-room and even happier that the heating was on and that the huge tea urn was bubbling away merrily on its table at the rear of the room. I quickly removed my boots and slipped on a pair of comfortable old mules, thanking my good fortune in batting at eleven.

'Shall I shower now, Gaffer?' I asked Carlisle as he passed.

He cast his eyes heavenwards. 'It's not over yet. We've still got to get those runs,' he snapped, as he went over to speak with Dench.

I smirked to myself as I sauntered over to get a mug of tea and a ham sandwich. Carlisle was humourless at the best of times – that was common knowledge – but on match days he was unbelievable. I looked over to where Dench was sitting, all padded up, listening to Carlisle's words of encouragement. Dench was due to come in at three in place of Carl Gaye who had gone down with flu.

After several weeks at The Oval I still did not know anything much about Dench and judging by what I heard from the others, they knew very little either. He certainly seemed to keep himself to himself and I was not even sure whether he was still commuting down from Worcester or whether he had found somewhere to live down south.

The pre-season article by his old Worcester teammate, Larry Helm, in the Guardian had seemed to question his move to Surrey and alluded to it being for financial reasons. It seemed common knowledge that his benefit year had not been a success, although full figures had not to my understanding been released. There was also talk of relationship problems, but I knew nothing of that. Either way, his presence in the dressing-room left me feeling uncomfortable. He was generally moody and uncommunicative. I bet that the Worcester boys were glad he had gone.

Rennie and Driver went out to start our reply and I settled back into my corner with another mug of tea and a plate of chocolate biscuits, glad that it was them going back out into the cold and not me. I looked at the stack of mail that had been put in the pigeon-hole above my locker and suddenly remembered the message from Sally. '*M is a monster*'. I was pretty sure that Miller had been in the group that held up play earlier down at the Vauxhall End. I decided to go and see if I could find him – although I was not sure what I was going to say if I did.

I decided not to say anything to Carlisle. He was still in deep discussion with Dench, and besides, he would no doubt have refused. He likes to keep the team focused, which I quite understand, but he can be too rigid. With his back still turned to me, I looked up and caught Pallant's eye, and made walking fingers in the direction of the door. Pallant smiled, nodded towards Carlisle, and mouthed back, 'Be quick!' Grinning, I stepped quietly to the door and looking back quickly towards the manager, I slipped out into the empty corridor.

I called in on Jackie Kray first to see if she knew where Miller was. She told me that he was having a meeting with some people from Frederic Prinz's team, having earlier showed them around the ground. So it was them that I had seen earlier up in the Vauxhall End. There was still talk of replacing the ramshackle collection of stands at that end of the ground and I imagined that Prinz's team were perhaps undertaking more scoping out work on the project. I wondered if Surrey were planning on a re-design. Given the huge praise that the original plans had garnered that seemed unlikely but maybe it was to do with costs.

'I think they're meeting up in the library.'

I grimaced. 'I can't bring myself to speak to Sally's mum, although I really feel I should,' I said.

'We had a nice letter from her today to thank us for the flowers that the Club sent. The funeral is tomorrow. Will you go?'

'Tomorrow? I want to, but we've another B&H game the next day.' I doubted that Carlisle would give me time off to attend, but it made me more determined to call on Sally's mother.

The top deck of the pavilion was populated with a couple of dozen hardy souls, braving the arctic conditions. The view from up there was almost worth it. As I started up the steps towards the library at the rear of the stand a little ripple of applause sprang up amongst the members up there. I smiled in acknowledgement.

'Morning, Johnny. Think we'll win?' It was Mr Brown. He was a member of the Supporters Club and never seemed to miss a day's play – home or away. I had no idea of his real name, but he was always dressed in brown. Brown suit, shirt, tie and shoes – of different shades. He was a serial correspondent with the Club and had complained about the one-day pyjamas we used to wear, pointing out that most of the counties played in their club colours but that Surrey seemed to prefer the colours of our sponsors. This had been the case since Fosters had been our main sponsor and the team had gone out in blue with red and yellow details. When Thoren Investments had taken over the shirt sponsorship they had suggested a new strip based on Surrey's traditional chocolate brown and silver. Mr Brown was delighted and immediately contacted the Club, proposing that the Surrey Lions one-day moniker be dropped in favour of the Surrey Feathers – a reference to the Prince of Wales feathers in our crest. No one was quite sure why we had ever become the Lions, but most felt that 'the Feathers' did not project the right image either.

'Win? I reckon so – and I don't think I'll be needed either,' I replied with a smile.

'Come on you Feathers!' Mr Brown chanted nasally, in his speaking voice.

I playfully clawed at the air and roared quietly, sending Mr Brown and his easily pleased little group of friends off into gales of laughter, as I quickly mounted the steps to the library door.

The meeting must have broken up, as I found Miller sitting alone at Sally's PC. As I opened the door his head snapped up towards me. I thought for a second that I detected a guilty look but if there was, it dissolved immediately into the oily smile that Miller employed to charm everyone with. Sitting at the computer screen I was struck by how big a man he was. Well over six-feet tall and probably seventeen stones. I had a sudden image of Miller forcing himself on Sally and of her trying to fend him off. She would have been no match for him. She could only have weighed eight stone at most.

'The wanderer returns,' he gushed. 'Johnny, how good to see you.'

I accepted his outstretched hand. 'Barry,' I said coolly.

'Just wrapping up a few things from this morning's meeting,' he continued, as he busily clicked with the mouse in his right hand, closing down whatever documents he had been working on. 'It's all looking very good on the development front – shame you won't be covering it for the magazine. I could have put you in touch with Prinz's team to get the inside info.'

So, he had heard already that I had been taken off *Oval Eyes*. I wondered how that had spread so quickly.

'I just hope your successor is as interested. I'm sure the members will want to know what's going on.'

'Why was Prinz's team in the ground today?'

Miller tapped his nose conspiratorially as he replied. 'Plans afoot to upgrade the Vauxhall End. We saved a bit on the double-deckers and we might be able to sort that end of the ground too – it certainly needs it – but, mum's the word, eh?'

'Are you going to Sally's funeral, Barry?'

He looked taken aback for a second and then embarrassed. 'That was a dreadful business, wasn't it? Poor thing. And such a nice girl too. I don't think the funeral has been arranged yet, but I certainly intend going.'

I felt suddenly angry; angry that I would not be able to go, but that he would. I was pretty certain that Sally would not want him to attend – if what her note to me suggested was true. 'It's tomorrow, Barry.'

He immediately pulled out a diary from an inside pocket and I noticed for the first time that he was wearing his old England blazer – probably in an effort to impress the team of architects. He had played once for his country as far as I could remember and one of those matches had been at Lord's, where it is customary for the monarch to attend. He had been presented to the Queen on the second day and had barely been seen in anything else since. With its embroidered three lions crest and silver lion buttons down the front and on the cuffs, it looked very smart, but I could not help wondering if it was appropriate to wear it so casually.

'Oh, damn it! tomorrow you say? No, I have an important meeting up at Willby Construction in Leicester. I really don't think I can move that one, though I'll try.' He looked at me with exaggerated sadness. I was secretly pleased that he might not be able to go but annoyed at the same time that he might be able to escape it.

'That would be a shame, Barry. You got on well, didn't you?'

'Very,' he began, enthusiastically. 'I didn't see an awful lot of her, of course, but she was very good at her job – very conscientious. You probably got to know her better than me – working in here together.' It seemed more of a question than a statement.

'I guess so, but we never got a chance to really socialize.' I wanted to see if he admitted having been out drinking with her, and to my surprise, he did.

'We only managed one session. Well, it was hardly a session, but we did have a nice couple of drinks together. It was the night she died, actually.'

I suddenly had a thought. 'Had she drunk much?'

'No – not a thing! If I remember, she was on orange juice the whole time. She told me she had to drive later. It was a nice evening, though,' he added quickly.

'She liked Covent Garden,' I said evenly.

'Covent Garden? We didn't go there. We were in Fleet Street – at the Cheshire Cheese.'

That would give me somewhere to start, should I need it.

I managed to slip back into the dressing-room without Carlisle noticing. Rennie and Driver had both gone early but Dench and Pallant were making inroads into the Gloucestershire lead. I strolled out onto the enclosed balcony with a fresh cup of tea and leant on the back of Molander's chair.

'Dench looks good,' I said, noticing from the scoreboard that he was rapidly approaching his fifty.

'He does,' the big Swede responded, in his lilting voice. 'It looks true what they say about Dench's running between the wickets though.'

Dench had a reputation for selfishness – on and off the pitch. His batting partners certainly had their work cut out and as if to illustrate the point, Dench suddenly called Pallant for what looked from our vantage point an impossible single. Pallant hesitated for a split second and then dashed for the striker's end. Cover swooped in and in one smooth, fluid motion, picked up the ball and rolled it in at the base of the stumps. Pallant was struggling to make it, and still two yards short of the white chalk line, he flung himself despairingly forward. There was a blur of tumbling bodies, bat and ball, stumps and bails and cries from the Gloucester fielders of 'Howzaat?' Umpire Farmer at square-leg remained statue-like. Under his helmet, it was impossible to see Pallant's face clearly – but his body-language was eloquent, as he brushed himself down and shot a meaningful glance down towards Dench. Dench limply raised a gloved hand in apology, before turning to talk to Umpire Schlatter.

'Arrogant too,' Molander concluded. 'By the way, Johnny, you had a couple of calls on your mobile.' I had left it switched on in my jacket pocket. 'Carlisle was doing his pieces, so I'd keep a low profile if I were you.' Molander laughed as he handed the Nokia back to me.

Carlisle had issued strict rules about mobiles – he had spoken to the team about new ECB guidelines focused on illegal betting in India and had said that mobiles would have to be locked away. I had never received calls from bookies, unless you count Summers, but I knew a few players who had, sometimes during matches, and the authorities were making increasingly loud noises about taking action to stamp out this possible contamination of teams. I had forgotten that I had left it on.

'Who called, Hammy?'

'Your wife and Mark Summers,' he replied, keeping his eyes on the cricket.

'Elisa? What did she say?' I was a little annoyed to have missed her again.

'Said she was in San Antonio and that she was off to a video shoot. She'll try you later. Summers wants you to call him.'

'Did Elisa leave a number?'

'No, and I didn't ask – I assumed you'd have her mobile number. She also said something a little odd; something like "don't believe everything you read"?'

'Oh dear, what's that all about?' I replied, making light of it but wondering if Elisa was aware of the piece in The Star. 'Mobile calls from the States are so expensive she left hers at home,' I explained. 'I guess she'll call back later.' I had no idea when that would be though, and her strange comment further dampened my spirits.

I was annoyed with myself for leaving the mobile on and hoped that Carlisle was not aware that Summers now worked for a spread-betting firm, but I managed to avoid direct contact with the gaffer for the rest of the day and as I reached the car park at the rear of the pavilion I caught a glimpse of Alan Dench standing over by one of the concession stalls, still shuttered for these early season games. He was in earnest conversation with another man, a big fellow dressed entirely in black, who seemed to be doing most of the talking. I was about to stroll over when Dench, scowling angrily, suddenly brushed past the man and headed for the main gates.

'Alan! Where you going? Need a lift?' I shouted across the car park.

He stopped in his tracks, glanced back quickly in the direction of the man he had been talking with, and crossed the tarmac towards me. 'No, it's okay thanks. I'm taking the Tube into town.'

'Well played today by the way. Shame you missed out on the ton though.' Dench had made an unbeaten 93 and with Pallant had knocked off the Gloucester total without further losses.

Dench grinned – the first time I had seen him smile since his arrival at Surrey. 'Thanks. We won though, that's the main thing.'

I hoped the look of shock did not show too clearly on my face. This new commitment to the team's cause, from Dench, was most unexpected. 'I'll see you at training tomorrow, then.' As he turned to go, I had a sudden thought. 'Alan, save taking both cars, do you want a lift up to Cambridge?'

'I'm sorted, thanks – Pallant offered me a ride. Mine's at the garage.'

'Gone wrong already? Must be all that commuting you do from the Midlands,' I said with a smile. We had only had our sponsored cars for a matter of weeks.

'I guess so,' Dench replied, a little uncertainly. 'I don't know much about motors,' he added, 'but this one just never handled right. Steering was stiff and I was always having to correct it. They reckon it will only take a couple of days. And I'm not even doing that many miles, now I'm living in London.'

'Oh, you've moved down have you? Where are you staying?'

'I'm with friends in Twickenham at the moment – been there a couple of weeks now. I will have to find a place to rent when I get the time.'

From what Dench said, and no mention of a partner, I had the feeling that his wife had not made the move south with him. Maybe the talk of his having marital problems had substance to it. Or maybe they had decided that she would stay in Worcester. I said goodbye to him and went in search of my car amongst the ranks of identical silver saloons.

CHAPTER 15

I felt an immediate sense of enormous sadness when I awoke to the 6:00 a.m., alarm. It was the day before Sally's funeral, and despite my pleading, Carlisle had refused to budge on his decision not to let me miss the next day's match to enable me to attend. He had tried to assuage my feelings by telling me exactly who was representing the Club but that just infuriated me even more. A couple of people from the admin team who probably had never even met her did not do it for me. Of course, I knew that it was an important B&H match, but it was against the British Universities and I felt confident that the team could have managed that one without me; no disrespect to the students. And for some reason Jackie's place had seemingly been taken by someone more senior.

I stood on the outfield at The Oval and looked around me as my team-mates worked in small groups on catching and fielding drills. There was a sharpness about training that either comes naturally at elite level or is more evident when a mercurial coach is scrutinising every move from under furrowed brow. Carlisle caught my eye and started in my direction.

'How's the shoulder, Johnny?'

Taken aback by what for the gruff Australian passed as empathy, I instinctively gave it a rub as I said it was okay.

'Get yourself involved then,' he growled through almost closed lips as he turned to go.

That did it for me. 'Thanks for your concern, Gaffer, though I won't forget about the funeral.'

His head snapped around. 'Well don't forget that you are a professional cricketer and that Surrey pays your wages!'

'Nice, Carlisle, very understanding,' I replied, sarcastically. He simply ignored me and continued over to a group working on the other side of the square.

Rennie and Driver were waiting for me to resume our drill. Driver threw me the ball. 'That seemed to go well,' he laughed.

'What a bastard,' I said loudly enough that Carlisle might have heard. 'I mean, we are playing a bunch of students tomorrow and he can't rest me for that to go to the funeral of a colleague.'

'That's rough,' Rennie agreed. 'You lot reckon *I'm* bolshy but he takes it to another level.'

'Compared to him Renners, you are Mother Teresa,' Driver quipped.

'Who?' Rennie queried, in all seriousness.

'You are a hopeless case, Rennie,' I laughed, pulling off his ancient, sun-bleached Surrey cap and giving him a noogie.

Sally's funeral was set for 2:00 p.m. the next day down in the Surrey countryside, not far from her home. At 1.30 p.m., Carlisle called us all into a huddle, announced that he was pleased with what he had seen and gave us the rest of the day off.

'Good work today, gents. Get some rest before the match. Stay off the booze. There are no easy games and if you think that we are just playing a bunch of students, don't fool yourselves. This is the season's biggest banana skin. If we cock it up against them it takes cricket from the back pages right onto the front. I won't need you all tomorrow and I am finalising the team this afternoon. You will get a call one way or the other around 6:00 p.m., so keep an eye on your phones. For those in the squad, we meet here at 6:00 a.m. For those not, you meet in the Barrington Centre at 9:00 a.m. All clear?'

I strolled back to the Bedser with Gus MacLaine. He knew that I was close to Sally and he threw an arm round my shoulder. 'He was wrong not to let you go, Johnny. That was bang out of order.'

'What was?' It was O'Brien, immediately behind us.

'Carlisle,' MacLaine explained. 'My fellow countryman has no grace about him. Banned Johnny from Sally Framsell's funeral.'

'Grace?' O'Brien sneered. 'Grace has nothing to do with it. We are professional sportsmen. We have a job to do. Can't let sentiment get in the way.' With that he brushed past us and hurried towards the Bedser's steps.

I stopped in my tracks. Speechless.

'Was that Mark O'Brien?' MacLaine muttered through his huge, droopy moustache. 'I've never heard him say so much. Classy guy...not.'

At that moment Alan Dench walked past us, seemingly deep in his own thoughts.

'What do you say, Denchy?' MacLaine grabbed at Dench with a huge paw.

Dench turned, looking highly irritated and very pointedly picked MacLaine's hand off his shoulder as if it were a stray hair.

'What do I say about what,' he asked, a supercilious look in his eyes. He really was hard work.

MacLaine has a wonderful self-confidence and Dench's approach seemed to faze him not in the least. 'Just saying, Denchy, that Carlisle banned Johnny here from attending Sally Framsell's funeral. I think that was bang out of order – they were great mates. O'Brien thinks Carlisle is right, says we are professional sportsmen and all that. What's your view?'

'I don't have one, MacLaine.' Dench made a move to go.

Gus grabbed Dench's shoulder even harder. 'Well have one for me, then, would you?'

There was no physical response from Dench. He stared icily back at the huge Aussie bowler. 'Okay, let me formulate a view for you. Let me see.' Dench paused for effect, finger to temple in a show of deep thinking. 'I've got it! Carlisle's decision is the right one for the reasons he gave. Now, take your hand from my shoulder and try being a little more professional.'

MacLaine released him and watched Dench walk up the steps to the dressing room. 'Boy, he is something, isn't he?'

'Sure is,' I agreed.

The call came at a little after 6:00 p.m. I was in the starting eleven. I had hoped that Carlisle might have had a change of heart.

CHAPTER 16

Friday May 2 1997

The forecourt at 6:00 a.m., looked like a Vauxhall showroom as I parked up. Carlisle was already barking orders as my teammates loaded their kit into the coach's huge storage space. I retrieved my bags from the Vectra's boot and waited behind Lenderman for my turn to stow. Even at this early hour he was all tics and fidgets and talking to himself as usual. I reminded myself not to sit next to him.

Carlisle waited until all the bags had been stowed and then called us all to gather round. Clipboard in hand he proceeded to call our names. It was like being on a school trip. My name was one of the first called and I took my place on the coach not fully knowing who had been selected for the match. I kept my eye on the coach door to see who was coming in. Rennie, Driver and Pallant were followed by four lads from the seconds. By the time the coach door hissed shut and we started to pull out through the Hobbs Gates I was pretty sure that MacLaine and O'Brien were missing. It was not until we spilled out at Fenners that I realised that so too were Snipe and Dench. For all that talk of banana skins Carlisle had rested some key players. Dench was in fine form and no opening bowlers? I did not get that at all.

In the event it was a fairly short day. Pallant won the toss and, in conditions in which against a county side we would have had a bowl first, he elected to bat. Rennie and Driver plundered the student quicks for plenty and after our allotted overs we were 339 for 3, with tons for Rennie, Driver and Pallant. Their reply was meek. Molander took 5 for not many, opening the bowling with Reynolds from the seconds. He took a couple and I wrapped things up with three cheap ones at the end. The winning margin was a rather embarrassing 273 runs and simply added fuel to the calls for British Universities to be removed from the fixture list. Still, a win is a win and it was a banana skin avoided.

CHAPTER 17

Saturday May 3 1997

I awoke with a start and soon found the alarm clock but, having slapped down the rocker switch on top of it, I quickly determined that it was not the clock that had awoken me. Realising that it was the telephone, I started to pull myself out of bed, when the answerphone cut in after the sixth ring. I did not recognize the voice for a minute but suddenly realised that it was Elisa. Throwing off the bedclothes and leaping from the bed in one swift movement, I was down the stairs in a matter of seconds; not fast enough to speak with her though. When I picked up the handset the line was dead. I angrily stabbed a finger at the button marked 'play'. The tape rolled.

Elisa's voice sounded faint and tremulous. I could hear laughter in the background.

'Hi Johnny, guess you're still asleep – won't disturb you – I'll call you later....'

'Shit!' I cursed.

I threw the handset onto its cradle and stalked into the kitchen, filled the kettle at the tap and ripped the plastic from a fresh box of teabags. I saw the pack of Marlboros on the side and was about to open it but, annoyed with myself, I threw them back down. I had bought them during the week on a whim and it had become a real personal test of will – between me and the cigarettes. I thought about chucking them in the bin but half of me wanted to smoke them and I guess it was to spite Elisa, as it was for her that I had really given up. The boiling kettle made the decision for me and I slid them to the back of the worktop.

I had called Elisa's office at the beginning of the week and they had immediately promised to send a copy of her itinerary. True to their word, it had arrived the very next day and I had pinned it to the cork noticeboard in the kitchen. As I poured steaming water into a mug, I looked up at the sheet of paper and scanned down until I came to the right date. She was in Seattle and, judging by the time difference, the gig was probably just finishing. I had visions of her calling me from a party backstage. There had been enough background noise for it to have been a party and I did not find the thought comforting. Her colleague had professed ignorance as to what hotels Elisa was staying in and sounded a little surprised that I did not already know. Feeling embarrassed, I claimed that Elisa had given me a list before she flew out but that I had mislaid it. I could not imagine that her magazine did not know how to reach her and was left with the distinct feeling that this was what Elisa must have wanted.

I gulped down the first mug of tea and made a second whilst the toaster browned a couple of slices of thick, crusty bread. I slopped butter and marmalade on these and took my breakfast up to the bathroom where I showered quickly, dodging out every now and then for mouthfuls. I dried myself with a small hand towel, the only clean one I could find, and reminded myself to get some washing done later. Still partly wet, I rifled through my side of the vast wardrobe in our bedroom and settled on the only really smart clothes I own; my England blazer and a pair of chinos. I smiled ruefully at the indignation I had felt when I saw Miller wearing his England blazer at The Oval as I slipped mine on. I pulled out a Surrey tie, stuffed it into a pocket of the blazer and dashed downstairs for the car keys which were hanging in their usual place in the kitchen. I reached the front door and was about to close it behind me, when I ran back to the kitchen and snatched up the pack of cigarettes. I tapped my pockets – mobile and spare house key. My one had not yet shown up. I wondered if I had somehow scooped it up with rubbish for the kitchen bin.

Eleanor Framsell had sounded pleased when I called and immediately invited me down. We settled on ten o'clock after she told me that she was going away for the evening and would be leaving around lunchtime.

I sped down the A3, slowing every mile or so for the speed cameras that had apparently been breeding along there. The morning was cool, but the clear blue skies promised a fine day. All along the busy road trees were springing into life and my lifting spirits were boosted again when I saw my first house martins of the summer, soaring and swooping across the road in search of invisible insects. I turned the music up louder as Mama Cass's voice started to belt out *Sing Hallelujah*. The flip side of the Jay and the Americans tape had The Big Three, Cass's first group from the early sixties; if these two bands could not raise my mood, I knew I was in trouble. Singing along loudly and badly as ever, I pulled off onto the Farnham road and arrived a few minutes later in Elstead, feeling good.

Sally's mother had told me to look out for the old Elstead Mill pub on the left and that from there she was just a half-mile or so further along on the right. I was to look out for a yellow Lotus parked on her drive. The pub looked wonderful, set in its own lawns with water all around it and I determined to check it out after my audience with Eleanor. Sally had told me once that her mother could be quite intimidating and that knowledge, coupled with the awkward nature of my visit, had left me feeling a little nervous. The little yellow sports car stood out from some distance away. I slowed down, and seeing that there was room for me, eased the Vectra onto the gravelled driveway and pulled up behind the Lotus.

Eleanor Framsell was a striking woman – and surprisingly young; possibly no older than forty. She was about five-feet-six, slim, and had jet black, straight, shoulder-length hair and sparkling green eyes. I had conjured up an austere image of her, as a woman in her late fifties and the look of surprise must have shown.

'What did you expect, Mr Lorrens, an old dragon? What has Sally been telling you?'

Her smile faded as she mentioned Sally's name.

'I must say, Mrs Framsell, that I am awfully sorry about what happened...'

She raised a hand, and her smile returned. 'I know you are, Mr Lorrens – that's why you are here.'

'Please – call me Johnny,' I replied, relieved that she had not gone to pieces.

'And I'm Eleanor,' she smiled as she held out a hand.

She led me through the house and out onto a vast patio which overlooked a vast lawn. I could see a silver-haired figure working in a far corner and I assumed he was a gardener for he looked far too old to be Eleanor's husband. Trees dotted around dappled the lawn into a chessboard pattern. On the patio a wrought iron table, surrounded by a cluster of heavy-looking metal chairs, had been laid for two, with an unusual tea service; brightly coloured, it was all triangles and circles. I commented favourably on it.

'Clarice Cliff,' Eleanor explained. 'She was a leading English designer in the thirties.'

'Art Deco?'

'Absolutely! Famous for combining geometry with nature,' she enthused, pointing to the gaudily coloured trees and clouds painted on the ceramic. 'That's classic Deco. Not to everybody's taste, though.'

It seemed more of a question than a statement. 'No, I like them,' I insisted, feeling, however, that Summers would have liked them a lot more.

The small talk continued for a while longer, Eleanor asking me, as she poured the tea, about my cricket career; it transpired that like Sally, she was not a follower of the game.

'It always struck me as odd that Sally ended up at Surrey, given that she really did not like cricket,' I said.

Eleanor looked up at me slyly from over the rim of her cup. 'Oh, but she did like cricketers, though.'

'She did?'

'Surely she told you about her boyfriend – he was involved with cricket. I didn't like him though; he was nearer my age than hers.'

I must have looked surprised for the sly grin spread into a big smile. 'Surely you knew that she adored you?'

I felt my face smart with a mixture of embarrassment and pleasure, a pleasure tinged with sadness at Sally's absence.

'No, I really did not,' I spluttered. 'Of course, I knew we had struck it off well...'

'She never should have got involved with him... silly girl...' It was Eleanor's turn to let her words fade away.

I left an appropriate pause, took an elaborate drink from my teacup, before continuing. 'I never had any idea about the boyfriend.'

Eleanor's eyes had glazed over and she was staring blankly across the well-manicured garden. She looked round at me and I could see she was trying hard not to cry. 'She went to university up in the Midlands to study psychology and when she graduated she had hoped to use her degree to become an educational psychologist. Then she met this cricketer and she lost all her senses – or at least, to me she did.'

'Who was he?'

'Mm?' she was drifting off again.

'The cricketer – who was he?' I asked again.

'She never said. It didn't last long, thankfully. All I know is that he did not treat her very well.'

'You said you didn't like him?' I reminded her.

'If he had treated her okay it might have been different,' she replied. 'You don't need to meet someone to dislike them.'

I was still reeling from the shock of Sally's secret and wondering feverishly who the mystery cricketer might have been, when Eleanor spoke again.

'He was the reason she left the Midlands... for a fresh start. If it hadn't been for him she would still be alive.' I looked back towards her; she had lowered her head and I could see her shoulders shaking. I quietly stood and walked a few paces away from the patio and made a point of inspecting one of the immaculate borders.

A few minutes later Eleanor appeared at my shoulder. She pointed out a few of the more exotic flowers and told me their names. I recognised the tulips and the daffodils without prompting.

I was just starting to reverse the Vectra out of her drive when she leant into the open window.

'That cricketer – I think he was at the funeral. At least, there was a guy about my age standing on his own at the back, wearing an England blazer.'

I stopped the car and put the handbrake on. 'Are you sure?'

'Yes, absolutely. I mean, I didn't know it was an England blazer, but one of Sally's old friends recognised him.'

'Barry Miller.'

'Was it?' She did not sound too bothered what his name was. 'You know him?'

'Yes,' I replied grimly. 'Oh, yes.'

The Elstead Mill was as good close to as it looked from the road and as I pulled into one of the many free, grassy parking spaces a little family of ducks scattered in front of me. I slipped off my Surrey tie and left it on the seat next to me, my blazer back on its hanger in the rear. I ordered a pint of a local brew I had never heard of and a cheese ploughmans, took my drink out onto the terrace at the rear and found a seat overlooking the millstream. The bright morning sunshine was dazzling on the still water and I regretted not bringing my sunglasses.

The meeting with Sally's mother had been far less painful than I had feared and as I sipped my beer I reflected on what she had said. The plough-mans arrived as I was dialling Jackie Kray's number on the mobile. I crumbled off a corner of the generous slab of cheddar as the phone started to ring. Jackie picked up immediately.

'Bunking off again?' she laughed.

'I got permission this time – from Carlisle, because I couldn't get to the funeral.'

Jackie asked me how Mrs Framsell was holding up and I said that I thought she was doing okay and that she had asked me to thank Jackie for the flowers.

'And did Miller go?'

'Apparently, yes – the bastard.'

'Johnny!' she reprimanded me.

'Jackie, I am not sure, of course, but I have the feeling that Miller is in-volved somehow.'

'What do you mean?' she replied with sudden interest.

I explained about Sally's references to M, her concerns about the build-ing project and her determination to have it out with Miller. I also mentioned Miller's reputation and why he was forced from the game.

'We don't know anything for sure yet, Johnny,' she replied, a clear doubt now in her voice.

'Oh, I think we do,' I replied impatiently. 'First the note from Sally about 'M', and then he turns up at the funeral even though he told me he had a meeting he could not reschedule...'

Jackie cut in sharply, her voice lower and harsher. 'He *was* her boss!'

'I know that,' I snapped indignantly, 'and I also know now that Sally, unbeknownst to all of us, followed her cricketer boyfriend down to London and that that boyfriend was almost Eleanor Framsell's own age. I reckon she is no more than forty-two at most; Miller is, what, forty?'

'Ish.' Jackie sounded less sure of herself.

'Do you know where Miller was immediately prior to coming back to The Oval?'

Jackie paused for a moment and I heard her muffled voice speaking to someone in the office, before she replied. 'Project management, I think.'

'I know that, but who for and where?'

'I'm not sure, Johnny – want me to find out?'

'Please. I always thought it odd that Sally came to The Oval when she hated cricket and it makes more sense if she followed Miller here – although her with Miller makes no sense at all to me.'

'I'll see what I can do,' Jackie said quietly. 'I shouldn't be nosing around in personnel files as you know, so I shall have to do it when the office is empty.' Jackie would be in big trouble if she was caught. She was just about old enough to be my mum, but I think she had more than a soft spot for me and would do pretty much anything for me.

The traffic on the A3 was thin and I was back home within forty minutes. My good mood took a dip as I looked at the sink-full of washing up I had left from the night before and the mound of dirty washing that I had dumped onto the kitchen floor before I went to Elstead. Groaning inwardly, I started to load up the washing machine when the telephone sounded in the hall. I reached it just before the message cut in. It was Krishnan Singh from The Mirror.

Singh had played a couple of seasons with Warwickshire after leaving Cambridge, but a knee injury had forced him out of the game at just twenty-two. Ten years on, he was the chief cricket correspondent of The Mirror and a well-regarded and well-connected critic.

'I just want a quick reaction, Johnny – sorry to call you at home.'

I tensed up as I remembered The Star piece about Elisa. 'I really don't think I want to talk about that, Krishnan.'

'Really? I thought you'd be delighted,' he replied in a surprised tone.

We were clearly at crossed purposes. 'About what?' I asked hesitantly.

'Your recall – thought you'd be over the moon about it.'

'My what?'

'Recall. I just spoke with Gorton and he told me you had been selected for the one-day squad. I thought they'd have called you by now...'

'They may have tried, but I've been out all morning. But if it's a re-action you want, I can say that that is the best news I have had in what has been a crap week!' I laughed as I said it, but Singh paused, clearly unsure of what I meant.

'Crap?' he asked. 'But you won all three Benson and Hedges matches in the past week, which puts Surrey in good shape to go through to the knock-out stage – and you picked up a wicket or two on your return from injury.'

I realised afterwards that his subtle probing had worked. 'When your wife makes the front page of the tabloids and one of your friends dies it tends to overshadow a handful of wickets,' I snapped angrily.

'Do you know the Toadlust lot?' His nose for a story was highly tuned.

'No, I do not.'

'It must have come as quite a shock to see her photograph splashed across the front page.'

I said nothing.

'And you said a friend died?'

I was glad to move on from Elisa. 'Sally Framsell – a young girl who was working with the building development team. It was her funeral yesterday. She died in a car accident two weeks ago.'

'Where was that?'

'Putney. Putney High Street – hit and run.'

'I know Putney well,' Singh said. 'It's quite near where I live. Busy road. I saw some yellow incident boards down there a week or so ago which were probably for the accident. Plenty of CCTV there I would have thought.'

I was not really interested in what he was saying and longing for the call to end. He had one last question.

'Have you spoken to your wife about the photo?'

'For fuck's sake, Krishnan,' I exploded. 'That really is none of your business.'

'But you *are* pleased about the recall?'

I slammed the handset down and pulled the cord from the wall, went and found a bottle and glasses and took a large brandy out onto the patio. I picked up the pack of cigarettes as I passed them in the kitchen and rummaged in the drawers for some matches. The combination of the thick, strong-smelling drink and the heady rush of my first cigarette in two years left me feeling slightly nauseous. I mashed the cigarette out beneath my feet after a couple of draws and felt a little ashamed at having lit up.

CHAPTER 18

Sunday May 4 1997

A Sunday League home game against Kent is always a big fixture and the crowd was building up nicely by the time Pallant went out for the toss. From my vantage point on the balcony the weather looked perfect. I had had a close look at the strip and it had enough green in it to give me hope but The Oval is renowned as a batters' paradise so I was not going to hold my breath. Pallant was hoping to bat first, get the runs on the board and then have a go at them, reasoning that they would be remembering our B&H win at their place less than a week before. As he strolled back from the middle, it was clear he had lost the toss. Kent would bat.

And bat they did. We did manage to get the openers out cheaply but they put on 203 for their third wicket and a century stand for their fourth, leaving us a challenging target of 318 in our 40 over reply. Sadly we did not rise to the challenge, went for it too soon and when I came in at eleven, we still needed 92 more. I was run out responding to Molander's urgent call for a quick single, for 1.

Carlisle berated us for our ineptitude and when MacLaine noted that we were flying high in the B&H, our Aussie coach simply walked out of the dressing room. We did not see him again that day. His man management skills were really something to behold.

CHAPTER 19

Monday May 5 1997

I finally got a call from Alex Gorton on the Monday morning, forty-eight hours after Singh had broken the news to me. Naturally I was pleased to hear it officially but the excitement that should have been there was largely absent – partly because I already knew but also because I felt the selectors had not tried very hard to tell me first. Any excitement I did feel vanished the moment I saw the front cover of The Mirror.

I saw the strapline from across the forecourt as I filled up at the Esso station next to the A3 at Tolworth:

England recall for unlucky Johnny.

I picked up a copy from the rack outside the door to the shop and felt self-conscious as I paid for the fuel, wondering if the cashier would recognise me. I was relieved to find her disinterested in serving me and I hurried gratefully back to the car. The forecourt was not busy, so I unfolded the paper and scanned down the article, which carried over onto page three.

Johnny Lorrens' long-awaited recall to England colours has been overshadowed by the death of a close friend – and marital problems, writes our chief cricket correspondent, Krishnan Singh, in an exclusive interview. Lorrens, age 27, was effectively banned from international cricket after a tour to Australia two years ago when he was suspected of having been involved in an illegal betting incident and of having smoked pot in the dressing-room at Sydney.

I felt my face getting hot and saw that my hands were shaking. With a steadily rising anger I turned the page and read on:

Lorrens' recall has been the subject of much speculation in cricket circles and there is also reasonable doubt as to whether he was actually involved in either of the incidents that led to his ban. Although Lorrens is delighted at the opportunity to play for his country again, this has been overshadowed by two very personal tragedies.

His journalist wife of less than two years, Elisa, age 25, is in America covering the tour by the controversial English shock-rock group, Toadlust. She has apparently resumed her relationship with lead singer Crispin LeDare – a shock to Lorrens who only found this out from the front page of a national newspaper last week. It was also the funeral last week of close friend and colleague, Sally Framsell, who worked at The Oval on the redevelopment of the ground. She died in a hit and run accident in Putney, South West London. The Metropolitan Police are treating the incident as 'suspicious' and are appealing for information.

I jumped at the sound of a horn and saw in the rear-view mirror a car waiting behind me. I flung the paper down onto the passenger seat and, waving an apology to the car behind, nosed the car out into the traffic.

It was becoming embarrassing to turn up for work and as I drove north on the A3 I ran through in my mind how I would explain things. Singh's assumptions about Elisa stung particularly hard and although I was pretty sure that I had told him very little, I was acutely aware of his perceptiveness. The bit about her 'resuming' her affair with LeDare had me puzzled though; puzzled and sickened. I glanced back at the paper on the seat next to me, but it had closed itself when I threw it down. My impatience got the better of me and checking my mirror, I pulled off the A3 at the entrance to Richmond Park and quickly parked up.

I turned to page three and continued to read.

Elisa and Johnny met on the disastrous Australia tour in 1994/5 and married shortly after. Elisa wrote the story up for a lads' mag having recently broken up with her long-term boyfriend, Crispin Gates. Gates, 27, apparently the son of a senior Government figure, has since found fame as part of Toadlust, the British band currently on a sell-out American tour. He now goes by the stage name, Crispin LeDare. The loss last week of close friend Sally Framsell, 23, has been the second big blow to Lorrens.

Employed in the Ground Development office, Framsell was a newcomer to The Oval, coming from Warwick University where she studied psychology. She reported to former England and Surrey cricketer Barry Miller, who is project manager on the redevelopment of the famous cricketing landmark. Eleanor Framsell, her glamorous 43 year-old mother, thinks the police are right to treat her daughter's death as suspicious.

This comment was surprising as Eleanor had not said anything about this to me, although in fairness she had, not surprisingly, seemed in something of a daze. She had said nothing about talking with Singh either. I checked my watch – it was just gone nine o'clock; I was going to be late, but I wanted to finish the article.

"Sally called me at around nine-fifteen for a quick chat on her way home. She had been out with someone for a drink after work – it was early still – she didn't sound drunk but she did sound really happy and said she had some exciting news to tell me about work. Her phone was low on charge and she said she would call me when she got home. By ten o'clock she had not called back and I was beginning to get worried. I didn't hear anything until the police called me at eleven to say they had found Sally. They said she had been hit by a car that didn't stop. She has lived in London long enough and I know she is always ultra-careful around roads as that's how we lost her father."

The police have so far been unable to find any CCTV footage despite it happening so close to a major thoroughfare and have erected yellow incident boards throughout the area in the hope of sparking memories. Anyone in or around Putney High Street between 9:00 and 10:00 p.m., on April 17th is urged to contact the police urgently.

I let the paper close slowly in my hands and let out a long, low whistle. I did not know what to make of it either. What was the exciting news from work? Surely it had something to do with whatever she and Miller had discussed when they went for a drink. It was certainly a brief evening out if Eleanor's timings were correct and that was corroborated by what Miller had told me.

I was late and Carlisle did let me know that he was aware, but the way everyone pointedly left me alone confirmed that some at least had seen The Mirror. I tried hard to make out that everything was perfectly normal but found it very difficult and was relieved when the five-minute bell finally sounded for Pallant to lead us down the steps and onto the pitch.

The sun was shining brightly from an azure-blue sky and but for the stiff north-easterly breeze that was tugging and tearing at the flags on top of the pavilion it would have been pleasantly warm. Instead, on the pitch, it was another three-sweater start. Beyond the advertising boards the sparse crowd was huddled together in little pockets in an attempt to keep warm, the steam from vacuum flasks dotting the boundary.

Hampshire's captain, Marvin Clegg, had called correctly and elected to bat and as we waited for their openers to appear Pallant gathered the team together into a huddle. He reminded us that although we had won the first three B&H matches and that another win would as good as put us through to the quarter finals, Hampshire were a strong outfit and batted down to number eleven. I was sure his eyes flickered towards me as he said that – or perhaps I was being overly sensitive.

MacLaine opened up from the Pavilion End, into the breeze, and seemed fired-up from the start. He came close to getting both openers caught behind in his first over. Snipe took the new ball from the Vauxhall End, the wind appearing to give him an extra yard of pace. He had an LBW appeal rejected in his first over – an appeal that looked a good one to me judging by the excited response from Lenderman, and Dench at first slip.

After a shaky start Cashman and Luff settled and as the fielding restrictions were lifted after fifteen overs the scoreboard showed Hampshire at 88 for none. Pallant had sidled over to me after MacLaine's seventh over and nodded at the footprints the big Australian had left on the neatly mown strip; large, dark patches where his spikes had gripped and torn the thin top surface.

'Fancy a bowl on that?'

I smiled and nodded. Fielding down on the boundary was giving me too much time to dwell on the newspaper story and I had let one snick slip through for four already. MacLaine had scowled at me but restrained himself from venting his anger in his normal whole-hearted manner. I supposed that he too had seen the paper.

I had to wait for three more overs and went through a series of bends and stretches down by the boundary rope. A couple of young Hampshire fans, huddled up against the cold, enquired after Elisa and I laughed along with them through gritted teeth, but aside from them, there were no other comments. I was quite relieved that the combination of a mid-week fixture and the cold weather had kept the crowd numbers down, and glad too to get the ball in my hands at the end of Molander's first over.

I glanced up at the huge electronic scoreboard on the Bedser Stand and saw my name replace Snipe's. Hampshire were looking threatening at 98 without loss. My first couple of balls were decent enough yet Luff smashed them through the covers for boundaries. I felt a stab of doubt as I ran in for the third delivery and tried to give the ball an extra flip – it was meant to be a top-spinner. It was actually one of the better long hops that I have ever bowled. It caught Luff completely off-guard and, too soon with his pull shot, it struck the toe of his bat, looping up to give O'Brien an easy catch at silly mid-on.

The departure of Luff was the catalyst that saw Hampshire falter to 123 for 3 before MacLaine returned to take three more quick wickets. After thirty overs the visitors were reeling at 149 for 6 when a light sprinkling of rain sent us hurrying from the pitch.

Fifty overs in the field without a break is quite a strain, even when you are doing well, and it was a relief to be able to get into the warm half-way through the Hampshire innings and have a cup of tea. I had that craving for a cigarette again and had just propped my feet up on my coffin and closed my eyes when I felt someone sit down next to me. I looked up to see Carlisle.

'Gorton called earlier – wants to speak with you. Congratulations by the way.'

I shook Carlisle's outstretched hand and smiled. 'I've spoken to him already, Gaffer - this morning, before I left home.'

'I know. He told me. But he wants to speak to you again. Give him a call now if you like,' he said, handing me a slip of paper. 'Use your mobile – looks like we'll be off for a while.'

I followed his gaze towards the windows and saw that the rain was falling more heavily. I thanked Carlisle and, having grabbed another mug of tea, slipped off my boots and tapped out the number printed on the slip of paper. Gorton's bluff voice answered immediately.

'Lorrens? Listen lad, I know you are having some problems at the moment, but I would appreciate it, and so would the other selectors, mind, if you would try to keep your private life out of the papers. So that means no interviews on anything but cricketing matters. And that's on *the field* matters. Understand?'

Gorton was about sixty years-of-age, a Yorkshireman, and forthright. He had captained his county until a dispute with the board had led him to

Gloucestershire, where he ended his career. He had captained England on two overseas tours at a time when our fortunes were at a low ebb and managed to inspire his team to beat both Australia and a strong South Africa. With England once again at a low ebb on the cricket scene Gorton had replaced my nemesis Richard Lees and it was beginning to look like I was going to have trouble with the new chief selector too. He was not afraid to speak his mind and did not mind to cause offence. He was causing me offence now.

'Now wait a minute...' I began, before Gorton rudely cut across me.

'No! You wait a minute, young man. Our sponsors will not accept this type of adverse publicity and I do not need to tell you how important they are to us, I am sure.'

The newly formed ECB had started the year without a sponsor after the expiry of the previous contract which had ended at the conclusion of the winter tours to Zimbabwe and New Zealand. The results there had been so variable that the brewery had decided not to extend and there had been a frantic search for a replacement. With the new season only a matter of a few weeks away a deal was finally inked with KidsownTV, a relatively new children's satellite cartoon channel; a deal that the ECB was particularly pleased with as it seemed to ensure a raising of awareness of the game amongst young children.

I tried to explain that Singh's article had been largely supposition on his part and that I had certainly not given him an interview, but Gorton was not listening. I did neglect to tell him that the article was at least partly true, however. The part about Elisa and Crispin Gates/Le Dare was a curveball; I had no inkling of any prior relationship and resolved to investigate that part. I slipped the mobile back into my blazer pocket and suddenly any euphoria over being selected was replaced by a feeling of despondency. I glanced over to the windows and saw the rain lashing down out of leaden skies. It looked like being a long afternoon.

It was announced at two o'clock that an early interval would be taken and that the umpires would inspect the pitch afterwards – provided the rain stopped. After my conversation with Gorton I did not feel in the mood for lunch and decided instead to go for a stroll. Besides, I needed to see Jackie Kray to check whether she had been able to find anything about Barry Miller and where he had been before taking on the development role at The Oval. I found the Club Office full of people, caught Kray's eye and mouthed that I would call back later.

There are few sadder sights to me than a cricket stadium in the rain. The skies above south London looked dark and menacing and judging by the soggy flags on the pavilion roof the wind had swung around from the north and was now coming in from the direction of Brixton. I found it hard to see a resumption of play and, not caring too much that my cricket gear was getting thoroughly soaked, I decided to walk the long way back to the dressing-room – right the way around the ground, along the walkway between the back of the terraces and the high, red-brick perimeter wall. There were no spectators in sight and it appeared that those few who had braved the chilly start had given up and gone home.

For the public there is very little cover at The Oval and I reflected that the new double-decker stands would be a real bonus and provide some much-needed protection. I glanced through a gap in the terracing towards the jumble of stands at the Vauxhall End, showing brightly despite, or perhaps in contrast to, the dark skies above. Once the double-deckers were complete and if the Club was able to get the funding to replace the old stands The Oval would rank with almost any ground in the world outside of Australia. I looked forward to that but had a twinge of sadness – modernisation threatening to iron out all the quirks of our county grounds; memories of long, happy summer days as a young boy watching Surrey with my little group of friends, the whole ground almost to ourselves. The perimeter wall had been largely reconstructed since then but in those days there were gaps every twenty yards or so where fibrous expansion boards had been inserted. As these had decayed over the years, gaps would appear; gaps just the right size that, with a deft flick, it was possible to launch through a membership card from the inside to waiting friends in the road outside. The thought made me smile and I remembered the day we were spotted by a keen-eyed steward and the subsequent chase around the ground trying to evade him. Stewards back then all seemed to be about eighty and the chase was an unequal one.

I found shelter at the back of the Vauxhall End, in one of the concession stalls, the door to which was invitingly open. They were normally locked when not in use but there was clearly some remedial work in progress on this one, so I stepped inside and stood at the doorway watching the rain coming down in sheets outside. I found myself thinking about my conversation with Gorton and suddenly realised that Elisa did not yet know that I had been reselected. Almost immediately I realised that I did not really care, and the realisation shook me for a moment. A flood of mental images tumbled past as I gazed fixedly into the pool of water outside the stall, the rain bouncing a foot into the air off the tarmac. This one was surely going to be abandoned.

My international ban had largely been sealed by the article that Elisa had written about me when we first met. At times since then, especially when I was down and fearing my England career was over, she had apologised and expressed regret over writing the piece. I had always waved away her protestations but as I stood in that doorway, watching the rain beat down, for the first time I started to feel really resentful. It was not a feeling I liked. My eyes glazed over as I stared into the pool of water. Images continued to flash by: Elisa on The Star's cover with LeDare draped over her; Sally Framsell lying in the road; I pictured Miller's leering face; the Chelsea Hotel words on Elisa's PC; Gorton's warning; Summers's betting scam and suddenly – Lori's smiling face. I realised with a start that I had not spoken with her for too long and more importantly, that I suddenly really wanted to.

CHAPTER 20

Thursday May 8 1997

This felt like getting in too deep. I tiptoed to the door, opened it as quietly as possible and then with a quick look behind to check that I was unseen, slipped out into the corridor. I stepped into my shoes, patted my trouser pockets to check that keys, wallet and mobile were there and hurried along to the stairs. It looked like a Travel Inn judging by the colour scheme. I trotted down two flights and came out into the lobby and was about to ask the receptionist where I was when I saw a flicker of recognition in her eyes. I did a swift about face and headed for the revolving doors which spilled me out onto a busy London street. This was an assumption as my last clear memory was of drinking in the Green Man and French Horn and informed by the stream of black cabs and red buses that were now streaming past me. A couple of turns later and I found myself in Leicester Square. It was a short stroll to the Tube and within minutes I was heading south on the Northern Line to Waterloo.

I buried my head inside a copy of the Standard, which I found on the seat next to mine, affording me some protection from scrutiny and time to think. Lori had been keen to meet and we had had a curry in a little place in Covent Garden before pub-crawling through Soho, ending up at the pub in St Martin's Lane. She was easy company, laughed at my jokes and was, frankly captivating. When I realised that I had missed my last train and started searching for a taxi it was Lori who simply took my hand and led me around the corner to a hotel. I knew then it was not the best idea but did little to dissuade her; that is, until we got into the room. Then I suddenly felt sick, spent forty-minutes in the bathroom waiting for the nausea to subside, and came out to find her tucked up in the double bed, fast asleep, a pile of clothes on the floor. Was I meant to get in? I was tempted but there was a chance, albeit a slim one, I had misread things. I flopped down on the single bed and before I had had time to reflect had fallen asleep too. When I awoke, light was seeping in at the bottom of the thick curtains as I tried to work out where I was. I looked over at the other bed and could see Lori lying on her back, her hair splayed on the pillow, the white duvet covering most of her body with one perfect breast revealed. She looked like a Greek goddess and I had to question my self-restraint as I grabbed up my shoes and scarpered.

With a day to myself and still no contact from Elisa I decided to head back to The Oval for a net. Summers' plan was never far from my mind and, whilst it made me rather uneasy to say the least, it had got me reflecting on his observations about my batting. I wanted to have a session to try out the different stances but knew that if it was busy in the indoor cricket centre I would have to give it a miss; Summers was probably right that I needed to keep this quiet – at least if I wanted his spread betting plan to work. I was coming to the conclusion that it hurt no-one if I waited for the one-day internationals to focus on the new stance. Anyway, in some way I still felt that I owed him.

At 9:00 a.m., the Barrington Cricket Centre beneath the Bedser Stand was empty aside from a couple of Surrey coaches who were preparing for the day. I didn't know either of them very well as they had only started at the club fairly recently but the young, slim blonde setting up one of the nets smiled at me as I came in. There was a hint of Elisa about her – or was I now seeing that in every girl I spoke to?

'Morning,' I began, checking her name badge. 'Samantha, how are you on the bowling machines?'

'Call me Sam,' she replied with a broad grin. 'I can load the balls as well as anyone or I can send a few down if you want.'

'What do you bowl?'

'Fast-medium or some leggies if you prefer?'

'Well let's start with the machine and if I get my eye in we can see where we go from there,' I offered, presuming, perhaps unfairly, that the bowling machine was likely to provide me more useful practice.

'Let's,' she smirked suggestively.

'I meant that we could start with the machine and then try some of yours after maybe,' I explained, feeling my face redden as she led me to a different net where a bowling machine stood waiting.

'I know,' she replied with a curious grin and a hint of mischief in her eye. 'But...'

She let that linger. I hurried off to the changing rooms and the locker where I keep spare kit, changed quickly and was back in time to see Sam loading balls and adjusting the aim. Seeing me, she paused and with a sparkle in her eye asked if I wanted 'fast, very fast or super-fast?'

'I thought we could start with something gentle and work our way up?' I suggested.

The broad grin was back. 'That sounds nice, but you are going to be facing the Aussies, remember? They are basically your options for the rest of the summer – as far as the bowling goes ...'

Emboldened I enquired, 'Are there other options non-bowling wise?'

Sam paused. 'Now that would be telling but first you need to get down the end there,' she said with mock severity as she nodded towards the stumps at the far end of the net. 'We are starting with 80mph and working up to the ton.'

'That'll be nice,' I muttered as I walked past her. 'Set it to a good length.'

I reached the end of the net and let my eyes acclimatise to the lighting down there for a few seconds. I saw that Sam was standing on the high step at the rear of the bowling machine and adjusted my protector as I took guard.

'Comfortable?' she smiled.

Everything she said seemed to be loaded or was I flattering myself? 'Let's get this started.'

Sam raised her hand to show me the ball before lowering it and dropping the ball into the funnel at the top of the machine. A momentary pause before a blur of red and the 'thwack' of ball hitting netting behind me. We repeated this a couple of times before Sam paused.

'We've started, you know?' She grinned.

'Amusing,' I retorted. 'Next!'

This time the blur focused into a red sphere and I connected imperfectly and sent it like a laser straight between second and third slip.

'Turn it up,' I ordered as I needlessly re-fixed the Velcro straps on my gloves.

'Chin music,' I heard Sam mutter with a giggle.

This promised to be a fun session.

I had started with my normal stance, the overly closed one that Summers had identified, and every now and then I managed to connect fairly well. For most of the time I found myself getting a little tucked up, with my front foot, my left, tending to point a little too much towards cover point. Sam turned the bowling machine up to 85 mph and this started to cause me real problems. Sam slowed it back down to 80 mph.

'You prefer it nice and slow?' She said with a sly grin.

'Turn it back up!' I snarled, as I shifted my body weight, making a determined effort to turn my left shoulder a little more towards mid-on, sliding my right foot to point more towards the cover area, my left towards mid-off – a much more open stance.

'Fair enough – here comes 85 again!'

I let the first one go. And the second and third. Sam looked quizzically as she loaded the fourth. Pitching on a good length I watched the ball exit the machine, stepped forward and creamed it through the covers.

'Where did that come from?' she called, with a smile, as she loaded the next ball.

'Same place as this,' I called as I cracked the fifth ball to the right of cover. I couldn't miss from then on and after half an hour, and dripping with sweat, I shook my head as she indicated another bucket of balls. I could see some of the seconds coming in for a net before the start of day two of their match with Somerset and I did not want them to see me trying out the new stance. Carlisle had not picked me for the first Championship away game up at Derby because of my shoulder and I had an appointment with the physio at 11.30 a.m.

'You were great,' Sam said. 'I get off at three today,' she continued, smiling shyly now from under her blonde fringe.

'Sorry?' I muttered.

'Nothing, forget it,' she said, reddening suddenly. She seemed really sweet.

'That's a shame, I was going to ask if you fancied a coffee later...'

'I'd love that,' she quickly returned.

'Great – see you out by the clock at three then?'

I left the sports hall with a wave to my Surrey colleagues and a spring in my step and for the first time the feeling that perhaps, just maybe, Summers might have been on to something.

I showered quickly, packed my gear into my locker, folded the damp kit into a bag to take home for washing and, wiping my face with a towel, made my way round the ground to the pavilion entrance and up the several flights to my office at the top. The kettle was full enough and as I waited for it to boil, I found the makings and set about making a brew. Sitting at my desk I looked across at Sally's. It was exactly as she had left it the day she left for the last time and that immediately dampened my mood. Her tea mug sat empty next to her notepad, the pen laying on top of it. As I stood up to make the tea my eye was caught by a doodle in the top corner of her pad. I walked round for a clearer view, reluctant for some reason to move anything. She had drawn a stylised 'M' and then scribbled it out. Under that she had scrawled 'bastard'. I slumped into her swivel chair forgetting the kettle that was boiling fiercely by the sink. 'M'; what had happened that night? What went so badly wrong that Sally Framsell had wound up dead? Hit and run they said but was it an accident? I resolved then and there to do something about it – I needed to talk to Miller again. I tore off the pad's top sheet, folded it and slipped it into my trouser pocket.

There was no answer to my knock on Miller's office door and when I tried the handle I found it locked. I hurried back down to the Club Office to see if Jackie knew whether he was in the ground.

'He was in earlier, Johnny, but I think he's popped out for a meeting. Is it urgent?'

I said that it was not and that I would catch him later. I climbed back up to my office with the intention of clearing my stuff out. Carlisle had ensured that my editorship of *Oval Eyes* was terminated, or at least on hold until the end of the season, and the office that Sally and I shared was being returned to its usual library use. In truth there was not much for me to take away but I thought I should pack up Sally's stuff and return it to her mother and I had a couple of calls to make.

'Hello, Jack, how's it going?' I had not spoken with my brother since my visit to him in Bledington and I thought that he might have had a chance to look at the plans I had left with him. 'What are you up to? Had a chance to cast your eye over those plans yet?'

'Up to my ears in an assessed piece on compressive loads and yes, I did have a look at the plans. They look pretty good to me – nice design but I am just looking closely at some of the numbers.' I could hear Jack's fingers on a keyboard as he spoke.

'Do you mean the costings?' I asked, remembering that Willby had come in as the cheapest bid and of course, the latest.

'The plans don't show me those,' Jack corrected. 'No, it's just some of the dimensions I am pondering. Might speak with one of my uni professors, if you don't mind?'

I had visions of the stands being designed too large for the available space. 'Don't mind at all – that could save us some embarrassment.'

'Embarrassment wouldn't come into it, Johnny. But let me check it out first.'

I could tell he was busy so ended the call quite quickly and it was only then that I reflected on what he had said. It was not the embarrassment he was thinking of so it must have been something more serious.

I pressed the power button on my PC and whilst it hummed into life, I re-filled the kettle and absent-mindedly set about making a couple of teas before realising with a sad start that I only needed to make one. I walked over to Sally's desk, picked up her used mug and placed it on the draining board. I slumped into her chair and, feeling somewhat disloyal, started to open her desk drawers. They were all empty. Her diary, which she normally kept on her desk had gone too along with the row of lever-arch files that she had stored on the windowsill next to her desk. The pad that had been on her desk just ten minutes earlier too had gone. Looking around I could see no other signs of a visit from the cleaners – mugs on the side still and the bin half-full. Miller, if it was him, had beaten me to it. Jackie had said she thought he had gone out but maybe he had stopped by here first.

I mashed the teabag, spooned in a couple of sugars and some milk. I strolled over to the huge window and gazed out across the ground. A perfect spring day was forecast, and the pale blue sky and perfect, early-season light-greenness of the outfield certainly boded well for a full day's play for the seconds. Finishing touches were being made to the white lines on the strip and another member of the ground staff team was straightening out the boundary rope in front of the Bedser Stand down below to my left, where the heavy roller had just left the field. I took a swig of scalding tea as I tapped out Eleanor's number on the mobile – I was keen to probe a little more about this mystery boyfriend of Sally's. I was also puzzled as to why Sally had never mentioned the fact that she had apparently followed her former boyfriend to The Oval. Miller was my best bet – why else would he have hired a personal assistant who knew nothing about the business he was in? I did not have any feeling of warmth towards Dench either and he had appeared at Surrey at pretty much the same time. And then there was O'Brien, another relative newcomer down from the Midlands. But 'M is a monster' was still worrying me the most.

Eleanor picked up on the third ring. 'Oh, hello Johnny, how lovely to hear from you,' she said brightly.

I could hear a lawn mower in the background and the chink of a glass. I pictured her sitting on her terrace, enjoying a late lunch on her own, her aged gardener toiling away as she relaxed. Nice life. Except for the death of her daughter, I pondered grimly.

'I'm good, thanks, Mrs Framsell...' I began.

'Eleanor,' she interjected.

'Oh, yes, of course – Eleanor.'

'How are things at work?'

'Not bad. I have a few days off, actually. We have a 4-day match going on up at Derby at the moment, but I am being rested until the one-dayer on Sunday.'

'You have time off already? Hasn't the season just begun?' she said with a gentle laugh.

'It has, yes,' I smiled, 'but I have been carrying an injury for a while now so they're not risking me in the longer format.'

'I remember Sally talking about her boyfriend. If it wasn't his knee it was an ankle. I thought he was a malingerer, if I'm honest. She wouldn't have it, of course. Said he was taking advice from the physiotherapist. She was so keen on him at the start...' she tailed off.

'So her boyfriend was still playing?' I asked, realising that this could rule out Miller.

'Oh, I don't know about that,' she replied. 'Sally just mentioned various ailments he seemed to have.'

There was silence again and I began to think it was not the best idea to have called. Suddenly she snapped out of her reverie.

'So, Johnny, what can I do for you or did you just call for a chat?'

'Well, I have been thinking about Sally a lot since, you know, since...' I began.

'She died?'

'Yes, since she died.' I said quietly. I found the word hard to say to her mother and seemingly harder to utter than she did. 'There is something not sitting right for me about all of this. Sally was going for a drink with Miller, her boss, that evening. We thought there was something off about the whole building project and she went off with a bee in her bonnet, determined to have a show down with him over it.'

'Johnny, you are not making a whole lot of sense. It was a hit and run. The police are looking for the driver, but you are not telling me it was deliberate, surely?

I paused for a moment, unsure for a second as to how much to share. 'I get that, Eleanor, but this is a big project. The numbers are huge.'

'Huge enough to kill someone for?' she replied, a tone of incredulity in her voice. The lawnmower had stopped. A bird was singing somewhere in Eleanor's garden. Suddenly I heard my own words. It did seem far-fetched.

'I don't know,' I said. 'Sounds like a movie, doesn't it? Look, you said you never met the boyfriend?'

'That's right. I only knew he was a good deal older than her. Look, I don't want you to think I wasn't interested. Sally only told me about the relationship a couple of months back, when she had decided to go for The Oval position. I think she thought I would be opposed to her going with someone that much older than she.'

'And would you?'

'Absolutely I would. But I would not have told her, and I would have done my best not to show it either. The thing that saddens me is that I never did meet him. It quickly all went wrong for them. I would like to have given him a piece of my mind. Although I don't know exactly what happened...'

I heard a different tone in Eleanor's voice – a sadness at what might have been had she known earlier about her daughter's relationship.

'Eleanor, you told me that there was a cricketer at Sally's funeral. If I was to show you a picture of him do you think you would be able to recognise him?'

'Possibly. Like I said, there was a guy in an England blazer there, about my age, but I didn't take much notice.'

'I remember you saying that someone at the funeral recognised the England blazer. Would they be able to identify him, do you think?'

She paused. I heard her glass chink against her teeth. She swallowed and answered in a weak voice that sounded slightly the worse for drink. 'I doubt it, he's not a real cricket follower.'

'That's a shame but would you be okay if I whizz down to show you a photo of Miller?' I persisted.

'I'll try, Johnny, but I am not sure I can remember anything about him.'

'Don't worry, it's worth a go,' I said, reaching for my diary. I flipped through until I reached May 8. The only thing written was 'Call Elisa – Houston.' Given my singular lack of success in reaching her at any city on the tour I pondered for a moment whether I would even bother. I had not heard from her since the previous Saturday and was beginning to wonder if I had deliberately been given the wrong tour schedule. On a whim I suggested that I pop down that evening and was pleased that she immediately agreed. We settled on 8:00 p.m.

Replacing the receiver, I saw that it was a minute short of 3:00 p.m., and with a pleasant sense of anticipation dashed out of the library and raced down the several flights of stairs to meet Sam under the cricketers clock.

She proved to be excellent company. We had coffee at a little café close by Oval tube. She knew her cricket and for a moment I thought I had been rumbled when she remarked upon how my batting had improved when I shifted my stance. I think I covered this quite well by rambling on about the lighting down there in the underground sports centre and saying I was attempting to get rid of a strip light from my line of vision. She was not that interested in my stance, to be fair, and thankfully the conversation moved on. Summers' words were in my head and I told myself that I would be more careful. It was still two weeks until the one-day series with Australia and I determined to get some more batting practice in. Sam had asked if I wanted to do some extra bowling practice with her and seemed surprised that I said I would rather practise my batting. She gave me her number so I could arrange another session and reddened as she kissed me when we parted at Vauxhall Station, suggesting a proper drink after the next session.

I was back in Epsom forty-five minutes later and by 6:00 p.m., shaved, showered and eating a sandwich as I caught up with the sports news on Sky. The Australians were doing well at the start of their tour; early days but unbeaten so far. That piece was followed by an update on England skipper, Ted Glynn. The Worcestershire batter was still struggling with a hamstring problem and was a doubt for the one-dayers. I raised a full mug of tea to my lips as the presenter suggested that his place might be taken by Alan Dench of Surrey. Cue tea all over the place. Dench? At 38? He had not played for England for three or four years and certainly last appeared well before my Australian tour. In fairness he had settled into the Surrey line-up quickly and was scoring well but I would never have put money on this. Not that I am a betting man, of course, as you well know.

The A3 was slow and much as expected but sometimes I don't mind a traffic jam. It can offer a rare moment of calm in what can be a pretty frantic summer of cricket, what with travelling up and down the country trying to cope with what seems every year to be a more and more insane fixture list. As we stopped yet again, at the Painshill junction, I fumbled in the glovebox for a cassette. At the third attempt I found it; The Marnies – *Quiet but Dangerous*. I slipped it into the player, rewound to the beginning, wound up the windows, pressed play and turned it up. Elisa's voice introduced the first number, *You're Mine and Don't Forget It!* with a dreamy, crystal clear stanza – wistful and yearning. This was the lull before the musical storm. 'One, two, three, four!' screamed the bass player as the band launched into a multi-tracked barrage driven by the tightest of rhythm sections, bass line moving sinuously at pace and Elisa's vocal now with a grittier edge. But the melody! Oh my, I could still not see why they did not become huge even if just for this one song. But then I guess I am rather biased. Hearing Elisa's voice again left me feeling a little conflicted. My feelings for her were still strong but she had not been in touch for five days and if there was any truth in the paper's coverage, which I should have taken very cautiously, she did not seem to have quite the same feelings for me. As the traffic finally started to move again, I found myself thinking of Lori and, feeling bad about running out on her that morning, realised that I wanted to see her again.

Eleanor came to the door, glass in hand. It looked like she had moved on to shorts and the mix of alcohol and cigarette smoke on her breath was a heady mix for a recently retired smoker. She looked younger than her forty-three years and was once again beautifully dressed in flaring, orange, silk trousers with a white, silk, polka-dot print chemise with most of the buttons undone.

'Johnny!' she exclaimed, as if surprised to see me. 'How darling of you to come,' she slurred, suddenly grabbing the architrave for support. 'Drink?'

'It has been noted!' I replied with a smile, as I steadied her with a hand on her elbow. 'Though not when I am on duty.'

'A little one won't hurt,' she replied as she turned clumsily and waved me in as she made a weaving turn into the lounge, leaving me to close the door. I left my shoes at the door and followed her in.

Eleanor turned from the well-stocked bar which took up a large corner of her huge lounge.

'Getting undressed already? I heard you were a quick worker,' she said, with a hiccup as she tumbled ice into a glass, nodding at my stockinged feet.

Awkward. I started to mutter something about always taking my shoes off in my own house as she pressed the glass of bourbon into my hand and put a well-manicured finger to my lips. She then took my hand and led me across the large, geometric-patterned rug over to a ship-sized, leather sofa and almost pulled me on top of her as she misjudged the descent. She managed to save her drink with a practised hand, and I managed to save the lush, arctic-white carpet by spilling mine on my polo shirt. Eleanor still had hold of my hand and pulled herself back up with surprising agility, placing her own glass on the occasional table next to the sofa.

'Oh, Johnny, that was my fault,' she scolded herself. 'Let me get that shirt sorted for you.'

'It's not a problem, Mrs Fram –, Eleanor. I'll sort it out later.'

'No, I won't hear of it, take it off now and I will wash it,' she commanded.

She had already started to pull the shirt upwards from its hem and as she lowered her head to the task, I caught another breath of the alcohol-cigarette mix and felt powerless to stop her. As she pulled the shirt higher to the point where I had to raise my arms above my head, she stumbled forwards once again and her face planted against my chest. My instinct was to catch her, and with my arms restricted by the bunched-up shirt, Eleanor was for a second trapped. A sudden sharp pain made me instinctively step back and, with my foot catching on the rug's thick edge, I fell backwards dragging Eleanor down and on top of me.

Our faces were centimetres apart. I had the urge to kiss her. But she was very drunk and given all of the circumstances that seemed highly inappropriate. I opted for conversation. 'Did you just bite my nipple?' I was still taken aback by that.

My arms were still trussed by the polo shirt and she remained trapped, but she managed to push herself up so that I could look into her face, her long, jet-black hair falling into my face. 'I did,' she said without a trace of embarrassment. 'And what are you going to do about that?' she challenged.

'Bite yours,' I replied, matter-of-factly. I had sensed a lack of bra when I had arrived and as she straddled me I could see that I was right, her fall having apparently loosened further buttons.

Her eyes seemed to light up as she somehow wriggled out of my grasp. She took hold of my hands and lifted my arms over my head so that they lay flat on the carpet behind me, unbuttoned her chemise fully, kneed her way a little further up my body and lowered her small, but beautifully proportioned breasts into my face. I gently kissed one.

'Bite me,' she whispered urgently.

CHAPTER 21

Friday May 9 1997

Her bed was huge but then so was everything in the house. Her appetite for sex was huge too. What started on the lounge floor continued in the shower and then moved on to the bedroom. I had heard that older women know a thing or two and Eleanor certainly did. We continued drinking throughout and after several hours fell asleep in mid throw, exhausted. It all started again the following morning before breakfast and a little after too. But by then I was sobering up and reflecting with the clarity that comes after drunkenness that I had just slept with Sally's mother and been unfaithful to Elisa. The former seemed perhaps bad form, the latter, clearly wrong but I reminded myself that Elisa seemed to be doing the same to me, would not care, and very probably had not done for some time.

As I opened the front door, I suddenly remembered why I had driven down to Elstead the evening before. I fumbled for the photograph in my jacket pocket.

'This is Miller, Eleanor. The one you said saw at the funeral. Is this him? Is this the man you saw?'

She took the photo from my hand, looked at it for a second and, returning it to me said, 'No. Never seen him before.'

I thought about nothing else all the way back home. No traffic this morning but The Marnies left me feeling uneasy, guilty, and I quickly ejected the cassette. Eleanor had asked me to go back that evening and I had fudged it, saying I had appointments, but I do not think I was very convincing. She looked disappointed – hurt, even. *Smashed* had called me an 'all round bad boy' and for the first time I actually felt like one. I would have to think about the Miller development too – if it was not him at the funeral, then who was it?

The house seemed unusually quiet as I entered and I immediately saw the red, blinking light on the answerphone. Surely not. I pressed the play button and, as I listened, any slight feelings of guilt ebbed away, replaced at Elisa's final words, by a sense of crushing self-loathing.

'*Hiya lover! I am so missing you – you can't believe how much. The schedule has just been crazy; it's gig, after-show, hotel, freeway, media, soundcheck, eat, gig, after-show …. you always said that you never got to see anything on tour and I can see what you meant now. But why can we not get to talk to each other? I'm going crazy without you. Where were you last night? I called five times! It must be 9:00 a.m., your time now – I guess you are still asleep. I can just see you sleeping and if I was there, I would be climbing all over you…*'

I stabbed the stop button, unable to listen to anymore.

After a shower and shave I felt slightly more human, made a strong, black coffee and took it out onto the patio which by mid-morning is in full sunlight. The sky was a perfect, baby-blue and perfectly cloudless. A dark flash caught my eye – my first swift of the year, swooping over the rooftops, and for me the sign that summer is truly on its way. The warming rays of the sun, the hot, bitter edge to the coffee and the swift's sudden appearance made me feel a little more positive. I had summoned up the courage to play the rest of Elisa's message and was relieved to hear that she was due back at the end of the tour, sometime around May 23rd; that would give me time to work out what I was going to say to her. At this safe distance I was planning to come clean but knew that as her return came closer, I would likely feel less keen on this tactic.

I took a long sip of the still-scalding coffee and resolved to contact Jackie Kray to see if she had managed to find out more about Barry Miller's background. I realised that I knew very little about him. The start of my first-class career overlapped the end of his for a season or so, but we only played in a handful of matches together. I remember him having a really coarse sense of humour and whilst that normally does not worry me there was always a cruelty to his as well. It was mid-season when it hit the fan at Surrey with allegations from three separate women that Miller had got physical with them during what were agreed by all to be consensual relations. The media would have had a field day, but Surrey officially released him because of a well-publicised, though not career-ending, knee injury. I remember the day he left as if it was yesterday; doors slamming, bats flying, and we were all told quite clearly where we could go. Quite how, seven years later, Surrey had hired him as project manager for the ground redevelopment was puzzling. Perhaps Jackie would be able to help there. The only positives I could come up with were that Eleanor had described Sally's boyfriend as a cricketer, and not an ex-cricketer, and that it was seemingly not Miller that she had seen at Sally's funeral. Perhaps that ruled him out?

My call went through to her immediately and I asked if there was any news. She told me that my office had now been cleared, returned to use as the Club's library and that the artist had been recalled with a brief to finish the 150th anniversary painting. As expected, and with little fresh interest from members, the Club had decided to fill the remaining places with current dignitaries, players and their wives or partners with the plan to unveil it sometime in July. Whilst this was interesting, I was more interested in what she might have uncovered about Miller. In the event it was not overly exciting, but she was able to tell me that he had moved to Leicester, took a Masters in some aspect of project management at De Montford University and had a quietly impressive curriculum vitae. From small projects at Leicester City FC's training ground and Leicester Rugby Club's Welford Road Stadium he had moved on to some larger projects across the Midlands and, more recently, in the City of London. Nothing he had done was on the scale of what he was working on at

The Oval, however. I asked Jackie to dig around a little more to find out if there was any link between any of the projects? I was about to end the call when I suddenly remembered.

'Oh, Jackie! Sally's funeral. I meant to ask, did Miller attend, like he promised?'

'No, he did not,' she replied tautly. 'What a creep.'

'Jackie, this is important, do you know who did represent the Club in the end?'

'Let me think,' she started. 'Um...there was Sir Ken, of course, and a couple of board members plus Snipe, MacLaine, O'Brien and Dench of the players.'

'Who? Are you sure, Jackie? I wasn't given permission to attend because of our match the next day. The first three maybe; they've been here a while, not that they probably ever met her, but Dench? He's only just joined – that's ridiculous!' I stormed.

'I did ask Carlisle about that too,' Jackie replied. Before I could explode again, she continued. 'The way I heard it was that they were rested for the game up at Cambridge against the Universities, so they were basically told to represent the playing staff.'

That did not make it much better, but it helped a little.

'Oh, and by the way, Eleanor Framsell has called you three times already this morning. Have you two got something going on or what?' she chuckled.

'No!' I replied, a little too sharply.

'Okay, only joshing,' she replied, sounding a little taken aback.

I ended the call a little too quickly. No smoke without fire. I probably should have laughed it off.

I was in the shower when the landline rang twice, a few minutes apart. Dried and in a fresh pair of jeans and a crisp, white Nike T-shirt, I trotted back down the stairs with a sense of foreboding. If it was Elisa I had not had time to plan what I was going to say to her. I pressed play. Thankfully, it was not.

'Hi, Johnny – Ralph here. I imagine you must be missing Elisa but from what she tells us she is having a fine old time in the States. Not that I like the idea of her hanging out with those hoodlums. Used to be... anyway was thinking about popping up to Derby for the Sunday game. That's if you are playing? Let me know, okay? Bye for now.'

That was a surprise. Ralph had never called me before to see if I was playing, rarely went to away games and, being an arch traditionalist, avoided the one-day games like the plague. I remember meeting him and Kitty for the first time shortly after Elisa and I got together. She had never mentioned that her father was a cricket obsessive so when we went for dinner at their pile in Esher I was surprised to find that he was a long-standing Surrey member and we had chatted long into the night about the Club. He wanted to hear about cricket from the inside; I wanted to hear stories of the greats he had seen from the sixties onwards. We became great friends at that point. I called him back straight away, said I was driving up the next day and readily agreed to swing by his place to give him a lift. It would be good to chat though my discomfort over what I had done to Elisa threatened to provide a painful backdrop to our journey.

The next call gave me a little start. It was Lori. I had meant to call her after running out on her the previous day but with everything that was going on had clean forgotten to do so. Her call was brief and thankfully she did not seem to be harbouring any grudge. Her last words sent a chill through me though. This promised to make things awkward tomorrow. She was planning a trip to Derby too. Had I mentioned the game to her the other night? I did not recall doing so. More importantly, how was I going to keep her and Ralph apart?

CHAPTER 22

I met Summers in the Hole in the Wall, a dingy real ale pub set deep in the arches of the Charing Cross line just outside the main entrance to Waterloo Station. I had not exactly been avoiding him and had been experimenting with the new stance, but he quickly reminded me that I had not responded to his calls.

'Rude bastard,' he grinned, thrusting a frosty pint of Castlemaine 4X into my hand.

'Coffee, I said,' I replied. 'I have a net in an hour.'

'Won't hurt you,' he laughed.

'You drag me to a real ale pub and buy me a pint of this?' I said, nodding at the lager in my hand.

'Fair point. That real ale stuff is like liquid fart, though, isn't it?'

'Well, I'm not a great fan to be fair,' I agreed. 'Cheers!'

We chinked glasses and chatted about this and that for a few minutes. I wondered when Summers would raise the issue of the spread bet and it didn't take long.

'So,' he began, 'have you had any more thoughts on the spread. You're back in the squad and the series is just a couple of weeks away.'

I took a long draft of the amber liquid. 'Thought you said that you were going ahead with it anyway?'

'I did, and I am, but it would give me more confidence to quote the higher price I need to attract sellers if I knew you were taking it seriously, mate.'

'Taking it seriously,' I started, loudly enough for him to cough and shush me, looking around him as he did to see if any of the three old men supping beers in the bar had heard us. They did not seem to have noticed us at all. 'Taking it seriously?' I started again, more quietly this time. 'If I am picked for England, I *will* be taking it bloody seriously, *mate!*'

He took a huge gulp of lager, wiped his mouth with the back of a huge hand and, setting his pint down with a thump, looked at me intently. 'Why the silence? I called you at The Oval and I must have left three or four messages on your home phone. Thought you had had second thoughts.'

'Second thoughts?' I was getting fed up with this already. 'Second *thoughts*? This is your plan, Mark, I am just glad to get my chance again.'

Summers could see that I was fuming, put up both hands in surrender. 'You're not remembering it all, Johnny. It's not just the spread; I know you don't want any part of that but if you are practising just be discreet with the new stance, okay?'

'I am not broadcasting it, if that's what you are saying.'

'I am not,' he replied calmly. 'But you seem to be forgetting the beers.'

'Like I said, I am having a net in an hour so I don't want to be drinking.'

'Not these beers,' Summers corrected quietly, nodding at the two pints on the table. 'I am talking about the New England beers – my saviours?'

In fairness, with all that had been going on I had given little thought to his beer idea. As I did reflect on it, that plan seemed a little daft too. 'What do you need from me?' I asked tiredly.

'Woah, mate! Like you're doing me a favour!' he retorted, a grin creeping across his broad features. 'This could be a nice little earner for you too. I put your ugly mug on the labels, you promote the beers. We push the 'New England' angle to tie in with your return and you get ten percent of the profits. All it costs you is a couple of hours of your time with a photographer for the publicity and advertising. Only trouble is that we have got to move quickly on this if we are going to tie it in with the one-day series. And that's why I have been trying to get hold of you.'

I looked at my watch, downed the remnants of my pint and stood up. 'Gotta go, Mark. Net at midday.'

'How's Elisa?'

'Elisa? Okay. Well, I think so. Had a call yesterday from the States.'

'*Has* she been playing away, then?'

Summers' bluntness stopped me in my tracks. My face must have shown my rising anger?

'Just asking,' he said, hands once again raised. 'Seen the stories in the papers...'

I regained my poise somewhat and managed a reply as I turned to leave. 'Don't believe everything you read, remember?'

'I do mate,' he laughed. 'Keep your nose clean – claim the moral high ground, eh?'

I paused. That was an odd thing to say.

'Call me with your diary, Johnny, so we can set a date for the photos?'

I waved a hand at him as I left the pub and hurried across the road to the main steps into Waterloo station. On the train for the one stop ride to Vauxhall I stabbed out the number on my phone; Lori picked up on the first ring.

'Hey, Johnny!' She sounded pleased to hear from me.

'Hi, Lori. I got your message. What's all this about Derby?'

'Well, I kind of thought it would be nice to see you play,' she said, her soft voice vaguely suggestive in my ear.

'That's a nice thought,' I started, 'but to be fair it is always freezing up at the Racecourse Ground.'

'Racecourse?'

'It's where Derby play – it's really open. So, it's always really cold and, to be honest, it won't be much of a match as they are one of the weaker county sides.' With Ralph now coming I really did not need Lori there too, but I was aware that I was offering a limp excuse.

'It's no bother, Johnny. I am up there for a conference actually, so I am not going out of my way. In fact, the conference promises to be a dull one so it will be a good excuse to escape.'

'If you are sure you want to come I can leave you a ticket at the ground?'

'Let me call you on the morning if that is okay? Just in case I can't escape,' Lori said.

I hoped she would not be able to get out though reflected that, had Ralph not been coming too, I would have welcomed the chance to meet up with her. 'Where are you staying up there?'

There was a pause. 'In a Trust House Forte place near the town centre. Why, are you planning to finish what you never started?' she challenged, with a hint of smile in her voice.

'Lori, I'm sorry about the other night. I was out of order.'

'How so? Taking the room with me or running out?'

I paused this time. 'Both, I guess,' I replied sombrely.

'Oh, lighten up,' she laughed. 'You're only young once. Anyway, I need to speak with you about...' she tailed off.

'Lori?'

She mumbled something quietly, seeming to choke back a sob.

'Phillipe? Is it? What's he saying now?'

I heard a whimper just before the line went dead. That settled it for me. I suddenly wanted to see her again. She had a knack of tugging at my heartstrings.

Sam was ready with the bowling machine fully loaded in net one. The other nets were in use, but they looked like private sessions; there was certainly no sign of any of my teammates. I went for a hi-five with Sam, but she had already leant in for a kiss on the cheek. We laughed at the contradiction and settled on a fist pump before I strolled down to the business end.

'What's it to be today, Johnny?'

'Ramp it up – let's start with 80mph,' I replied with a casual grin.

'Ooh! Okay, big fella,' she replied. 'Slightly full?'

I nodded as I adjusted the straps on my gloves and checked that my box was positioned correctly. Her little grin was back; suggestive somehow but not brazen. I liked her.

The new stance worked well. My timing was getting better and I do not think I have ever hit the ball more cleanly. As Sam reloaded the machine, I found myself thinking about Summers' plan. The price he was planning to quote was based on his theory that England would be hammered by the Aussies in the one-day series meaning that we would probably have to bat down to eleven. In all likelihood it all hinged on me batting in all three unless I took a whole bunch of wickets or scored a stack of runs in at least one of the innings and, even with the improvements with the new stance, I found it hard to see that happening. The venture looked highly risky to me.

We moved up to 90mph during the session and re-calibrated the bowling machine a number of times so that by the end of the hour I had faced a barrage of short-pitched, 1997 Aussie-style deliveries. I was dripping and completely exhausted as I trudged back towards Sam, who was tidying things away.

'That was great, Sam, thanks very much.'

She brushed back a tress of blonde hair out of her eyes and returned my smile. 'Anytime,' she said with a grin that said much more. Starting to think that I was imagining this in every interaction with women at the moment, she continued. 'Coffee again?'

'Would love to but I have a meeting up in the Club Office in a few minutes' time, Sam, sorry. Next time?'

She looked a little crestfallen but laughed it off as she quickly kissed me on the cheek before bending back down to her work.

I said I would call her to arrange another net after Derby and, reddening slightly, she gave me a thumbs up without actually looking up.

I showered quickly and grabbed a Diet Coke from the vending machine outside the changing room before heading towards the Club Office. Jackie was in and for once was not on the phone. She nodded towards a smaller office in the corner of her larger one and I followed.

'Johnny, you asked me to look into Miller's background a little? Well, you know all about the allegations that ended his playing career?'

I nodded that I did.

'And you know that he did his MA at De Montford. Well, he worked for a while with a project management outfit in Leicester; quite a junior role from what I can gather. Then after about two years with them he went solo. He's been fairly busy by the looks of it with a number of small projects apart from the ones we spoke about. But you asked me if there were any links between his projects.'

'And?'

'Every single one has been on behalf of Willby Construction.'

I took a sharp intake of breath.

'What do you think it means?' Jackie asked.

I paused, reflecting on the fact that I had been taken aback by that news but was then unsure why I was surprised; perhaps because Willby was building the new double-deckers and Miller seemed to be tied into them but perhaps more so because of the seemingly unorthodox bidding process that had won them the contract. 'I really don't know, Jackie. There just seems something off about the whole thing. Maybe it's just the way that they got the contract or maybe it's Miller.'

'You're still worried about him?'

I nodded. 'Do you know the full story?'

Jackie looked puzzled.

'Right, where to start?' I muttered. I could not remember what I had shared with her.

'Just tell me from the top,' she suggested.

I told her everything, from Sally's appointment, Willby's late bid, Sally's '*M is a monster*' comment and the fact that Sally and Miller had gone for a drink with Sally set on a showdown the night she died. Though I did say that I was not sure enough to point a finger at Miller for that and acknowledged that the police seemed to have made no progress as they were still appealing for witnesses.

Jackie was quiet for a minute after I stopped speaking. She looked at me with a frown. 'This stinks, Johnny.'

'That's what I think,' I muttered.

'What do we do?'

I spread my hands. 'I don't know.'

I left Jackie a few minutes later and strolled down to Vauxhall Station for my Epsom train, thinking about what she had told me. Was it that odd that an independent project manager would work exclusively with one building company? Perhaps not. Was it odd that a contract be awarded on a late bid? Probably.

'Hiya!'

I jerked my head up as I passed the little school playground that ran alongside the Harleyford Road. It was the same young teacher with whom I had chatted a few weeks before. The gentle breeze was playing havoc with her long, black hair. She had a wonderful smile, her class playing happily next to her on a climbing frame.

'No trip today?' I asked as I waved at the children who had stopped their play to look at me.

'Not today,' she smiled. 'And when we got down to the Thames last time the boats had been cancelled.'

'What a shame. Listen, I am in a hurry now but would your children like a cricketer to visit, do you think?' I am not sure where that idea suddenly came from.

She smiled and spread her hands to indicate her class of 4-year-olds. 'Might go over this lot's heads, but I am sure Year 6 would love it,' she replied. As an afterthought she added, 'And so would I, of course.'

'It's a date then. Let me have your number and I will call with my diary.'

She came closer to the railings, recited her number and as I turned to go, I asked her name.

'Elisa,' she replied.

I am not sure what my reaction was, but I must have shown my surprise.

'I know,' she grinned, 'same as your wife, Johnny.'

I walked a little quicker towards Vauxhall to make sure I caught my half-hourly train. I was surprised that she knew my name, let alone Elisa's. Perhaps she had seen the papers. Anyway, it got me to thinking about Elisa, my wife. I was beginning to wonder what I did feel about her now.

I arrived in Esher at a little after 5:00 p.m., with the radio tuned to Surrey's Championship match at Derby. It was coming to the end of the fourth and final day and we were clinging on with two wickets remaining but still 80 adrift. I turned the engine off and had just reached the front door as Ralph emerged, overnight bag in hand. He shut the door before I had chance to say hello to Kitty.

'Best to leave her, Johnny. She's 'in the zone',' he explained, making rabbit ears.

'Is she still doing that, what does she call it … Action Art?'

'I am afraid so. I just don't get it, Johnny. She studied fine art at college, can produce paintings that look like photographs and yet she seems to think thrashing a canvas with a whip and running over it with a kid's scooter is the apex of art.'

'She gets bored quite quickly, though,' I noted as I stowed Ralph's bag next to my coffin and overnight bag in the boot of my car. I noticed that we had both brought the same chocolate-brown Surrey CCC holdall.

'Normally she works in phases of about three months but this one is dragging on a bit,' Ralph grimaced.

'She should have a word up at The Oval,' I suggested. 'I hear the 150th painting is being kick-started and that they're hoping to unveil it in the summer. Seems that Elisa is going to be added to the picture, next to me.'

'I did put her name forward, actually, but Goldrich said he could complete it on time and anyway, when I told Kitty she said she was too busy with her 'Scooter' series.'

'Well, you have to admit, Ralph, that she is certainly committed to her art,' I offered.

I turned on the radio as I pulled back out of his driveway, catching a glimpse of Kitty through the front window, whip raised and dripping with yellow paint and steered the Vectra towards the A3. I glanced quizzically at my father-in-law.

'She's moved into the lounge to work on a new painting. Everything's covered in tarps but I'm glad to be getting out,' he smiled.

Surrey had capitulated in the few minutes that I had been at Ralph's. He wondered why we were making such heavy weather in the Championship but cruising in the one-day format. I suggested that it was too early in the season to make any real assessment and he grudgingly agreed, recalling some barren years in the seventies when Surrey always promised but rarely delivered.

With the radio off again we chatted amiably until we came onto the M25 at Wisley. I was just nosing my way into the slow line, trying to squeeze in between two articulated lorries when Ralph said the thing I had been fearing.

'So, Johnny, what is going on with you and Elisa?'

I shot a look at him as the lorry behind me suddenly loomed large in my rear-view mirror. 'Shit!' Holding up a hand in apology, I floored the gas pedal and sped away from that danger but had to swing quickly into the next lane to avoid the lorry in front, causing the car I had cut up to honk furiously.

'What do you mean?' I asked.

'Johnny, I know you think I am a died in the wool Tory, but I am aware of what the red tops have been reporting, you know.'

'Oh, that,' I mumbled, easing the Vectra up to eighty as the traffic ahead thinned out.

'It doesn't make for happy reading.'

'No, it doesn't,' I agreed. 'But you know what they say about the tabloids.'

'I do, but what do you say about it?'

'I think they can go stuff themselves. Elisa is doing her job. I trust her and she assures me that the papers have it all wrong.' She had not actually done that, but her last call had on the face of it been very positive about her feelings for me.

'Is Elisa in touch with you?'

'We do seem to be missing each other. She doesn't call very often, and when she does I seem to be out so it's answerphone messages really. And I can't call her because apparently she can't give me an itinerary.'

'Unusual for a big tour I imagine, but this one seems to be quite unique. That band seems to be making things up as they go along. Getting bigger by the day, apparently.'

'It's a good story for Elisa to cover, that's for sure,' I replied, managing to sound more generous than I felt. 'Not sure I like the sound of them, though.'

Ralph looked across at me. 'Johnny, it's all a veneer. Think of the Sex Pistols twenty years ago. A few swear words on television, some ripped up clothes and safety pins, a 'shocking' musical statement about the Queen in her Jubilee year. They were just kids. Look at them now. The Fat and Forty tour last year – they're national treasures now.'

I looked back at Ralph. Hearing him talk like this surprised me. Perhaps he was more clued up than I thought. 'One of the papers described Elisa as Le Dare's long-time girlfriend.'

Ralph looked straight ahead as we curved northwards on the M25 towards the junction with the M1, the blue sky above changing to a darker, more forbidding colour ahead.

'Like you said, Johnny, you know what they say about the tabloids.'

That surprised me too. I had expected an immediate refutation of that story but did not want to ask him the truth.

Our Travel Inn was easy to find and by 8:00 p.m., we were sat at the bar having a quick drink before dinner. The forecast heavy showers had started twenty miles south of Derby and by the time we parked up it was torrential.

Tomorrow's game was already in doubt and the projection was for more of the same all night.

Ralph had said he would not hang around once my teammates appeared and as they began to drift down from their rooms he quickly downed the last of his whiskey, nodded a welcome to the Surrey boys and, as he headed back to his room, paused to ask, 'How's Jack?'

That took me by surprise. I am not sure we had ever talked about him before or even if Ralph would even have been aware of Jack. 'Jack? My brother?'

'The very same,' Ralph smiled.

'Okay, I think,' I began, realising that I had not spoken to him in a while. 'Why do you ask?'

'He's been phoning me, but I keep missing him. Just wondered why he was calling me. Would you happen to know?'

'No idea, Ralph.' As I said it, I remembered my conversation with Jack, the plans I had left with him and my suggestion that we consult with Ralph. 'Although, Jack and I were talking about The Oval plans a few weeks back and he had some questions I certainly couldn't answer, so I mentioned you. Must have given him your number, I guess. Sorry if he is being a pest; he is like a dog with a bone when he's on one,' I said with a smile.

'Pest? Not at all, Johnny,' Ralph replied, a hand on my shoulder. 'Any idea what he wanted to know about?'

'Not really. Said something about the numbers not adding up but he didn't elaborate. He's doing an engineering Masters at Bath,' I added by way of explanation.

'How did he get the plans?' Ralph asked with what seemed like renewed interest.

'From me. I was planning a piece on the ground redevelopment for *Oval Eyes* before I got pulled and I just had a few questions about the process.'

'And how would an engineering scholar help there?'

That was a good question and I realised that I would have to share more. 'Ralph, do you remember when I came to your place a while back and told you about the odd goings on with the bidding process and how Willby Construction secured the contract despite missing the bid deadline?'

Ralph nodded.

'Well, Jack just seemed a little concerned but like I said, never said much more than it being something about the numbers. I thought at first he meant the value of the contract because Willby came in cheapest but I think it is more to do with the dimensions.'

Ralph smiled, 'Have you got another copy of the plans?'

I said I had a copy with all my stuff from the old library office and agreed to get it to him as soon as I could.

'The thing is, Johnny, your brother will not have full access to all of the financials. I'll take a look and let you know, okay?'

As Gus MacLaine slapped me on the back with a cheery, 'There you are you soft, Pommie bastard!' Ralph waved a 'goodnight' and left me with my teammates who were clearly expecting an abandonment the following day, judging by the amount of lager they were consuming.

'Where's Carlisle?'

'Had to rush back for a last-minute meeting at HQ,' MacLaine replied, taking a second pint from Pallant, who had just ordered another round. 'So, when the cat's away...'

I took the pint that Pallant thrust my way, nodded my thanks, and said, 'Curry tonight, skipper?'

'For sure,' he agreed readily. 'The Golden Temple round the corner is meant to be excellent.'

'Really? On what basis?' Molander had joined the conversation.

'Proximity, basically,' Pallant replied drily, stretching to hand a pint to Dench, who was sat at a table on his own a little behind me. He looked a little cheerier than usual. I was surprised to see him drinking. I was sure he had told me just a few weeks before that he did not drink.

'Good enough for me,' I grinned. 'Let's down these and get round there.'

'Who was the old bloke?' MacLaine asked as we headed for the door.

'Father-in-law,' I replied, realising that Ralph had seemingly focused on the financials rather than the dimensions that were Jack's main concern.

We managed to get drowned in the forty-yard dash to the curry house and ten minutes later we were sat around a long table the waiters had constructed by a quick alteration to the restaurant's layout, and tackling the mound of poppadums that had arrived with the pickle trays and a round of Kingfishers. All were present except for Lenderman, who is obsessive about most things and his sleep pattern in particular, Dench and Molander. The big half-Swede is more of a raw fish type and will not touch a curry after an early experience at a dodgy little place in Durham. And I had not expected Dench to join us.

It felt good to be back with the boys. Being rested from the Championship matches was good for my shoulder but it was leaving me feeling a little removed from the team. Back together again we soon fell into the usual banter. I had missed it. The lads did not seem too worried about the loss to Derbyshire earlier that day. They also seemed to be pretty pleased at the prospect of a day off the next day. I, on the other hand, was disappointed that I might not get the chance to try out the new batting style in battle conditions. Another round of Kingfishers helped offset the disappointment.

We were just leaving the curry house a little after eleven when my mobile rang. I had just been grilled by the lads over Elisa. Tongues loosened by beer, there was little of the reticence or awkwardness from earlier in the season and I seemed to be fair game for their wit. Some of it, in truth, was very funny. As we stood to go, I had just finished telling them how I was unable to get a tour itinerary either from Elisa or from her office and that consequently I was not sharing my whereabouts with her. I did not mention that she seemed to care little about my whereabouts anyway when the mobile went off. Cue cries of 'Oi, oi!', 'He's been rumbled', and the like. I flicked them a couple of fingers and turned left, away from our hotel as they all trooped off laughing, to the right.

'Lorrens,' I answered.

'Hiya, Johnny, time for a nightcap?'

I had clean forgotten about Lori, but emboldened by my teammates' hectoring and a growing sense of independence due to Elisa's continued absence and apparent indifference, I agreed but did give myself a get-out by saying it would have to be fairly quick owing to the match the next day. She gave me directions to the Trust House Forte which proved to be less than five minutes away. The rain was coming down in sheets and, having dried out a little in the curry house, I reached the hotel's lobby looking like a drowned rat. Lori was sat in a club chair next to a fireplace just to the left as I navigated the revolving door. She looked dressed for an important business meeting, soft, cream silk blouse, well-cut black trousers and heels. She looked up, covered her mouth and roared with laughter.

'Come on,' she commanded, 'let's get you dried off.'

I followed her to the lifts like an obedient child and seconds later we were in her room. Without a word she peeled my soaking polo shirt up and over my head, took a towel from the bed, wiped my chest down and with a quick kiss pushed me towards the open bathroom door and told me to get undressed. I had just stripped off completely when she opened the door wide enough to pass through one of the hotel's fluffy, white bathrobes. She looked me up and down and lingered just long enough on my lower half that I nodded my thanks and covered up with the robe.

'Prude,' she laughed as she pulled the door to. 'Nothing I haven't seen before,' she called through the closed door.

Seconds later I plucked up the courage to return to the bedroom, slightly nervous about what I would find. What was I doing? Surely, I knew my visit was not going to be a business meeting and here I was once again bottling it. I put my hand on the door handle, cranked it as quietly as I could and eased the door open. Lori was sat in a chair in the corner of the room, mobile to her ear. She was fully clothed. My relief must have been obvious. She covered the mouthpiece.

'Don't worry – I won't eat you,' she grinned. And as an afterthought, added, 'Yet!'

I gave her a dismissive wave meant to suggest I was not in the least concerned.

Lori nodded towards the mini-bar and indicated drinks and, as I obliged, she spoke into the mobile. 'Look I have told you I don't know how many times – you have no right to use those photos. They were just for us; we agreed that. I will be seeking legal advice if you sell them to any magazine and take you for everything you have...'

Lori listened for a moment. 'No, I told you, I cannot get that sort of money and to be honest, if I could, I would still say no.'

Her ex was clearly on a rant. Lori apparently could not get another word in and suddenly burst into tears as she threw the mobile to the floor. I picked it up to make sure the call had disconnected and, kneeling in front of her, put my hands on her shoulders and held her close.

We stayed that way for fully five minutes until her sobs started to subside. Eventually she looked up at me through her tears with panda-eyes, mascara streaking her face. My heart melted and I gently wiped her tears away. She looked so vulnerable and as she raised her lips to mine, I fell into those deep, blue eyes. I had not been kissed like that for a long time and as she eased the bathrobe from my shoulders, I started to unbutton her blouse. She either went to important meetings bra-less or had slipped that off for my comfort. And then my mobile went off again. I was tempted to ignore it, but Lori said she was going to freshen up, so I accepted the call.

'Johnny, you better get back here, mate.' It was MacLaine. 'Carlisle has just turned up and wants us all in the lobby in fifteen.'

'Damn it! Okay, mate, thanks for the heads up.'

Lori was disappointed but I think I was more so. I apologised profusely, we had one last, lingering kiss and I said I would see her at the ground the next day.

CHAPTER 23

Sunday May 11 1997

That never happened sadly as the match was abandoned shortly after we arrived at the Racecourse Ground. The square was under water following torrential rain that lasted all night and, despite the best efforts of the ground staff, the damage had been done. Scanning around the dressing room at my teammates I had mixed emotions. With the England-Australia series looming I badly wanted some more match practice but looking at the shape of them I was relieved; we would have been slaughtered out there and Carlisle would have gone mental. Again. By the time I got back to the hotel the night before, the team was just assembling in one of the corporate meeting rooms off the lobby. I managed to sneak in with the later arrivals, catching MacLaine's eye and nodding my thanks to him. Most of what Carlisle said, or screamed, is unprintable. The gist, however, was clear. Final warnings for all, a fifty percent deduction in our week's wages and the promise of second-team cricket for the remainder of the season for any repeat offence. The journey home on the team bus must have been a quiet one. Thankfully, I had driven and, even better, Ralph had decided to stay another night to give himself time to explore Derby. I would have some time to myself on the way home, but I had planned to bring up the apparent link between Barry Miller and Willby.

We met in the restaurant, after I had checked out, for coffee. The rest of the team were already on the bus home and we had the place to ourselves. The room was over-warm and with the high alcohol levels in me I could feel a light sweat on my forehead.

'Shame about the game, Johnny; I was looking forward to it.'

'We're on a good run in the one-dayers, too,' I agreed, blowing across the top of my scalding Americano and mopping my brow. 'So, what's the big attraction about Derby, then?'

Ralph put his coffee mug down on the small table between us. 'Cathedral. Second tallest perpendicular tower in the country,' he smiled.

'Busman's holiday, eh?'

Ralph grinned, and pushed the sleeves of his sweater up to his elbows. I noticed again his forearms; they were huge, sinewy. For his age he looked in very good condition. 'Kitty gets a bit cross with me to be honest. Whenever we go anywhere there is always a building I want to check out so as she is not here I am going to make the most of it.'

'Here's to that,' I agreed as we chinked coffee mugs.

'I had another call from Jack this morning,' Ralph added, seemingly as an afterthought.

'Oh?'

'Spoke to him this time. Nice chap.'

'Jack? Can be, when he wants,' I said with a grin. 'Did you allay his fears?'

'Oh yes,' Ralph paused. 'He was questioning the vomitory dimensions.'

'Ah, was he?' I had not a clue what he was on about. 'But you put him right?'

'I did. He went away happy.'

We chatted for a few minutes more before I made my excuses and went to check out.

'Send Elisa my love,' Ralph said as we shook hands. 'Tell her not to forget her mum and dad, would you?'

'I will, after I've told her not to forget about me,' I replied.

Ralph smiled as he pushed through the revolving door and into a perfect, sunny spring morning; perfect for cricket but for the underwater pitch. As he disappeared around a corner I suddenly remembered that I had wanted to ask him about the link between Barry Miller and Willby Construction. Missed opportunity; I would have to catch him later.

I dialled Lori's number on the mobile but there was no answer so I obtained the number for the Trust House Forte hotel she was staying at from the desk but there was no answer from her room and the hotel receptionist there refused to say whether or not she had checked out. I nosed the Vectra out into the thin Derby traffic and found myself thinking about Lori's problem. It sounded as if Phillipe was upping the ante and, judging by her reaction, Lori was really upset and worried about the ramifications. I called her again from the services at Watford Gap, but she was still not answering.

Back in Epsom I discovered a message from Elisa. I only half listened as I made trips back and forth to the car to bring in my bags, blazer and bat.

'Hiya! Dallas today – managed to check out the Grassy Knoll! Oh my – the Texas Book Depository is still there; it's like the place has been preserved in a time warp. Eerie! Oh, and we had an amazing party last night. You'll never guess who was there? Pearl Jam! Oh, and did you see my n...'

I stabbed at the 'stop' button but in my growing anger I missed and hit 'delete' instead. I did not have the heart to listen to Elisa's babble. I found myself more worried about Lori this morning. I still could not get hold of her but, remembering a promise made a few weeks earlier, I went to the study and rummaged in my box of odds and ends until I found it. The card was one of a set of Hitchcock postcards I had picked up on a whim at a festival for the great director at the BFI a few years before but found I had no real use for. I returned the rest to the box, found a pen on the desk and scribbled on the reverse of the one with the *Strangers on a Train* poster: *You do mine and I'll do yours! Johnny* xxx

Pen poised over the space reserved for the address, I realised that I still did not know where Lori lived. Slightly frustrated that I was not able to send it immediately I propped it up against the PC and determined to get her address later that day, although my repeated calls to her mobile achieved nothing more than a series of left messages that remained unanswered.

Carlisle had called us in for training at 2:00 p.m., so I had a little time to catch up on mail at home, writing cheques to settle bills and to do a couple of loads of washing. Carlisle's decision was in part due to our Benson & Hedges match against Sussex the next day and, I suspected, as punishment for the Derby misdemeanours. The day was warm with a strong breeze which helped get everything dry before I got into the Vectra again for the drive up into London. The south had missed out on the torrential rain up in the North Midlands and the forecast was decent.

I called in on Jackie Kray who reminded me that I had been planning to ask Ralph about Miller's apparently exclusive arrangement with Willby. I had missed the chance to ask him about that but had already decided that there was probably nothing sinister in it, that perhaps Miller did sufficiently well from the relationship that he did not need to look elsewhere. Jackie agreed with me but suggested I ask Ralph anyway.

The session started in the nets and although I did not get a bat, I did have the chance to turn my arm over and was pleased to find that the discomfort I had been experiencing was easing. I caught Sam's eye as she was loading balls into the bowling machine in the next net where Pallant looked to be in supreme form. The addition of the captaincy seemed to be suiting him just fine. I made a 'c' for coffee sign at Sam and she smiled broadly as she mouthed 'soon'. Dench was in my net and he frowned at me, gesticulating that I should hurry up.

'Lorrens, do leave the women alone,' he barked.

'Calm down, Alan,' I replied sweetly, wishing not for the first time that I was a fast bowler and that I could send him down a bouncer. Instead, I gave the next delivery a real rip, pitched it just outside his leg-stump and watched as it gripped the artificial surface, spat viciously and, clipping the inside edge of his Gray Nicolls, hit middle stump. My exaggerated celebration annoyed him and that rather pleased me too.

Training moved outside for some fielding practice. Starting with some long-range catching drills, Carlisle lofted balls for each of us in turn, high into the deep-blue, cloudless sky. My first one, a real steepler, came out of the sun and, without sunglasses on, I completely misjudged the trajectory and had to make a final, desperate lunge before missing it completely. The look of disdain on Carlisle's face was clear even from a forty-metre distance. Sniggers from my teammate spoke as much of a 'glad-it's-not-me' reaction as it did of our normal bantering ways. I determined that that would be the only catch I dropped and made sure the sunnies were on for the next one. We moved on to slip-catching and finally some throwing drills, both long-range and short-range. No more dropped catches for me and a couple of decent shies at the single-stump target. Carlisle gathered us together at the end of the session, close to the square, which at Surrey's headquarters is made up of twenty-five or more strips and consequently is actually a very large oblong in shape, and reminded us that the Derby antics would be regarded as a one-off. He reiterated the penalty for any subsequent offences and gave us his thoughts on the next day's B&H encounter with Sussex. He went through their key threats and reminded us, not that we needed it, that like us Sussex had won three of their first four matches too and that a win for Surrey would in theory leave us with a more favourable draw in the quarters. He stressed the importance of not assuming another easy win against them like we had enjoyed a few weeks before.

I showered and popped into the pavilion's Long Room to take a look at the anniversary painting. It was cool in there after the warmth of the late-spring sunshine and with the blinds halfway down it had the feeling of an art gallery what with the old paintings on the walls and the original Victorian features of the old building. The painting was on a large easel in one corner, by the fireplace, cordoned off with a plum coloured rope. Andrew Goldrich was sat before it on a high stool, wearing his cliched, paint-daubed smock, one finger laced through his palette as he put the finishing touches to the face of one of the VIPs who stood on the grass in front of the pavilion's white, picket fence. By this time I had reached Goldrich and stood silently behind him, watching as he expertly created a likeness from a small photograph propped up on the easel, in front of the huge canvas.

'Good God,' I breathed quietly.

Goldrich gave a slight start and swung around with a furious expression.

'Do not creep up on me like that,' he growled with his famous temper clearly on display. It was widely discussed that he was a volatile character, liked a drink and was well-known for painting lifelike but not necessarily flattering portraits of his subjects. I decided not to rattle him any further lest he elect to paint me in too honest a fashion.

'Sorry,' I began, 'I didn't mean to startle you. It was just a shock to see Barry Miller in the front row with the VIPs.'

A smile broke across his craggy features, his trademark shock of curly, grey hair barely contained by his, I hoped, ironic French beret. 'Complete tosser,' he said quietly. 'Paid his money so I have to paint him where I am told. Not my decision.'

His bitter tone perhaps reflected the pain of the loss of an artist's independence. For me, it did seem a bit rich. Miller had effectively been thrown out of the Club but all these years later his money had been gladly accepted and for that he had a place alongside a group of dignitaries which included a couple of famous pop stars, a former Prime Minister, a group of senior political figures alongside a few Lords and an even greater number of Knights of the Realm. Upon consideration, perhaps Miller's inclusion amongst this group was more appropriate than I had first considered. Smiling, I asked Goldrich if current first-team players were still in the plans.

He sighed again, lifted his brush from the canvas and without turning to face me said, 'That is my instruction. You lot are going to be up here somewhere.' He indicated, with a dismissive wave, the general area in the huge canvas that had been mooted a few weeks before.

'Hope you have a nice picture of me,' I said with a grin.

He half-turned. 'I have a nice one of your wife,' he said matter of factly. Charmer. But it made me suddenly reflect on the prospect of being sat next to Elisa in the painting. It could be hanging in the Long Room for decades to come but would Elisa and I still be together?

I was on my way to visit Miller in his office on the floor above Jackie's when I suddenly realised that I could not recall supplying photos of either Elisa or myself for the painting but supposed that the Club had done it on our behalf. Would have been nice to have chosen them really. Elisa's would have been fabulous whatever, whereas I would have had to spend a little longer finding a good one of me. I was surprised to hear a cheery, 'Come in,' to my knock.

I was not certain but felt that Miller's initial reaction on seeing me lacked warmth at best and reflected unease at worst. Either way, he quickly assumed a friendly, smiling, professional demeanour.

'Johnny, old chap, how lovely to see you,' he beamed.

'Barry,' I replied noncommittally.

'And what brings you in today? Social or business?'

Given that we did not really know each other very well, a social call was presumably unlikely, I thought, but I wanted this to be a positive exchange. I was not sure what I wanted to achieve but his relationship with Sally was still puzzling me as was his relationship with Willby. I could not get past Willby's successful, post-deadline bid. And I could not quite satisfy myself over the details of Sally's last night.

'Bit of both, I guess,' I replied, lowering myself into the seat opposite him that he had indicated. The office was tiny, Miller's desk practically filling the space, showing why Sally had been relegated to the library with me. I declined the coffee he offered; I did not want to be with him for one second longer than was necessary. In my mind he was involved in Sally's death in some way even though there seemed to be nothing whatsoever to link him with it. That 'M is a monster' comment and the scribble on Sally's notepad seemed like evidence to me but evidence the police were totally unaware of. I wondered if perhaps I should be sharing that with them.

'How are you doing without Sally? I imagine things are busier here now on your own.'

'Oh, Johnny, what a sad state of affairs. She was a lovely girl with her whole life ahead of her. So sad,' Miller replied sombrely. His sadness seemed plausible.

'And the police are still none the wiser?' I assumed that Miller had no information that was not already in the public domain but wanted to see his reaction.

'Not that I am aware of, no. We had that quick drink in Fleet Street that I told you about. I thought we would be dining too, to celebrate the building contract being signed, but Sally said she had arranged a drink with a friend on the way home so had to bail early.'

'Did that make you angry, Barry?'

The look of surprise on Miller's face was what I wanted to see. I wanted to see guilt too, but I did not see a trace of that.

'What?' he asked uncertainly. 'What do you mean by that, Johnny? I don't think I like the tone of this. Are you making an accusation?'

I sat silently looking intently at him. The silence lasted several awkward seconds. Miller broke it.

'If that's what you are doing you had better be careful – I can make life very difficult for you. I suggest you go and find that friend she was going to meet; that's who the police should be looking for.'

'Who's threatening who, Barry?'

Regaining his composure, Miller's clubbable persona quickly reappeared. 'No threats, old boy. I know how close you two were; you are just lashing out – I get that.'

'Why would Sally have left me a message then? *M is a monster.*'

He spread his hands wide. 'Not a clue, old chap. I really doubt that that is about me,' he laughed.

'Barry, you do have something of a reputation in that department,' I retorted.

'Unproven!'

'Yeah, right. Barry, another question. Why do you only work for Willby?'

He paused for only a second, a slight flicker in his eyes as he responded. 'Firstly, none of your business; secondly, I like them and they like me and thirdly, what the fuck has that got to do with anything?' Composure gone again.

I locked eyes with his, cupped my right hand across my mouth and mumbled, 'Missed deadline.'

The look of pure hate in his eyes was extraordinary. 'You just do not understand the process, Lorrens. You stick to the cricket and let me do my job. If you don't, I will need to take this higher – tell the management that you are interfering.'

I stood up and, reaching the door, opened it and turned to face him. 'Do your worst, you corrupt bastard.'

I stepped out into the corridor and looked at my hand as I let go of the door handle. It was shaking. I trotted back down the stairs to the Club Office and had just reached the door when I heard raised voices from further down the corridor. I paused to listen. The voices were muffled but both were clearly angry. I walked closer quietly until I was immediately outside Sir Kenneth Parslow's office. I could only make out the odd word here and there, but I was sure I heard 'stands' and 'construction' and I thought possibly, 'Miller'. One of the voices, on the law of averages, belonged to Parslow; the other was familiar despite the muffling but I could not place it. Though they were both angry they did not seem to be angry with each other but not wishing to be caught listening I hurried on my way.

Jackie was alone in the Club Office and I told her not to worry about exploring the Miller/Willby relationship, that I had already done it.

'And?'

'He was very cross,' I grinned. 'Definitely something dodgy going on and he threatened to go to 'the management' if I don't let it drop.'

Jackie looked concerned. 'Be careful, Johnny. Don't give anyone a chance to ruin things for you; if you rock the boat too much bang goes your England recall and it could mess things up here too. Check it with Ralph, first?'

'I meant to do that up in Derby and was waiting for the right moment, but he ended up staying there for another night, so I travelled back alone. He did bring up the plans, though. Seems my brother has been calling him to talk about the numbers.'

'Oh?' Jackie looked up from her PC where she had been tapping away as we spoke.

'Ralph seems to have answered his questions so no drama there, at least. Any idea what vomitory dimensions are?'

'Not a clue,' she laughed. 'Doesn't sound very pleasant, though.'

I smiled. 'Internet working?'

'Barely,' she grimaced. 'It's on the go slow today; took ages to load up this morning. Let me check it out and I'll call?'

I nodded my thanks, blew Jackie a kiss and headed for home. The sun was warm, and with the Surrey flag fluttering proudly atop of the pavilion and the cloudless, blue sky I felt my mood lifting. As I approached the Hobbs Gates I stopped in my tracks. Ralph's ancient, red E-Type was parked over against the boundary wall.

CHAPTER 24

Monday May 12 1997

A decent crowd was already building up by the time we finished our warm-up drills and, having signed a couple of sunhats, a copy of my 'How to bowl ... spin' book and a few scorecards and scrapbooks on the Bedser Stand steps, I made my way out onto the balcony with a steaming mug of tea. The sky was a light blue with thin clouds scudding high above on the firm southerly breeze. The forecast was good for a full day's play and, with our opponents level on points at the top of the group, today's winners would top the group and get the better of the quarter-final draw. I had looked at most of the papers in the dressing room and, of the few which bothered to preview the day's matches, not one predicted a Sussex win. Pallant had won the toss and took a nano-second to bat on what promised to be a real belter. Great news for us – not so good for me; with the one-day internationals fast approaching I desperately wanted to get out there with a bat in my hand. As I took a large gulp of tea, I thought of Summers' call to me earlier.

I was finishing my breakfast at about six o'clock when the mobile went off and, supposing it to be Elisa calling at such an early hour, ran back up to the bedroom where it was on charge. Nothing to be gained by avoiding her. If I had known it was Summers I would likely have let it ring; I really was not in the mood. He was his normal, larger-than-life self, wishing me well and predicting a huge Surrey win and a bagful of wickets for me. I had said something about time at the crease being more important to me, but he waved that away, arguing that a few wickets would seal my place in the starting eleven. This, of course, was central to his plan. Or, at least, one of his plans. He also told me that he had a photo session booked for the following day at a studio in Pimlico and asked could I get away from training for an hour. On reflection, my obvious testiness towards him was already feeling a little unreasonable. He was trying to rebuild his life and, whilst I was uneasy about his betting plan, I could at least reassure myself that I was not really involved in that, though the benefits of his analysis of my batting promised to make a big difference to me with the bat. I was sceptical about the beer importing to be honest, but it was not costing me anything save an hour or two for the publicity pictures and if it went anywhere could bring in a few quid too. I determined to call him later and to be a little more gracious.

There must have been around three thousand in the ground as Rennie and Driver followed the Sussex team out onto the field and they received a great reception from the largely home crowd in recognition of our qualification through to the knock-out stages of the Benson and Hedges Cup. It was a competition I have always had a soft spot for, probably because my cricket-loving father had made me watch the conclusion of Surrey's only successful campaign to date, back in 1974. Back then, as a five-year-old, I had sat on the hugely uncomfortable wooden seats in the old Grandstand alternately enjoying the cricket and asking when it would be over. I cannot say that I really remember Younis Ahmed top scoring for Surrey, Ken Higgs' hat-trick or John Edrich lifting the golden trophy, but I can at least say I was there. We now had a chance to do what none of the Surrey teams since had been able. That was incentive enough for me.

Our openers set off at a furious pace and by the time the opening bowlers had been withdrawn for the eleventh over we were already at 70 without loss. The onslaught continued and Sussex bowler after bowler received the same treatment. The away supporters grew increasingly quiet as the score mounted apart from one, periodic booming call of 'Sussex by the sea', which sounded ever more mournful as Rennie and Driver both approached their tons, neck and neck. It was the younger of the two, the left-handed Driver who got there first with a slashing cut through point for four, followed two balls later by Rennie as he smashed one back over the bowler's head for a steepling six that was dropped by a gentleman in the pavilion's middle tier. In fairness to that gentleman, he had probably never had a sniff there in the past several decades. And we still had fifteen overs remaining.

Although our two openers went pretty much as soon as they had posted their centuries, the runs kept coming and with five overs remaining and our score on 322 for 2, I put my bat away and found a corner to do some light stretches. Pallant had a few minutes earlier passed me the binoculars which we keep on the balcony, indicating the large patches of rough that the Sussex quicks had churned up in their follow-throughs and told me to expect an early entry into the fray. When our innings ended on 378 for 2, agonisingly ten short of Essex's record Benson & Hedges team score, the game looked as good as won. The Sussex supporters were silent as their team trudged off the field and up the steps to their dressing room next to ours. They looked like a beaten side, but we knew they were a dangerous one as evidenced by their position alongside us at the top of the group.

The between innings interval seemed to last forever. I could not wait to get started and although I had to wait for eight overs of pace from MacLaine and Molander I was ready with sweater half off before Pallant threw the ball to me. My first over was decent as I explored the patch outside the right-hander's leg stump. A couple went for singles down the legside and Pallant brought fine-leg up to close off that scoring option, but the other deliveries suggested there was plenty of turn down there. I was pleased that Sussex had ten right-handers in their line-up. O'Brien's off spin from the Vauxhall End would not benefit from the rough patches that I would enjoy but he bowled a tight line and length and tended to frustrate batsmen into making poor judgements.

This promised to be fun.

As I led the team off the pitch a little over an hour later, match ball in hand, I acknowledged the applause from the pavilion to my left and the Bedser Stand ahead of me. 6 for 23 from my seven overs were my best one-day figures to date and would do my England starting eleven plans no harm at all, especially given the quality of Sussex's in-form batting line up. The 250-odd winning margin was huge and a real statement to the other teams left in the competition. Perhaps this would be our year.

I only stayed for a couple of quick drinks in the dressing room as most of the lads were pretty swiftly heading out on the town. I had sneaked my mobile into the dressing room toilets and called Lori. She had not answered my calls since I had run out on her in Derby and I needed to know she was okay. Her ex was clearly being a complete bastard and I felt I had let her down too. I felt a little helpless as I had no address for her. She was still not answering. And she still did not answer me when I continued calling from home. I had just clicked the mobile off having reached her messaging service for the tenth time when it rang in my hand.

'Lori?' I started. 'At last, I've been trying to get you all afternoon,' I said with relief.

There was a pause and a strange echoing silence for a moment.

'Johnny, it's me. Who is Lori?'

Shit. It was Elisa. Thinking on my feet I came up with the best lie I could. And perhaps I could use it to my advantage.

'Bitch from News of the World, pestering me for a quote about your antics in the States.'

'My what?' she demanded heatedly.

'I know! Where do they get this stuff from,' I seemed to agree. 'She said you were having an affair with Le Dare, that you had been seen coming in and out of his bedroom in various hotels and that you two had been an item way back.'

'And what did you tell her?'

'Told her to get stuffed and that that was my quote.'

'Oh, Johnny, I'm sorry that you have had to put up with that crap. How dare they!'

'Don't worry about it, babe,' I reassured her. 'She also asked me what I thought about the photos in the papers with you draped all over Le Dare.'

'What did you say about that,' she asked with a hint of uncertainty in her voice.

'I didn't. And I didn't give her the satisfaction of denying that you and LeDare used to an item either.'

There was an awkward pause before Elisa spoke again.

'That part does have some truth to it,' she said quietly.

My turn to pause. I suppose I should have realised that this part of the story might be true – it was too specific. I felt a little nauseous suddenly and saw my knuckles whiten as I gripped the handset more tightly. My eyes stung a little and at the same time I felt acutely guilty of betraying Elisa, first with Eleanor and then with Lori.

'Johnny?'

'Still here,' I mumbled. 'So how is the book going?'

'Which one?' she replied, her voice back to normal.

'How many are you writing?' I laughed. 'The tour diary, of course? You seem to have access to all areas, so I imagine there's going to be plenty of scandal in there?'

'Well, when the cameras are not around they are not quite the hotel-trashing yobs they would have us believe. Cris actually asked me to spice up some parts to maintain the bad-boy image.'

'Cris? Well at least you are there to tell your readers what goes on in the bedroom,' I said, rather unkindly.

'Johnny, that is not fair. As for being seen going into bedrooms your contact fails to realise or to mention that the band is staying in suites of rooms. The bedrooms do not come directly off of the corridors.'

'Methinks she doth protest too much,' I said with a chuckle. 'Anyway, Elisa, I do think it would have been reasonable for you to have told me that you and Le Dare were once partners before you went travelling round the States with him. Don't you?'

She paused before replying sadly. 'Yes. But I didn't want to worry you and that was a very long time ago.'

'Look, let's sort this out when you get back home. I'll keep the tabloids at bay the best I can, but they will just not let this drop, especially as I am back in the England squad.'

'You are? Oh, Johnny that is fabulous news – I am so pleased for you. Why didn't you tell me? When did you find out?'

'I don't know, a week or so ago, I guess.'

'A week ago?! Why didn't you tell me?'

'You were busy, you weren't calling, I had no idea where you were and I had no idea you were interested.'

There was a muffled sob. It gave me a perverse pleasure to hear that she was upset. 'Look, Elisa, I have a lot to do today so as I say, let's sort this when you are back. When is that likely to be?'

There was a snuffle as she replied sadly. 'Middle of next week. Wednesday earliest.'

Later that evening Lori finally picked up. She seemed brighter and she did not seem to be harbouring any ill will. I had the *Strangers on a Train* postcard in front of me as we chatted.

'You know, I still have no idea where you live,' I said.

'And best you don't,' Lori replied with a laugh. 'I think Phillipe's having me watched. I don't want you getting dragged into this, Johnny. Not this side of the Australian series, at least.'

It all seemed a little overly dramatic and had me wondering whether she was being completely honest with me. Did she actually have a partner, perhaps one that she lived with? This business with Phillipe seemed increasingly far-fetched. Would he really go to the lengths of having her watched? There had been a lot in the press in recent years about stalkers, but I somehow could not quite believe it.

'Look, Lori, I have something I need to get to you. Where do I send it?'

'Why not wait until we meet again,' she said. 'You can give it to me then,' she said in a husky voice.

'When will that be?' I replied as I touched the postcard where it remained propped against the PC in the study. I realised that I really needed to see her.

'Be patient. It'll be a surprise.'

The line went dead.

CHAPTER 25

Tuesday May 13 1997

The papers were very complimentary about Surrey's Benson and Hedges campaign and about my bowling spell the previous day. A couple of them went further, suggesting that my 6-fer demanded a certain start for the one-dayers. Krishnan Singh, in his Mirror column, was even more forthright, arguing that the selectors would be mad to overlook me, though he cautioned that:

Lorrens's private life remains a concern. If he can just focus on the cricket, without the distractions of his wife's involvement in the Toadlust saga, he could be the difference this year.

If Singh only knew about my other various distractions he might not have been so positive about my return. I guessed it was only a matter of time before he rang me again.

As I pulled out of Longdown Lane and headed down the Reigate Road towards Ewell Village, the sun finally broke through the thick cloud cover. Ten o'clock. Bang on time. The rest of the day was supposed to see the cloud burn off and a high of 22 degrees – a perfect spring day. I nudged the cassette back into the car's player and turned the volume up. I was in the mood for some old punk and as the brief drum intro to Buzzcocks' *I Don't Mind* boomed out of the Vectra's stereo, my spirits lifted and I sang along, all the way to Tolworth. The A3 was unusually quiet and by the time I had treated myself to some classics from a bunch of old favourites like Sham 69, The Heartbreakers, The Lurkers and The Vibrators, I was pulling into the underground car park next to Wimbledon station. Within minutes I was on a District Line tube heading into town.

Summers had called earlier with the studio directions and after a change at Victoria it was one stop down on the Victoria Line to Pimlico. I quickly found the Alderney Street address Summers had given me, saw the sparkling, new-looking, *Sebastian Moran – Photographer,* brass nameplate on the wall next to the door and rang the bell.

Summers was already there and showed me through into one of the ground floor studios, a large one with white ceiling, walls and floor. A huge, white paper screen covered one entire wall and curled onto the floor to eliminate the wall/floor join. Three very expensive looking cameras were set up in an arc, each with its own attached silver umbrella and flashlight combination, and all focused on an arrangement of a couple of dozen large, white cardboard boxes, each emblazoned with *New England Beers* and my grinning, pointillist face in black and white. Summers waved a hand expansively towards the set up.

'What do you think, Johnny?'

It looked really professional. 'Impressive,' I replied. 'Wasn't expecting anything on this scale.'

'Well, mate, if a thing's worth doing, and all that. Look we have got to get this right and we are on a really tight turnaround. Sebastian is an old mate and owes me a favour or two. He's normally booked for months in advance but squeezed us in, so we only have an hour tops. Did you bring all the stuff I told you?'

I had. My full cricket gear, a lounge suit and rather oddly, I thought, swimming trunks. I patted the large suitcase I was still holding. 'Yep, it's all here. What's the plan?'

'The plan,' Summers began, grandly, 'is a series of photos aimed at different markets. I have already bought a half-page ad in next month's Cricketer and we will be promoting initially in the Evening Standard and in some of the lads' mags too. So, it's cricket clobber for the Cricketer, lounge suit for the Standard and...'

'Swimming trunks for the lads' mags?' I groaned.

'You betcha,' Summers boomed, slapping me jovially on the back. Even his jovial slap sent a minor shockwave through me, packed as it was with 20-stone of ex-cricketer.

At that moment a tall, thin man of about thirty-five swept into the studio; unfashionably long hair, heavily greased back so that it lay perfectly flat on his head, finishing in little upcurls around the back of his neck. An open, white silk shirt with paisley cravat, jodhpurs and knee-length, tan riding-boots. He was quite a statement.

'You must be Johnny,' he lisped, holding out a hand.

I was not sure whether I was meant to shake it or kiss it. I plumped for the shake. 'Sebastian,' I said, with a nod.

'How divine to meet you, dear boy. Mark has told me a lot about you,' he replied as he hurried off to adjust a camera. 'Mark, shall we start with the cricket scene?'

Summers gave Moran the thumbs up and started to open my suitcase. It was as if I was suddenly invisible. Moran continued to busy himself with cameras and lights and made miniscule adjustments to the crate arrangement, creating a central stack of four boxes surrounded by several lower ones. Summers pulled out all of my cricket gear, hung my suit up on a hanger and hung that on a coat stand in a corner of the room as a young lady appeared and beckoned me over to the dressing table in the opposite corner and waited to apply my make-up as I put on the white cricket shirt that Summers thrust into my hands. Time was clearly of the essence.

With only about thirty minutes of our studio time remaining, I was fully kitted out and ready to bat. Sebastian seated me on the highest stack of boxes and propped my bat up against my pads as Summers appeared with a tall, frosted half-pint glass full of beer and the bottle. Once again, my pointillist face from the boxes on the bottle, but with text. *'New England Beers – Raspberry IPA'*. I have to say it looked good. I went to take a sip.

'No!' Summers barked. Then more calmly, 'Don't want to spoil that frosting on the outside, Johnny.'

I grinned. 'Fair point. Smells good, though.'

'Tastes great too,' he agreed. 'We are competing with other beers, but I think we can drag people away from those dreadful alcopops...'

'Are we ready, gentlemen?' Sebastian interrupted. 'Time is money!'

Moran took charge and in ten minutes must have shot over two hundred frames with me in my cricket gear: different angles, poses, shirt and bat logos covered, uncovered, batting helmet on, batting helmet off, his voice increasingly hysterical.

'And breathe,' he lisped. 'Great work, Johnny. Get changed into your suit and let Sharelle touch up your face. Back on set in five.'

The same format was in place for the lounge suit photos and after a little attention to my face I slipped out to the toilet to slip on the Bermudas. As I walked back into the studio I heard Summers answering Moran.

'Yes, they are here, don't worry.'

'Who is here?' I asked, but Summers was busy with another change to the set. Gone was the central stack, replaced by a sun lounger.

I guess I should have known the minute Summers told me to bring my trunks and as the six very pretty young women entered the studio in dressing gowns, I was immediately fearing the worst. I shot a 'what the heck?' look at Summers but he simply smiled and gave me the thumbs up. Moran had clearly briefed them and, with me lying on the sun lounger, a bottle of beer in hand, they handed their gowns to Sharelle and proceeded to take their positions on the beer crates around me. They were wearing the tiniest bikinis, striped, in the egg and bacon colours of the MCC. I was not sure this was a particularly wise move but had little time to think as Moran was becoming increasingly strident in his commands.

He worked at a furious pace, alternately snapping away and issuing instructions. Moving a hand here, a foot there or tilting a head as if the women were mere mannequins. I began to have misgivings before Moran paused, took a couple of steps back, turned his head on one side and closed one eye.

'Lose the tops please, ladies,' he ordered. 'Sharelle, the lotion, please.'

I would be a complete charlatan if I tried to claim that what happened next was completely awful but, with Moran snapping away with the three static cameras and a hand-held and Summers nodding knowingly in the background, I could see this set of pictures curtailing any comeback that was just about to happen. By now I was completely smothered in suntan lotion with twelve hands all over me. I could see by the clock on the wall over Moran's head that the session was almost over when he suddenly exclaimed, 'Get the spliff!'

That was enough for me and, with an 'excuse me, ladies', I literally slid off of the lounger and skidded past Sharelle, dripping lotion and, snatching one of the robes she was still clutching, dashed from the studio.

I did not say much to Summers when I returned to pack my case. He had already done it. The women had gone as had Moran and Sharelle. Summers could tell I was not happy.

'That seemed to go well, Johnny,' he said cautiously.

'You think?'

'I do,' he replied confidently now. 'Sebastian knows what he is doing, Johnny.'

'Do you, though?' I snapped.

'Don't fret, my friend. You will get a first look at the prints and we will choose together. I know you are cross about the spliff, but you were probably wise to walk out at that point, so no harm done.'

'No harm done?' I retorted, incredulous that he could not see how damaging the sun lounger pictures would be.

'Look, Johnny, I'm not stupid. The powers that be at Lord's will hate *those,* but you have a sort of maverick image based on your music background, marriage to Elisa, the Aussie tour with the big spliff picture on Bondi Beach – you know the stuff. But it's all gone a bit quiet on that front. This could just remind people that there is more to Johnny Lorrens than a disgraced player who has served his time, reformed his character, regained his England place...'

Summers could see by the look on my face that I was not buying this. 'It's not like I have been having good press lately, though, is it?'

Summers paused before replying. 'Seems to be Elisa with the rock'n'roll bad girl image these days, Johnny. You are more in the role of the rock'n'roll widow.'

I could not even reply to that. From his point of view it was true. But from my side of things, I had not exactly been a model of virtue since the Elisa stories had emerged. I simply glared at him.

'Let's decide once we have seen the photos, okay?' Summers said with a chuckle as he held the studio door open for me.

I was on the District Line, heading back to Wimbledon, when my mobile rang. I was right, it had not taken long for Krishnan Singh to make contact. He was well informed. It was from Singh that I had learnt about my England recall, from Singh that I learnt about Elisa's relationship with Crispin Le Dare.

'Any comment on the Toadlust developments?'

'Krishnan, what the hell have Toadlust got to do with me? Aside, of course, from your allegation that my wife used to go out with Le Dare.' I was not going to admit to Singh that I knew he was right.

'Are you saying I am wrong, Johnny?'

'Just saying it has nothing to do with you and I would ask that you stop writing rubbish about me and Elisa. Elisa being on the Toadlust tour is not a distraction to me. Period.'

'Fair enough,' he replied. 'But what's your comment on the news from Shreveport?'

'Shreveport?'

'Louisana.'

'I know where it is. What of it?'

'You haven't heard? Toadlust played there last night and caused something of a riot. The good ol' Southern folk didn't like their brand of cross-dressing, sacrilegious imagery and highly offensive language. A bunch of rednecks stormed the stage, beat up Le Dare and the group had to have police protection to get out of the concert hall. Then back at the hotel there was a record-burning in the street outside.'

'News to me,' I replied tersely. 'And, no comment.'

'Have you been able to speak with your wife?'

'Not since the gig, no. I am sure she will update me in due course.'

'Are you not worried about her safety, Johnny? They do not seem the safest people to be around.' Singh's persistence was beginning to grate.

'Krishnan, go pester the Home Secretary. The story is about his son, not my wife.'

'Oh yes, I've been checking that one out. It's a great story but is not in the least bit true. The twins' father is a senior police officer and their mother works as a CEO in a large hospital trust I am told.'

'Whatever,' I replied as I clicked the mobile off and sat from Southfields to Wimbledon, weighing up the mobile in my hand and wondering what could possibly happen next.

CHAPTER 26

Wednesday May 14 1997

We chinked glasses and I took a large gulp of the Old Hooky. Delicious, one real ale I do like, and just what I needed after a very warm drive down from Epsom. The M25 was at its hideous worst, making me rethink my thoughts on traffic jams, but thankfully the M40 was largely clear. Under a clear, blue sky with not a cloud in sight, the Cotswolds looked at its very best. Burford was awaking from its sleep as I drove through around 9:00 a.m., and the A424 north towards Stow was clear enough to let me put my foot down. The field edges were alive with scarlet splashes as poppies responded to the early morning sunlight. I took a right to take the narrow road through Idbury and Foscot and once again pondered a move away from the London area. That would realistically mean a move to one of Gloucestershire, Somerset or Warwickshire but there were worse things to consider. I was beginning to feel that perhaps a change was what I needed. That thought took be aback. I had been fixed on playing for Surrey from a very young age. It almost shocked me that I was even admitting to myself the possibility of leaving. And what shocked me more was that I was thinking of a change for me but no thought of Elisa.

I *was* thinking about Eleanor Framsell again, though. Jackie Kray had called as I was about to set off that morning. She had forgotten to tell me that Sally's mother had called three times the day before saying that it was imperative that she spoke to me. I groaned inwardly and wondered why I had let myself get involved with her. This was unlikely to end well but I supposed I would have to call her.

'How are the studies going?' I asked, wiping froth from my top lip.

The King's Head was quiet at this post-lunch hour. I had parked up around 9:30 a.m., before the old pub had opened and taken a walk through to Adlestrop and back round to Kingham before meeting Jack at 2:00 p.m. It was great to walk along deserted footpaths thinking of absolutely nothing and I sat opposite my brother feeling refreshed.

'Slowly,' he grimaced. 'Trying to balance it with earning some money.'

'I meant to ask about that. How are you supporting yourself?'

'Maintenance loan and some bar work in Bourton. Nothing glamorous, I'm afraid.'

I smiled at the thought of Jack in the role of friendly barkeep. I couldn't quite see it. 'Ralph tells me he managed to reassure you about your concerns with the building plans,' I said, taking another slug of Old Hooky.

Jack nearly dropped his glass. 'He what? He did nothing of the sort;

the opposite, in fact!'

My brother's vehemence startled me. 'But Ralph told me that he had reassured you about the vomit dimensions.'

'Vomitory.' Jack corrected.

'Yeah, whatever they are,' I said with a smile.

'Vomitory dimensions are one of the most essential parts of the build,' Jack said heatedly. 'They are the points of ingress and egress to the seating areas in a stand. They need to be wide enough to get people in quickly and, more importantly, out at the end of the game or in the event of an emergency evacuation.' He thumped the table to emphasize his point causing the few people in the bar to look our way.

'And?'

'And yours aren't,' he replied, downing the last of his pint as he headed back to the bar for two more.

I pondered his words as I waited for him to return, wondering why Ralph had been so casual when we talked about my brother up in Derby. Why would he make the bold claim that he had reassured Jack when if anything, he had done the very opposite? And why was Ralph's car at The Oval on Sunday? It suddenly dawned on me! It was Ralph's voice I had heard in that heated discussion with Sir Ken Parslow. I certainly had no idea that they were in any way connected but it seems that they must have been; parking at The Oval is severely restricted so for Ralph to be permitted to park suggested that he was no ordinary Club member but I had known him for two years and had had no hint of him being anything more than a long-standing Surrey supporter.

Jack placed the pint glass on the beer mat in front of me and skidded a pack of Walkers salt and vinegar crisps over to me.

'Tell me more about vomitory dimensions then.'

'Not much more to tell, Johnny. Key principle is to cram as many seats as you can into the stand because that makes more money. But because most people don't arrive well in advance of the play, you need wide enough pathways to get the fans in quickly and, like I said, out as quickly as possible at breaks, end of play and especially in the event of an evacuation.'

'And our stands are not consistent with that?'

'Sadly not,' Jack replied, tersely.

I reflected on that. 'Isn't it a pretty simple matter of just tweaking the drawings? You, know, lose a few seats, widen the exits?'

'It would be, yes, but the Club is clearly working to a tight timeframe and don't want anything holding this up. Besides, that would also reduce income over time.'

'Surely planning permission will not be granted if the authorities are unhappy with anything on the plans; or am I being naïve?'

Jack drained his pint. 'Look, I am no expert, Johnny – I'm still training, for goodness sake. But I do not trust these big building companies. They'll cut corners wherever they can. What worries me more, though, is your father-in-law telling you that he had reassured me. Far from it and I told him!'

'Well, he seemed pretty relaxed about it to me. What did he say?'

'It's not so much what he said,' Jack began. 'It is more the fact that he didn't even want to see the plans.'

'Yeah, I'm sorry, Jack, I promised to get a set of plans to him, but I just haven't got round to it,' I replied.

'Well, he told me that I had probably made a miscalculation. He just seemed overly defensive. I just would have expected a little more from him, I guess.'

I sat looking at my beer quietly.

'Johnny?'

'Um, sorry, what?'

'Ralph. I said he seemed rather defensive. Why would that be? Some sort of architects' mafia?'

'It's odd,' I replied. 'Ralph was at The Oval on Sunday. I didn't realise it at the time. I mean, I saw his E-type parked in the forecourt as I was leaving but it has only just dawned on me that before I left, I heard him in heated conversation with Sir Ken Parslow.'

Jack was looking at me quizzically.

I explained. 'I was outside Parslow's office – he's the Club President – and I could hear two raised voices. Not arguing but clearly agitated and the only words I could make out were 'stands' and 'construction'. I'm pretty certain one must have been Parslow's as it was his office and, although I recognised the other one, I could not quite place it. It makes sense now; it must have been Ralph, and his car parked outside is the clincher.'

'Fair enough, but what does that mean?'

'Not sure,' I mused. 'What worries me is that in the two years I have known him, and in all of the cricket talks we've had, Ralph has never revealed anything about his relationships at Surrey. He portrayed himself simply as a long-standing supporter.'

'Just because he doesn't drop names...' Jack interjected.

'It's more than not dropping names,' I snapped. 'Something dodgy is going on.'

'I have to admit I don't like the way he thinks he has shut me up. I mean, I am sure I'm right about those measurements and if I am, it's a disaster waiting to happen. Even if nothing goes wrong those stands are going to be pretty uncomfortable to get in and out of. I think I will have another word with Ralph.'

'I'm not sure that is wise just yet. Why don't we see what the planning authorities have to say? Surely, they will spot it?'

Jack looked glum. 'I don't trust any of them.'

I drove back to Epsom, checking in on the radio for news from The Oval, where we were starting our Championship match with Gloucestershire. I was feeling increasingly uneasy and wondering if I should wait for planning or speak with Ralph. I had suggested Jack not do anything rash but was more than a little concerned that he was now on a mission. It would be me in the firing line if Jack did cause a fuss because I did not have permission to share the plans.

I was home by 5:00 p.m., and as I motored up the A3 towards London I had half a mind to take the Elstead turn and go see Eleanor Framsell. Things had got a little out of hand there and I felt pretty bad that maybe I had taken advantage of her at a time when she was clearly very vulnerable. Having thought that, I immediately reflected that I had not exactly had to fight her off. I opted for a phone call.

'Johnny! You are an elusive man,' she laughed.

'How are you doing, Eleanor?'

'Oh, you know – good days, bad days...'

'I can only imagine,' I sympathised. I meant it too. I may have only worked with Sally for a few short weeks, but we had struck up a great friendship, one that I was sure would have lasted. 'Do the police know anything more? Are they keeping you updated?'

'I don't hear much from them, Johnny. My Family Liaison Officer calls me every day but that's more of a welfare call. As for the investigation, it seems to have run aground. Apparently, CCTV showed nothing after she turned off the High Street and they have come up with no witnesses. Incredible, isn't it, that in a city of 10 million no one saw a thing.'

'Alone in the crowd,' I mused.

There was a pause. Eleanor was choking up.

'Look, maybe this was the wrong time to call,' I said.

'No, I am glad you did, Johnny. I found something and wanted you to see it.'

'Found something?'

'Sally's diary. I found it in her flat.'

'And?'

'Nothing dramatic, I don't think. I mean, the police looked at it but can't have been too concerned as they left it in her flat. It's not a 'Dear diary' sort – more of an appointments diary really. She kept the ones covering her university years. The one I'm talking about is a couple of years old.'

'What makes you think I can help? Obviously, I am happy to, but if the police couldn't find anything...'

'I think they were looking for names. Recent stuff. This diary is for 1994/95 – it's one of those academic diaries,' she interrupted.

'Well I wouldn't know anything about her life before she came to Surrey, Eleanor.'

'Did you two never talk? Surely she must have told you about life before The Oval?'

'Not much, to be fair. She talked about you quite a lot; talked about uni...'

'Boyfriends?'

I thought for a moment. 'Not sure she ever did, actually. Why?'

'Just some of the scribbles in her diary. She seems to have been meeting 'M' quite frequently though.'

'M?' I half shouted. Hearing that sent a shudder through me.

'Do you know who that is?' Eleanor asked, with sudden interest.

Within half an hour of returning home I was back in the Vectra and retracing my steps back down the A3 again. Maybe I was simply tired but driving the thirty minutes to Elstead was like the last lap of a 10k race. Well, it was how I imagined it to be, having never run more than a few laps of The Oval. Even the Frankie Valli tape could not raise my mood and I ejected it before I had even reached Painshill. In the silence, I had time to reflect on Eleanor's words. I had no idea what she was about to reveal but wondered why she was calling me and not the police. Unless she had tried them and they were not interested. I was slightly nervous that I might we walking into an ambush.

Eleanor looked stunning; in her tight-fitting denim shorts and loose pink, silk chemise and black Wayfarers she looked the epitome of cool, lady of leisure, and far more 33 than 43. The top had six buttons, but Eleanor seemed only to require the lowest couple. She led me through to the garden where the early evening sun was warming the patio. The table was set for two. I presumed she was expecting a guest.

'Eleanor, we could have done this another time,' I said, apologetically.

'I thought you would be hungry. Will you stay for tea?'

From the look on her face it seemed she needed company and she was right about me being hungry. She disappeared to get drinks. I pushed my chair into a semi-reclining position and closed my eyes, enjoying the warmth of the late sun. A sudden shadow over me caused me to snap to and I found myself looking straight into Eleanor's face.

'Johnny, you must be tired too,' she said gently. As she leant forward to place my drink on the gaudy coaster my eyes were drawn to the tanned torso beneath. She paused long enough to confirm my suspicion that she knew what she was doing. I *was* about to be ambushed.

'So,' I began authoritatively, putting my chair back to its upright position, 'what have you seen in this diary?' I took a sip of the beer. Ice cold, perfect. My face must have revealed my thoughts.

'Hogs Back Brewery,' Eleanor said. 'Our local one.'

'Very nice,' I replied, wiping away a spot of froth with my index finger. I took another sip. 'Very nice, indeed.'

'I'm glad you approve,' Eleanor said, smiling demurely.

'I do. In fact, it runs my own beer very close.'

She looked surprised. 'You have a brewery?'

'No, not a brewery,' I laughed. 'Old pal of mine from Surrey is a man with a plan. He's signed me up as the face of his 'New England Beers' range.'

Eleanor looked completely puzzled.

'I played for England once a couple of years ago,' I explained. 'There was a bit of a hoohah down in Oz on an Ashes tour and we both were suspended. In his case, fired, to be honest. I've now been recalled to play against Australia in a couple of weeks and he wants me to promote his beer range. And these beers all come from the States – New England, of course'

She looked impressed. 'England? Congratulations, Johnny. But do you have time to do all of this promotion business?'

'Nothing much to it, really. We've done a photo shoot for the ad campaign – it shouldn't take any of my time. To be fair, I'm not sure if this will come off but he's an old mate and I owe him.'

'How so?' Eleanor asked, topping up my glass.

'Long story short, he wasn't playing in the Sydney Test, bet against us and cleaned up.'

'And is that a problem? If he wasn't playing, I mean.'

'Yes, that's a pretty big problem in sport. You definitely cannot bet on a game you're involved in and, although he wasn't in the team that day, he was still in the touring party.'

'I see. But you said you owe him?'

'Well, I knew he was planning it.'

'Ah, so you were duty bound to whistle blow?'

'Something like that,' I mumbled, keen to move on from this sudden interest.

'Well, here's to your beer venture and to your return to the team,' Eleanor said brightly, changing the subject and offering her glass up to mine. 'Let me go and find those diaries.'

She returned a few minutes later wheeling a trolley laden with food. A platter of cheeses, cold cuts, salad and crusty rolls in a wicker basket. There was an ice bucket with bottles of beer and on the lower shelf, three well-thumbed diaries.

As Eleanor set about transferring the food to the table, I picked up the most recent diary, the one for her final year at university, 1995/96. A quick flick through showed that she was using it mainly to record lectures and deadlines. I turned towards the trolley to reach for the diary for the previous year, the one that Sally's mother had mentioned earlier on the phone. Sally's mother. I looked at Eleanor as she busied herself. She looked ten years younger than her age, but she somehow seemed ten years older in her manners. It was an oddly intoxicating mix. I accepted a fresh bottle of chilled Hogs Back with a nod and returned to the diary.

'The post-its are where Sally mentions M,' she explained, nodding towards the diary from 1994/95 that still lay on the trolley. Sticking haphazardly from the spiral-bound student diary was a fringe of dayglo post-it notes, each one bearing at least one date.

'So, Sally came to us pretty much straight from university?'

'Yes, kind of. She graduated in summer 1996 and then spent a while looking for a job up in the Midlands. She really liked it up there, especially Warwick. Had a good little circle of university friends and a fair few of them were from the surrounding areas so it made sense for her to start looking for work up there.'

'Did she find anything? I don't remember her talking of having a job up there before she came down to us.'

Eleanor paused. This was hard for her.

'She managed to get some bar work in Warwick in '95. It fitted around her studies, but I think she quite enjoyed it. There wasn't much work around. When she graduated she managed to pick up some more shifts. If you look in her diary, she mentions it. Somewhere around late July.'

I picked up the older diary. It covered the academic months, September to July, but also extended to August 1995 with a few pages for notes after that. I started at July. It seemed that the bar work was irregular at first and I assumed that she was bank staff, only called in when needed. There were a few entries that suggested job interviews. These were generally accompanied by sad faces penned by Sally. Evidently rejections. It felt improper studying her diaries, intruding on her private life.

It seemed that she hooked up regularly with a group of uni pals. Sally, Beth, Tilly and Cat seemed to alternate between going to the cinema or drinking at a bar in Birmingham. Or, at least they started there. One of the other girls must have had access to a car, I presumed. I flicked to the address pages hoping that, unlike most people, Sally had actually used it to note down the addresses and phone numbers of her friends. I could not find Beth or Cat, but Tilly's details were there. It might be worth a call to her.

'You say the police weren't interested in these, Eleanor?'

She was putting the final touches to the table. The spread looked fabulous and I gladly accepted another bottle of the ice-cool ale.

'No, they flicked through all three of them and I asked them to be sure to return them to me, but they said they would not be needing them. They've decided it's simply a hit and run, Johnny.'

'Well, let's hope they are right,' I said grimly, as I returned to the well-thumbed pages.

By the end of July 1995 Sally was still looking for regular work and in the August pages there were another three interviews, one in Warwick and two in Birmingham. Sad faces next to each. What caught my eye, as it was the only one I had seen so far, was the smiley face next to the entry for 7th August 1995. It seemed that Sally and her friends had met in their usual Birmingham venue. No further details, just the smiley. I determined to give Tilly a call to see what she could recall about that night.

'Johnny?'

I was not aware that Eleanor had spoken, so engrossed was I in the old diary.

'Sorry, yes?'

'Eat. We can look at those later.'

I put the diary down as Eleanor lit candles on the table. I had not realized how dark it had grown and I could no longer see to the end of her garden. As we ate, the candlelight flickering between us and alternately catching sparkles of joy or glimmers of sadness in her eyes, I was finding myself feeling increasingly protective towards her. Eleanor spoke at length about Sally's childhood. They seemed to have been idyllic days deep here in the Surrey countryside; a small village school, friends round all the time, summer holidays in a small cottage they owned in Brittany, horses, hockey and happy memories. Until Sally's father went out to work one spring morning and never returned. He was struck by a bus as he crossed a road up in the City. She leant across the table and took my hand to emphasize a point when my mobile rang. Spell broken.

It was Summers. I gave an apologetic nod to Eleanor and stepped away from the table to the edge of the patio which was by now in almost complete darkness, the flickering light from the candles not reaching much beyond the table.

'You ok, Mark?'

'Can't complain, Johnny. Are you home?'

I said that I was not but did not say where I was, despite his pause suggesting I tell him.

'Never mind. Listen, I've given Singh a nudge about the beers; he wants you to call him unless you're at Surrey tomorrow, in which case he'll hook up with you there.'

I prickled a little at being told what to do but breezily agreed and went to end the call when Summers cut in.

'I'm putting the bet out tomorrow, Johnny.'

'Isn't that a little hasty? I mean, I may not make the starting eleven.'

'No drama. If you don't make it, the bets are cancelled.'

'Fair enough. Look, mate, I've got to go.'

'Last chance for a piece of your own action,' he said quickly.

'Sod off!' I laughed, clicking to end the call.

After dinner and another couple of drinks, Eleanor and I continued to pore over the diaries. First on the patio, and as it grew cooler, in the lounge. I focused on the post-its to start with. More nights out with the girls and then, in mid-August 1995, a scribbled entry that simply said, 'M @7 @CC Bm'. Eleanor had no idea what it might mean but we both agreed it was surely a date, or a meeting of some sort at least and it was the first mention of 'M'. 'Bm' was perhaps Birmingham and was the abbreviation Sally had been using for most of the girls' nights out. I wondered if CC might mean cricket club. It might not be the same 'M' whom Sally had scribbled angrily about on her pad at The Oval; it could be coincidence, though I doubted it. The diary for 1995/96 had a good number of post-it notes sticking out from September to March and then, nothing.

'Did you ever meet these friends, Eleanor?'

'No, sadly not. Sally mentioned that she had a strong group of friends at Warwick but never mentioned any names, or if she did, I don't recall any.'

'Do they even know that she died? Did they not come to her funeral?'

'I had no idea who to contact, Johnny,' Eleanor said sadly, welling up.

'I think it's time to call Tilly,' I decided.

Eleanor glanced at her watch. 'It's nearly eleven, Johnny. Isn't that a bit late to call a total stranger?'

I paused, frustrated at what would delay us, and realising too that I was over the limit. As if reading my mind on both counts, Eleanor smiled. 'It's probably not too late if you are 23, I suppose, and the spare bed is made up – you are welcome to stay.'

I felt an uneasy mixture of relief and disappointment, if I am honest. Relief that she was seemingly dismissing our recent intimacy as a one-off; disappointment, at the same time, that that was how she apparently viewed it. I accepted her offer as I turned to the back of Sally's diary and tapped out Tilly's number on my mobile.

A woman's voice answered after half a dozen rings. There was a hub-bub in the background. It could have been a television or perhaps bar noise. She sounded, young, bubbly and intelligent – exactly as I expected a friend of Sally's to sound. I was probably the exception to the rule there. I apologised for the late hour, introduced myself as one of Sally's friends from work where-upon she interrupted me with a giggle.

'Are you Johnny? Johnny Lorrens? The cricketer?'

I said that indeed I was, puzzled that she had guessed so easily, or actually, at all. The sound muffled as she seemingly covered the mouthpiece with her hand, but I could hear her telling someone that she was talking to 'Johnny Lorrens, the cricketer!' She reappeared on the line.

'And how is Sally? She's been quiet for a few weeks. Most unlike her.'

'Tilly, you haven't heard?'

'Heard what?' The bubbly quality had been replaced by a querulous tone.

'I'm sorry to have to tell you that Sally passed away about three weeks ago.'

I heard Tilly's gasp as Eleanor's shoulders slumped. I pulled her gently towards me and she sobbed into my shoulder as Tilly recovered enough from the initial shock to answer.

'Sally's – dead?' she said with incredulity in her voice. 'No, no, no – you must be mistaken?' There was desperation in her voice now.

'Tilly, I'm so sorry to have to give you this news...'

'But how?' she interrupted.

I explained what we knew. I could hear her crying between the questions she asked. She and Sally had clearly been close and I could feel her pain from a hundred miles away. Pain at losing such a close friend; anguish at not having known for the past three weeks.

'I missed her funeral,' she sobbed. 'Did you go? She talked about you a lot – she really liked you.'

That made me feel instantly worse, and angry again with Carlisle for not allowing me to attend.

164

'Tilly, I need to ask you about Sally's relationships. Is there anyone who would wish her to come to harm?'

'Harm?' she spluttered. 'Sally?'

'I know this is hard to talk about, but please think. Had she fallen out with anyone?'

'Not to make someone want to kill her, no!' she replied hotly.

'Would you have a think about it, Tilly? Let me give you my number and if you remember anything just give me a call, okay?'

Tilly took down the number and said she would but that she did not think she would remember anything that could help.

'Tilly, there's an entry in Sally's diary from August 1995. It seems she was meeting an 'M' at CC at 7:00 p.m. Any idea what that meant?

There was a pause.

'Tilly?'

'I remember that!' she replied angrily. 'We told her not to go. Didn't like him from the start – arrogant prick. And he was far too old for her.'

'Who was she meeting, Tilly?' Eleanor's head shot up from my shoulder; she could hear the urgency in my voice too.

'A cricketer she met. We used to hang out at a bar in Birmingham – *The Cricket Club*. Nice bar – quite an upmarket place really. The cricketers from Warwickshire used to come in on matchdays. Sally was always keen on sporty types and most of the players were really decent – and fit,' she giggled. 'I think it was owned by some bigwig at the club. Anyway, one night the boys sent drinks over to the four of us and we got chatting, some numbers were exchanged and a couple of days later Sally met up with this guy.'

'Who was it?' I said, trying to mask the excitement in my voice.

'Mark O'Brien.'

I nearly dropped the phone. O'Brien had joined us just a few months after he and Sally met but I had never seen him go anywhere near her and had never heard her talk about him. He had always seemed okay to me; that certainly jarred with Tilly's view of him.

'Johnny? Are you still there?'

'I am,' I replied, mustering as much calm as I could. 'I know him quite well – we play in the same team here at Surrey.'

'Oh, I knew he moved away but I assumed he still played for Warwickshire?' Tilly puzzled.

'He did up until the end of the 1995 season, then he joined us for the following year.'

'Well that's why Sally moved south then,' Tilly said, almost to herself, with perhaps a hint of disappointment.

'Well, I think she moved south because she got a job at The Oval,' I challenged, keen to hear more of Tilly's thoughts.

'You are probably right', she agreed, 'but as soon as he said he was moving away from the Midlands she was desperate to follow him.'

'But he moved over a year ago. Was Sally still in touch with him?'

'She talked about him a lot when he first moved down. But look, after that night in the bar I never saw him again. To be honest, I am not sure this much later that I would even recognize him. But Sally was smitten. Hook, line and sinker. She hadn't known him long, but she had decided, Mark O'Brien was the love of her life. Did they move in together down there?'

'No. No, they didn't, Tilly,' I replied cautiously.

'What's the matter?'

'Tilly, this is really odd. I knew Sally for only a month. We shared an office. But in that time we worked together quite a bit even if we were always both in and out a lot. We still had plenty of time to talk together, though. She never once mentioned O'Brien. I never saw them together and he never once mentioned her to me. They were both at The Oval but their paths never crossed; at least, not as far as I could tell.'

'Well that is desperately sad,' Tilly decided. 'She followed him all that way and it sounds like he didn't want her to. Did she seem sad?'

'No, not a bit of it. Are you certain that she was following O'Brien? I mean, could it be a coincidence?'

'No chance. One thing I do recall is Sally telling me that Mark was living down south and that she was going to look for a job down there too.'

'When was this?'

Tilly breathed out through pursed lips as she cast her mind back. 'Early January, perhaps?'

'So, O'Brien had been with us for almost a year by then. I wonder if he encouraged her to join him? You said that you and Sally kept in touch?'

'We did, up until she moved down in early spring. Then our calls dwindled a little. I assumed she was all loved-up and didn't pester her. I guess we kept the calls going for a while but...' Tilly tailed off, apparently lost in her thoughts.

'Tilly, you have been really helpful. And sorry, again, to give you the sad news.'

She asked me a few more details, wanted to know Eleanor's address for flowers and where Sally's remains were. She also promised to call me should she remember anything else.

Eleanor sat quietly for several minutes, her head still resting on my shoulder. She eventually sat up slowly, wiping her eyes on a tissue.

'Did you hear any of that?'

'Most of it,' she replied. 'Who is this Mark O'Brien, Johnny?'

I took a swig of my beer. 'O'Brien? Decent guy. At least, I always thought he was. Keeps himself pretty much to himself; not unfriendly, just reserved. We brought him in as skipper last season, but he has stepped down for this one. It's odd though, neither one has mentioned the other.'

'Perhaps whatever they had had fizzled out before she moved south,' Eleanor wondered, her hands fidgeting nervously with the wine glass in her hands.

'Possible,' I mused. 'That's the only explanation I can think of.'

'How old is he?' Eleanor turned to face me directly.
Thirty-eight.'
'Oh dear.'
'Guess I am gonna have to speak with him.'

CHAPTER 27

Thursday May 15 1997

I slept fitfully. The bed was supremely comfortable but for an hour or so after I retired I half-expected Eleanor to appear. We had talked until late about Sally and what may or may not have happened. Neither of us could quite fathom why the police were seemingly so disinterested. Case apparently closed. She sat very close and was clearly struggling. For a moment I thought she was going to lead me into her room. She certainly paused at the door before showing me to the guest room.

Breakfast on the patio in beautiful late spring weather. Pure blue skies and a very pleasant breeze making the twenty degrees at this early hour suggest a perfect day for cricket ahead. I was looking forward to being fit enough for the Championship games but was also quite enjoying a little more time out. Eleanor's question startled me.

'Your wife, Johnny – what does she do?'

I had not paused for a second to wonder if Eleanor knew if I was married or not. Did she know? Perhaps she was just probing. Either way, I felt like a complete rat.

'My wife,' I replied, reddening I am sure, 'is an editor at *Smashed* magazine. You've probably not heard or it, Eleanor. It's a monthly music magazine – rock music.'

'You are blushing,' she said, teasingly, as she wiped her mouth gently with a napkin.

I busied myself with the full-English in front of me. 'She's on duty at the moment, touring with a band in the States. Been away for a few weeks now. Busy schedule – haven't spoken to her in days.'

I felt I was saying too much. Almost trying to excuse my behaviour with Eleanor.

Eleanor shushed me with a well-manicured finger to my lips. 'It's between us, Johnny. You are welcome here any time.'

Now I did redden. Secrets. Never good.

I was pretty sure that Carlisle would not let me keep coming in just whenever I fancied for ever and was not surprised when he showed his feelings at The Oval later. I had parked up at eleven-thirty in the players' spaces at the back of the pavilion, snuck into the dressing room in the Bedser Stand and walked straight into our Aussie coach having a massive rant. Wrong moment to arrive. We had bowled Gloucestershire out the previous afternoon for 237 and had reached stumps with Rennie and Driver unbroken on 87. As I walked in our fourth wicket had gone down and we were teetering at 101 for 4.

'And you!' he screamed at me. 'Where the fuck have you been, you lazy bastard?'

My response was ill-considered. 'And a very good morning to you too, coach.'

A few sniggers from my teammates, even more averted gazes and a clipboard slung in my general direction by a very irate coach as I slipped back out the way I had come.

I took the several flights of stairs down into the bowels of the Bedser hoping to catch up with Sam. I owed her a coffee. Apparently, she was not on duty, so I decided to go for a head-clearing stroll around the ground's internal perimeter road.

The modernity of the Bedser quickly gave way to the antiquity of the soon-to-be replaced terraces. They were indeed a shocker. And, catching sight of the terraces on the eastern side of the ground, it struck me that naming the terraces on that side, the May Stand, did not improve their look and was a disservice to the great P.B.H. May. The '90s seemed in so many ways to be a bright new age. In the City, towering, shiny new buildings were going up on any available patch yet in this corner of south London parts were still positively prewar and, more importantly, looking positively war-torn. Hopefully that was all about to change. The Club had a vision for the future and I could not wait to see the work start. Just those niggling worries of Jack's.

I had almost completed the full circuit when I stopped dead at the rear of the Lock/Laker stand. Emerging from his E-type was Ralph. He was becoming quite the regular. It was a match day so perhaps no surprise there, but parking inside the ground? That did not come with Club membership. I ducked into the entrance to the toilets underneath the stand's overhang and watched as Ralph made his way to the pavilion entrance beneath the cricketers clock.

I hung back for a couple of minutes to allow Ralph time to get wherever he was going. It was just possible that he was here for the cricket but parking inside the ground on a match day is a strict no-no, Member or not. Ralph's involvement in the Club was beginning to suggest a whole new level. I had been at the Club a good few years but had probably only been in Parslow's office twice in that time. My father-in-law seemed quite a fixture now. If that was where he was headed.

I strode quickly across the car park, now half sunlit, half in shadow thrown by the Lock/Laker Stand. A couple of men, old enough to know better, stopped me for autographs and wished me well for the one-dayers. I signed an old bat for one that had room for only a very small version of my normal signature, covered as it was by countless other scribbles many of which were faded to a very pale blue.

'Looks like you've been busy with this a very long time,' I noted.

'Surridge,' the old man mumbled, pointing at an almost invisible inking at the top of the blade. 'First one I got when I was a boy.'

'Then I am flattered to be in such illustrious company,' I replied with a smile, returning the bat reverentially to its owner, as I took the large volume held out to me by another gentleman of about sixty-five. He had opened the book to a double page spread with my name at the top of each page. There was a dozen or more photos of me taken from various papers, magazines and match programmes. 'Which one?' I asked, nodding at the spread.

'Can you do all of them, Johnny?'

I groaned inwardly. I remembered this as a child collecting autographs at Surrey myself. I preferred getting players to sign the scorecard from that day's play, but I did find it a little odd that players were frequently asked to sign multiple photos of themselves in scrapbooks. 'Really?'

I signed anyway. I guess I enjoy the reputation of being good with the fans and the guy was grateful and wished me a bucket load of wickets against the Aussies.

'Might even have a little punt on you too,' he grinned; toothlessly, I noticed.

'How's that?' I asked, squinting into the sun.

'Not out,' came the call behind me accompanied by a girlish giggle.

I turned. Mr Brown was just coming in from the turnstiles, cameras slung around his neck. He had excitedly shown me his collection of new cameras a few weeks before, explaining that he was going to record as much of the season as he could, hoping to self-publish a Surrey diary of the season.

I giggled back, not girlishly, shook his proffered hand and, nodding towards the autograph-hunters, followed Ralph's steps into the cool, semi-darkness of the pavilion.

No sign of Ralph by that time, so I mounted the stairs quickly to Sir Ken's office. The door was closed but I could hear the low rumble of male voices from within. I paused for a second and leaned in towards the door. Just at that moment I heard the door at the end of the corridor swish open and a booming voice.

'You okay, Mr Lorrens?'

I snapped upright sharply and must have looked like the boy with his hand in the biscuit tin. 'I, um, er, yes, thanks Tommy. Think I dropped a pound,' I said, now bending back down as if to look.

Tommy, the blazered steward in charge of the pavilion on match days, was ex-marines. Tough as you like and larger than life.

'Don't think you'll be needing that, Mr Lorrens. Not if you have a cheeky punt on yourself,' he added with a pantomime wink.

'I'm sorry?'

The door to Parslow's office opened at that instant and I came face to face with Ralph, on his way out. Tommy, unfortunately, continued.

'No disrespect, Mr Lorrens, but it's a must sell if you ask me. I mean 77/80? No one in their right mind is gonna buy tha...' Tommy's brain had just caught up with his mouth.

'Ralph!' I exclaimed, hoping he had either not heard or cared about what Tommy had just blurted out.

'Johnny,' he said curtly as he brushed past me and went the way I had come, face like thunder.

'Lorrens? In here now!' barked Parslow.

I showed a face full of false bravado to Tommy who, out of Parslow's sight, mouthed a sorry as I entered the Club President's office for only the third time in my career. The other two times were to sign contracts. The omens for this meeting looked less positive.

'Sit down, Lorrens.' It was an order, not an invitation.

The view across the ground was as good as any in the house and I was relieved to see from the scoreboard that we had rallied a little to 137 for 4. I waited as Sir Ken, a large, powerfully built man in his seventies, his full head of grey hair neatly brushed back and gleaming with Brylcreem, walked around the huge desk and eased himself into his ancient swivel chair.

'So', he began ponderously. 'Tell me about your brother, Jack.'

I let out a silent sigh. I was sure this was going to be about the bet. However, as that good news sank in I realised that this was potentially a problem that Ralph had raised – about my brother.

'Jack? What's to tell?' I started breezily. 'You won't have met him, Sir Ken, and you are unlikely to do so. Not a cricket fan,' I explained.

'Mmm.' Parslow sat back in his chair, laced his fingers together and half-turned towards the play.

'Looking forward to the Australia series?'

I was a little taken aback at the abrupt switch of focus, but relieved.

'I certainly am, yes. Can't wait to get stuck into them. It's been a long wait.'

'It most definitely has,' he agreed, his voice deep, rich – from an altogether different age.

There was a silence just long enough to be awkward. I am not great with silences and tend to fill them, not always usefully. I tried to say nothing but failed. 'Of course, I can't wait to get playing again in the Championship.'

'I was coming to that. Look, Lorrens, you have been a good servant of this club.'

I did not like the sound of this.

'You got away with one on the Australia tour. You have served your time and you deserve the recall. But.' Here, he paused ominously. 'I have concerns.' With that he swung sharply back towards me, eyebrows low over eyes that pierced mine and pinned me back in my chair.

'Oh?' was all I could muster.

'What do you think I am concerned about?' He had elaborately taken a sheet of paper from a stationery holder on the corner of his desk, laid it on the huge, leather-cornered blotter in front of him and uncapped an expensive-looking fountain pen. He was about to make a list. I felt sick.

'My shoulder?' I offered, weakly.

'Well, let's start with that, shall we?'

I was transported back ten years to my high school. My headteacher was just like this; domineering, patronising and all-powerful. My future at Surrey was in this man's hands and that thought gave me no confidence at all.

'My lack of match fitness?'

'Yes, we can add that too,' Parslow muttered as if dealing with a naughty infant, as he added to the list.

I bit my tongue, deciding that I did not want to offer anything that he may not already have thought of. Sadly, he had thought of plenty. And he let me know it once he realised that I had suddenly taken the fifth.

'Well, let's add, your relationship with Mr Carlisle, your apparent pre-occupation with the sad demise of Miss Framsell, your very public marriage difficulties and now this very odd bet that has appeared this morning on City Sports. Oh, and your brother's meddlings in our business.'

I remained silent but inside my mind was racing. How did he know all of this?

He remained passive, towering over me in true big-business mogul style – his chair much higher than mine.

'Apart from that, okay?' I managed. Not the right response on this occasion.

He looked furious. 'Get out! We will return to this later.'

Jackie Kray was alone in the Club Office, dealing with an issue on the phone. She nodded towards a chair so I guessed it would take a while. I called Summers from my mobile but there was no answer. He had warned me the spread was to be published that day, but I had not envisaged such an immediate impact. Clearly Parslow knew about it already unless he had heard Tommy speaking with me. But then, Mr Brown knew too. I did not want to call City Sports now, not from work. I was lost in thought when Jackie spoke.

'Johnny?'

'Mmm, what, sorry?'

'Are you okay?'

'Not sure. Just been balled out by Parslow.'

Jackie looked concerned. 'Why?'

'Says he has 'concerns' about me.'

She smiled. 'We all have, Johnny, so what?'

I flicked her two fingers along with the grin. 'Listed in front of me all of the things that are worrying him.'

'Such as?'

I did not want to mention the bet, even to Jackie, but told her the rest. She looked a little uneasy.

'What is it, Jack?'

'Jack? No-one calls me that,' she laughed.

'They do now', I smiled back.

'Actually, it's about Jack. He rang here.'

'My brother, Jack?'

'Yes, just this morning. Maybe fifteen minutes ago. Asked to speak with Sir Ken.'

'Shitola! No wonder he was mad at me. What an idiot!'

'Sorry, I don't understand, Johnny. Why would your brother want to speak with the Club President?'

'Long story, Jack – ie.'

She smiled broadly. 'Okay, well, get your family in order!'

'Not you too,' I groaned. That was another gripe of his. Said my marriage difficulties are concerning him too.'

'What a cheek!' Jackie exclaimed. 'What does he know about anything? Actually, I was going to say, Elisa called you this morning. I told her you were in later.'

That surprised me more than anything that Parslow had said. I tried to make it seem routine but inside I was quite unsettled by the thought that she had tried to call and still wondering why her calls were so infrequent. It was not long ago but I could not remember the last time we had spoken.

I stood to go. 'Thanks, Jackie, did she leave a number?'

'Your wife?'

'That's the one,' I grinned.

'You don't have it?'

'She's still with Toadlust, on a tour that seems to be adding dates as they go, so I never know where to contact her.'

Jackie looked puzzled suddenly. 'She did, Johnny, but it's a London number.'

The door of the office opened at this moment as Sir Kenneth Parslow's large frame entered the small office. He smiled at Jackie Kray and without looking at me, muttered disparagingly, 'Are you still here?'

'Apparently,' I replied jauntily and, taking a slip of paper from Jackie, sauntered out, probably looking a lot braver than I felt.

I left Jackie feeling decidedly uneasy. Parslow's 'concerns' could be a big problem for me but in the awkwardness of being caught outside his office I clean forgot about Ralph's presence. Was it too much of a coincidence that Jack had called at almost exactly the same time as Ralph had arrived? Was it a prearranged meeting between the three? Jack had apparently, and rather unhelpfully, stirred things up plenty, and there was the City Sports angle too. And then there was Elisa. Why was she ringing from a London number? I checked my pocket to ensure I still had the slip that Jackie had given me and took out my mobile as I reached the car park.

Sitting underneath the cricketers clock I pondered ringing Elisa first. I did not know how I felt about that situation now. It was odd. A few weeks earlier, when she first mentioned going away, I was desperately keen that she should stay and felt rather childishly angry with her. The intervening weeks had been a crazy rollercoaster of emotions, what with Sally's death, Lori, Eleanor, my recall and Summers and his plans. Elisa had missed all of that. Normally we would have shared everything, but she had not been there. I had been unable even to call her and now I wondered if I even wanted to. And that was a miserable thought. I decided to call Summers.

As I waited for him to answer I gazed around the forecourt. Club shop away to my left, cars parked in the centre and, over to my right, the Hobbs Gates and a number of concessions stands. I could smell the chips from the fish and chip stall and realised I had missed lunch. I was just about to cancel the call and go and buy some when I was answered.

'City Sports,' a female voice snapped, the hum of a busy office in the background, punctuated by harsh male voices shouting numbers across the room, or so I presumed.

'Mark Summers, please,' I snapped back, hoping that my certainty would leave me less likely to have to explain my call or identity. Making this call from The Oval was, I suddenly realised, not my best idea.

'One moment,' she replied. As she transferred me, I faintly heard, 'Line three, Summo; the call you've been waiting f...'

I sat for several seconds waiting for my call to be picked up and was about to hang up when I heard a click.

'Summers speaking.'

'Mark, it's me.' I realised I was whispering but scanning the forecourt again, saw that I was still alone. 'I understand that you have published the quote?'

'The spread? That's right, buddy...' he began. '97/99!'

I quickly pulled the mobile away from my ear as he roared the numbers. '97/99? That's a joke, mate. How many do you think I am going to score?'

'Sorry, buddy, that wasn't your spread. No, I went with the 77/80 we discussed.'

'Woah, mate. Not discussed. This is all your idea, remember?'

'Fair enough.'

'Look, I am gonna do my best if I get picked, spread or no spread.'

'I know that, Johnny. I trust you.'

'So, the spread went live today?'

'This morning,' he clarified. 'And I have had a few decent sells already, mate. So, it's all down to you now.'

'Down to me?'

'Yup. You cannot get injured and you cannot get dropped.'

'Jeepers, Mark. Thanks for the added pressure.'

'You can handle it,' he said, before cupping the mouthpiece and shouting more numbers.

I thought back to the pricing that Summers had mentioned a few weeks earlier: wickets at 10 points each; 5 for a catch, 1 for each run. A quick calculation meant that if I did play to form, I needed to score 21 or so over the three matches for Summers to break even, with him on the bid at 77. All in all, I needed to score a quantity of runs from the three matches that would normally take me a dozen or more games. And this would be against Australia – the number one side in the world.

'You should have had a piece of it, Johnny.'

So, Tommy was right about the price. 'Blimey, Mark, you really think I'll score that many?' I exclaimed, ignoring his comment.

There was a pause as Summers seemingly covered the mouthpiece to shout more numbers, before he returned to me.

'Mate, I am trusting the stats. I have to assume at least 50 for the wickets and catches, leaving you to score just 21 for me to break even.'

'Wow – you have a flattering level of faith in me,' I laughed.

'That I do, old friend. Look, it's mad here, gotta go.' And with that he was gone.

I mused for a few moments on the bet and quickly decided that it was his brainchild and really had nothing to do with me so determined to put it out of my mind. I had enough other things to worry about.

A sudden roar from the other side of the pavilion woke me from my thoughts and I walked quickly round to the gap between the Lock/Laker and the Peter May Stand for a look at the scoreboard. Pallant and O'Brien were making a spirited fightback and had taken us to 175 for 4 in pretty quick time.

'Oi, Johnny! Did you see that?' It was a shirtless spectator who was, given the early hour, already surrounded by an impressive array of empty beer cans.

'What happened?'

'O'Brien!' he replied. He's gone berserk. Quickest fifty I've ever seen, and he got there with a six. Massive one over the terraces on the other side.'

I gave him a thumbs-up and, taking my mobile out again, set off for another lap of the ground as I dialled Elisa's number; the one Jackie Kray had given me.

'Hello?'

I almost did not recognise her voice, but then it had been a while.

'Hello, gorgeous,' I started. Despite any misgivings about the state of our relationship that I harboured, that greeting came naturally enough. There was a silence at the other end. 'Elisa, can you hear me?'

'I can, yes. Sorry, that just surprised me – the way you spoke to me.'

By now I knew. It was not my wife. 'God, I am sorry. That's not you is it? Is that Elisa from St Mark's?'

She laughed. 'Yes, it is, Johnny. I just wondered if we could fix a date. I mean, for you to come to my school to see the kids. You know, after that chat we had the other day.'

It was her turn to sound embarrassed. I said that I would give her a call when I could get to my diary.

I had just reached the dressing room door again when the mobile trilled. I turned abruptly around and darted off down the stairs again. If Carlisle saw me with the phone that would just give him further ammunition and it seemed like he had enough already.

'Johnny? Krishnan Singh.'

I groaned inwardly. I had been expecting his call. This was developing into a tricky day all round.

'Krishnan.' I acknowledged.

'So, you are a beer label now? Tell me about that.'

My mind raced. Summers put Singh on to the beer angle but was also intimately associated with the betting scandal of '95 and was now quoting what would be seen as an odd performance spread on me. My links to Summers were going to be questioned and I had to be careful in this interview.

'It's just a bit of fun for me, Krishnan. An old mate called me some time ago, had me sample some beers and asked me to be the 'face' of them.'

'New England Beers? Explain that.'

'Simple really. They are from a small brewery in the States – Vermont. He thought the idea of me returning to the England team and the beers' New England origins were a good match up.'

'Where can people buy these beers, then?'

I suddenly realised I did not know. We had not talked about that. 'The usual places,' I improvised.

'So, you and Summers are back together again?'

I groaned inwardly. This was precisely what I had feared. My worries about being linked with Summers to any betting issues had overshadowed my thinking and now, the links between me, the beers and Summers were going to be in the spotlight. I was angry with myself for not thinking about that earlier.

'Well, I would not exactly say that, no.'

'But he is the brains behind the beer business?'

I could hardly deny this. 'It is something he has been working on for quite a while and I guess he saw my recall as an angle.'

'So how do you see this fitting with your England future?' he asked, with a sudden cooling in his voice. 'And at Surrey?' he added, as an afterthought.

I paused for a moment, wondering where we were heading. 'Doesn't make any impact on either,' I replied firmly.

It was Singh's turn to pause. 'Tell me about this spread that's been quoted today.'

I gulped inwardly. For all that Summers was keeping me out of the actual bet, my links to him could certainly pose me problems if it ever got out that he was behind it. I just hoped that Singh did not know that Summers worked at City Sports. I decided to play it dumb.

'Spread?'

'Oh, I thought you would have known,' Singh said, a hint of doubt in his voice. 'City Sports have your performance in the one-dayers at 77/80. Unless you take a bagful that has to be a huge sell. No offence.'

'I know nothing about that. And none taken,' I replied curtly, wishing immediately that I had not lied so easily.

By now I had reached the forecourt again and was once more starting on another circuit of the ground. There were short queues at the concession stands and bars and I realised just how hungry I was.

'What news from the States, Johnny?'

'I thought this was a call about New England Beers,' I said, rather more forcefully than I had intended.

'I just wondered if Elisa had been in touch. I see the tour is continuing but it does seem to be causing a lot of offence, especially in the southern states.'

'I can't help you with that, I'm afraid,' I replied, mustering a calmness in my voice that I did not feel, visions of Gorton reading this and pulling me out of the team.

'Are you two not talking?'

'Are you with Hello! magazine now, Krishnan?' I replied, forcing a chuckle. 'I thought you were better than this.'

'One last thing, Johnny. What's your reaction to Ted Glyn's injury?'

I had seen in the morning papers that the England skipper had been injured at Northampton the previous day but had seen no details. 'What's the latest?'

'He's out for the season – ACL in shreds.'

'Ouch! Poor old Ted, we will miss him. He is a fantastic bat and a brilliant captain – I feel very sorry for him and wish him all the best. We will just have to regroup behind whoever the selectors choose.'

'Can I quote you on that?'

'Sure can,' I replied confidently.

'Oh, and they've chosen already.'

'Really?'

'Teammate of yours – Alan Dench.'

'Dench? Seriously?'

'Not a good choice?'

'No, it's not that,' I replied, thinking how my words could be twisted by Singh. 'I just haven't seen the man-management skills that suggest he'd be a good skipper. No, he's done alright for us this year. I am just surprised. I mean, he hasn't played for England for three years or more.' I was saying too much but then I was genuinely surprised.

Carlisle left immediately after stumps so I joined the boys for a couple of pints in the Tavern at the rear of the pavilion; a dark, rather uninspiring, old-fashioned watering-hole but one that used to be a magnet for players of both teams after play each evening until just a few years ago. Tonight, it was just a group of seven or eight of us and a smattering of fans stopping off for a pint before heading for the Tube and home. No sign of Dench. He was not the most sociable, but I thought he might have joined us to celebrate his re-call. Had the coach not rushed off we would not have risked the pub – not on a match day. But we were in a strong position again and what harm could a couple of beers do? Quite a lot as it happens.

Gus MacLaine was just regaling the lads with a story about me from my Australia tour. I knew where this was heading and cut him short.

'And there was no truth at all, sadly, in the story about me smoking pot in the SCG dressing-room. But there was truth in my ability to down a pint, in one, from the wrong side of the glass.'

At this point I demonstrated the skill on my almost full pint glass, spilling barely a drop. Huge cheers from my teammates as Pallant called across to the barman for another beer for me. At the same time, I was aware of movement to my right. The two men who had been deep in conversation at a small, round table just a yard or two away from us were getting ready to leave. I instinctively moved to allow them to pass when I felt a hand on my shoulder.

'Nice trick, Johnny. All part of the training for next week?'

I swung round sharply as I reached for the foaming pint that Pallant was holding out to me and came face to face with Krishnan Singh.

'Ah, good evening Krishnan. Yes, all part of my intense training plans for the one-dayers,' I replied with a grin, my smile fading fast as I saw who he had been talking with. It was Alex Gorton, Chairman of Selectors and not my biggest fan.

'Mr Gorton,' I nodded, humbly.

'Outside,' he said curtly.

My group fell into an immediate and very awkward silence. As I have mentioned before, I do not like silences and tend to fill them, not always helpfully. For some reason I made little doggie-paws with my hands and gave a little, acknowledging bark as I followed him towards the door. The Surrey lads erupted into laughter as I turned to follow Gorton. Even from behind I could see he was cross.

When I reached the street outside and the Chairman of Selectors swung around to face me, I could see he was incandescent, fists balled and face purple.

'If you ever do that to me again, you scrawny little bastard, I will see to it that you never play for England again. Now my suggestion to you is that you go straight home and think about your actions. You are about to represent your country. That is a massive honour and your re-selection is one that I am really concerned about now. I would not have picked you, let me be clear. My colleagues on the panel spoke for you and your recent one-day performances do seem to warrant consideration of your return, at least. But you are a loose cannon. Your marriage problems are plastered all over the papers, you are promoting beers at a time when we are trying to tie cricket to the healthy pursuits agenda and your old mate, Mark Summers, is pushing a very dodgy looking spread bet on you.'

I stood in silence. Partly in shock at this tirade and partly because I could see Krishnan Singh loitering just a few feet away and certainly close enough to hear Gorton's rant. I replied quietly.

'Are they?'

Gorton stared at me, his mouth open, purple face contrasting with his white hair. 'Are they what?' he roared. I could feel his spittle peppering my face. I decided not to wipe fearing that would simply antagonise him further.

'My marriage problems. Are they all over the papers?' I asked quietly.

'You need to get a firm hand on your wife, Lorrens. She is a disgrace.'

'Well then, I suggest you talk with her about that and I hope you have more luck contacting her than I have had.'

With that I turned on my heel and walked straight back into the pub, leaving Gorton to make of it what he would. I had managed to avoid responding to the issue of Summers and his bet but was left with the nagging worry about Krishnan Singh. I would have to check out the Daily Mirror in the morning to see what he had made of it all. As it happened, he made quite a lot of it.

CHAPTER 28

Friday May 16 1997

My heart sank as I strode across the forecourt of the Esso petrol station at the junction with Reigate Road and the A24. The papers behind the protective plastic flap in the display unit outside the shop were easy to read. The Mirror led on a story about Tony Blair, but in the top right-hand corner, next to the paper's red banner in the top left, was an old photo of me taken in a bar after a match somewhere with a splash headline: *'Bad boy Lorrens upsets selectors.... again.'*

I knew the staff in the shop by name. It was my nearest fill-up. I took a copy of the paper up to the till and handed the correct money over.

'Morning, Mr Lorrens, thank you.'

'Morning, Suhail. How are you?' I wanted to get out quick but the Sri Lankan family who ran the place were big cricket fans.

'Good, thank you. I see you have made the papers again,' he said, nodding at the copy in my hand.

'Oh, have I?' I lied, none too convincingly. 'Let's hope it's nice,' I smiled.

'It isn't, I fear.'

He was right. Singh had not done me any favours at all. I took the paper back to my car and sat in a parking space for the few minutes it took to read the article on the back page.

Johnny Lorrens concerned about new skipper

England spinner and reformed bad boy, Johnny Lorrens, is shocked to hear that Surrey teammate, Alan Dench, has been handed the England captaincy for the upcoming one-day series with Australia. Lorrens questions Dench's man management skills but concedes that the veteran batsman has made a good start at Surrey this year after his surprise move south from Worcester in the spring. The 37-year-old Dench has been called in to replace Ted Glyn; the Worcestershire and England captain suffered a career-threatening ACL injury at Northampton two days ago and is out for the rest of the season. It is not completely new territory for Dench, who last played for England in 1994. Twenty years ago, he skippered England Schoolboys in a three-match series against the old enemy – a series England won, two games to one.

Lorrens has not featured so far this year in Surrey's Championship fixtures but has been a key feature of their one-day success this season to the extent that he has been recalled to the England one-day squad for the upcoming series with Australia. There does seem to have been some debate over his return with an apparent split in the selectors over his recall. Chairman of Selectors, Alex Gorton has read the riot act to Lorrens over the Surrey man's profile in the media. Of great concern to Gorton is that there are too many distractions in Lorrens's life at present. Not only is his magazine editor wife on a very controversial tour of the United States with shock-rock outfit, Toadlust, where she has been romantically linked to former boyfriend and lead singer, Crispin LeDare, but Lorrens has hooked up again with former Surrey teammate and disgraced England cricketer, Mark Summers. Lorrens celebrates his return to England colours, following the betting scandal on the 1994/95 Australia tour that threatened to end his international career, by promoting a range of Summers' beers, which is inconsistent with the English Cricket Board's focus on healthy lifestyles. Tapping into the moment, they are being sold as 'New England Beers', with Lorrens's face on each bottle. I have yet to sample one, but knowing Lorrens's fondness for a pint or several, I would expect them to be perfect for a day at the cricket.

Summers in the meantime is working for spread-betting outfit, City Sports, and he is celebrating the upcoming one-day series with a range of cricketing spreads. The one that stands out to me is the 77/80 quote on Lorrens's perform-ance. What, indeed, does Summers know that the rest of us don't?

I let the tabloid fall onto my lap as I let out a groan. They say any publicity is good publicity. I was not so sure. I did not like Gorton's suggestion that I take a firm hand with Elisa. Very 1950s of him of course, although I was growing increasingly uncomfortable with that situation too. It now seemed accepted in the media that Elisa had rekindled her old relationship with Le-Dare but I could not contact her to pursue that. I would only have to wait a little longer, though, as she was due back in about five days' time.

And then there was Dench. He would not be happy about Singh's por-trayal of my thinking about him. And he was about to be captain on my return to the England team. That could be awkward.

CHAPTER 29

Sunday May 18 1997

The weather was perfect. Powder blue skies, strong for the time of year sun and zero chance of rain. It was five before two and the ground was filling up fast. Well, not filling up but certainly a better than usual turnout. I was sat on the balcony, cup of tea in hand, enjoying the prospect of watching us bat. The balcony at The Oval is really a seat by an open window but the views are superb. Rennie and Driver were making their way down the steps of the Bedser Stand about to start our innings. We had beaten Gloucestershire easily in the Championship match and with our current one-day form I felt comfortable about this one. With the form we were in I thought it highly unlikely that I would get near a bat. Carlisle had been rather sniffy with me until I said to him that I was going down to the nets for some throw downs. That seemed to impress him.

With only 40 overs per side, a good start was essential and our openers set off at a gallop. When I padded up for my net we were 75 without loss from ten, with Rennie closing in on an excellent 50. I had seen Sam taking a break outside the external entrance to the sports centre on my way in and she had readily agreed to give me some time. When I reached the subterranean nets she had the lane ready with a bowling machine in place. She had also put on makeup and flashed me an entrancing smile as I arrived.

She threw balls to me for fifteen minutes, on a slightly full length and I very soon found the middle of the bat, the balls crashing into the netting on the off-side. We had the place to ourselves and I experimented with my stance until I found again the perfect position.

'What's your batting average?' Sam asked, as she collected up the balls ready for another round.

'First Class or one-day?'

She paused. 'Either?'

'Very low,' I replied with a grin.

'Which one?'

'Both, sadly,' I laughed.

'Well I can't see why. Let's get the machine cranked up, shall we?'

I nodded my assent as she switched the machine on.

'Shall we start with 80?'

I shook my head. I was seeing it like a beachball. '85, please,' I ordered.

'Sir!' Sam replied with an awkward left-handed salute, raising her right hand to show me the ball clutched in it. She lowered the ball, dropping it into the machine and a nano second later it fired out towards me. We had agreed to keep the length about the same as we had used on the throw downs so I left the first three to allow my eyes to refocus.

'Too fast?' she quipped, playfully.

'Just load 'em.'

The fourth clattered into the base of the bowling machine, the next hit the netting at cover. And the rest of that bucket were hit hard in an arc between mid-off and cover point. Sam refocused the machine so that I faced yorkers, full tosses, bouncers, the lot. And they all or pretty much all, got dispatched. I walked back up the net towards Sam, wiping sweat from my brow as the door barged open and in rushed Rick Pallant.

'Johnny! You're in – hurry up!'

'What? In? But I'm eleven surely, unless Carlisle has suddenly realised how good I am,' I said with a laugh.

'Seriously, Johnny, it's been carnage. You'd better hurry, mate.' Pallant spun around and dashed back out of the door.

I felt quite exhausted. Perhaps, with hindsight, the net was not my best idea. I thanked Sam, who smiled and planted a kiss on my sweaty cheek as I passed. 'Anytime', she smiled.

I returned her smile and headed for the stairs.

Somehow, I managed to avoid being timed out but as I walked out to the middle I felt my legs shaking from the exertions of the last fifty minutes. A few calls from the terraces behind me made me smile to myself; one wag called, 'It's alright, folks, Johnny's here now!' I half-raised my bat in the general direction of the voice and received a ripple of applause in return. I reflected on the fact that my batting had perhaps never generated any applause before as I blinked a few times to allow my eyes to become accustomed to the brighter light. I took my first look at the scoreboard. Carnage was the right word. I had left the game at 75 without loss and now we were positively teetering at 113 for 9. There was something strangely comforting about the situation; desperate but there was nothing expected of me.

Dench strolled towards me and we met just off the square.

'One ball to come. He's moving it away most of the time but the odd one stays straight. Just block it and I'll shepherd the strike.'

I nodded, but with no real intention of following his advice. My net session had left me tired, but I felt like my eye was in.

Umpire Stainforth nodded to me from the bowler's end. 'One?' he asked, expecting me to affirm.

I simply nodded and moved my bat until I had aligned it with leg-stump whereupon I set about scratching a mark with my bat. I still had on my indoor cricket shoes, having had no time to change them. I stood up, looked carefully around to check on the position of the fielders and ignored the Gloucester keeper who loudly wondered why I bothered looking at the fielders as I rarely ever hit the ball. I smiled inwardly. Dench at the other end was discreetly showing me the back of his hand, gloved fingers pointing downwards, reminding me to block.

'Right arm over, one to come,' Stainforth noted as Gloucester's big West Indian quick, Collins, steamed in from his long run. For a second, I found myself wishing the Sunday League matches still limited bowlers' run ups. I knew that Collins' slower ball was around 80mph. Dench still had his hand down and that annoyed me. I knew what I was about to do and could not stop myself. Collins had reached the end of his run, leapt into the air and suddenly a white blur came hurtling at me. I think I probably closed my eyes. I certainly do not remember seeing the ball pitch, but I felt it snick off my Gray Nicolls as I threw everything at the ball. An 'Oooh,' from the crowd, shouts of 'Howzaat?' from the slip cordon, followed immediately by Dench's scream of 'Run!'

The ball had cannoned off the keeper's outstretched glove and was racing away to the empty third-man boundary, being chased by two slip fielders. I turned for a third, but Dench was once again standing impassively, hand raised in a stop sign. I ignored that and kept running forcing him suddenly to do the same.

'You cocky bastard,' he shot at me as we crossed. I simply smiled.

The next over, from the Pavilion End, was from Beatty, a dibbly-dobbly medium pacer who normally poses us little threat. Today, however, he had taken 5 for very little from his first five overs. I took my strike. Leg stump again. I shifted into the slightly more open stance – the one Summers had forbidden until the internationals - and waited for Beatty to stop polishing the ball on his whites. He was an unimposing figure, slightly overweight, with a bit of a crinkly mullet going on. I get easily distracted when batting, which is probably more than half of my problem, and found myself wondering if he was modelling himself on a mid-80s Ian Botham.

I let the first ball sail gently past, well outside off.

'Bowling, Kev!' growled Mitchell from immediately behind my stumps as he took the ball into his gloves and slung it across to first slip.

Kev? Distracted again, I pondered this as the bowler trudged back to his mark. Brian Beatty. Nickname, Kev. As the bowler turned at the end of his run, I looked behind me at Mitchell.

'Kevin Beatty – Ipswich?'

Mitchell nodded. 'Focus, Johnny, you could beat your highest score today. Four, isn't it?'

I let the next one drift down the leg-side as the umpire signalled a wide. The scoreboard was beginning to tick over, just.

'Actually, I scored 9 against Kent a couple of years back,' I muttered, without looking back.

'Ladies?'

I laughed at that. Beatty was still walking slowly back to his mark, polishing the ball furiously. 'Why not Warren?'

The next delivery was slightly full, outside off and I stepped forward and connected perfectly, the ball crashing past extra-cover who could do no more than trot after it as it sped to the boundary underneath the Bedser

Stand scoreboard. A shocked silence, followed by a roar of appreciation from the Surrey fans. This felt oddly easy.

'Do what?' Mitchell said, as I returned to the batting crease.

'Warren Beatty. Why not Warren?'

'It's the hair.'

'Oh yes, makes sense,' I replied, assuming my stance once more.

A shorter one this time but I had time to readjust and turn it off my hip for two to fine leg. Dench signalled for a mid-wicket chat.

'What on earth are you doing, Lorrens?' he snarled.

'Equalling my highest score, Alan. What's your problem?'

Dench was silent for a moment. 'Just remember who's the senior batsman here and give me the strike.' With that he turned on his heels and went back to the non-striker's end.

The next delivery was a yorker which I just managed to jab the bat on, the ball squeezing past short leg. I turned Dench down for a quick single, more out of exhaustion than contrariness but that did nothing to improve his mood. I padded away the fifth ball and, going against all advice from the training manuals, decided that on the sixth ball I was going to hit it straight, whatever it was. Beatty leapt and released, I stepped forward and met the ball perfectly on the half-volley and watched lovingly as it arced over the umpire's head, one bounce into the boundary boards at the Vauxhall End. New top score achieved and even Dench felt compelled to bump gloves with me in the centre of the pitch.

'Now leave the batting to me,' he commanded.

'Whatever,' I thought.

Between us we put on a further 24 of which I contributed just 3, Dench managing to dominate the strike. It at least gave us something to defend.

We did not manage to, sadly, and recorded our second AXA one-day defeat of the season. Carlisle was in a foul mood although to be fair it was pretty much the same mood whether we won, drew or lost. As a player who had made a handful of appearances in a strong Australia team in the late '80s, he was always described as 'taciturn'. This seemed generous to me. If he had caught me with my phone between innings he would have been rather more than taciturn and I knew that having it out in the dressing room was a huge no-no but when it vibrated in my kitbag I snatched it up discreetly and headed for a toilet cubicle.

'Mark,' I mumbled in reply, as quietly as I could. It was Summers and he did not sound happy either.

'What the bloody hell are you doing, Johnny? You were meant to wait for the one-dayers!'

'I couldn't help myself, mate. That idiot Dench was getting under my skin – I just wanted to shut him up.'

'Well it hasn't helped me, Johnny. I now have punters sniffing around the offer and that was not any part of the plan.'

I was not a huge betting man, but I knew enough to understand that if he now had punters buying the spread, and if I scored well, he stood to lose his long position. This would drastically reduce his winnings and he could conceivably end up short; and that could cost him a lot if I ended up scoring some.

'Apologies, Mark. Like I said ages ago, I would find it hard not to do my best if I knew how to improve. I've managed not to do it earlier this season,' I added, weakly.

'Yeah, well the damage is done. My long position has already been badly eroded and sellers are not showing now,' he replied angrily.

Having apologised, there was not much I could say. 'Can you still make decent money?'

'Only if you bat like that in all three games.'

'Well, you never know,' I ventured as Summers ended the call.

CHAPTER 30

Monday was meant to be a day off but after the loss to Gloucestershire the day before, Carlisle called us all in for batting practice. It started at the ungodly hour of 9:00 a.m., and as we formed a circle around him, steadying ourselves for the inevitable tirade, I caught sight of Sam, adjusting one of the bowling machines. She smiled back, mouthing 'well done', just as Carlisle was saying that the only batsmen who came out of it with any credit were Rennie, Driver, Dench and Lorrens. This prompted a giggle from my teammates, quickly suppressed when they saw Carlisle's face tinge with purple.

I bowled for an hour to Pallant, MacLaine and Lenderman. To be honest I did not try too hard, preferring them to look good in Carlisle's eyes today. I checked my mobile when I returned briefly to the changing room to stow my sweater away. I had missed a call from Summers. For a moment I thought to ignore it but after the previous day's debacle I decided I ought to reply.

'Mark, it's me. Gotta be quick – we've been called in for extra training.'

'Seen The Mirror yet?'

My heart sank. What had Singh done now? 'No, what's in it today?'

'Let's just say that Elisa is not going to be best pleased. She's due home tomorrow, you said? Silly boy.'

I could feel the beginnings of a cold sweat on my forehead. 'Doubtlessly something invented by Krishnan, Mark. You know how he is.'

'He knows people, Johnny. And I know you.'

The phone went dead. What did that mean? He knows people. I needed to see a copy of the paper quickly. Elisa was due home the next day and I feared that I might need to enter damage limitation mode.

Risking Carlisle's wrath, I legged it back up to ground level and dashed round the back of the pavilion and up to the Club Office. Jackie was there and just finishing a call. I was breathless.

'Papers?' I gasped.

She reached below her desk and pulled up a stack of that morning's newspapers.

'Are you keeping cuttings after your personal best yesterday?' she laughed.

'No point,' I replied, breezily. 'There's more where that came from.'

I did not feel breezy in the slightest. I fumbled through the pile until I found The Mirror. Nothing on the front page, nothing on the back. So far so good. I turned to the inside back and found Singh's column on the opposite page. Skimming down the columns of print I saw nothing to alarm me. I was starting to feel a little calmer when I saw a small piece tucked away in the bottom corner of the page.

While the cat's away... reformed, returning England bad boy is up to his old tricks. With magazine editor-wife, Elisa, on tour with Toadlust, Johnny Lorrens has been spied on the town with a mystery blonde, adding to rumours of marriage problems for the one-time golden couple.

'Anything wrong, Johnny?' Jackie must have read my face.

'What? Um, no. No, all is good. Can I keep this?' I asked, nodding at the paper in my hand.

'Sure. I'll search through the others if you like?' she said with a grin.

I waved a farewell and dashed back to the training session, wondering just how much worse this could all get.

Once the session was over, I climbed back into the Vectra and sat for a few moments, relieved that no-one else had seemingly seen the piece in The Mirror. I had not seen Lori since Derby, but she must certainly be the 'mystery blonde'. Sadly for me, there was truth in me being on the town with her, and more. I felt a mixture of shame and indignation. Shame for what I had done in betraying Elisa; indignation in that she was apparently doing the same and even more publicly, with Crispin-bloody-LeDare. I was just about to start the engine when I jumped at a rap on the driver's side window. Dench was glaring at me. I rolled down the window.

'Everything okay, Alan?'

'Not really, Lorrens. What you did yesterday. That showed a total lack of respect to me as the senior batsman.'

'Yes, you indicated that to me at the time,' I replied calmly. More calmly than I felt. I realised, with him towering over me as he leaned in towards the car, just what a powerful man he was.

'You are a bowler. Just remember that.' With that he turned and walked a few yards across the forecourt towards an identical silver, Vectra.

'You got your car back then?' I ventured, stating the obvious.

'Evidently,' he muttered without looking back.

I drove back to Epsom deep in thought. With Elisa due back the next evening I was going to have to decide whether to come clean or deny.

I opened the front door to a blinking red light on the answering machine, dumped my bags down and pressed the play button. A call from Jack, who wanted an urgent reply. Another from Ralph, wanting the same. The third message caught me off guard.

'Hiya, lover. Long time no see. So sorry about that – I have really missed you. Anyway, I am on a flight out of LA which gets into Heathrow at about nine so don't go to sleep without me. Oh yes. You never did tell me what you thought of my novel idea. I guess that can wait. Knowing you, you haven't even looked at it. Can't wait to see you. All of you!'

With a playful giggle she had hung up. Mixed emotions ran through my mind. The sense of betrayal over the LeDare issue outweighing any excitement at the thought of seeing her again. But her novel? What was that all about?

I shut the front door, slid my bags to one side and set to making a cup of tea in the kitchen. I looked out across the lawn. It still needed a cut. I caught sight of the notice board and saw the photo of me. The one I had snipped Elisa from. I took out my wallet, looking for her half but could not see it. Emptying the contents and spreading them across the work surface confirmed it was not there anymore. Strange. And disappointing as that was my favourite picture of her. My eye was drawn to a pink slip tucked between two bank cards. I pulled it out. It was the note that Lori had left behind when she stayed over.

Johnny, thanks so much for being there for me – and yes! You get rid of Phillipe and I'll sort your problem out too!! Love you – Lori

Damning evidence, that could certainly come back to haunt me. I read it one last time and with a tinge of regret, tore it into a dozen pieces and threw it into the kitchen bin.

I mashed out the teabag, sloshed in milk, heaped in a couple of sugars and took the drink up to our study room. I powered up the PC and read Singh's piece again. How on earth did he know about me and a mystery blonde? Someone must have told him, but I could not fathom who that could be. The only person who I could think of was Terry Court, the ECB liaison guy, but that seemed so unlikely. He was part of my rehabilitation into the England team so leaking that to the press would have been highly unhelpful.

As I waited for the PC to open up, I tapped out Jack's number on my mobile. I had only to wait for a couple of rings. Time enough to catch sight of the *Strangers on a Train* card I had written to Lori – the one where I 'offered' to do hers. I picked it up, half-turned and flicked it towards the bin in the corner.

'Lorrens,' my brother snapped.

'Afternoon, Jack. How goes it in deepest Oxfordshire?'

'Oh, it's you,' he replied, a sense of relief in his voice.

'You left me a message to call?'

'Hold on a sec, let me just finish this...'

I could hear a scratching of pen on paper. I assumed he was working.

'Right,' he continued. 'We have a problem with your father-in-law.'

'Go on,' I encouraged, fearing that this was going to happen. When Jack gets his teeth into something he is like a highly irritating dog with a bone.

'Well, I had what I would consider a rather threatening call from him yesterday.'

'About the plans?'

'What else? He always sounded like a nice guy, but he's vexed over this one. Vexed and aggressive.'

'Have you been calling him, Jack?'

'Yes. I cannot get him to accept that the vomitories are all wrong...'

'But, Jack,' I interrupted. 'He's an experienced architect and, with respect, you are still training. Besides, we only shared the plans to get his thoughts. If he doesn't agree with us that's not the end of the world. We can take the concerns elsewhere.' I was not sure where that would be but I could see nothing good coming from pestering Ralph; certainly not given his obvious ties to Sir Ken Parslow.

'It's simple maths, Johnny,' he snapped back.

'Look, I need to return a call to him too. Let me see what I can do.'

Jack was not satisfied with that. 'You might want to find out why it means so much to him,' he commanded. 'Which firm did he work for?'

I paused for a moment to think. 'I'm pretty sure he has always worked for himself.'

'Well you said yourself that he's tight with the Surrey president, didn't you? I am certain there is more to this.'

'Like I said, let me see what I can do.'

'But what does that mean, Johnny?'

'Like I said, I will speak with Ralph and I will have another word with Windy too.'

'Windy?'

'Miller. Barry Miller. Last time I spoke with him he got very agitated. Might just wind him up again and see what happens.'

'He's the one you think might have something to do with Sally's death?'

'Not so sure now to be honest. But he'll be fully involved in any shady dealings if there are any.'

'Windy? Do all you cricket types have daft nicknames?'

'Pretty much,' I chuckled. 'And we are cricketers, not cricket types.'

'Yeah, right,' he replied before clicking me off.

The PC had come to life and I started to look through the few emails that Elisa had sent since she went to the States, searching for the novel that she had mentioned. If Elisa had been home I could have asked her about her father's career. Instead, I clicked on Ask Jeeves and typed in his name: Ralph Wilton. I waited a few seconds as the screen populated and took the opportunity to dash down to the kitchen to make another brew.

When I returned to the study I saw that the search had been successful. I learnt that Ralph was still a consulting architect, though semi-retired, and had clients in the worlds of business, entertainment and sport. Perhaps that explained his apparently close ties with Surrey. Further sub-headings promised details of his business interests, early life and personal life but by now I was keen to find Elisa's novel ideas and elected to further my research of Ralph a little later.

It did not take long to find the email. She had sent it more than a month earlier.

I'm gonna miss you, darling. Hope you miss me too – if you know what I mean. I'm due back Tuesday evening, late. Don't wait up, but if I'm in bed before you get in, don't be afraid to wake me!!!

There was an attachment. I took a swig of the scalding tea as I clicked on it and began to read. It was a fairly brief synopsis (that's what she titled it) of a novel she was planning. It was a warts and all account of a young band suddenly making it big in the States. I had an uneasy feeling as I continued to read. The lead singer, Cash, was a wild, untamed youth, living dangerously in the moment. The novel was written from the perspective of a photographer who had been assigned to cover the tour by the band's management. The next few words sent a chill down my spine and a feeling of nausea enveloped me:

I woke up to find C's hand in my pants. I thought about screaming but, seeing that there were already half a dozen people already in the room, I pulled him down on top of me – it was exciting knowing that we were being watched. I loved it – decadent, dangerous and very Chelsea Hotel.

I'd seen those same words before when I had been looking for some information for Elisa. I felt sick. When I had read those words the first time I had assumed it to be a diary. Maybe I had been wrong about Elisa. I mean, there were photos in the paper but it was LeDare draped around Elisa, not the other way round. Perhaps she really had been unable to keep in touch, like she said. I mused on my recent behaviour. I had certainly won back the 'bad boy' tag, even though the press did not know all of it. They now knew about a 'mystery blonde', though, and that was enough.

Ralph answered on the third ring. 'Wilton,' he said languidly. His voice oozed calm, expensive, professional.

'Ralph? Hi, it's Johnny. You called?'

Immediately his tone was cooler, more distant.

'I did. Two things, Johnny. Firstly, please tell your brother to stop calling me or I will need to take further steps.'

'Is he bothering you?' I asked, rather needlessly.

'That is an understatement,' he replied drily.

'It's still about the numbers?'

'It is. Look, not to be rude, he is not qualified to comment on these aspects. I have personally checked the calculations and they are more than adequate.'

'Fair enough,' I replied, not willing to get into an argument about this. 'And secondly?'

'Well, this is rather more awkward,' he began.

I felt a knotting in my stomach, gulped down some more tea and ventured, 'How so?'

'It's not for me, or Kitty, to involve ourselves in your private affairs, Johnny, but when our daughter is involved...'

'I don't know what you mean, Ralph,' I replied with as much innocence as I could muster.

'Oh, I think you do.' There was a harsh edge to his voice that I had rarely heard before.

I left a silence, which I always find nigh on impossible. It was Ralph who broke it.

'If I find that any of this stuff in the papers is true...'

He let the rest hang. I was not sure what he would do in that event, but I thought back to his shirtless figure, working the ground at the end of his garden and remembered thinking then what an impressive physique he had. He might be a tricky physical opponent, but surely it would not come to that.

CHAPTER 31

Tuesday May 20 1997

Elisa was due back and I had had plenty of time overnight not to sleep but to lie there wondering how I could have got it so wrong. To be honest I had not decided whether or not to come clean with Elisa. If I was going to do that I felt it was best to do it immediately though I feared that might just force her away. The best plan I could come up with was to break things off with Lori and to quietly forget about Eleanor. Both would be hard to do but with Eleanor it was perhaps more difficult due to my link with Sally and our shared concerns over her death.

Stowing my breakfast debris into the dishwasher I found myself thinking about O'Brien. I found it really hard to see him as the type to run down an innocent girl but then I puzzled over how someone capable of that *might* present? The only way I could think of finding out was to confront him with it. We rarely socialised unless it was with a bunch of the guys and he was surprised to hear from me.

'Aren't you meant to be in Leeds?'

'No, practice day is tomorrow – I'm going up really early. Elisa comes home late tonight and I want to see her first. She's been gone for weeks.'

'Well, yeah, that's fine with me. A quick beer would be good. Where do you fancy?'

'You're at Parsons Green? Why not make it Putney? Some decent pubs there.'

'Good plan. Why don't we make it the Eight Bells?'

We set the time for 1:00 p.m., which gave me time to have a clear up at home and to put off calling Lori. I eventually plucked up the courage.

'Oh, hi Johnny!' she answered happily. 'Day off?'

'Sort of,' I began quietly. 'Look, Lori, you are a fabulous person, but...'

'But you are married.'

I stopped short. Was she about to make this really easy for me? 'Well, yes, I suppose so,' I mumbled in embarrassment.

'Look, I totally get that. I don't want to make things difficult for you.'

This was going better than I could have imagined. 'Lori, you mean a lot to me...'

'Don't say anything more. We had fun. We probably shouldn't have but we were both having issues with our other halves or ex-partners. You have sorted your issues and, as for mine? Well, mine will sort themselves out I am sure.'

I felt like a complete rat. Not only for betraying Elisa's faith but now giving Lori the cold-shoulder. I bit my lip as I was about to say something like 'let's keep in touch', when she spoke.

'Busy at work here, Johnny. I've still got that surprise for you.'

'Oh, you don't need to worry about that.'

'No, but I want to. It's been fun, Johnny. Good luck.'

And with that she was gone. I felt totally drained. Relieved. And a total cad.

The Tube from Wimbledon was empty and I had less than fifteen minutes to plan my strategy. Parsons Green, one stop on from Putney Bridge. Putney High Street was where Sally was mown down. O'Brien lived in Parsons Green. Coincidence?

I pushed open the dark green, half-glassed door of the old pub, stepped inside; two steps and I was immediately at the bar. I had a quick look round the horseshoe-shaped bar but could see no sign of O'Brien. There was just a handful of drinkers, mainly solitary men. I ordered a pint of Coors, a light beer for lunchtime, and spent a few minutes looking at the memorabilia on the walls, most of it linked to Fulham Football Club, just up the road. I had been there a few times over the years with friends who were avid fans, following the club as it teetered almost out of existence and languished in the lower divisions. A tap on my shoulder snapped me from my reverie.

'Beer, Johnny?'

'No thanks, Mark. My round, what's it to be?'

He easily found us a couple of seats in a quiet corner as I bought him a pint of Guinness.

'Cheers', he said, offering his glass up to mine.

I had always liked O'Brien. Well, since he joined us a year ago. He always seemed positive, generous and thoughtful. The only glimpse of a different side was a few weeks earlier as we came off the pitch after a practice session.

'Is it just us two?' he continued.

'It is, Mark. Let me get right to the point.'

He paused, with his glass just about to touch his lips. 'The point?' he echoed with a note of uncertainty.

'Sally Framsell.'

O'Brien put his pint glass back carefully on the beer mat in front of him.

'The girl you worked with at The Oval? What about her?'

'Nothing to tell me about her?'

O'Brien paused. A flicker in his eyes made me wonder if he was deciding to tell. Not enough to suggest he had been rumbled but he looked uncomfortable.

'Like what?' he challenged.

'Like what happened the night she died.' I retorted.

'Whoa, there!' he said through clenched teeth. 'I had absolutely nothing to do with that hit and run, if that's where this is going, Johnny.'

'I'm not making any allegations, Mark. It's simply that the police have decided that this was all a tragic accident.'

'And you think it's not?' He seemed a little calmer.

I was not sure how much to share but this seemed like as good a time as any now that I had caught O'Brien off guard.

'I'm not convinced. Tell me about your relationship with Sally.'

A flush appeared on his cheeks. O'Brien toyed with the beer mat unable to meet my eyes. 'Nothing to tell.'

'Well why not start with the time you two dated up in the Midlands in the Summer of '95.'

Now he looked up sharply.

'How do you know about that?'

'Doesn't matter. What went wrong?'

O'Brien paused for a few moments. 'I made a mistake,' he started glumly. 'I was already in a relationship, got tangled up with Sally so when the offer from Surrey came I jumped at it.'

'Did that work out?'

'Not really. The Sally issue went away.'

'And your partner?'

'She didn't come down with me.'

'Did she know about Sally?'

'Not so far as I know. Just didn't want to live in London.'

I drained the last drops from my glass. 'And since Sally came to The Oval?'

'Do you mean, did we carry on with our relationship?'

I nodded.

'No. I had rashly assumed that she had followed me down. Got a bit of a slap down, to be fair, for being presumptuous.' Here, he gave a small laugh, at his own expense.

'Did you two go out together at any time down here?'

'Just the once. The night she died,' he said with what appeared to be genuine sadness.

So, perhaps he was 'M', after all.

'How did that go?'

'Bloody hell, Lorrens! What are you, a copper or something?'

'Well, they're not interested so, yeah, I guess so.'

O'Brien took our empties to the bar and returned a couple of minutes later with replacements.

'So, how did it go?'

'Badly. I suggested that we start dating again and she said no. We didn't even order a drink. She made an excuse about rushing off to meet someone else. Couldn't have gone worse really.'

'Except, it did for her. Much.'

'I know. I could not believe it when I heard. I left her outside the Kings Head just across the river and decided to walk home. It must have happened a few minutes later. I am haunted by that.'

O'Brien looked genuinely broken by this. I found myself feeling for him.

'Any idea who she was meeting?'

He simply shook his head.

'Did you speak to the police, Mark?'

'No. I wasn't sure enough. I didn't actually see anything,' he replied. 'Think I should?'

'I do. You never know, you may have seen something without knowing it.'

Back at home I packed my bags for the trip to Leeds and double checked I had all my gear. The actual kit would be new and supplied up at Headingly. I just needed to worry about pads, gloves, bat and the like.

Elisa would be home in less than 5 hours' time if her plane was on time and I was excited to imagine seeing her again. Now knowing that it was an excerpt from her novel that I had read changed everything. The phone rang as I was zipping up the final bag. I dashed down the stairs, hoping that it was not going to be Elisa telling me her flight had been delayed, or worse.

'Hiya!' I answered, panting from my sudden dash. It was Summers.

'We have a slight problem here, Johnny.'

Again, the noise of the trading floor, numbers being hurled hysterically around. I reflected briefly on the difference for Summers. Long, sunny days on the cricket field replaced by the claustrophobia of a City trading room.

'We have?'

'Your little shenanigans against Gloucester the other day have complicated things this end.'

'They have?'

'My long position has been whittled away by punters who saw what you did.'

'You told me that already and I'm sorry about that, mate. But, in the moment...'

'I did ask you not to change things too early,' he said with feeling. 'But what's done is done. Now we need to sort it.'

'We?'

'Yes. We. The only way to straighten this out is either for you to bowl and field well below your normal standards or for you to fail with the bat.'

'Shit, mate. You can't ask for that,' I replied angrily.

'That's as may be,' he replied tersely. 'But that's exactly what I'm asking for.'

'How is that going to help?'

'Simple. You get dismissed for none, with your old stance. That'll scare the buyers off. And if you're crap in the field, even more so – might even draw out some more sellers. And my long position is restored in time for the second match.' He had it all worked out.

'Well let's just see what happens, Mark. If I am too bad, I won't even get a second match.'

'So that's a no, then, is it?'

I simply put the phone down.

Summers called back an hour or so later, full of apologies. He explained that he had been working really long hours and that his bosses were keeping a close eye on the 'Lorrens spread'.

'I meant to ask, how did you manage to create a long position? Presumably there are rules on that sort of thing?'

'Yeah, there are but I called in a few favours from friends and had them take the positions for me. Like I said, though, when you had that mad half-hour against Gloucester more buyers soon appeared. That has left me pretty much square so...'

I decided not to mention his latest plan.

'Listen, can you meet quickly?'

I groaned inwardly. 'Mark, I am rushing around trying to get ready for Leeds. What do you need?'

'It's not what *I* need, mate. I have ten thousand pounds here for you.'

'Ten grand?'

'For the beers, Johnny. We never sorted that. Does that sound fair? I mean, there could be more, but I thought ten grand for the use of your face seemed reasonable.'

I thought it sounded more than reasonable and had not expected anything until the beers sold – if they ever did. 'That is most generous, Mark, but I don't think I can get up to see you today. Why don't we leave it until after the one-dayers?'

'No, tell you what, I'll sneak out early, pop down to Epsom on the train if you can meet me at the station? I won't take any of your time. I just don't want the cash hanging around any longer.'

I thought for a moment. It did not help me, timewise, but it seemed churlish not to at least meet him if he was keen to give me ten grand. We agreed to meet at Epsom at 5:00 p.m.

As I left the house to drive down into town I reflected on Summers. Radio silence for a year or more and then suddenly he popped up with his analysis of my batting and what still seemed something of a hare-brained betting scheme. It was the way he had turned on me a couple of times recently that left me feeling uneasy. My old, best mate had returned, to be replaced at times by an unpleasant bully. I was glad that this was going to be a brief meeting and pondered returning to a life without Summers once the one-dayers had finished. The beer deal might prolong things, but I could not see Summers retaining his interest in that for too long. I parked in the tiny car park on West Hill and strolled the quarter of a mile downhill to the station.

For a fairly well-known, historic town like Epsom, the station is a bit of a dump. I walked through the low, wide entrance into its dingy interior. The station clock said it was a couple of minutes to five so I picked up a copy of The Mirror at the kiosk and turned to the back pages. It was a relief to read nothing about me and, just to be sure, I flicked through the front pages as well; nothing about Elisa, either. The paper gave me something to hide behind too. It's not like I am David Beckham, or anything, but I do sometimes get recognised out and about. I had a quick look around me. Across the other side of the concourse was a woman, wearing over-sized shades and an old-fashioned, red and white-striped headscarf, hunched behind her paper and I wondered, with a smile, if she was doing the same as me. Aside from her, I was alone.

I looked up as passengers from a just-arrived train started to descend from the elevated platforms. Summers was easy to spot as he picked his way down the steps. He looked bigger than ever and seemed to be finding this simple act a little difficult. He smiled as he neared the bottom of the staircase and flipped up one hand from the wrist in discreet greeting. He rolled towards me and stood close. No handshakes today, just a rather furtive fumble in his inside-jacket pocket before he thrust a brown-paper wrapped package into my hands. I went to put it straight into the pocket of my Harrington.

'Check it first,' he said quietly.

'Really? Here?' I was surprised. Counting out ten-thousand pounds, even in a safe town like Epsom, seemed ill-advised.

I opened the package and looked carefully around me; still just the lady engrossed in her paper. I pulled out the wad of cash and flicked through it. It was made up with stacks of mint fifty-pound notes, banded together in amounts of one-thousand pounds. There were ten packs. 'Thanks, Mark. Thanks very much,' I said quietly. 'Much appreciated.'

'Well, like I said, there should be more where that came from if they sell well.'

There was a slightly awkward pause. Two old friends that perhaps have discovered they no longer have that connection that made them great friends not so long before.

'Well, thanks again, Mark. I'd better dash. I want to get packed and an early night ready to beat the morning rush hour on the M25.'

'Understood, Johnny. Just remember, though. You are not going to have any Botham moments up at Headingly. Save those heroics for Lord's, okay?'

He smiled as he said it, but I felt uncomfortable; underneath I was sure I detected a threat.

'Like I said right at the start, Mark, I very probably won't get to bat and I would need to take a stack of wickets to cause you problems.'

'Oh, I think you will bat. These Aussies are seriously good, despite a few recent poor results, and our top order is flimsy. Either way, don't be ashamed to have a poor one. I need the punters to start selling.'

I gave him one last, withering look, turned on my heel and went to leave the station.

'Give my regards to Elisa, Johnny. Is she still back tonight?' Summers called across the concourse.

'Nine-ish,' I replied, 'but I'll be well asleep by then.'

Summers made a lewd gesture with his right hand as I walked out back into the sunlight.

I was all packed and ready to go by early evening, made myself some pasta and was just sitting down at 8:15 p.m., to watch a few minutes of television when I suddenly remembered that I had forgotten to buy toothpaste in Epsom. I jumped in the Vectra and dashed down the Reigate Road to the Esso station and grabbed two tubes of Colgate. One for me, one for home, and by 8.50 p.m., I was parking up back in front of the house. The light in our bedroom flicked off suddenly and I realised with a jolt of anticipation that Elisa must be home for I had not switched on any lights upstairs. Either that or we had burglars. Just in case, I grabbed an old bat from the car's boot and slipped quietly back into the house.

On the hall floor in front of me was a red suitcase. Not one that I remembered but clearly Elisa was home. I put the bat down in the porch, checked all of the downstairs doors were locked, put the chain on the front door, went swiftly upstairs and took a quick shower.

I went quietly across the landing, avoiding the creaky board, and eased open our bedroom door. A glow of light seeped through our curtains from a street light outside and I could just make out the halo of peroxide-blonde hair on Elisa's pillow. At the same time I caught a waft of *Balahe* – Elisa's favourite perfume and the one that I can always 'smell' when I think of her. I slipped off the boxers and slid into bed next to her, disappointed that she appeared to be asleep. She turned onto her side, with her back to me and made a small murmuring sound in her sleep. I moved in closer to her until our bodies were in sync. She moved back slightly, putting pressure on me in just the right spot. I responded in the most natural way and with a little manoeuvring of her hips, Elisa allowed me to enter her. I reached over and felt for her breasts. Firm as ever, but strangely fuller.

'These have...'

'Shhh.'

'But they feel diff...'

'Johnny, just shut up and do me!' she breathed as she began to work her hips harder.

She did not have to work too hard. After weeks of waiting for her to return it was all over rather too quickly. Thankfully, Elisa did not seem to mind and, within seconds she seemed to be asleep again.

My phone ringing on the bedside table next to me awoke me suddenly at midnight. I grabbed for it quickly so as not to wake Elisa. She stirred but did not wake.

'Hello?' I whispered.

'Sorry to wake you, lover. Plane was delayed and I've just got through customs so will be home in an hour or so. I was going to say, don't wait up, but you didn't,' she laughed.

By now I was wide awake. And sitting up, terrified to look to my right. I knew what I was going to see. Or rather, who.

'No problem, darling, I can't wait to see you. Coffee or tea?'

She laughed. 'Oh, go on then. Coffee would be fab.'

When the call had finished, I pulled my boxers back on and walked to the bedroom door and slapped my hand against the light switch, flooding the room with harsh, electric light.

Lori sat up in bed, the duvet around her waist, perfect breasts exposed. 'Hi, Johnny,' she said, her voice husky from sleep, blonde hair tousled and half over her eyes. 'What's happening?'

'What's happening?' I started in incredulity. 'What the fuck are *you* doing here?'

'I just came to give you your surprise. Didn't you like it? You seemed to?'

I looked at my phone. Elisa would be back in less than an hour and I had to shower again and had sheets to wash now too. I went to the windows and opened them all to try to remove the *Balahe* scent from the room.

'What are you doing? Come back to bed,' Lori said, pulling the duvet back up as she lay down again.

'Lori, you need to get out now!' I said urgently. 'My wife is coming home in less than an hour and you need to be long gone.'

She sat back up, duvet dropped again. 'So, you meant it when you said our relationship is over?'

'Well, I'm not sure I'd call it a relationship, but yes, I did.'

'That's such a shame,' she said, with a look of genuine sadness.

'How did you even get in here?'

'Research,' she said, ambiguously.

'Right, well it's time to go now,' I ordered, snatching the duvet off of the bed and realising at the same time that I was about to throw out of my house someone who I had actually felt very close to for a while. I now had deep misgivings about her.

I waited impatiently as she got dressed and then led the way down the stairs, opening the front door for her as I handed her the case and stepped aside to let her pass. As she did, she suddenly leant in to plant a kiss on my lips, handed me a door key and, with a wistful smile, stepped out into the night. So, *she* had taken the key that went missing a few weeks earlier. I had little time to dwell on that, though.

I dashed back upstairs, stripped the bed linen, filled and set the washing machine going, re-made the bed, showered again and dived back under the covers just in time as I heard a vehicle pulling up outside.

When the bedroom door opened a few minutes later I caught a hint of *Balahe* again and for a terrible second thought it was Lori coming back in. Perhaps my sudden dash to Epsom had afforded her the chance to slip in the house. Presumably she had been waiting outside to creep in once all the lights were out. That felt just creepy. I heard a rustle of clothing slipping to the floor and faked a stirring from sleep.

'Elisa? Is that you?'

'Who else is it gonna be?' she chuckled as she slipped into the bed and snuggled up against my back.

'Welcome back, gorgeous,' I mumbled, still feigning a recent sleep.

'Mmm, fresh sheets, thanks Johnny.'

I felt a hand slide over my side, reaching.

'Do you have a few minutes?' she asked in her husky, bed voce.

Inwardly I groaned slightly. I felt in several ways like a spent force, but Elisa's soft hands combined with the sharpness of her nails soon did for me and seconds later she had straddled me and I let her control things. Second time that evening, and she was pleased that I outlasted her. I eventually fell asleep around two a.m., painfully aware of the early start and the long drive up to Leeds.

CHAPTER 32

Wednesday May 21 1997

I pulled in at Leicester Forest services at a little before 9:00 a.m. It had been something of a struggle to get up and Elisa had pleaded me to stay a little longer when I brought her up a coffee at six. I was surprised how good it felt to have her back and was beginning to wonder what had possessed me whilst she was away. In fairness, the whole Toadlust thing was nagging away at me still, but I was pleased to have rediscovered what I had been missing. That left me feeling conflicted over Lori, though. I really liked her and was unhappy about the way things had gone the night before.

I would have loved to have stayed longer at home but knew that I had to beat the rush hour if I was to get to Headingly by 11:00 a.m. The practice session was due to start at midday and I had to be there on time. Incredibly, I had received special dispensation from Alex Gorton, Chairman of Selectors, not to stay over in Leeds the previous night with the rest of the squad on the grounds that Elisa had been away for several weeks. He made it very clear that were I to be late to the session he would have no problem in putting me on a disciplinary. I was not about to give him that chance.

A quick comfort break and I was back on the M1, heading north, cruising at a little over eighty. The drizzle in Epsom had given way to a misty start in the Midlands with the promise of fine weather and temperatures of 25 degrees in Leeds. The inane banter from the radio DJ was grating and, as I turned the radio off, I found myself thinking ahead to the match. In some ways I could not quite believe that I was going to play for my country again. I am not jingoistic but to have played a Test for England gave me enormous pride. Even with just the one cap I was often referred to as 'England cricketer, Johnny Lorrens', and whilst I pride myself on not being overly status conscious, my goal from a very young age was to represent Surrey and England. The first I had done many times but as for England and me, well, that was unfinished business.

I ran through our batting order in my head. I knew all of the boys, but it was a very different side to the one I played in just a couple of years earlier. A few senior players had retired and a couple more were really 5-day specialists, but we had a promising mix of youth and experience, leading off with Dench and Carter at the top of the order. Dench I knew plenty about from playing with and against him over the years; Carter, from unfashionable Glamorgan, at 27 was just entering his prime. A dashing left-hander who, if he managed not to give the slips an early chance, was capable of scoring damagingly quickly. The trouble was that this season he had been giving too many early chances.

A low score tomorrow might mean a chance for one of the other guys in the squad. Da Silva at three was having a cracking season and this match was at his home ground. A product of the Yorkshire Academy, I fancied he might be pulling on an England sweater for years to come.

I checked the time as I pulled out to overtake a string of three supermarket articulateds and relaxed. It looked good for a pre-eleven o'clock arrival.

At four, Hassan of Worcestershire. Right-handed, immensely strong on the off-side, quick scoring and bowled some useful off-spin. I knew that only too well; he had got me out on several occasions, in one-dayers and in Championship games too. But then, so have most bowlers in the County game.

Temple of Middlesex was down for five. A bit of a nurdler but hard to get out and a fabulous slip. Bright at six, the Somerset wicketkeeper and their number three, which gives a sense of his quality, followed by Corbett of Essex – fast-medium with a preference for steepling bouncers aimed at the head. Useful with the bat too, a big six-hitter. Leander and Swartz were next up. The Derby quick had come quite late into the County game via the northern leagues so was still a bit on an unknown quantity for most bats, whilst Swartz's South African upbringing had made him a hard-as-nails, very fast, fast bowler. He qualified for England whilst with Lancashire two seasons before and promised to be a complete handful. In most teams, Yorkshire's fast-medium Barrett would be number eleven. With me in the side he was a definite ten. If there was any movement he could be lethal on his home ground. As for me, well I did not expect any favour from the Western Terrace, having been picked over their local favourite, Cotton, whose line and length seemed completely to have deserted him. If they did not mention my 'marriage difficulties' or spliffs, I would be both amazed and highly relieved.

I parked up inside the Headingly ground with ten minutes to spare, grabbed my bags and bat from the boot and, acknowledging the cheery greeting from the steward on the back door to the pavilion, mounted the steps as quickly as I could. Slightly breathlessly, I pushed open the door to the home dressing room and glanced at my watch as I did so. 10.57 a.m.

I immediately came face to face with Alex Gorton, stood squarely in the centre of the large dressing room, left arm, bent at the elbow, raised horizontally, right hand gripping the bezel of his wristwatch. As the lads erupted into an ironic cheer, I was sure I detected a look of disappointment on Gorton's craggy face.

'What ho, lads,' I offered with a grin. 'Mr Gorton,' I added deferentially, with a nod, as an afterthought.

I saw my changing space over between Da Silva and Hassan, my name above it on a card embossed with the crown and three lions badge. I felt a surge of pride as I put my bags down and carefully leant my Gray Nicolls against the seat.

'Just the one bat, Johnny?' Hassan asked, surrounded by wood.

Dench's voice from the other side of Da Silva, muttered something unintelligible.

'Morning, Alan', I smiled, leaning forward to see him. 'What was that?'

Da Silva grinned and said, 'He said that that's one more than you need.'

I feigned a laugh. No loyalty from my Surrey teammate, then.

Brian Dean, the England coach, came through the door at that moment. 'Morning, lads! Sleep well?'

Mutterings and nods of assent all round, although I simply nodded. It was good to have Elisa back, but I had got less sleep than I needed.

'Good. Okay, let's get out there and put in some hard work. We have just this morning session. The Aussies will be in by two o'clock so we have a couple of hours to fine tune. Nets first, then fielding practice.'

As he turned to leave he caught my eye, walked directly over and with a smile, offered his hand. 'Great to have you with us, Johnny. It's been a long time, but you deserve your recall. You found your kit. Good.'

I was just pulling on the crisp, white shirt, England crest in blue on the left breast, green KidsownTV logo on the left sleeve and right breast. I had a choice of two sweaters, one short-sleeved, the other long but I hoped not to need either.

'Thanks, Gaffer. I appreciate that. Really looking forward to it.'

The session was good and for once I felt a little appreciation towards Carlisle. He worked us mighty hard but today's session under the genial Dean was even harder. I bowled well in the nets, completely owning Dench to the point where Hassan, who was padded up ready to bat next, told me to ease up.

'You're gonna wreck his confidence, Johnny.'

That's a shame, I thought. 'You're right, Hassy, I'll send down a couple of full tosses,' I said.

Dench smashed the first two back over my head, or would have had the net not had a mesh roof. The third one he left to smash into his stumps.

'Don't patronise me, Lorrens,' he snarled.

'Boy, it must be fun at Surrey,' Hassan said quietly.

'He's not the captain there, thank the Lord,' I said with a grin as I sent down a ripper that took the edge of his bat and would have been snaffled by any half-decent slipper.

Dean deemed the practice session to be a success, identified a couple of the guys to do the press and took me to one side.

'Gorton wants to see you, Johnny. You are probably aware that he is not your greatest fan.'

I nodded.

'You have been selected for press duties, but he wants to speak with you first. My advice, is nod, agree with everything and avoid controversy, okay?'

I said that it was. I appreciated his quiet word; it felt like I had an ally.

Gorton made no bones about it.

'You know my view, Lorrens. Would not have picked you but my colleagues were adamant that we needed you. I, however, have the final word and if you let me and your country down, I will not hesitate to send you packing back to Surrey. Understood?'

In a game ever more full with sports psychologists and motivational coaches, one had to question Gorton's old-school motivation techniques. Sadly, he was the ultimate authority and I could do little but take it on the chin.

I slipped into the back of the pressroom for the last few questions to Alan Dench. Sat next to him was Terry Court who noticed my arrival with a smile and a nod towards me.

'So, Alan, what was it like to get the call? Most unexpected, I suppose.' It was Larry Helm from the Guardian, Dench's old Worcester teammate.

'Overdue, Larry. I would have thought it would have come sooner, to be honest.'

Cue an awkward silence, save for the furious scribblings of half a dozen hacks. The three television crews continued to film, their reporters speaking quietly into mobiles or making notes like their print-media peers.

'How's life down in London? Must be quite a change from Worcester?' Helm continued.

'I've settled well at Surrey, as you can see from my scores. The team is playing well and there were things I was keen to get away from,' he added, ambiguously.

Never one to miss an opportunity, Krishnan Singh spoke up. 'People, do you mean?'

Dench gave him a hard stare but did not reply.

The reporter from The Daily Express was one I did not recognise. Thirty-ish, long, dark hair, pretty face. 'What do you make of this Australian side?' she asked.

Dench looked relieved at a straight, cricket question and noticeably relaxed. He went on to outline their strengths.

'And weaknesses?' she probed.

'If they have any, I am not about to tell *you* am I?' he said with a strained smile.

Larry Helm again. 'Alan, your benefit year at Worcester was a complete disaster, you won't mind me saying. Was your move south a purely financial one?'

Dench looked furious. 'As opposed to?'

Helm paused, for effect. The atmosphere in the room was electric. 'Personal,' Helm answered.

'I'm here to talk cricket, Larry,' Dench responded through gritted teeth.

'So am I,' Helm replied calmly. 'I'll take that as "personal" then,' he added, scribbling in his notebook.

'Take it how you like,' Dench muttered angrily, pushing back his chair and starting to stand.

Terry Court had been surprisingly quiet throughout this exchange, almost as if he was as shocked as the rest of us. He suddenly came to, stood and said, 'I think that's enough for now. Thank you, Alan, very much for your time.'

Suddenly, Krishnan Singh stood too. 'So, is there any truth in rumours of your gambling debts, Alan? And, will you be having a punt on the Johnny Lorrens spread? The price looks like an absolute sell, doesn't it?'

A deathly look from Dench towards Singh was immediately followed by Dench's chair flipping over as he stormed from the dais, past Terry Court and out through a side door.

The small group of reporters all started to talk at once as Terry Court tried to restore order, reminding the assembled group that players were forbidden to gamble on any games, especially ones in which their team was involved, as I took my place before the press.

The questioning I faced seemed a lot less hostile. In fact, I felt a great deal of support from the assembled media. What was it like to get the call again? Could we beat the Aussies? And much laughter when Larry Helm asked if I had any beer samples to share? The female reporter from The Express, announcing herself as Maggie Sumpter, asked when the beers would be available and then Krishnan Singh, not waiting for my answer, asked if I did not have too many distractions.

'Focused solely on the series, Krishnan,' I replied confidently, and then, smiling at Maggie Sumpter, 'I haven't seen a date yet but supposedly to tie in with this series.'

'With your wife touring the States with Toadlust and back in the company of her old, long-term boyfriend, Crispin LeDare, can you really focus on this important series and your return to the England team?' Singh, again.

'As I said, focused on the job in hand,' I said as calmly as I could. Inside I was boiling.

'Another from me,' said Sumpter. 'How do you honestly feel about your wife's very public relationship with her ex?'

'Elisa is now home. She had a job to do out there and she will have done that very well. You of all people,' I added, scanning the room full of journalists, 'should know not to believe everything you write.'

Cue much scribbling in notebooks until Singh spoke again, just as Terry Court gave me the nod that time was up.

'This spread that City Sports have quoted on you. What can you tell us about that?'

I had feared this moment but had decided to play it casual. 'Not much more than you can, I doubt,' I replied, fixing my gaze firmly on Singh. 'You will probably know that they are essentially a spread-betting outfit and that they are known for offering quirky bets.'

'What do they know that the rest of us don't, Johnny?'

'I don't get you,' I replied calmly.

'The price is so high. They must know something.'

'Well, you will need to take that up with them, I'm afraid.'

'Will you be having a piece of that?' Now it was Helm.

Before I could answer, Terry Court cut in. 'The rules on gambling as far as players are concerned are well-established. None of the England squad will be betting on any of the matches that they are involved in.'

'What about Sydney, Johnny? Did you have a little flutter there?' It was Maggie Sumpter again.

'I would not be sitting here if I had,' I replied with a smile that I hoped did not look too forced.

'Not if you'd been caught,' Singh mumbled as he bent back over his notebook.

So, the Sydney business was not going to go away anytime soon. I would have to watch my step very carefully. One slip-up and the press would be all over me.

CHAPTER 33

Thursday May 22 1997

The big day dawned at last with clear, blue skies and a forecast of a warm, dry day with temperatures expected to top out at 26 degrees. Perfect cricket weather. As Dench and the Australian skipper, Matt Kelly, strolled out across the immaculate, emerald green outfield for the toss, I had my fingers crossed that we would bat first; that we would bat and that I would not have to.

It seemed likely that, if Summers had a position still, it was a small long one. He wanted me to have a bad game which would send the buyers into hiding and probably induce some selling, meaning that he could reinstate his bigger long position. It all seemed highly risky to me. Either way, with the press now keenly aware of the spread and with the speculation that I might be involved, I thought it best that I did not score highly. That in theory would help Summers in bringing out the sellers again helping him to reinstate his long position. Gorton had pulled me to one side after the press conference the previous day seeking my assurances that I had nothing to do with the City Sports' spread. The assurances I gave rang a little hollow to me as I clearly had known all about it before it went live. I was going round in circles but it dawned on me that whatever I did, the fact that the price was deemed odd, put me in a difficult position.

By now the two captains had reached the middle and were being interviewed by the BBC's anchor-man, surrounded by ground staff making last-minute repairs to the crease markings. There was a clear focus from both skippers on the strip and looks to the sky as a coin was produced, shown to both captains and flipped high into the air, as tradition dictates, by Dench as home captain. The two skippers shook hands and Dench turned towards the pavilion, set at almost ninety-degrees to the square, making a cover drive with his left arm, signalling for Carter to start padding up. We had clearly won the toss and elected to bat.

On the opposite side of the ground the Western Terrace was fast filling up. The rowdiest stand in English cricket, matched perhaps only by the Hollies Stand at Edgbaston; I was grateful for the distance between us and hoping that Dench did not field me at either deep extra-cover or deep backward square. Somehow, I knew what he would do. But for now, I could relax and hopefully enjoy not batting at all. Whatever that did to Summers' plans I decided not to worry about it. The spread was all his idea and so it was all his lookout.

I looked at the scorecard in my hand. The Australia line-up was deeply impressive. They were not the best one-day side in the world by accident. They batted pretty much all the way down the order and with four very fast bowlers and a cracking good leggie in Tim Pocket there would be no let-up. In club cricket you might get three bowlers in a team who you feel happy to face. In county cricket one, or perhaps two. But at this level you would be lucky to find any. There would be no respite today. Sitting on the balcony to the right of me were the four quicks. Kenny Barrett was tackling the Times crossword and had been for several minutes; it was still blank. Swartz and Leander had a new ball and were swapping finger positions and theory. Ben Corbett looked pensive, unsurprisingly, on his debut. As he looked up, he caught me looking at him.

'How are you feeling?'

'Bit nervous,' he replied with a shy grin.

'Me too, if it makes you feel any better,' I offered.

'Thanks, mate. That was a tricky press conference for you yesterday. I thought they threw you to the wolves, if I'm honest.'

'I've had better ones,' I laughed, 'but after Sydney I would have been a mug if I thought they'd give me an easy ride.'

'Then they should not have had you do it. Any one of us could have done it instead.' At this point he stood and squeezed past the other three to come and sit on the other side of me. Lowering his voice, he said, 'What did you make of Dench's grilling?'

'Dench has been around a long while; you can make a few enemies in that time.'

'Well, they certainly got pretty personal with him. All that stuff about financial problems and personal issues.'

'They're just digging for a story. Best thing we can do is stuff the Aussies and their focus will soon change.'

'Make you're right,' he replied, the Essex-boy in him coming out. 'But do you think there's any truth in that about Dench?' he persisted.

'I think the Benefit year was a huge flop and he did suddenly arrive at The Oval this year, but I've not seen anything to be fair.' As I said that I thought back to the incident a few weeks before, in The Oval forecourt, when I saw Dench in heated discussion with the guy dressed in black. That had certainly looked personal.

With the fielding restrictions in place for the first fifteen overs Dench and Carter made the most of some untypically wayward bowling. Barambah and Vernon were generating a huge amount of pace, but their control was not there today. Barambah was pitching far too short to a back-foot specialist like Carter, and Vernon's direction was off too, allowing both bats to leave pretty much anything that they did not want to hit for four or six. After 40 minutes with the score rattling along nicely to 85 from just eight overs, the two quicks were withdrawn and replaced by a pair just as fast. Calton and Yardley managed to slow things a little but after fifteen overs, as the fielding restrictions were lifted, we were 134 without loss and looking supremely comfortable. Pocket, the leggie, was brought on from the Kirkstall Lane End and immediately had us tied up in knots.

Dench looked extremely uncomfortable with the transition from searing space to artful spin and twice missed the googly in Pocket's first over. The Western Terrace which, just an over before, had been raucous was suddenly silenced. Ironic cheers had greeted Vic Nguyen removing his sweater as it became clear that Kelly was depending on spin for a breakthrough. Nguyen had had a couple of seasons with Nottinghamshire recently and had gone for 34 in a single over in a County Championship match against Yorkshire, here at Headingly. The Western Terrace, already a few beers into their day, were a knowledgeable crowd and chants of 'six sixes' were soon ringing from that side of the ground.

Carter checked his guard with the umpire as he set himself to face Nguyen's occasional off spin. He prodded at the first ball uncertainly and missed it completely. Lots of noise from behind the stumps with Queensland's stumper, Bob Lee, making his usual fuss about it, urging the bowler for more of the same. Carter, who just minutes before had looked as comfortable as I had ever seen him, suddenly looked like a complete novice. He played at and made a hash of the next four deliveries, none of which seemed to turn, although from the pavilion's square-on position to the strip it was never easy to tell for sure. On the sixth delivery he was in such a muddle that when the ball hit his pad and rolled through the vacant short fine-leg position he started to run. Dench was stationary and reacted late. As Carter hared down the wicket, Dench suddenly lurched into life and headed for the striker's end. Bob Lee had thrown off his right glove, chased the ball down and, as he turned, arrowed the ball in towards the stumps, where Stu Taylor took it wide and swung his hands at the timber. Dench was still flying horizontally through the air and well short of safety when the bails came off. Silence in the ground, as Dench picked himself up, snatched his bat from Taylor who had retrieved it for him, and shot an evil look at Carter as he trudged off.

'Take cover, boys!' I called over my shoulder to my teammates inside the dressing room. 'You might all just want to squeeze out here with us.'

Geno Da Silva, the local lad, was all ready to go and met Dench on the external staircase. I heard Da Silva's 'Bad luck, skipper,' but could not make out Dench's reply, drowned out by the roars for Da Silva from the fans on the Western Terrace. Dench's response came seconds later when his bat went flying across the dressing room. I decided to stay on the balcony a little longer. It had been a squeeze before; now it was positively rammed.

Da Silva made a decent start but was stumped for 20 off Pocket and from there it did not get much better. Carter followed soon after, bowled by Pocket's googly for 77 and then it was a steady stream of wickets. I was padded up from the thirtieth over and at 187 for 9, with fifteen overs left, I finally got my chance. More cheers from the Western Terrace, ironic this time, which I acknowledged with a very slight bat-raise. This elicited more cheers as I passed

Dean Swartz who had just holed out at long-on to give Pocket his fifth of the day. Batters had crossed so at least I would not have to face him first ball. Only one bowler has got me out in Test cricket, and that's Tim Pocket. Twice. Admittedly I have only played one Test, but I did not fancy becoming his rabbit in my first one-dayer. I need not have worried. Kenny Barrett edged the next one to Thompson at second slip. Innings over. Nought not out. Could have been worse.

The Gaffer took a positive line with us, which surprised me. He noted that we had runs on the board but did not point out the obvious; that there weren't many of them. He went on to highlight our qualities in the field, whether it was as bowlers, catchers or deep fielders. It made a pleasant change from the histrionics of Carlisle and, for me at least, made me ready to take the Aussies on. Pocket had taken five with his leg-spin and seemed to generate much more turn than Nguyen had from the Football Stand End. As we trotted out onto the field I caught up with Dench.

'Kirkstall Lane End for me, please skipper,' I said with a grin. 'Pocket did well from that end – used the bowlers' marks well.'

He gave me a withering look and threw the new ball to Kenny Barrett who was taking the first over. Dench seemed to have no interpersonal skills. Quite why the selectors had picked him, aside from the fact that he had long ago led England Schoolboys, was a mystery to me.

The Western Terrace reached a crescendo as Barrett raced in from his hugely long, retro run-up, reaching a deafening peak as he leapt into his delivery slide. The ball hit midway down the wicket and soared over batsman, stumps and keeper. Four wides. Not the best start. Cheers from the Western Terrace. Their knowledge now compromised by lager.

The Australians reached 120 without loss by the time fielding restrictions were removed and by then my warming up routines were becoming quite ostentatious. The bowlers' marks, started by the Australians, were now perfect for me and, although Dench kept me on the boundary as I had expected, I made sure that he was aware of my extravagant warm-ups. The Aussies now only needed another 60 to take this first match, and a lead in the three-match series. My actions seemed to be falling on deaf ears.

Barrett and Swartz had by now given way to Leander and Corbett. No wickets yet but I was pleased to see Corbett looking a lot calmer and beginning to move the ball away nicely from the two right-handers. Dench eventually admitted to himself that pace was not working but it was not to me that he turned. Instead, he threw the ball to Mo Hassan. As a very occasional offie, he was not going to benefit from the bowlers' marks and to say that I was bemused by this decision is an understatement. By the embarrassed glance Hassan shot at me, so was he. The change did not completely help and Hassan's only over of the match went for twenty-four, though he did make the breakthrough.

As I had feared, Dench had me fielding the whole time in front of the Western Terrace and I was spot on about the kind of stick they would be handing out. Some of it was funny, some of it funny but not to me. I grinned along with them. On the last ball of Hassan's over, he dropped it short. Taylor rocked back and swung hard, catching the top edge, sending the ball high into the sky. It was coming my way, but I was looking up into the sun. It was one of those chances where you simply have too much time; the ball seemed to hang in the air. I was aware of a huge, growing roar from behind me. Suddenly the ball was hurtling towards me. At the very last second, I adjusted my position and had to lunge forward to reach the ball. Flat on my face, eating grass, I heard the cheers, looked down the length of my arms and saw the ball, nestling in my hands.

That was as good as we got and the Australians wrapped things up four overs later for a nine wicket win. As we trudged off the field Corbett trotted up alongside me.

'Are you injured, Johnny?'

'No,' I replied tersely.

'How come Dench didn't bowl you, then?'

I stopped to allow Dench, who was just ahead of us, to make some space between us.

'Your idea is as good as mine.'

And that would be the same tone in the papers the next day, although questions were being asked immediately after the game. Dench was taken to one side by Dean as we came off the pitch. I don't know what that was about but when Dench was wheeled out before the BBC cameras a few minutes later he credited the Australian bowlers with restricting us and their batters for taking us on. He was asked why he didn't bowl me and, rather obliquely, noted that he had his reasons. He had seen something earlier that concerned him and decided not to bowl me.

'What the hell was that all about Alan?' I had caught up with Dench in the car park after the match.

'You didn't look as smooth as usual.'

'Hang on a minute! I owned you in the nets yesterday,' I retorted angrily.

'I didn't mean that. I was referring to your press conference. You seemed rattled. With so few runs to play with I just thought...'

'Don't question my professionalism!' I stormed and abruptly walked to my own car.

Elisa was waiting up for me when I got home a little after eleven.

'Beer? I reckon you need one after today.'

'Please,' I replied, kissing her and slumping into an armchair. 'Did you watch it?'

'Woeful,' she replied, handing me a glass. 'Why did Dench not bowl you? That's what everyone is asking.'

'I asked him about that. He said it was something he had seen the day before in my press conference. Thought my mind wasn't on it. The only thing I did get to do I did okay.'

'The catch was brilliant,' Elisa enthused. 'But Pocket took five on that pitch so you might have done too.'

I nodded as I took a long sip of cold beer. 'Well, at least that's 5 points in the bag,' I said, only too aware that that left another seventy or so to get, with only two matches to do it in. That's if Summers was going to get what he wanted.

'Five points for a wicket?' Elisa queried.

Damn! I had slipped up there. She knew nothing about Summers and his spread bet.

'Any calls while I was away?' I changed the subject quickly.

'Only one for you. Jack. Said it was no big deal.'

'I'll call him tomorrow. He's been upsetting Ralph.'

'How so?'

'He's got a bee in his bonnet over the plans for the new double-deckers at The Oval. Says the vomitories are all wrong but he keeps pestering Ralph over it.'

'What's Dad got to do with it?'

'Well, until recently I would have said that he had nothing to do with it aside from the fact that I had given him a set of plans to look at after Jack raised his concerns with me. But, the last couple of times I've been up at Surrey, Ralph has been there in closed-door meetings with Parslow.'

'Didn't know he was that interested,' Elisa pondered. 'I mean, I knew he loved his cricket, but I had no idea he was pally with the bigwigs up there. He certainly never said.'

'Elisa. What is your Dad's status now?'

'Status?'

'Yes, you know, retired, working, semi-retired?'

She paused. 'Pretty much retired, I think. Has been for a while but he does do some consulting as far as I know. Why do you ask?'

'Well, I think he is acting as a consultant for Surrey on these stands.'

'I thought you said that *you* gave Dad the plans to look at?'

'I did. But I overheard a bit of his conversation with Parslow the other day and they were talking about stands and construction.'

'Well that doesn't mean that Dad's involved, surely?'

'No, but he's getting mighty defensive about it,' I said, taking a long swig of beer. 'By the way, what does 'Willby Construction' mean to you?'

Elisa looked up from her notepad. She was working on the Toadlust book. 'Willby? That was Grandad's company.'

'Ralph's Dad?'

Elisa nodded. 'Why do you ask?'

I paused, not sure for a moment how much to tell Elisa. 'Does Ralph still work there?'

Elisa put her notepad down. 'No, he's pretty much retired, like I said. Does bits and pieces for them though, I think. Why?'

'No drama. Think that's why he has been so vexed with Jack and the way my brother has been questioning the numbers.'

'Good old Jack,' she smiled, returning to her work.

I sat there for a few minutes, mulling over the thought that Ralph was massively linked to Willby, thought back to the botched contract award when their tender came in late and of Ralph's anger towards Jack and his frostiness to me at The Oval a few days earlier. When the phone suddenly burst into life Elisa moved first.

She came back in from the hall with a severe look, hand over the mouthpiece.

'Summers,' she said tersely.

I took the phone from her, with a questioning look that was meant to convey surprise, stood and walked out through the lounge door into the garden.

'Mark.'

'Well what the fuck happened today?' he hissed.

'You must have seen it?' I replied calmly.

'Five points! Five, fucking points, Johnny! Do you know how much I've got riding on this?' he stormed.

'That's not really my concern, Mark. You were set on doing this stupid spread. I told you I wanted nothing of it.'

'But you didn't even get a bowl!'

I was well aware of that and perhaps only marginally less angry about it than Summers appeared to be. 'What am I meant to do if Dench won't bowl me? And in any case, I thought you wanted me to have a 'poor one'; no Botham-style heroics, you said.'

Summers was quiet for a moment. 'Yeah, I know, mate. I'm sorry – I shouldn't be having a go at you. It's just that I've found myself a bit longer than planned and wondering if I need to shed the position. Trouble is, after today those buyers will almost certainly have vanished.'

Elisa popped her head out of the door at this point and held up my empty beer glass. I nodded for another.

'Look, mate, it ain't over yet. After the post-match furore I don't think Dench will dare to not bowl me next match and you were right about me getting a bat. That looks likely for Lord's too.'

Summers seemed to calm a little, apologised again and added that he was sending over a crate of the New England Beers either tomorrow or the next day. Soon, at any rate.

When I returned to the lounge my beer was waiting for me.

'Are you two back together?' Elisa asked, a stern look in her eye.

'What, Summers and me? No,' I replied calmly. 'Not together but we do have a little shared business interest.'

Elisa had returned to her notebook but at this, looked up sharply.

'Beers,' I explained. 'He's gone into the beer importing business and signed me up as the face of 'New England Beers.' Not sure if it'll work out but it's costing me nothing. And actually, he gave me ten grand just yesterday.'

'Ten grand?' Elisa looked shocked.

'For using my face on the labels. Said there would be more to come.'

'Nice work,' she said, impressed I thought.

I elected not to tell her that it was paid in cash at Epsom station or that Summers worked for a spread-betting outfit and was quoting an outrageous price on my performance.

Elisa put her notebook down. 'So, you didn't bowl and didn't really bat?'

I nodded.

'Right then, you can't be too tired.'

With that she stood up, took my hand and led me upstairs.

CHAPTER 34

Friday May 23 1997

I was just pulling in through the double green gates into the Nursery End at Lord's when my mobile rang. I parked quickly and grabbed for it. Just in time. Expecting Summers, it was a relief to hear Jackie Kray's voice.

'Hiya, Johnny. Shame about yesterday. What was Dench thinking about?'

'I really don't know, Jack,' I laughed. 'He's not my biggest fan, I guess.'

'Clearly not,' she agreed. 'Listen, I went through the long room last night to see how Goldrich was getting on.'

'Hasn't he finished it yet?' I smiled.

'No, but it's certainly taking shape. Actually, he's made a really good likeness of you.'

'Quite right too,' I replied. 'Happy with yours?'

'Not really, Johnny, he's made me look so old.'

'Bastard,' I laughed.

'When you get a chance, stop by. I don't think he's got Elisa right at all. You might want to bring a better photograph.'

'Well to be honest Jack, I think that the Club supplied that one. Not sure where they got it but I'm back with you in a couple of days just as long as I don't get dropped. I'll bring one then.'

She wished me good luck as I ended the call.

I walked around the back of the old Grandstand. A large building with too few seats for its size and some pretty dark seating areas they were too. Iconic from the pitch, for sure, but past its use-by date and, with the still new-looking Mound Stand opposite, its jaunty sail roofline puncturing the London sky, the old building's days were surely numbered. I reached the pavilion, passing the museum and fives court on my right, climbed the grand staircase as quickly as I could with my bags and soon found myself in the dressing room. I immediately noticed that my space was right next to Dench's. He was already there, lacing his boots.

'Morning, skipper.' I elected for a positive, appropriately respectful start and was surprised to be met with a warm smile.

'Johnny,' he said, extending his hand.

I shook it firmly, rather unsettled by this new Dench.

'I'm sorry about yesterday.'

'Me too, skip. That was a tough game.'

'No, I meant about not bowling you. That was a mistake. Especially after what Pocket did to us.'

'No drama. We've got two matches left. We can still win the series.'

'That's the plan,' he smiled back. 'You'll get a bowl tomorrow.'

I nodded and started to change.

After the training session we were given the rest of the afternoon off. We were staying in the Danubius Hotel just across the road from Lord's, so I went back to my room for a shower and decided to go for a stroll down to Baker Street and from there into the West End for a couple of quiet pints. I called Elisa to ask her to remind me to take a photo of her to The Oval.

'There's that one of me you like on the kitchen board,' she started. 'Oh, it's not there. Did you cut me out?' she sounded concerned.

'I did. You are in my wallet,' I lied, still not sure where the photo had gone.

'Aw,' she mumbled. 'You could use that one then. Oh, Johnny, no sign of those beers yet but you have had a postcard from Mr Brown.'

'Ah, I was getting worried about him,' I lied, again. Mr Brown often wrote to me and, ahead of big games, just as at the start of a new season, it was not unusual for him to send a 'good luck' postcard. 'Is there a poem?' I winced.

'I'm afraid there is,' Elisa intoned grimly. 'Here goes.'

You're so good at this game cricket,
Let's hope you take a stack of wickets,
Batting may not be such fun,
But fingers crossed you get a ton!'

PS I will have my new camera at Lord's and The Oval

I was silent for a moment.

'I mean, should we be reporting him?' Elisa said, with a hint of seriousness.

'Nah, he's just a harmless cricket saddo,' I replied. 'Actually, I was wishing he'd write letters instead. At least the postman would not be able to read this stuff.'

Elisa laughed. 'Johnny, I just remembered. Had a call here from Jackie Kray? She said something about a stack of bats coming that you have to sign?'

We have to sign a whole lot of bats before the season starts but Surrey had just made a deal with a new sponsor and needed another batch inked.

'Want me to pop up for the night?' Elisa asked, her voice full of suggestion.

'I most certainly do, though I would be straight out of the team,' I replied with exaggerated sadness.

'Well, good luck for the match,' she said breezily as she ended the call.

My mobile rang just as I was about to return it to my pocket.

'Johnny?'

It was Eleanor Framsell. I groaned inwardly. I had hoped that that was all over. 'Oh, hi!' I managed with forced cheer.

'Johnny, did you get to speak with that O'Brien character?'

I had clean forgotten to go back to her. 'Eleanor, yes I did. Sorry I didn't get back to you yet – so wrapped up in this Australia series. My apologies.'

'What did you discover?'

'Not a lot, really. Seems O'Brien went for a drink with Sally in Putney, said goodbye outside the pub and walked home. That was the last he saw of her.'

'How do we know he's telling the truth, though?'

'I have to say he seemed genuine. Said Sally was dashing off to meet someone else. He thinks she was probably hit just minutes after they parted...'

Eleanor gasped. 'Oh, Johnny.'

'He asked me should he go to the police and I said that he should.'

'And did he?' She asked quietly.

'I guess. I mean, I haven't chased him up on it.'

Another pause before she spoke again. 'Johnny, I remembered something odd that Sally said to me a week or so before she died. She said that someone at work had got wind of the fact that I have money and was pestering her for a loan. Could that have been O'Brien?'

It was my turn to pause. 'I suppose it could, Eleanor, but Sally never mentioned anything like that to me. O'Brien has his own flat in Parsons Green – not the cheapest area.'

'It doesn't mean he can afford to pay the mortgage though, does it?'

'Fair point,' I agreed. Another odd piece of this odd puzzle. I promised to let her know if I heard anything.'

CHAPTER 35

Lord's is a beautiful sight empty but with a full house and in perfect spring weather it simply cannot be beaten. Worcester and Cheltenham might stake a claim, but it is hard to beat Lord's. As I sat on the balcony watching our openers making their way to the middle, I felt confident about our prospects, despite the hammering we took at Leeds. I was surprised that the selectors had stuck with the same eleven but winning the toss was a positive. A fine morning and early afternoon with a prospect of cloud cover from after the break, just in time for the Aussies to bat. I had thoughts of that legendary 1972 Ashes match, when Bob Massie took an absolute bagful with a wildly swinging ball. We needed something like that to get back into this short series. Winning the toss was a good start.

Dench and Carter kept the scoreboard ticking over nicely in the first three or four overs. The Australian pair, Barambah and Vernon, were bowling extremely fast and accurately. Lucky are they who can swap a very quick opening pair with an equally fast duo, but key in these moments is to keep getting those quick singles to swap the batters around and to irritate the pacemen. Keep the scoreboard ticking over.

I slipped my shades on and, resting my elbows on the stone balustrade, rested my chin on my hands and thought back to the hotel at breakfast. I had sat with Mo Hassan, Nick Temple and Charlie Bright at a table next to Dench, Dean and Gorton. Gorton was going on as ever and saying how there would be wholesale changes if we didn't perform better today when a message was brought over by a member of the hotel staff, for Dench. He read it quickly and excused himself before heading off to the lobby. I did not pay much attention to it but a few minutes later followed his footsteps to find the toilets. The lobby was pretty much empty save for a couple reading newspapers by one of the large, plate glass windows near the hotel's main door. As I crossed the marble floor towards the restrooms, I suddenly noticed Dench in a far corner, deep in conversation with a tall man dressed entirely in black. It looked like the same guy I had seen a few weeks before with Dench at The Oval. Dench had his back to me and was unaware of my presence. I knelt quickly to re-tie my shoelace and watched as Dench pulled out a brown envelope from his pocket and furtively handed it to the other man. As I stood to walk on, the man glanced into the envelope and, tucking it into his own jacket pocket, walked quickly towards the revolving main door. No handshake. No goodbyes.

As I reached the middle of the lobby, Dench turned to come face to face with me. If he *looked* awkward, I certainly felt it.

'All okay, skipper?'

'Yes,' he snapped, rather too quickly.

'That's good,' I had replied, before disappearing into the toilets. That little transaction had not looked too kosher.

Sitting on the balcony I wondered if I should be speaking with someone about this. Well, I knew I should, being well aware of the damage that match-fixing does to sport around the world. But, having been the victim of a match-fixing investigation after the Sydney Test, I was less keen to start one myself. Actually, 'investigation' would be too generous. It was a witch-hunt and it was for that reason I guess that I said nothing about it that day.

After twenty overs we were going along very nicely. The slow, steady start wore the Aussie bowlers down a little and, as Dench and Carter picked up the scoring rate, a big total looked likely. Another century partnership for our openers with good contributions from Da Silva and Hassan, who were both on the attack from the outset, saw us on 180 for 2 when the collapse came. When I joined Phil Leander in the thirty-seventh over, we had reached 241 for 9, a huge disappointment after an incredibly good start. I had seen Leander, coming in at ten, score a fifty against us at Chesterfield a year or two before and, when I met him in the middle of the strip, he advised me to block the last two balls of the over from Pocket and said that he would nurse us through as many overs as possible. I nodded in agreement, but had my fingers crossed, as much as that is possible in a pair of Gray Nicolls batting gloves.

I took leg stump and looked around me to check the fielding positions before I settled into my new, slightly more open stance.

'Right arm over, two to come,' intoned the umpire.

'Don't know why you even bother with a guard, Johnny,' said Lee, the diminutive 'keeper immediately behind my stumps.

Pocket's five-step walk to the crease could hardly be called a run in, but the ball was well-flighted and full. I stepped out and flailed it on the full toss, through the empty cover area for four. A look of shock on Leander's face followed by a big grin as he walked down the track to fist bump.

'Oh my! Where have you been hiding *that*?'

'Oh, you know,' I replied, with mock modesty.

I returned to the striker's end. Bob Lee behind the stumps was nodding at me with a smile. 'I didn't know you had it in you,' he said through barely parted lips.

'Let's see if I've got another, shall we?'

Pocket approached the stumps at the other end. He did not look as amused as some of his teammates. He gave it a rip and as it pitched on middle I waited just long enough for it to turn towards gulley, stepped back and out towards the slip cordon and, with an almost horizontal blade, eased the ball over them for a quickly run three. As Lee passed me at the end of the over, I looked him in the eye.

'Oh, I did have another!'

'Pommie bastard,' he drawled as he threw the ball to Matt Yardley, the young Western Australian quick. 'You know what to do, Matty,' he instructed.

Yardley, brought up on the WACA's concrete strips, was rocket fast. The kind of fast that, if you were to watch him bowl from square on, you would not see the ball. Normally that would have filled me with dread. Not today.

He came hurtling in from his very long run, leapt into the air and the first one whizzed past me at face height, seam screaming as it went through to Lee.

'That's it, Matty,' he growled from behind me.

The umpire had a quiet word with Yardley, presumably telling him that another like that would be no—balled. Leander sauntered down the pitch.

'Careful, Johnny,' he said quietly. 'Want to nudge a quick single and leave him to me?'

'Thanks, Phil. Should be okay – I'm seeing it like a beachball,' I laughed.

I knew what was coming next. Very short and rearing dangerously to head height. I rocked back and heaved it over square-leg for a one bounce four. The crowd was by now fully on my side. Leander stopped for a word as we re-crossed in the middle of the strip.

'Perhaps you'd better keep the strike,' he grinned.

'Happy to share it, mate,' I laughed as he slapped me on the shoulder.

Between the two of us we managed to drag the total to a more respectable 310 all out when Leander went for 29. I was delighted and devastated at the same time. My 42 not out was way, way my best ever score and ridiculously higher than my average. The reception I received on my way back to the pavilion was something I will never forget. Even the Aussies applauded me off. As I took my pads off I suddenly thought about Summers. At least this would help him too. Only another 30 points needed to save his position and with two bowls ahead of me and another bat, I felt for the first time reasonably confident. My confidence was misplaced.

The Australian openers did to us what we had just done to them, Taylor and Nguyen both notching up quick, brutal half-centuries. After twelve overs Dench waited for me to run in from deep square, where I was fielding from both ends, and told me to loosen up. A couple of overs later, the ball was in my hand as I readied myself from the Pavilion End. At Lord's I had normally taken the Nursery End, gaining full advantage of the ground's legendary slope. I was not exactly sure how this would work but I decided I would just have to give it even more rip.

The first couple of balls were dealt with respectfully by Taylor. The third he padded away and the fourth he played firmly back to me. He took a quick single from the fifth as he nudged the ball through the vacant third slip area. That brought Nguyen on strike. He is an even more combative player than Taylor and I fully expected him to go at me, so I knew I was going to give this one some real rip.

Nguyen settled, having just checked his guard with the umpire. I took my short, smooth run-up and gave the ball everything I had, so much so that I could feel a worrying pull in my just-recovered shoulder. The ball hit a good length, spun viciously, and darted off towards the slips. Nguyen had clearly made his mind up and, eyes actually closed by the time his bat met the ball, swung hard across the line succeeding only top-edging it feebly to Charlie Bright behind the stumps who had just enough time to readjust to take a fairly simple catch.

57 points. That was my first thought and then I realised how much this spread of Summers was getting to me. My teammates mobbed me and the packed crowd went wild. Game on.

I was rubbing my shoulder as I passed Dench again on my way back to deep square.

'Is that giving you trouble again?'

'Nah. It'll be fine,' I said, lightly.

At the end of the next over as I walked in towards the strip, pulling my sweater off over my head, I was more than a little surprised to see Dench throw the ball to Ben Corbett.

'Skip?' I enquired as I reached the Pavilion end, where Corbett was pacing out his run.

'You got us the breakthrough, but we need to look after that shoulder. Let me know how it feels for later,' Dench said, as he walked to take up his position at mid-off.

'But I can...' I started, watching his back as he walked away from me.

No point trying to discuss it here, I decided, so stomped off to deep square again, feeling less than happy. Of course, I was going to feel something after such a long lay-off, but to take me off after one over. I did not get that at all.

The wickets eventually tumbled at the other end, Barrett and Swartz taking four apiece and we won by 23 runs with a couple of overs to spare. As I walked off, I caught up with Dench.

'What was that all about?' I shot at him.

'I told you. Your shoulder,' he replied tersely.

'Yeah, and I told you that it was okay.'

At this he suddenly stopped and stared me straight in the face. 'That last one was a chuck.'

'You what?' I replied, in complete shock.

'What I said. You chucked that one.' With that he turned to acknowledge the crowd's cheers as he trotted up the pavilion steps.

I was stunned. If that's what he thought I would surely be dropped for the third match. I did not think that even my 42 would be enough to save me. I decided that I would say nothing and see if I could find footage on the highlights later that would provide an answer. I knew that I had given that ball an almighty rip but as far as I knew I had never chucked a ball in my life.

Elisa was in when I got home at ten o'clock, dressing gown on, ready for bed. She brought me a beer from the fridge. I took a long, slow drink.

'Well done today, Johnny! What a bat!'

'Thanks, lovely,' I replied, putting my arms around her.

'Still no sign of your beers, though,' she said, kissing me on the lips and licking the beer froth from hers.

'You know Summers.'

'But I thought he was tying the release of these beers with the one-day series? There's only one match left surely,' she queried.

'Must be a hitch with the import side of things I guess,' I replied, as I fumbled with the remote controls behind her back.

'Why did you only get one over, Johnny?' she asked as she slipped from my arms.

'Bastard said I chucked the one I got Nguyen with!'

'He called you a chucker?' Elisa said incredulously.

I turned on the television and checked the TV guide. Highlights were due at 10:30. I grabbed another beer and flicked to Ceefax to see what the match reports had to say. No mention of me chucking, just some confusion over why I had been given just the single over. Thankfully there was much more about our excellent series-levelling win and lots of surprise and kind words about my knock.

When the highlights package eventually started, I sat waiting nervously for that wicket. Elisa was telling me bits about her US tour and I suddenly realised that I was so wrapped up in my own issues I had not asked her anything about her trip. Not that I really wanted to know too much about it, to be honest. As I watched the match on television I nodded along and asked the odd question, but my mind was still really on the cricket.

'So, he's popping by tomorrow around twelve to drop them off.'

'Sorry, love, who is?' I asked, without taking my eyes off the screen.

'Crispin,' she replied simply.

'See! There's nothing wrong with that delivery. The bastard!' It then dawned on me what she had just said. 'LeDare? Coming here?' I said, as lightly as I could.

'It's no big deal, Johnny. He's just dropping off some interview tapes from the tour that I need for the book.'

'Why does he need to come? Don't they have, I don't know... servants to do this kind of stuff?'

'Servants?' she laughed. 'Oh, you are silly.' With that she got up from the armchair, unbuttoned her dressing-gown, revealing a complete lack of clothing underneath, straddled me and planted a big kiss on my lips.

My LeDare worries subsided; for now.

CHAPTER 36

Sunday May 25 1997

I woke with Elisa still draped all over me. It was great to have her back, but she had some serious needs and I slid out from under her at ten o'clock more tired than when I went to bed. I was making fresh coffee when my mobile went off. It was Jackie Kray.

'What's news?' I asked, looking out across the lawn, the sun streaming into the kitchen windows.

'Just checking it's okay to drop those bats in around lunchtime. Did Elisa warn you?'

I said that she had and that that was fine. 'Stay for coffee, Jack?'

'Would love to but I have offered a lift home to Alan Dench. I wasn't sure you'd want to see him just yet.'

'Dench? What's he doing up there this early?'

'Came in for an early net but he's got trouble with his car again so as I was coming down...'

'Yeah, not sure I do want to see him to be honest, but I'll have to see him tomorrow so what the heck.'

We agreed sometime about twelve. I let the coffee brew and took two mugs up to the bedroom where Elisa was stirring. I told her that we would briefly have company around midday and waited whilst she slid up the bed and pushed her pillows up behind her to make a backrest. I passed her the mug of strong black coffee and stood admiring her body, uncovered from the waist up. She took a sip of the hot drink and, putting the mug down on the bedside table, grinned.

'Well don't just stand there,' she ordered.

When we had finished the coffee was still hot and we sat shoulder to shoulder in companionable silence.

'Midday, did you say?' she said, breaking the quietness.

'Yeah, sometime around then. Dench is coming too, more's the pity.'

She looked at me sharply. 'What is he coming for?' she demanded angrily.

'Seems he's been in for an early net and Jackie's driving him home. His car's off the road again,' I explained.

'Well, I've not met him,' Elisa said firmly, 'but he sounds dodgy to me.'

'I'm not keen myself. Not just because of the way he refused to bowl me at Leeds and kept me to just one over yesterday.' I told Elisa about the brown envelope business from the day before the Lord's match.

'Oh my god!' she exclaimed. 'That has got to be corrupt. Didn't you report it?'

I felt a bit foolish. Of course, I knew it looked dodgy at the time and now wondered why I had not at least shared it with Dean.

'If I was you, I'd phone that in today,' Elisa said decisively.

'Guess you're right,' I muttered, pulling on a polo shirt over my head. The time had raced to eleven and I was just off to pick up the papers, keen to see what had been written about me. I had seen enough trash stuff lately it would be good to read something positive.

'Hope your head fits through the door when you get back,' she teased.

I bent forward to kiss her and cupped a breast as I did so.

She cupped me in return and I thought for a moment to let the papers wait.

I ambled back from the village with an armful of papers. A quick flick through had shown most of them leading with pictures of me batting on the back page. My favourite headline was in the Express. They led with 'OMG! He **can** bat!', whilst most of the others were in similar vein. I did not read through all of the reports but flicked to Krishnan Singh's straight away. If there was going to be any negativity I felt sure it would come from him.

His match report pretty much summed up what happened objectively, but his last paragraph left me with a feeling of unease.

So, Johnny Lorrens, in the news recently for the wrong reasons, showed us all yesterday why cricket is the most fabulous of games. The lowest batting average of any current England-qualified player, rejected as a bowler in the previous game by his skipper (and County colleague) and restricted to just one over in this, goes out and bats out of his skin to record by far his highest score using a new batting stance. No sign of his 'New England Beers' yet, but anyone who went long on City Sports seemingly ridiculously priced spread might just be feeling a little more confident ahead of tomorrow's series-decider at The Oval. If he gets a bowl. Someone knew something...

Singh had unhelpfully managed to weave into one paragraph, the spread, the beers and my new stance. What was he trying to do, I wondered?

I arrived back at home at a little after twelve and saw a Nissan Micra parked outside. As I opened the door, I heard Jackie's laugh and nearly tripped over a couple of dozen bats, lined up in several rows neatly underneath the coat pegs in the porch. I straightened out my England blazer on its hanger, re-righted the two bats that I had stubbed my toe on, and walked into the lounge. Elisa and Jackie were on the sofa, smiling at something one of them had said. Dench sat in my normal armchair looking interested in their conversation. Jackie looked up as I came in.

'Oh, hi Johnny! Elisa was just telling us all about her USA trip. It sounds fabulous!'

With a guilty pang I reflected again that I had shown very little interest in it, wrapped up as I was in the one-day series and my antipathy towards LeDare. 'Yes, it does sound exciting, doesn't it,' I replied rather disingenuously. 'Are you a Toadlust fan, skip?' I asked, turning my gaze towards Dench.

'Me? Oh no, not really. More of a Sinatra fan to be honest.'

That did not surprise me somehow. He seemed out of step with everything. His dress sense was not great at the best of times. Sat in my lounge in his England blazer, slacks and loafers, he came across as much older than he even was.

'Me neither,' I agreed. 'Awful music and the Pistols did the shock'n'roll thing first and much better. And as for LeDare. Well, he's due about now isn't he, love?' I said with more bitterness than I intended. 'You can decide for yourselves.'

'What? He's coming here?' Jackie exclaimed, with more excitement than I think she intended to show.

'He's dropping some tapes off to me for the book I'm writing on the tour,' Elisa explained. 'I'll ask him in so you can meet him.'

'Don't bother on my account,' I said with a grin as I went to make more teas.

'Is that okay with you, Alan?' Jackie asked.

I did not stay for his answer and when I returned to the lounge a few minutes later with four, fresh brews I saw the empty armchair.

'Where's Alan?'

'Loo,' replied Jackie. 'I just have to meet Crispin LeDare!'

She suddenly sounded like a teenager. 'Jack, you are old enough to be his mum,' I laughed.

'Don't be so rude, Johnny,' Elisa chided.

Jackie laughed. 'No, he's right. But I am not his mum,' she said with a wink to Elisa.

'Oh, god help me,' I groaned.

'He's very different in private,' said Elisa. 'Quite charming, actually.'

There was a rap at the door. I stood up to go. 'Well, Elisa, your taste in men is questionable.'

The two women laughed out loud at this. I had been meaning LeDare but saw the irony of my argument. I opened the door laughing and continued to do so as I found myself face-to-face with the legendary Crispin LeDare. The shock rocker with the lurid wardrobe was wearing a woollen tank-top, jeans and DMs. Too young to remember Gilbert O'Sullivan, he would have been devastated to know who he looked like.

I don't think I actually spoke to him, merely standing aside and gesturing to the lounge. As he passed, I made pathetic hand gestures behind his back. I really had no words for him. I straightened the blazer again. What was wrong with that hanger?

The outrageous clothes might have gone but, even with a tiny audience, he slipped easily into rockstar mode. Jackie was like a schoolgirl, entranced by the man. Elisa sat beaming proudly by. Proud of LeDare? Proud to be associated with him? Either way, it made me feel sick.

'Yaar,' he drawled, 'it was just the most, Jackie!'

Jackie's smile widened even further. He knew her name!

'Wasn't it a blast, Lise?'

Lise? No-one calls her Lise! She sat there still beaming.

'Oh, it was too cool, wasn't it, Cris?' she agreed.

Oh my god! I couldn't bear this. My wife was almost drooling over this dweeb. Jealous? Yes, I was, but honestly. I did feel Elisa let herself down there. Fair enough, I had not covered myself in glory recently and had been giving myself a pretty hard time over it, but I felt a twinge of justification now.

'It was like we were The Beatles, Jack! You just would not have believed it,' LeDare whined on.

'Don't flatter yourself,' I mumbled, a little louder than I intended, provoking a furious glance from my wife. 'And it's Jackie, not Jack,' I said grimly.

I returned to the porch and, with a marker pen, quickly signed each of the bats. When I got back to the lounge Le Dare was regaling Jackie with tour stories, telling her all. And I mean all. Every gig, TV date, women he had bedded, drugs he had snorted, the lot. 'And that time at the Chelsea Hotel, Lise! Oh my! It was just like the Warhol days. So decadent. A massive orgy. We all took part, didn't we?' He looked at Elisa for confirmation. Her smile had slipped for the first time.

'Get out of my house!' I roared, still standing in the doorway and towering over him.

'Steady, man,' he whined, not moving. Jackie and Elisa looked shocked.

I grabbed LeDare by his tank-top, hauled him to his feet and launched him towards the door.

'Nice meeting you, Jack,' he lisped over his shoulder. 'Bye, Lise!'

'Just go,' I growled, shoving him hard into the porch and into the stack of bats that fell all over the floor.

'Trouble, Johnny?' It was Dench descending the stairs.

'No. It's all sorted,' I smiled at him. Turning to LeDare, I gave him one final shove out through the front door and, picking up a bat, waved it angrily at him as he walked down the path to our gate. 'And if I see you around here again, I'll kill you with this!' I yelled.

As I returned to the lounge, I felt a little sheepish. I had lost complete control there for a moment and was met with an embarrassed silence.

'Think he thought I meant that,' I said with a forced grin.

'Sounded like you did, Johnny,' Dench said, brushing past me and out through the open doors, stumbling through the mess of bats on the porch floor. 'What's up with him?'

'I think you shocked him, Johnny,' Elisa said. 'That was pretty rude. I mean, I am effectively working for Crispin at the moment.'

'Well, I guess it's him or me, then,' I said, returning to the porch to re-right the bats again, and my blazer, on the floor now, though I was sure I had just straightened it on its hanger.

Jackie stood to take her leave. 'I'll go and see if I can find Dench,' she said. 'I'd promised him a lift home.'

'He's a big boy, Jackie,' I replied.

'I think Jackie feels uncomfortable, Johnny,' Elisa said quietly.

Jackie Kray stood awkwardly in the middle of the lounge. I felt bad about that. 'Well if Jackie has not seen the photos of you and LeDare in the press, I can certainly go and find them,' I said, raising my voice again. 'Jackie probably feels uncomfortable hearing about orgies at the Chelsea Hotel, *Lise!* I know I did,' I said grimly, using LeDare's pet name for her out of spite.

I helped Jackie carry the bats out to her car.

'I'm sorry you had to be here for that little session, Jackie. We're not normally like that,' I said, stowing away the last couple of bats in her car's boot.

'That's twenty-three,' she muttered. 'There should be one more, Johnny. I'm sure we brought two dozen over.' She ignored my apology and I decided not to press it.

We both returned to the porch, now completely clear of bats. 'Oh, I guess it was twenty-three,' she said simply.

Seconds later she was gone and I felt uncomfortable as I walked back into the house. I had upset someone who I felt very close to and one I valued very highly. I had also upset my wife, though my concerns about the exact nature of her relationship with LeDare had not been assuaged by what he had said and by what she had not said. When I entered the lounge Elisa had gone. I looked for her in the kitchen and looked through the window to see if she had gone outside. I heard noises upstairs and went up to see how she was. She had a small suitcase, the one she had only just unpacked from her States trip and she was quickly throwing in handfuls of clothes from her dresser.

'Off again already?' I said with a smile.

'Johnny, I can't stay here when you are like this,' she said through a veil of tears.

'Oh, Elisa, love,' I said going to put an arm around her. She shrugged it off sharply.

'Don't touch me!' she hissed.

'Oh, so it's okay for LeDare to drape himself all over you but your husband cannot so much as touch you!' I retorted, childishly.

'You were pathetic down there, Johnny. You have probably cost me a job. And that's all it was. A job!' She burst out crying again, slammed her case shut and, brushing past me, dashed for the stairs.

I slumped onto the bed. This was not the homecoming I had planned.

I sat there for a while, not really thinking about anything, a mess of images juddering through my mind, when I heard the front door close quietly. Elisa had been gone for several minutes. I stood to go downstairs when I heard the kettle being filled. With some caution I walked silently down the stairs and up to the kitchen door. There was Elisa, standing at the sink, suitcase by her side.

'El?' I said softly.

228

She turned, mascara streaking her face. She looked beautiful. I simply took her in my arms and we both cried.

Summers called at five. Elisa and I were still in bed where we had spent pretty much the entire afternoon. She was laying on top of me, half asleep, so I had answered quietly.

'Speak up, mate, you are very faint,' he boomed.

'Is this better?' I asked, a little louder.

'That's it,' he replied. 'Listen, tomorrow's the big one, Johnny. You need just 20 points now, so a couple of wickets or maybe three and a dozen runs and...'

'And you are off the hook,' I laughed.

'Well, that's not quite how I would put it but, yes, it would do me no harm,' he said brightly.

'Yes, well, the matter might have been taken from my hands, old pal,' I started with insincerity. 'Dench was just here. He clearly doesn't want me in the side and witnessed me giving Crispin LeDare a hard time.'

'LeDare? At your place? But weren't he and Elisa...' He let his thought trail off.

'That's all sorted now, mate. But I could tell that Dench was unhappy with my response. I reckon it'll only be a matter of time before Gorton calls to tell me I'm dropped. Dench will not hesitate to use this against me.'

'He can't do that, surely?' There was desperation in his voice.

'Can't he? I don't trust him one little bit. So, I am not going to wait for him to do me in. I am calling Gorton today to pull out. I'll tell him that Dench was right, that my shoulder is still playing up.'

'Whoa, there! Don't let that mother ruin your comeback.'

'No, I've decided. I want to make things right with Elisa, mate. She comes first.' I looked down at my chest. Her eyes were still closed, breathing still rhythmical.

'No, mate, you need to take a bit more time on this one. Don't rush at a decision you will live to regret. Think of all the work that's gone into getting a recall. Think of that 42, Johnny!'

He seemed genuinely concerned for me, but I had the strongest feeling he was more concerned about his long position. 'No, like I said, Elisa comes first.'

He was silent for a moment. 'Fair enough. Like you were completely faithful whilst she was away. Who came first then, Johnny?'

I clamped the earpiece close to my head hoping to prevent any spillage of sound. 'And what is that supposed to mean?'

'Well let's just say that you were seen out and about with a mystery blonde, for example.'

'Trash talk in the papers. Old hat,' I replied, calmly, although I hoped Elisa would not have seen that.

'Or the 10k I handed you at Epsom Station?'

'For the beers, Mark. What's that to do with it?'

'Have the beers arrived at your place yet?' he asked.

'What? No, as a matter of fact they haven't. But what is your point exactly.'

Summers paused. 'My point exactly is that you are in no position to pull out of the match tomorrow.'

'How so?' I challenged, comfortable with my decision.

'Simply because that 10k will look mighty suspect in light of the spread.'

'You bastard!' I exclaimed, vehemently enough for Elisa to stir. 'There are no beers are there?' I asked with mounting anxiety.

'Oh, there are,' he said vaguely. 'But that's not really the point here is it?' he challenged.

'Well, mate,' I replied with undisguised venom, 'I will simply deny that you ever gave me any money.'

'Up to you, old pal. Just have a look under your bed when you get a minute,' he said as he ended the call.

As gently as I could, I eased Elisa off me and slipped off the bed. Lying flat on the floor I reached under it and pulled out a plastic bag. I opened it quietly so as not to awaken Elisa. I put my hand inside and pulled out the contents. A pair of over-sized sunglasses and a red and white-striped headscarf. It took me a second to remember where I had seen those before, but it came to me pretty quickly. The woman battling with her newspaper in the foyer at Epsom Station, the day Summers handed over the cash. Was she taking photos too, I wondered? 'Bastard! You absolute tosser!' I muttered under my breath, slipping back into bed.

I woke sometime later, gently eased Elisa's arm from my chest and slid out from under her. It was dark outside now and I really needed to eat. I started a pan of water for some pasta and, as quietly as I could, set about frying some mushrooms to go in it. I heated the sauce in the microwave, tipped it over the pasta and took it over to the breakfast table. I sat eating quietly for a moment, memories from the past few weeks flashing past. I was just thinking how close I may just have come to losing Elisa when I put down my spoon sharply.

I had had a sudden uncomfortable thought, darted quickly up to the study and searched frantically for the *Strangers on a Train* postcard. I was sure I had left it propped against Elisa's PC but there was no sign of it. There were not many places to look. Perhaps I had moved it. I just hoped that Elisa had not found it. Did I address it to Lori? Probably. Lori? A cold chill ran down my spine. I felt sick. Lori. How could I have been so slow? Probably my sleep-clouded brain. I suddenly realised, she was the lady in the headscarf. She must have left the scarf and glasses under our bed the evening she snuck in. That meant... and at this point I started to feel physically sick; Lori and Summers were in this together.

Back in bed it was soon clear that sleep was not quickly going to come so I pulled on a pair of joggers and a T-Shirt, went quietly downstairs again, grabbed the car-keys and slipped silently out of the house. The streets at one o'clock were empty and I drove without a thought of where I was going. I put my toe down on the A3 northbound, realising that in just six hours' time or so I would be taking this very same route up to The Oval. This did not seem like ideal preparation for an important match; an important match for England but possibly a career-defining one for me.

I turned off the A3 at Roehampton and continued up Roehampton Lane, made a left on Upper Richmond Road and drove into Richmond and on through Twickenham and Hampton Court on my way back to Epsom. My mind had begun to feel a little calmer but when I saw the dashboard clock tick over to two a.m., I started to regret this early hours drive. I needed sleep.

Back in bed, sleep was still hard to come by. Still unsure about the match the next day, wondering if I should just come clean with Elisa and wondering what to do about Summers, I tossed and turned. And then there was Lori. That was the hardest part, struggling to understand why I had been so easily duped. They must have had it planned right from the start. I had pretty much fallen for her immediately and I knew that that was partly due to the fact that Elisa was away and seemingly focused only on LeDare. None of that was an excuse and none of that changed the situation facing me. I felt like a fool.

Summers was clearly not going to let me drop myself from the side; his threat to reveal all was undoubtedly genuine. I could defuse some of that by coming clean with Elisa although that ran the very real risk of ending our relationship anyway. No, the best thing, I decided, was to tough it out, make those points to satisfy Summers and then have nothing to do with him ever again. My only real hope was a call from Gorton dropping me for the final match. At least then the spread would be voided; at least, that is what Summers had told me. Even then, I suspected Summers would be vindictive enough to try to wreck my marriage so I finally fell asleep imagining how I might secure those twenty points.

CHAPTER 37

Monday May 26 1997

The alarm sounded at six. It seemed like I had only just dropped off, but I managed to silence it before Elisa stirred. Breakfasted and showered, I was ready for the drive up to The Oval by seven, glad that I had packed the night before. I popped my head round the bedroom door to say goodbye to Elisa, but she was still sound asleep, although she had moved across to my side of the bed. I blew her a silent kiss and went back downstairs, grabbing my blazer and bags as I did so.

If you only get to see cricket on television or perhaps arrive for a big game in the hour or so prior to the first ball being bowled, you cannot imagine the work that goes into putting the game on and getting it onto the screen. Broadcasting trucks on every available space, extra catering, stewards everywhere and extra policing, of course. As I arrived and drove through the Hobbs Gates I followed the steward's directions to where the players' cars were lined up. Having parked in the tightest of spaces, I was retrieving my bags and bat from the car's boot when Brian Dean approached.

'Johnny,' he started uncertainly.

'Morning, Gaffer, how's things?' I asked brightly. More brightly than I actually felt.

'Not so bad, thanks. Police are here to see you.'

A chill ran through me. It is odd. I have never had any trouble with the police but if I am driving and see a police car behind me, I always assume they are on to me, though for what, I have no idea. 'No, problem,' I replied breezily. 'Where are they?'

'Long Room,' Dean replied as he turned back towards the pavilion.

I did not rush, checked I had everything and, as I locked the car, I noticed that my blazer was still hanging on its hook in the rear. I decided to return for that later and followed in Dean's footsteps. Where the forecourt had been all hustle and bustle, the old pavilion was its normal calm, elegant, peaceful self. I took the first set of stairs quickly to the Long Room and, with some effort, negotiated the heavy swing-doors with my baggage. The large room was empty of life apart from two people, a man and a woman, seemingly engrossed in the anniversary painting, still on its easel, in the far corner. Dropping my bags with a noise loud enough to cause them to turn, I waited for them to speak.

'Mr Lorrens?' the tall, thin man asked.

''That's me,' I replied. It seemed the guy was not a cricket fan. 'What can I do for you?' I asked, with as much nonchalance as I could muster, as I walked over to them.

'DCI Baines,' he said, 'and this is DC Evans.'

'So, the painting is pretty much finished at last,' DC Evans stated flatly, nodding towards the canvas.

'Well it looks like it,' I replied, scanning it briefly. 'It's certainly taken long enough, though. First time I've seen it in a couple of weeks.'

'Where are you?' she asked pleasantly, leaning forward and squinting at the dignitaries standing on the pitch at the front of the painting.

'Ah, you won't find me there with the big cheeses,' I laughed. 'I'm up here somewhere,' I indicated towards the pavilion's seating. The lights were off in the Long Room and it was a little hard to see faces clearly. 'Let me see, I'm here,' I said pointing at a little pink oval, one of about thirty little ovals, in various shades, in that area of the picture.

She squinted harder. 'Oh, yes, I've got you. Next to the blonde?'

'That's it, next to my wife,' I agreed, leaning in now myself and squinting to get a better look. As I did so my heart felt like it stopped.

'Pretty girl,' DCI Baines noted.

'She is,' I murmured, wondering how on earth Lori had come to be sitting next to me in the painting, and remembering that Jackie Kray had told me that Goldrich had got Elisa 'all wrong'.

'Mr Lorrens. Where were you at one-thirty this morning?' DC Evans asked abruptly.

For a moment, with the shock of seeing Lori in the painting, I had forgotten that the police had come to see me. In the second or two before I replied I had to remember where I was and then decide if I was going to tell. If I told them I was driving around it might open up the conversation about the arguments of the day before. I made a snatch decision and lied.

'This morning? I was asleep at home. My wife can vouch for me.' I do not know why I felt the need to say that Elisa could vouch for me. That made it sound untrue and I was cross with myself.

'Why would she need to do that?' DC Evans asked.

'Why? Oh, just because she was there. You know, if you needed to check,' I rambled.

'And why, Mr Lorrens, might we need to check on that?' DCI Baines queried.

'Well, hopefully you won't need to,' I laughed. My laugh, echoing in the vast room, sounded hollow to me and I wondered if it did to them too. I already felt guilty. I just did not know what of.

Evans had a notebook out and was scribbling furiously.

'What exactly is this all about?' I asked, trying to mask the deep unease I felt.

'That'll be all for now, Mr Lorrens,' Baines said, with a nod to Evans, who closed her notebook. 'We know where to find you today if we have any further questions.'

'Yep, I'm here all day,' I smiled, with as much sincerity as I could muster.

'Good luck out there,' DC Evans said over her shoulder, leaving me alone, in front of the painting, looking at Lori's smiling face.

I carried my bags and bat up to the dressing-room in the Bedser, left them just outside, and returned to the car for my blazer. When I entered the dressing room the noise seemed to subside momentarily before picking up to its original volume. Brian Dean came over to me as I was hanging up my blazer, slapped me on the back and asked, 'What did the old Bill want, Johnny?'

'No drama, Gaffer,' I replied lightly. 'Wanted to know where I was last night.'

'Been tearing it up again have you?' Mo Hassan laughed. He was sat next to me, tying up his boot laces.

'Not me, Mo. Not before a match day,' I grinned. 'In bed early, with the wife.'

'Oi, oi!' It was Nick Temple, sat on the other side of me.

'Not before a match day,' I said with a broader grin.

'Yeah, right,' Temple laughed.

'Well, let me know if you need anything,' Dean offered, rather unnecessarily I thought, as he started to move away.

'Like?' I queried, at his retreating back.

Dean turned in the middle of the room. 'I just thought, with your wife being close to him. You know, according to the papers.'

'What are you talking about, Gaffer?'

'You don't know?' he started. 'Crispin LeDare was murdered last night. Clubbed to death.'

I was immediately numb. For a moment I could not think straight at all. But I knew I had to call Elisa to see if she had heard.

'You okay, Johnny?' It was Dench. He had been sitting two along from me and had probably heard our conversation. 'Okay to play?'

'Why would I not be?' That was more defensive than it needed to be.

'Well, you have just had a nasty shock. Elisa's friend has been murdered.'

'Yeah, well he was no friend of mine,' I said harshly. 'Not that I would wish this on him,' I added, aware that both Temple and Hassan were sat with us.

'No, I could tell he was not a friend of yours when we were at your place yesterday,' Dench continued. 'Shame though, for Elisa. What happens to the book now?'

'No idea,' I snapped, as Dean called for us to go and warm up.

'Hurry up,' Dench ordered, as he passed me on his way to the door.

'Whatever,' I mumbled, making a fuss over my laces. As the last member of the team left the room, I smuggled my mobile from my blazer pocket and darted into the toilets.

'Elisa,' I whispered, in case anyone had gone back to the dressing room. 'What the hell has happened?'

She was sobbing and struggled to speak in intelligible sentences. 'He, he's gone, Johnny. Murdered.' At this she broke down.

'Where? When? What's the news?' I could hear the desperation in my own voice, worried now that that explained the unexpected visit from the police.

'I've only heard a news flash, just a few minutes ago. All they said was that he had been found, clubbed to death ...' She broke down at this point.

'Where?' I asked urgently, suddenly very worried.

'Outside his house. Richmond Hill.'

Shit! Evans and Baines had asked me about my whereabouts at one-thirty a.m. I was very probably in the general area at the time. So that explained their visit to see me. I racked my brains to try to remember our conversation. I had claimed to be in bed with Elisa. That was a stupid thing to do. Why had I lied? I needed to sort this.

'Look, love, I am really sorry about LeDare. I know I have been stupidly jealous about him but that's only because I love you so much.' I could hear Elisa sobbing heavily. I was not even sure she could hear me. 'I am just glad that I was in bed with you all night.' As soon as I said that I regretted it. What a crass way of denying it.

The sobbing stopped abruptly. 'But you weren't,' she said calmly.

'I what?' My heart felt like it had stopped.

'I heard you go for a drive at one o'clock', she stated simply.

I sat stunned for a moment. She had ended the call and I wondered for a moment if she would actually contact the police. That last comment of hers suggested that she was at least open to the possibility that I might have done it, but I did not have time to dwell on that now. The rest of the team would be out there warming up already so I hurried back to my seat and quickly dropped the mobile back in my blazer pocket. As I did so I noticed a stray thread on the cuff of my blazer's sleeve. Pulling at it, I realised that one of the cuff buttons was missing. I had no idea when or how that had happened but knowing I would be wearing it later and remembering that the spare was still in its little plastic pouch and still attached to the inside pocket, I grabbed the kitman's bag from the corner of the room, found a needle and thread and quickly sewed it on. A little untidy, but it would do. Two minutes' later I puffed my way to the far side of the ground where the practice nets were set up at the Vauxhall End.

'Where the hell have you been, Lorrens?' Dean sounded irritable.

'Couldn't get off the loo, Gaffer,' I lied.

'Ah, touch of nerves, eh?' he empathised. 'Big matches always gave me a bit of that.'

'Yeah, there's a lot riding on this one.' I meant it being the series-decider.

'You haven't had a sneaky bit of that 77/80, have you, I trust?' he grinned.

'What? Don't be mad, Gaffer. Not my game, that,' I replied confidently.

Walking over to grab a ball from the kitbag at the bowlers' end of the net, I pondered my options and quickly decided that I had only one. I had to play, not that I felt in the least like playing. If I pulled out I was perfectly sure that Summers would follow through with his threat to tell Elisa about Lori. Lori being in the painting did not help either and I was not sure what I could do about that today. Maybe I could tell Jackie that Goldrich must have muddled the pictures and at least have him return her face to a pink oval until I could supply a picture of Elisa. I just needed to slip out of the dressing room for five minutes. And I needed to find a newspaper to see what was being reported about LeDare.

Warm-up over, I was walking back towards the Bedser Stand when Dench caught up with me.

'That was a shock. About LeDare, I mean.'

'Completely,' I agreed. 'Didn't like the guy but that was awful. I haven't seen any news yet today so don't know any of the details.' I omitted to say that I had spoken to Elisa who had told me it happened just outside his own house. 'Probably a deranged fan,' I ventured.

'Maybe. Lennon-style, you mean?'

I nodded.

'Could be a jealous husband though,' Dench said, raising his Gray Nicolls bat in both hands above his head, and fixing me with a weird grin.

'Who knows,' I replied tersely.

'Not us,' he agreed. 'Johnny, how's your shoulder? You looked a little tense in the nets today. Line and length a bit wayward too.'

'I'll be fine. Probably the shock of it.'

'Okay. Let's see how we go. If the quicks are firing we might not even need you.'

With that he slowed his pace to join Dean and one of the bowling coaches who were a little behind us, leaving me to ponder his words. Why would he even suggest at this early stage that he may not need one of his five bowlers. Fifty overs with a maximum of ten each. That made five bowlers at least, unless he thought we could skittle them out with pace alone, and the chances of that were slim.

In the event I was going to have a fairly long wait to find out about that. Dench lost the toss and, with some low, scudding clouds and brooding skies, came back to tell us we were batting. That at least would give me an opportunity to go and see Jackie about the painting, but first we had to don our blazers to be introduced to a group of International Cricket Council executives. They were in town for discussions about a proposed Test Championship and were stopping by for a pre-match photo with the two teams, out on the pitch. They might even stop to watch some actual cricket but, we were advised, their time was limited. Seems they would rather talk about cricket than actually watch any.

At five to eleven, when Dench and Carter walked down the steps through the seating in the Bedser Stand, I took the chance to slip unnoticed out of the interior dressing-room door and hurried along to the Club Office to seek out Jackie Kray. Typically for a big match-day she had a queue of people waiting for her. I managed to catch her eye and with a slight grimace, she left her desk and indicated for me to come to the side door that separated her part of the office from the public part. I slipped through quickly.

'Jackie, you were right about the painting,' I whispered, afraid that the line of people might be close enough to hear us. 'That's not Elisa.'

'Who is it, then?' she asked.

'No idea,' I lied. 'But he's got to change it immediately.'

'Well he's not due back now until the unveiling, whenever that is.' Jackie seemed different today. Detached, somehow.

'Are you okay, Jackie?'

'Yes,' she said in a quiet, clipped voice.

'Sorry about the other day. Just a build-up of stress I suppose.'

'Johnny, I have got to get back to work,' she said and turned back to her desk.

I imagined that she had seen the news. Did she suspect me too?

As I hurried back to the dressing-room, hoping to get back before I was missed, I reflected with annoyance that having Lori removed from the painting was not going to be easy. On a whim, I decided to go and see Parslow to see if he could do anything about the painting. I did not know who else to go to. Jackie was unsure when the unveiling would be, and I had to ensure that Elisa replaced Lori by then. My mobile went off just as I reached the Chairman's door. I dived into the nearest toilets, thankfully empty, and darted into the first cubicle.

'You bastard, Summers,' I snarled in a half-whisper. 'You filthy, bastard.'

'And a very good morning to you too, Johnny,' he smarmed. 'A word of warning. No, let's call it a gentle reminder. Make sure you get those points today or...'

'Or what?' I hissed.

'You know what, Johnny. The press get the photos.'

'Photos?' I said warily.

'That's right. Epsom Station. The lady with the headscarf and shades? Let's call that my insurance policy.'

I had no idea if he was telling the truth. I did not recall seeing her with a camera but then I really had paid her very little attention.

'So you and Lori were in this from the start?'

'Indeed we were, old pal. You just fell for the old honey-trap straight away. I mean, how long was Elisa gone before you started playing away? Disgraceful behaviour, mate.'

I slumped down to sit on the toilet seat. 'But I thought...'

'Yeah, you thought she 'lurved' you,' he laughed. 'I could not believe how easy that was. A flash of her tits and you were gone. Pathetic.'

'Who is she?' I asked quietly.

'Lori? Oh, we've been married a year or more now,' he said brightly.

'What is wrong with you, Mark? You let her sleep with me for what? A lousy spread bet?' I was genuinely shocked.

'Well it's a bit more 'Indecent Proposal' than that,' he corrected. 'Though to be honest it nearly all went wrong right at the start.'

I wondered just how long he had been waiting to do this. And there was me thinking he had been so gracious over the Sydney incident. I remained silent so he continued, seeming to enjoy his 'victory'.

'Do you remember that she would never tell you where she lived, even though you kept on at her? Well, of course, she lived with me, and you might remember the time you came round to my place? The doormat got caught up when I let you in?'

I did remember that. 'Yeah, and it didn't get caught up for me when I left.'

'That's right!' he said happily. 'That's because our wedding picture was on the table just inside the door. I had to quickly hide it because I was sure you'd recognise her.'

I could picture the scene; Summers struggling to get the door open as I arrived and me noticing a thin, clean line in the dust on that sideboard.

'Well, I have to say, that I thought you were better than this. And as for Lori, I really liked her – I thought she was a decent person.'

'Oh, she is, Johnny, but she's high maintenance. Costs me a lot. And to be honest, she's a bit of a whore. Said you were pretty good between the sheets, to be fair.'

'Mark?'

'Yeah?'

'Go screw yourself!'

He laughed, a big, hearty laugh. 'Oh yes, I meant to say. Watch out for Dench. Client confidentiality aside, he is well short on the spread so don't expect a long bowl. Or any, come to that. You'd better bat your little heart out.'

That certainly explained why Dench was so keen to prevent me from bowling. My only realistic chance to get the points I needed to save my marriage was by getting a decent bat or taking one hell of a lot of catches. Twenty points without a bowl looked highly unlikely despite my earlier innings of 42. Lightning was more likely to strike twice than me batting like that again. I was pretty sure that the original 77/80 price would have moved around, but I had to assume that Summers still needed me to make those 20 points. The obvious thing to do at this point was to report my conversation with Summers to Brian Dean but that would surely only hasten the complete collapse of my marriage; he would have to withdraw me from the team straight away. No, there was only one way. I had to get those points. I paced it back to the dressing-room hoping for a huge collapse.

Nick Temple saw me slip back into the dressing-room and told me we were 48 for none from seven overs. Not what I wanted to hear.

'And, Johnny,' he said as I went towards the plate glass windows that overlooked the ground. 'Your brother called the office about ten minutes ago. Said it was urgent.'

I grabbed my mobile from my blazer's inside pocket and once more headed for the toilets. It seemed to take him forever to answer and I tapped anxiously on the cubicle wall as I waited. If I got caught on the phone while this spread was 'live' I would be in serious trouble. Jack answered on the tenth ring.

'Why did you call, Jack? You know I'm playing today, don't you?'

'Yes, of course,' he replied casually, as if he followed my career. Which he never has. 'Was just wondering why you are in the team.'

'What? You rang me for that in the middle of an important match?' I was incredulous.

'No,' he said patiently, as if addressing a recalcitrant five-year-old. 'I know why you are in the team but was just surprised that your captain said on tv this morning that you were probably not fit enough to bowl. Why did they not pick one of the reserves, or whatever you call them?'

'When was this, Jack? When did you see it?' I asked urgently.

'I don't know, maybe half-an-hour before the game. It was a pitch-side interview, just before the toss.'

'Thanks for letting me know. There's more to tell but I can't just now, okay?'

'What's up with him then? If you are fit, why is he saying that?'

'Let's just say, he's not my biggest fan, Jack. But, like I say, there's more to tell.'

'Sure. Oh, and another thing, those plans.'

I groaned inwardly. He was still on about them. The longer this call lasted the more likely I was to be discovered.

'What about them?' I snapped.

'Never mind,' he said with a chuckle. 'Let's talk later.'

I was about to cut off the call.

'Does he have a daft nickname like the rest of your mates?'

'Who?' I asked, remembering our recent conversation about nicknames.

'Your captain.'

'Alan Dench? No, he's far too dull for that,' I laughed.

I returned to the dressing-room to find Dench coming in through the door. He had just been removed by Yardley for 33. I thought for a moment to challenge him about the television interview, but he seemed in a rush to remove his pads and moments later he was leaving the dressing-room. I gave him a few seconds and slipped out after him, trotted down the stairs and caught up with him at the back of the Bedser Stand. He had stopped just inside the stand. I stayed on the bottom step, pretty much out of sight, a few yards away. He was talking earnestly to a large man, dressed entirely in black. I was pretty sure he was the guy I had seen him with a couple of times before. These clandestine meetings perhaps made more sense now if what Summers had said was true, that Dench was short on the spread. From what I had seen it seemed he was paying this guy off so me doing badly today was important to him.

'Ah, there you are!'

The shout from behind me made me jump and made Dench and the man in black swing sharply round. My cover blown, I turned to face my father-in-law, coming down the stairs towards me.

'Ralph!' I said, extending my hand. He ignored it.

'What have you done to my daughter?' he demanded, towering over me on the step above.

'Elisa?' I replied, wondering if she had said anything about LeDare. 'What do you mean?'

He looked furious and once again I was aware of his size. His suit was well-fitting but seemed to be struggling to restrain his muscular torso. For his age, he really was in very good condition. His fists balled, he looked right on the edge. I glanced down. His shiny, black DM boots looked incongruous.

'She turned up at our place this morning in a terrible state and all she can say is 'Johnny', before bursting into tears. What have you done?' he demanded.

'Everything okay here?' It was Dench.

I turned. The man in black had gone. 'Have you met my father-in-law? Ralph, Alan – Alan, Ralph,' I said with a smile and took the opportunity to slip past Ralph and away up the stairs.

'And tell your brother to back off, Johnny,' he shouted at my retreating figure. 'Last warning!'

Dench made no mention of the incident when he returned to the dressing-room a few minutes after me, and neither did I. I was pleased to give Ralph the slip and was getting increasingly fed up with Jack and his meddling; it was not helping me at all. It was also a little odd that my sport-hating younger brother had suddenly become so interested in cricket.

A shout from outside, followed by a groan from twenty-thousand voices made me look up sharply. We were now eight down for 220. As I pulled on my pads I reflected on Jack's question about Dench. He was sitting a yard or so away from me, deep in discussion with Mo Hassan over the sweep shot. The rest of the lads were either watching the cricket, on their Walkmen, doing crosswords, sleeping or talking nonsense. I could see Mo's eyes glazing over. As I bent to re-tie by laces, Dench stood up, bat in hand and corrected Hassan.

'No, Mo, you did not have your knee to the floor. You were only halfway there.'

With that he practised a vicious sweep and I only caught sight of the Gray Nicolls at the last minute. Luckily, I had begun to lurch backwards but the blade hit me full on the side of the head. I felt a sudden, searing pain and slumped to the floor.

The next thing I remember is blinking my eyes open. I was flat on my back, surrounded by a group of players and medics, my head ringing like a bell. Blood was on the floor and all over my shirt front.

Dench was looking down at me. 'Dreadfully sorry, Johnny. Complete accident,' he said.

Another screamed appeal from outside, another groan from thousands. I was in.

'You can't bat, Johnny.' It was Dean, gently pushing me back down.

'Get out of my way,' I growled, pushing myself up, knowing that if I did not hurry, I would be timed out. And knowing that I had to get runs; for England and for my marriage.

Dench was the last to try to prevent me from getting up and once I did I swayed a little and needed Corbett's help to get me over to the steps down to the pitch. I must have looked a sight, crepe bandage wrapped tightly around my head, blood caked on my face and staining the collar of my shirt with spatterings on my whites too. A gasp of shock as I started my way unsteadily down the steps. I was grateful for the support of those sitting on the ends of rows. As I teetered from left to right a helping hand would re-right me and help me on my way.

Through the white gate in the fence and onto the lush, emerald grass, rather too springy for me in my disoriented state. Phil Leander had already reached the dressing-room before I left it and as I looked up to my destination, the wicket seemed to be miles away. I was not sure I could make it and I could see the umpires conferring, checking their watches. I shoved my helmet back on and with one last burst headed uncertainly to the middle.

'What, in, hell?' Bob Lee said with an unheard-of-before hint of sympathy.

'Cut myself shaving,' I grinned. That hurt too and I reminded myself not to do it again.

'Right arm over, one to come,' the umpire advised. 'That is leg,' he confirmed.

I spent a few moments digging myself in and then did a little unnecessary gardening before settling in for the first ball. I expected no sympathy from Matt Yardley.

As he came in from the Vauxhall End he seemed to move in and out of focus. My sight was blurred and I suddenly realised that this was potentially suicidal. As he reached the crease and leapt into his delivery stride I lost focus completely. The ball was invisible to me, but I felt it. Right in the box and down I went like a sack of potatoes. The only positive was that where that is normally excruciating, my head still felt worse. The ensuing five-minute delay at least gave me a little more recovery time.

At the other end Kenny Barrett tried to farm the strike but I was aware that he is not the best of number tens and I knew I needed to score a few. I let him keep the strike for two or three overs but the singles at the end of each over were absolute killers. Running made my head feel like it was going to explode and after one particularly quick one at the end of an over I had to dive headlong to avoid a run out. Eventually Barrett called for a runner. On reflection, I should have gone out with one at the start. I had been too dazed to ask for one and no-one had thought to offer. I reflected later that Dench would have been hugely reluctant to send one out.

'Blimey,' Barrett muttered, 'I didn't expect him!'

I looked up. It was Dench, of all people, and that made me worried. Not the fastest between the wickets, a reputation for running out partners and, according to Summers, not wanting me to score any. I had not yet got off the mark and was certain that our skipper would do all in his power to ensure that I did not.

'Kenny, there's no time to tell you anything about this. Don't let him make the calls. Just trust me, okay?'

Barrett nodded but looked confused. Dench approached us across the square.

'How are you feeling, Johnny?'

'Okay,' I mumbled, through gritted teeth. It hurt even to talk.

'Right, let's get the scoreboard ticking over now,' he said firmly.

Barrett nodded again and, as Dench moved off to his runner position, square with the wicket, he looked quizzically at me.

'Don't run, Kenny. Seriously.'

Barrett looked even more perplexed as he turned to walk back to the striker's end. He prodded at the first two from Vernon but the third delivery went for a possible single. He sent Dench back. Another couple of dot balls and, as the Australians moved in on the last ball of the over to cut off the single, Barrett let an overpitched one sail past off stump. I had the strike and Dench looked furious.

The cloud cover was thickening and the light, which had been good enough just minutes before, was looking increasingly gloomy. The umpires conferred and, to understandable groans from the packed house, we gratefully accepted the offer of bad light and I looked forward to a lie-down in a darkened corner of the room. At 237 for 9 with just three overs left we were not favourites to win the three-match series and Summers would be fretting over his position. My head was splitting but I was still able to fret over my marriage. As things stood, Summers was going to be sharing details with Elisa that I did not want her to hear just yet.

I stretched myself out on one of the physio couches with a cold, wet towel draped over my forehead. Brian Dean had suggested that we simply retire me hurt but there was no way I was not going out there again. My only worry was falling asleep and finding that Dench had persuaded Dean to pull me out. In the event, we were only off the pitch for about half-an-hour and walked back down the steps to huge applause from the home crowd.

Three overs to go. I was on strike and I knew what I was going to do. The only snag was the sight of Tim Pocket warming up. I think he definitely saw me as his rabbit and I was determined to prove him wrong. Barrett spoke quietly, so that Dench on the other side of me would not hear.

'Are we running, Johnny?

I gave a slight shake of the head. 'My plan is not to,' I whispered, staring straight ahead.

You would be forgiven for thinking that as a leggie I would find facing Pocket a breeze. To be fair I had only faced him in one Test and a couple of first-class matches, but I had not covered myself in glory. Yet.

I checked my leg-stump guard with the umpire, had a good look around me to check on the fielders though there was little point as I had already determined what I was going to do: whatever the delivery. Pocket made a slight adjustment to mid-off and, with a last rub of the ball on his trousers, stepped up. The moment the ball left his hand, I took a long stride forward, went down on my right knee and swept hard with my eyes shut. My eyes were still closed when the crowd roared. Six over deep-backward square. Barrett jogged down the strip to shake my hand.

'Bloody hell, mate, that was a cracker!' he smiled. 'Got any more of 'em?'

'Maybe,' I grinned back. 'Dench just taught me that one.'

The next ball was a little fuller, a little wider. I rocked back and slashed it just past a sprawling gulley for four. Pocket gave me a slight grin and walked back to his mark, waiting for the ball to arrive back from the boundary down by the Lock/Laker Stand. The next two I swung and missed at and then the fifth sailed back over Pocket's head for four straight ones. On 14, the last ball was pitching on leg, a fraction short, and I just gave it the faintest of nudges, against the spin, down towards fine leg. I turned to Dench and screamed at him to 'run one!' He could do nothing else and I had retained the strike. Five needed to save the marriage.

Barambah was brought back into the attack for the penultimate over so I knew what to expect: 90mph plus. The head was still aching badly and the eyesight was a little unfocused but I felt oddly confident. A genuine hush descended on the ground as the huge Queenslander came steaming in, his long, dark, curly black hair flowing behind him like a mane. I only noticed that on the replay to be honest; at the time all I could see was this monster of a man getting bigger by the second. First ball, a steepling bouncer that had me off my feet in an effort to evade it. Second ball, a wild slash to a ball too close to me, a big inside edge and I turned to see the ball racing to the fine-leg boundary. Even if I got out now and did not get a bowl, perhaps a catch would be enough to prevent Summers revealing all to Elisa. In my confused state I was struggling to remember what Summers actually needed. I knew he was long again and was pretty sure I needed to score 20 today if I took no wickets and the way my head was banging I was not sure I would last the whole match. That meant at least one run needed.

Barambah briefly conferred with Matt Kelly, before the third delivery and as the Aussie skipper trotted back past me to his position at first slip, he grinned at me.

'You've upset the big man now. You didn't wanna do that, Johnny.'

'Well, if he didn't like that, he won't like this,' I replied with false bravado.

The third ball, the replays show, was a 91mph full toss arrowing towards my midriff. I did not see it at the time but somehow was aware that I was in danger. I was taking evasive action when the ball cannoned off the outside edge of my bat, just below the handle. The ball flew sharply to first slip where it was spilt by Kelly. I looked up the wicket to where Barambah stood, just twenty feet or so away from me, at the end of his follow-through. Hands on hips, he looked snarlingly at his captain. I turned to Kelly and smiled broadly.

'Not what I had in mind, but he might like that even less.'

I knew for sure that the fourth ball would be a bouncer, Barambah's childlike response to having a catch put down. As he released, I simply ducked sharply and heard it smash into the keeper's gloves behind me. I did not see the fifth delivery but heard it cutting through the air just behind my head and I managed a jab at the final ball of the over, a yorker, the ball squeezing out towards a deepish midwicket. I called Barrett to run and he started to but suddenly stopped, looking towards the runner, Dench. Dench had not moved.

'Run, you stupid bastard!' I shouted at the skipper, who suddenly lurched into life. Thankfully the shy at the non-striker's stumps was wide and I had retained the strike. And I might just have saved my marriage, with an over to spare.

In the excitement of it all, I left the next ball, the first of the final over – a straight one from Pocket. Clean bowled for those 20 runs. The runs I needed for Summers to save his position and to give me time to talk everything through with Elisa. That's if I could trust Summers. 257 was going to be difficult to defend and, as I walked off to a huge ovation from my home crowd, I looked over at Dench. He looked apoplectic. If Summers had made good, Dench was apparently facing a sizeable loss.

There were lots of gentle back slaps and handshakes from my teammates when I reached the dressing room and resumed my place on the couch. I saw that the early edition of the Evening Standard had reached us. The back page had a story about the 1998 World Cup in France and delays in some of the building works there. 'Plus ca change', I thought, realising that my French GCSE had not been entirely a waste of time. I flipped the paper over and was shocked to see the headline. With the events of the morning I had forgotten about LeDare completely. The headline was huge.

BLUDGEONED

The sub-heading made me go cold:

Toadlust shockrocker left to die after frenzied attack with cricket bat – just yards from his Richmond home.

I read on, my hands shaking.

The police have eyewitness accounts of events leading up to Crispin LeDare's murder and have retrieved 'items of interest' found at the scene of the crime. A spokeswoman for the Metropolitan Police said that they have strong evidence and expect to make an arrest soon but are appealing for anyone with information to come forward.

The piece then went on to tell more of LeDare's rise to fame and the critics' growing opinion that Toadlust represented an important departure in popular music. I threw the paper down. They had changed their tune.

I lay there for a few minutes' longer, reflecting on LeDare's visit to our home the day before and wondering if I should be advising the police of that. I thought back to the conversation I had had with Baines and Evans before play started. Their line of questioning was now worrying me. I decided I had to call Elisa, wondering if the police had spoken to her too. Perhaps they had and that conversation had prompted them to speak with me? I had a sudden memory of waving a bat at LeDare's retreating figure – threatening that I would kill him with it. Had Elisa heard that? Had she remembered it?

I eased myself off the couch and returned to the main part of the dressing-room. The lads were eating and I suddenly realised how hungry I was. I grabbed a sandwich from a platter and took it over to my seat. My blazer was on the floor again. Groaning with the effort of bending down, I picked it up and hung it back on its hanger. As I straightened it, Brian Dean approached.

'Johnny, take a breather this afternoon. You've more than done your bit.'

I went to remonstrate but he had moved on. I turned back to the blazer and as I straightened the right sleeve, running my hand down the arm's length, I noticed that the button I had re-attached was missing again. That was odd. I was sure I had sewn it on well enough, albeit in a rush.

At the end of the break, the team filed out and down the steps to take the field. Dean and the coaches sat by the windows and the dressing-room went quiet. I took the opportunity to grab my mobile and sneaked into the toilets to make a couple of calls.

Summers was first.

'Happy now?'

'Well, happy is not quite the word, old horse, but let's just say that it could have been worse.'

'Right, so that's the end of it then?' I wanted to hear him say it.

'Any chance you can get on the pitch and take a bagful?'

'Sod off!'

'How about a beer then?'

I simply clicked him off. I had been thinking about what Jack had asked me, about the nicknames. I looked for a number on my phone and waited a few moments.

'Helm,' he replied tersely.

'Larry? Johnny Lorrens, do you have a minute?'

'Well, aside from the fact that I am sitting in the press box, reporting on the match, no,' he laughed.

'Did Dench have a nickname when you played together?'

'Seriously, Johnny? How about 'MOG'?'

'MOG?'

'Miserable Old Git.'

'That's apt.'

'Why do you ask?'

'My brother was asking me. I guess I was talking about players and probably using their nicknames. For some reason he asked about Alan. I just said he was too dull to have one, but I'll tell him 'MOG'. That'll satisfy him.'

Helm paused. 'Dull yes, but he always seemed to have something going on.'

'What sort of things?' I pressed.

'Never quite sure what it was, to be honest. Odd phone calls during matches and he seemed to have a few strange friends that would pop up every now and then. It all seemed very clandestine to me.'

'Remember any in particular?'

'One, yes,' he started. 'Like I said, there were several and Dench was always careful not to introduce any of them. But there was often a big guy, sinister looking, dressed all in black, lurking around. Can only have been to do with money. Like I said to you before, he did often seem to have money worries. Gambling I assume.'

I thought for a moment before replying. 'I've seen the same thing, Larry. Big guy in black. I've seen the two of them together three times now.'

Helm mumbled something to someone in the press box and then came back on the line clearly, laughing. 'Yeah, for a while we called him the Milk Tray Man, because of his mate, behind his back but one of the lads said he was like a spy, what with all the clandestine meetings. But MOG seemed to stick.'

I searched the mobile's directory and clicked. She answered on the third ring.

'Well, hello, Johnny,' Eleanor Framsell said, in her sultry voice. 'Long time, no see.' She had been drinking.

'Eleanor, have you heard of a guy named Alan Dench?'

'Dench?' she repeated, with a slight slur in her voice. 'Dench? No, I don't think so.'

There was something in her voice, a hesitation perhaps, that made me question her again. Eleanor, think about it!' I snapped.

'Dench, you say?'

'Have you heard of him? I asked insistently.

'Johnny, I don't know. I don't think so. Why?'

'Don't worry, Eleanor. If you think of anything, let me know.' I cut her off. There was something about her response that I was not sure about.

I jabbed at the numbers quickly and waited impatiently as the phone rang at the other end. Elisa eventually answered. She sounded tearful.

'Did the police speak with you?' I asked quietly, just in case anyone came into the toilets.

'They did,' she sobbed. 'Johnny, what have you done?'

'Done?' I replied, more heatedly than I had intended. 'What have I done? What do you mean?'

'The police,' she said simply.

'Yes, I know,' I said quickly. 'They came to speak to me before the game. What did they say to you?'

'They came to see you?'

'They did, yes, but what did *you* tell them?'

'That you were at The Oval. What did they ask you?'

'That doesn't matter, Elisa. What did they ask you?' I persisted.

'Where you were last night,' she said, sadly.

I heard the door to the dressing room open. 'What did you tell them?' I whispered urgently.

'That you got angry and went for a drive after Crispin had visited.'

I sat there stunned for a moment. I felt betrayed.

'What the fuck did you tell them that for?' I hissed.

'Because it's the truth,' she stated simply, and started sobbing again.

'Thanks a lot, Elisa, you bitch. You have no idea what you have done,' I snarled.

There was silence on the phone. Outside the cubicle I could hear some-one pushing at doors.

'You should have thought of that, Johnny, before clubbing Crispin to death.'

'What?' I said, more loudly than I intended.

'You do mine and I'll do yours?'

I went cold. Where had she found *that*? 'What do you mean?' I asked, uncertainly.

'It was behind the bin in the study. Who were you plotting with?'

'No, no, Elisa, you don't understand,' I stammered as she cut me off.

I sat quietly for a few moments wondering what else she and the police had discussed. I may have been driving at a very unfortunate time but hopefully there would be CCTV footage that would show me nowhere near LeDare. There could be no evidence against me surely, and that thought made me feel a little easier. Having just saved my marriage on the pitch it looked like I had lost it in the toilets. It suddenly dawned on me that it had gone very quiet outside the cubicle though I had heard no-one leave. I stood up, flushed the toilet to justify my reason for being there, slipped my mobile into my trousers and opened the door.

I only saw the fist as it made contact with my face, felt a searing pain and, for the second time that day, found myself crashing to the floor. My head hit the doorframe on the way down and as I lay on the floor and opened my eyes I caught sight of a pair of black DMs leaving the room.

When I returned to the dressing room, holding a handkerchief to my bleeding nose, I was met by silence. Silence and the two police officers from earlier. Brian Dean looked at me awkwardly and turned back to the cricket.

'Mr Lorrens,' said DCI Baines. 'Would you accompany us to the station, please? We have a few questions for you.'

I could hardly refuse and, as Dean had indicated that I would not be needed, I grabbed my blazer and followed DC Evans as she held the door for me.

My biggest mistake was waiving my right to a lawyer. I blame that decision on the unassailable conviction that I was innocent and on the concussion from Ralph's fist and the earlier dressing-room incident. The black DMs did it for me, not that I can be totally certain. It had to be my father-in-law who had floored me but quite why I was unsure. Either Elisa had been on to him or Jack was still nagging him over the plans. I certainly do not remember much about our conversation, but Baines and Evans questioned me about my whereabouts the night before. I apologised for my earlier denial. There seemed little point denying going for a drive and I was alert enough to know that CCTV would place me in Richmond at some point. I did deny having anything to do with LeDare's death, told them, in all truthfulness, that I did not even know where he lived but that until reading the Standard's article, I had assumed it was still somewhere in Twickenham, and did acknowledge that I resented him for his relationship with Elisa.

There seemed to be no actual evidence against me. That was a relief. I do remember clearly saying, 'Well if that is all, I'll be getting back to The Oval.'

'Not just yet, Mr Lorrens.' It was DCI Baines. 'Mr LeDare was found just a few yards from his front door, battered to death, it seems with a cricket bat.'

'So I read, and like I say, it has nothing to do with me,' I replied calmly.

'Well, Mr Lorrens, how do you account for the fact that the apparent murder weapon was a bat recently in your possession?'

'I don't think so,' I replied confidently. 'I only have the one and it is in my kitbag back at The Oval.'

'Were you signing bats earlier that evening at your house, Mr Lorrens?' DC Evans asked.

I turned my attention to her, feeling sick in my stomach. So, there *were* meant to be twenty-four of them! 'I was,' I agreed, feeling my face flush. My fingerprints would be all over it. 'Well, there must be a mistake,' I floundered.

'Is that your blazer?' DCI Baines asked curtly.

I returned my gaze to him, looked down at the blue jacket, and nodded. The atmosphere in the room had changed suddenly.

'A button was found at the scene. A button from an England blazer,' Baines continued, his gaze dropping to my sleeve.

I went cold inside as I instinctively felt for the missing button.

'I can explain', I stammered, my fingers toying with the loose threads on my right sleeve where the missing button had been. 'Someone must have pulled it off. They were all there this morning.' My mind raced. I neglected to tell them that I had had to replace one before the photoshoot that morning, fearing that this would simply seem to compound my guilt.

DC Evans fixed me in the eyes. 'Who, Mr Lorrens, would wish to do that?'

I thought quickly, my brain in a fog. Dench? Ralph? Either could be seeking to discredit me. Summers? No, Summers needed me on the pitch. It cannot have been him.

'Mr Lorrens,' DCI Baines said sternly. 'You really do need a lawyer.'

I was permitted a phone call and called Elisa. It was past midnight.

'Hello, love,' I said quietly. 'I won't be home tonight.'

'You need help, Johnny,' she said firmly.

'I need a lawyer,' I replied with as much levity as I could summon. 'They might keep me for a couple of days.'

'I'll find you one,' she said curtly, 'and then I'm going to my parents.'

'Don't worry, love, it'll sort itself out. They have nothing on me because...'

'Who *is* Lori?' she said, a sob catching in her throat.

'Who?' I asked, playing for time.

'Don't lie to me,' she snarled. 'The postcard?'

'It's nothing,' I replied. 'Just a joke.'

'Look, I'll call Dad, get you a good lawyer and that's it.'

'No,' I said urgently. 'Not your Dad!'

'Take it or leave it,' she replied coldly and cut me off.

CHAPTER 38

Tuesday May 27 1997

She must have been a good lawyer. I finally got home in the early hours of the following morning and was basically told not to leave town. I smiled at that thought as I climbed out of the cab; I thought that the police only said that in films. Now, I am not the most recognizable of sportsmen but the notion of me being able successfully to disappear was laughable. They had not told me much, but I assumed that any CCTV footage would have shown that I had only driven through Richmond and therefore that I could not have attacked LeDare. I was furious with myself for having pulled over for ten minutes down by one of the Park gates to smoke a cigarette. It seemed unlikely that CCTV would cover that area and so the police would have a mysterious ten-minutes where I was 'whereabouts unknown'. When my lawyer finally arrived I was completely open with her but I had clean forgotten my smoke break. I fumbled around for her business card thinking I should tell her about the cigarette break and, having paid off the cabbie, walked to the front door. The house was in darkness.

The car was on the drive but there was no response to my knock so I checked under the loose paving slab by the side gate. Elisa had left the key there. I let myself in through the front door. The house was silent. Elisa did not answer my call; she must have gone to her parents and I could just imagine the conversation there. My wife had clearly determined my guilt and I felt very let down by that. The kettle was soon boiling. The Metropolitan Police brew was foul and I was gasping for a proper mug of Yorkshire tea and another cigarette.

My call to Howletts & Co., went straight through to voicemail so I simply left my name and mobile number and asked for an immediate call back. Claudette Lieeuw seemed no-nonsense and, to be honest, worryingly disinterested in my innocence or guilt and the fact that Ralph had arranged for her to represent me left me feeling decidedly uneasy. He was surely not a disinterested party. I wondered why I even agreed to Ralph's solicitor, but I had used my one call, to Elisa, and felt I had little choice. I pondered calling another firm in the morning as I carried my tea out onto the patio. The night was warm and I was feeling a little nauseous what with the injury, the lack of food and the tension of the day.

As I breathed in the fresher night air, I thought back to the drive down from London. The cabbie was a cricket fan, recognised me instantly and was keen to know why I had not featured in the second half of the match, why I was still in my bloodied whites at close to two in the morning and why he was picking me up from the Elephant and Castle. Too many questions. I simply blamed the blow I had taken on the field for a bout of forgetfulness and was certainly not going to mention that I had spent several hours as the guest of the Metropolitan Police. He offered to take me to hospital for a check-up, but I said that that had already happened and I just needed to get home. I was keen to stop the conversation as soon as possible but was desperate to ask him who had won. I still did not know. There had been no contact with the England team and I had no idea if they had even tried. I wondered if I should call Brian Dean at least but decided it was far too late and thought it best not to. The lack of contact from anyone had left me feeling quite isolated, cast adrift.

My mind drifted back over the events of the last few weeks. I thought back to conversations I had had with Sally, her scribblings of '*M is a bastard*', and the events of her last evening. I was reflecting that we seemed no nearer finding the truth on that one when I suddenly remembered the postcard that Elisa had found; the one I had addressed to Lori but never sent.

The study looked like it had been ransacked. Elisa had evidently been searching for any evidence she could find, presumably having spotted the postcard first. That was nowhere to be seen but spread across the desk was a loose mound of letters and envelopes. It had been a stack of mail I had brought back from The Oval a month or so earlier and simply never got around to dealing with. Elisa had apparently dealt with it quicker than I. A half dozen or so had been opened and I tried to marry up the envelopes with the likely contents. Nothing controversial, so perhaps that was why Elisa had given up. Or maybe Ralph had interrupted her when he came to pick her up.

I slumped into the desk-chair and spread the mound out across the expanse of the desk to see if anything jumped out at me. I was not sure what, if anything, I was looking for but as I fanned the envelopes, one in particular caught my eye. It was a plain, manilla envelope, the exact type that we use at The Oval. The handwriting was instantly familiar and sent a shiver down my spine. Taking a quick gulp of tea, I slid the letter-opener along the flap and pulled out a single sheet of white A4 paper.

Hi Johnny – Dench is a complete creep. He scares me to be honest. I know I never spoke about him. I suppose I was trying to forget about him. I met him around the time I was going out with Mark O'Brien. You didn't know about O'Brien, did you? Well, to be honest that's why I took the job at Surrey. Once we met up again, though, it was clear to me that we had moved on. I wasn't upset about that, though, because by then I had met you. You being happily married did upset me and I know that sounds jealous and bitchy but I love you and because of that I am going to resign on Monday. I cannot sit in that room with you, feeling like this and knowing we cannot be together. All I ask, please, is that when we are next in together, you pretend this letter never happened. I just had to let you know why I was leaving. It's all for the best because there is another problem as well.

I knew Alan Dench from when I lived up in the Midlands. He would hang out in the same bars as me and Mark and the Warwickshire boys. He's a total creep and was always coming on to us girls even though he is married and far too old

(I know O'Brien is the same age but that's different – he's not a creep). Anyway, somehow he found out that my mum has money. He has a bad reputation for gambling and would bet huge amounts on anything. That's why his benefit year made a loss and why he moved to Surrey – for the bigger salary and bonuses – and to get away from his gambling contacts. He started leaning on me a bit back then when he had losses and I thought I had got away from him when I moved south. And then he turns up at The Oval! I don't think he knew where I had gone but he saw me one day in the car park and has not left me alone since. One night, pre-season, when I had driven in, he followed me back to mum's and invited himself into her house. It was really quite sinister. He was all charm and smarm and I think mum fell for it. You know, she's been on her own for a while now and he's a good-looking guy. Well, it seems he made a few visits down to Elstead and then one day last week mum said she was going to loan him some money. Twenty grand! I soon stopped that and told her about his gambling problems. Well he did not take kindly to that and threatened both of us. Mum would not let me go to the police but after last week I think I am going to.

Somehow he must have found out that I live in Putney and one night, a week or so ago, he was waiting for me in the High Street. He almost dragged me into the Old Spotted Horse. He said that if my mum doesn't come up with the money he will go and visit her and will not be so gentlemanly next time. That decided it for me. If he comes anywhere near either of us I will go straight to the police – and I told him that! You should have seen the look on his face – he was furious. Really, he's a very dangerous man. And I can't believe my mum slept with him. Yuck! He said he would expect to see me at the Spotted Horse this Thursday. I have decided that I am going to go to the police and I will tell him that on Thursday.

Just telling you all this so that:

a)   You know of my feelings for you and why I am resigning

b)   If anything happens to me you know who did it – but I don't suppose that will happen!

Love you forever, Sally xxx

PTO

I sat stunned for several minutes. Eleanor Framsell had told me, but I had had no idea of Sally's feelings for me. I knew we both clicked immediately but the strength of her feelings shocked me. I was pretty sure it was just a teenage infatuation, even though she was a little older than that. Her letter could have been written by a teenager and I felt sad to think that she thought she could take Dench on. How mistaken she was. I then noticed the PTO and turned over the sheet.

By the way, me and the girls had a secret name for him when we spotted him on the prowl. He was a real pest to us. We used to call Dench 'M' – you know, Judy Dench.... 'M' in the Bond films!

I took my tea outside and put my mug down on the patio table as I lit up a cigarette. The exhaled smoke billowed around me in the still night air as I processed what I had just read. This surely changed everything and I was about to call DCI Baines when I saw the time. Far too late and in any case, it could wait until morning. I was not going anywhere. Police orders.

I re-read the letter and it got me thinking about Sally's last night. There may be no way of knowing if she had kept the appointment with Dench at the Old Spotted Horse but if she had I imagined that she had refused him the money. Unless Dench's threats were hollow it seemed likely that he would be very angry. A memory suddenly flashed into my mind. I could see myself at The Oval in the early spring, Dench speaking with the big guy, dressed entirely in black, in a shadowy part of the car park and me offering him a lift for the next day. His new Club Vectra was off the road with a problem. A sick feeling centred itself in my stomach. Had he run Sally down? Was his car in the repair shop for bodywork damage and not the vague steering issue he had claimed? Or perhaps it was for both. The more I reflected, the more I favoured a swift call to the police.

Whilst the kettle boiled for another brew I lit up another cigarette and found myself gazing at the little noticeboard on the kitchen wall. My eyes settled on the photo of me, the one I had clipped Elisa from for my wallet. Me, on my own. Much of this had been my fault and, although Elisa had walked out on me for what I did not do to LeDare, she could have done so for what I *had* done behind her back. Either way, I was on my own and the picture of me on the noticeboard seemed now almost like a premonition from weeks before for where I found myself now.

The mobile woke me up a little after 6:00 a.m. I fumbled for it on the bedside table in my bleary-eyed state and spoke into it. It had been shortly before dawn that I finally fell into my bed, the several mugs of tea making sleep unlikely until then. It was Alex Gorton and I did not need to ask him what he was going to say.

'Lorrens? About this business,' he began in an even gruffer tone than usual.

I interrupted him. 'I am sacked, will never play for England again, blah, blah, blah,' I intoned robotically. 'Fuck off!' I threw the mobile across the room. That woke me up and, feeling a little daft, I hauled myself out of bed, retrieved the mobile from the jumble of clothes in the corner of the room and clipped the rear cover back on before I called the police.

'Baines.'

'Good morning, DCI Baines. Johnny Lorrens reporting.'

'Mr Lorrens, I said not to leave town, that doesn't mean you have to call me at six o'clock every morning to report in.'

'Good news,' I started, not responding to his comment. 'I think I might have some news on the death of Sally Framsell.'

He was suddenly interested. 'The young girl from The Oval?'

'That's right. I worked with her for a few weeks and never had a clue, but I found a letter from her last night that she had written back in April. She names Alan Dench, one of our players, as the likely culprit.'

'Hang on, Mr Lorrens. You are saying that Miss Framsell predicted her death?'

'Exactly! And what's more, I think there is more to this.' As I sat there, gripping the mobile ever tighter, it suddenly struck me. Dench was apparently short on the spread in a big way and had been desperate to keep me out of the bowling attack, tried to run me out and then did his best to keep me from returning to the crease after my injury the day before – the injury he had caused. It all added up. He was at my house when LeDare arrived having brought the bats with Jackie Kray. He had left just after LeDare. Surely he had followed Ledare. Jackie was sure that they had brought twenty-four bats but after Dench left we could only find twenty-three, scattered all over the lobby. Dench must have taken one and left it at the murder scene to implicate me. I blurted all this out to a silent DCI Baines.

'Interesting theory, Mr Lorrens, and it could account for your finger-prints being on it. But.'

'But?' I echoed uncertainly.

'A blazer button was found at the scene. You had one missing.'

'Yes, but I explained that!' I said angrily. 'It wasn't mine. All the buttons were on my jacket yesterday morning at The Oval but at the end of the day one of them was gone.'

'Can you be certain of that, Mr Lorrens?' Baines sounded unconvinced. 'And can you prove it?'

I sat quietly for a few seconds trying to focus. 'Mr Lorrens?'

'Look, all I know is there has been something funny going on. When Dench came to my place the other evening and I found the bats all over the place, my blazer was on the floor with them. It had been on a hanger on the coat-pegs by the front door. Same thing yesterday at The Oval. Blazer on its hanger on my peg and when I get back it's on the floor again. And that happened twice just yesterday. I mean, I have been in dressing rooms hundreds of times and my blazer or jacket has never been on the floor. Suddenly it's never off it. That's odd to me, DCI Baines.'

'Well, I'm no expert on cricket dressing rooms,' he replied disdainfully.

Baines explained that police enquiries would continue and that I needed to keep myself available. I realised I needed more to convince him but thankfully they lacked hard evidence to take me in again. For a moment I pondered mentioning my cigarette break but for some reason did not do so. Maybe deep down I feared that admitting to a ten-minute window might look especially guilty. I decided to let the police find out about my cigarette break themselves. I was not sure I had done the right thing.

In the bathroom as I shaved at the mirror, I looked at my bruised and battered face. I was almost unrecognizable. The side of my head where Dench had 'accidentally' clubbed me looked flatter than the other side. I had forgotten to tell Baines about that – another example of Dench's desperation to stop me racking up points on the spread. There was swelling all around the eye where Ralph had punched me, the eye was closing up and the purple-black bruising coming out nicely. It looked like I had gone a few rounds with Mike Tyson.

It was probably about half-past eleven when the doorbell rang. Fearing the press, or police, or Dench or Ralph, I slipped over to the bedroom window and gently pulled the curtain aside. Of all people it was Mr Brown. How on earth did he know where I lived and what on earth was he doing there? I let the curtain slip back into place and stood quietly, pretending to be out. I could not face his banal cheeriness just now. The bell rang again, and again, and again every thirty seconds for about three minutes. After a longer pause I peeked out again. He was gone. Relieved, I started down the stairs when I saw a large brown envelope on the doormat. Picking it up, I flipped on the kettle as I took the envelope outside to the patio where the sun was now shining brightly from a clear blue sky.

The envelope was printed in the top left-hand corner: John Stiles, Photographer. So that was Mr Brown's name. I turned it over. The envelope was secured by a small metal fastening clip. I opened it and withdrew the contents: a number of black and white photographs and a single sheet of light brown writing paper.

Dear Johnny, I am writing this in case you are not in when I call. I took these at The Oval yesterday, as you will notice, with my new camera. I am keen to hear your thoughts on my photographs and wanted to give these to you to keep. I have to say you did tremendously well at bat yesterday and we were all very concerned about your injury. How on earth did that happen? It was clearly bad enough to keep you off the pitch for the Australian's innings but thanks to your runs we managed to win! I hope you will be fit again soon but, in the meantime, enjoy the photographs and well done again.
John Stiles

So that was his name. John Stiles. And we had won the match and the best of three series. I reflected grimly that that was most likely my last match for my country and that coming back had not been the most fantastic experience. If I had not been selected it seemed very likely to me that Elisa and I would still be together, but I would never know that for certain.

I very nearly did not even look at the photographs but as I tipped them out onto the patio table, and they slid apart, one photo in particular caught my eye. It was a portrait-style one of me, lined up to meet the dignitaries before the game, in my England blazer. It was a 10 x 8 close up depicting me from the knees up. I picked it up. Held it closer. I was extending my right-hand towards another suited-hand, the wearer cropped from the shot. Clear as day, I could see all the buttons present and correct on my blazer's cuff. Admittedly I had hastily sewn one back on not long before the photograph was taken but I had left the house that morning with a full complement of buttons.

255

DCI Baines answered on the second ring.

CHAPTER 39

Saturday July 13 1997

I had been keeping a diary since the beginning of the season, anticipating my recall and hoping to sell it to a publisher. You know, '*The Season of a County Pro*', type of book. After my conversation with DCI Baines I had closed the diary and put it away, my plans to publish on hold. I was sick of it all and struggling on my own if I am honest. Surrey were good to me, gave me some time off and I had just watched the late-evening highlights of our Benson and Hedges Cup final win over Kent. I could not face appearing at Lord's, but watching the lads lift the trophy made me immensely proud and suddenly hungry to be a part of it again. No winners' medal for me, but I could comfort myself in knowing that I had put in some performances in the early games at least. Sitting here six weeks on from the one-day series I am ready to fill in the gaps since then.

Baines kept me up to date with developments on the LeDare murder, though he probably should not have. Maybe he felt sorry for me, getting dragged into it like that. Dench was called in for questioning and it did not take long for the police to put things together. It was true what Summers had told me; Dench was short on the spread and when the price dipped early on, he went even shorter. Not enough to kill for surely but he was clearly increasingly desperate, and this was his one last attempt to frame me and to remove me from the one-day series before the final match started. He tried to shift the focus onto me, telling the police that he had heard me threaten to kill LeDare with a bat. Elisa apparently backed him on this but thankfully CCTV showed him close to LeDare's house and after an appeal to the public for eyewitnesses, a cricket fan came forward to say he had seen Dench in an adjoining street just minutes before the murder. More importantly, Dench was seen carrying a bat that looked like it had signatures all over the face of the blade. Now, this information had never been revealed at that point and Dench's prints, amongst others, were found on it. The blazer button found close to LeDare's body was initially thought to have been my missing one, but it did not take long for the police to determine that Dench had ripped off one of my buttons on the morning of The Oval one-dayer to replace his missing one and to further incriminate me. I had eventually told Baines about my rushed repair job and the forensics team were able to show that one of the buttons on Dench's England blazer – the one he had ripped from mine – had also recently been reattached. Mr Brown's photograph certainly helped buy me some time though and I will ever be grateful to him.

Having been ruled out of the LeDare murder, I pestered Baines about the hit and run on Sally Framsell and my suspicions over Dench's involvement in that and specifically my theory that his car had gone into the repair shop for bodywork damage rather than the steering issue he had claimed. It did not take long to ascertain that this was correct and the case against him in Sally's murder was looking stronger. Eleanor Framsell admitted that she had had a fling with Dench and that he was leaning heavily on her for money to bail out his growing gambling debts. Tragically, Eleanor's refusal to pay and her daughter's subsequent threat to go to the police led directly to Sally's untimely death. The case against Alan Dench looks solid.

The whole gambling issue blew up around this time and the ECB quickly set up a committee to investigate the scale and depth of the problem. There was nothing illegal about what Summers had done, maybe apart from having contacts of his go long for him, and I was cleared of any direct involvement, although I was sternly rebuked for not having reported Summers' scheme to the authorities. It looks as if this is going to be one of the big challenges for cricket in the years to come. It is a sport dominated by statistics and because of that, is a sport subject to manipulation by the murky world of organised crime. The authorities are going to have their work cut out.

My brother Jack did not give up on his quest to unveil the safety issues surrounding the Surrey building plans and it also uncovered another irregularity. My father-in-law, Ralph Wilton, had closer ties still to Willby Construction than we knew. Jack kept digging away, discovered that whilst the family firm had been sold upon Ralph's retirement, my father in law remained on the board and uncovered reports of Willby Construction building irregularities in a couple of Chinese stadia, revealing this to the press. To Ursula Hamilton of the Guardian in fact. She dug into it even deeper and the whole business of the after-the-deadline bid was uncovered, without me having to reveal my knowledge of it publicly, and the whole deal was off. Ralph is now the centre of yet another police investigation. And it turned out it was Ralph who had me pulled from my *Oval Eyes* role, I guess because I was asking questions about the build. Miller was quietly sacked by Surrey. And I think Elisa knew much more about this whole business than she let on.

Summers lost his job at City Sports when the management there learned of his manipulation of the spread. His very large original position, albeit held for him by associates, broke their own house rules. I did not feel sorry for my old friend this time. Not after the way he entangled me in his scheming. I got wind that after his original position was turned round following my score against Gloucester, he managed to restore his long position but bottled it and cut out too soon. Those 20 runs that I spilt blood for were not enough to make him any decent sort of profit. Poetic justice, I guess. And those New England Beers? Surprise, surprise, they failed to hit the shelves. Well, that's not entirely true – they were on the shelves all along and it was Jack again, who discovered that. It seems that Summers simply obtained a small supply of a new, imported range of fruit beers from Tesco. Re-labelled with my face on them, it was all part of his plan to ensnare me and it certainly worked. More than he could have imagined when he set out on his plan. Sebastian Moran proved to be hard to track down. I did go to his 'studio', but the shiny, brass nameplate was no longer there, just a few splodges of adhesive. I doubt he even had film in his cameras.

Oh, and Summers' letter that he kept on about? That finally surfaced a couple of weeks ago when Jackie Kray sent me down some mail that had been found in a corner of my old office up in the library. From early April, it was not a sheaf of his unprintable jokes as I had surmised. Inside was a photo snipped from a magazine of a younger Elisa and a guy, backstage at The Marquee. The guy looked familiar. The caption read: *Elisa Wilton, guitarist with The Marnies, prepares for her band's London showcase performance.* It had been taken just a few months before we met. She looked beautiful but I felt nothing for her anymore. I looked at the guy again. My heart stopped for a second. It was a younger Crispin LeDare, minus the wild hair, looking wasted and disoriented back at me. Summers had tried to warn me. I had to at least give him that much, though I keep thinking back to the evening at his place, after he had sent me the clipping, when I mentioned that the papers were linking Elisa with LeDare. He dismissed my fears and chose not to tell me what he knew. Already he was plotting my entrapment.

Sally's death hit Eleanor hard, but we have not really spoken about the funeral. O'Brien was there but she never met him. I felt sympathy for him as he clearly loved Sally, but it was just not meant to be. Eleanor must have seen Dench there but has never admitted that. I guess knowing that her daughter's murderer had the nerve to attend her funeral must be too much to acknowledge. Eleanor and I do keep in touch. It is purely platonic, but she has a wicked twinkle in her eye when we do see each other.

And then there is Elisa. I still find it hard to understand how that all fell apart so quickly. What we had up to the moment she set off for New York on April 12th seemed unassailable. I could not have imagined life without her but, through a series of misunderstandings, our relationship which had been so loving was ripped apart in a matter of just a few weeks. She is still living with her parents and 'consoling' LeDare's grief-stricken twin brother. And that business about them being the twin sons of a senior Government figure? Or, as Krishnan Singh told me, a senior police officer and a hospital trust CEO? Simply wrong, and that told me a lot about the quality of his research. They were the sons of a pair of retired teachers from Hemel Hempstead.

So that just leaves me. Battered and bruised but ready to re-join the fray. Reputation damaged? I don't know about that. I am sure there'll be some banter from the crowd and for sure from the opposition, but I am starting to feel in a better place. Who knows, I may yet get another recall although I am not holding my breath.

'Johnny? Are you coming to bed?'

Ah! I knew I had forgotten someone. Lori moved in with me about a month ago now and things are going great. All that business about her ex,

Phillipe? She told me he was an allegory for Summers. I will have to look that one up in a dictionary when I have the time, but apparently he treated her dreadfully and was a controlling bully. Given the way he had manipulated me I did not doubt it. But I have to admit that his honey-trap worked like a dream – in intended and unintended ways. Not only was I easily ensnared in his scheming and plotting, I ended up with the loveliest woman and any guilt I felt over what I did behind Elisa's back quickly disappeared when *Smashed* printed their teaser for her new book. There was an extended piece on the Chelsea Hotel shenanigans. Let's just say I am not surprised that Elisa has moved on to LeDare number two.

The Anniversary painting is being unveiled next week and I am planning to go up to The Oval for that. It will be my first visit since the one-dayer and I am hoping Lori comes with me. Thankfully I never managed to have her likeness removed. Look out for us when you come to see it – we are in the top right-hand corner.

Printed in Great Britain
by Amazon

24554470R00148